INSURRECTION

JEFFREY POOLE

Jeffrey Poole's Epic Fantasy Books
Bakkian Chronicles:
The Prophecy

Insurrection

Amulet of Aria

Disneyland Debacle (short story)

Winter Wonderland (short story)

Tales of Lentari
Lost City

Something Wyverian This Way Comes

A Portal for Your Thoughts

Thoughts for a Portal

Wizard in the Woods

Close Encounters of the Magical Kind

The Hunt for Red Oskorlisk (short story)

May the Fang be With You (Pirates trilogy #1)

The Hammer is Strong with This One (Pirates #2)

These are Not the Stones You're Looking For (Pirates #3)

Blast from the Past

Dragons of Andela
Harness the Fire

Strike the Spark

Clear the Water

Mysteries by J.M. Poole
The Corgi Case Files Series
16 delightful cozy mystery novels featuring corgi
sleuths, Sherlock and Watson

INSURRECTION

Bakkian Chronicles, Book II

JEFFREY POOLE

Secret Staircase Books

Insurrection

Published by Secret Staircase Books, an imprint of
Columbine Publishing Group, LLC
PO Box 416, Angel Fire, NM 87710

Book layout and design by Secret Staircase Books

First Secret Staircase paperback edition: December, 2022
First Secret Staircase e-book edition: December, 2022

* * *

Publisher's Cataloging-in-Publication Data

Poole, J.M.
Insurrection / by J.M. Poole.
p. cm.
ISBN 978-1649141163 (paperback)
ISBN 978-1649141170 (e-book)

1. Steve Miller (Fictitious character)—Fiction. 2. Lentari
(Fictitious location)—Fiction. 3. Epic fantasy fiction 4. Dragons and
mythical creatures—Fiction. I. Title

The Bakkian Chronicles Trilogy : Book II.
Poole, J.M., Bakkian Chronicles epic fantasy series.

BISAC : FICTION / Fantasy/Epic.
813/.54

For Giliane —

What can I say? My eternal thanks for choosing to marry someone with an overactive imagination!
Love you always & forever!

Acknowledgements

There are several people who helped with the creation of this book. So here we go with the shout-outs:

Many thanks to my Beta Readers! Scott (IndieBookBlogger), Jamie (my sibling from a previous life!), and various family members who sacrificed their personal time to read through it and tell me where I went horribly wrong. I'd also like to thank Sandra Anderson and Susan Gross, from Secret Staircase Books, for all their invaluable help, too.

And finally, to my wife Giliane, who helped me with all kinds of intricate plot details that I never would have known, or remembered, or thought of. Love you, babe!

Table of Contents

Chapter 1 - Taken ... 9

Chapter 2 - Pursuit ... 20

Chapter 3 - Reinforcements ... 38

Chapter 4 - Liberation ... 53

Chapter 5 - Thwarted ... 80

Chapter 6 - Predicament ... 100

Chapter 7 - Decision ... 120

Chapter 8 - Divided ... 140

Chapter 9 - Apprehension ... 167

Chapter 10 - Infiltration ... 178

Chapter 11 - Incarcerated ... 194

Chapter 12 - Thaden ... 212

Chapter 13 - Explanations ... 238

Chapter 14 - Journal ... 258

Chapter 15 - Bakkian ... 273

Chapter 16 - Showdown ... 295

Epilogue ... 323

Chapter 1 – Taken

Peals of laughter, intermixed with the excited barking of a dog, shattered the calm of the quiet morning. With the grace (and noise level) of a pack of pachyderms, the stairs were taken two at a time as the manor's two earliest risers decided to embrace the beginning of the day with a noisy game of tag. Clearly there would be no sleeping in, not on this day. The slam of a door sounded from several stories below, the muted laughter eventually fading away until nothing remained.

An arm reluctantly emerged from within the warm cocoon of the comforter, fumbling clumsily toward the nightstand by the bedside. The lifeless hand flopped noisily along the small bureau, scattering change, books, and credit card receipts before finally settling on a hard plastic object. Slowly, the fingers felt along the remote. It was too skinny; wrong device. Continuing the search, the hand flopped to the next remote. Several comatose fingers felt the various buttons recessed into the device. With a grunt, the large flat panel video screen on the far wall was activated. An infomercial appeared. A loud, over-enthusiastic salesperson was praising the sheer genius of the creators of the latest kitchen gadget, one that could apparently enable the general populace to peel a hard-boiled egg just by smacking the handle of some cheap, plastic gizmo. God forbid you had the common sense to peel the egg like a normal person.

With a curse, the audio was silenced. Long having the layout of this remote memorized, the fingers slowly mapped out the buttons, searching for the bottom right corner. Ignoring the picture-in-picture option, the button directly above it was selected. The video instantly disappeared, replaced by a blank blue screen: no video source. The finger slowly hit the button three more times. The blue screen disappeared, replaced by a picture that was divided into four quadrants. Live streaming images from various locations around the manor filled the screen.

An eye, still heavy from sleep, grudgingly cracked open and scanned the images before him. Another button was pressed. The four images were then replaced by four other feeds. Another press. There, in zone 9, was the young boy, eagerly throwing a padded frisbee for his canine companion. The fabric disc zipped out of the frame while the Pembroke Welsh Corgi trailed close behind in hot pursuit.

"So where's he at?"

"Mmmf. Garden."

"He's playing frisbee? In my garden?"

"Hey, I didn't tell him to play in there."

"If Peanut digs anything up in there, I'm going to hold you personally responsible."

Yawning profusely, Steve propped himself up on an elbow, still watching the antics on the screen.

"Peanut hasn't dug anything up since she was a puppy. Besides, didn't I end up replacing that entire section of carnations for you?"

"Yes," she admitted, "you did."

* * *

"What are your plans for today, Mikal?"

Busy wolfing down his breakfast, the young boy glanced up, piece of toast halfway to his mouth. "I am still teaching Peanut how to catch the disc with her mouth."

Months before, while channel surfing one night from the comfort of his media room, Steve had come across one of those dog agility programs. It was the type of show which had various obstacles placed before the dog and the dog was then timed as it raced through the course. Mesmerized by all the different and amazing tasks the dogs were put through, Steve had wondered aloud if Peanut would ever be capable of doing something like that. Passing close by on one of his evening romps, Mikal promised himself that he'd teach the young corgi to do all the cool tricks that the other dogs could do.

"Making any progress?" Steve asked.

"She seems to be more interested in watching it spin," Mikal answered, sighing.

"You'll have to keep at it. Don't give up. Would you like me to give you a hand?"

The boy's eager face lit up. "Aye, I would!"

"Tell you what," Sarah began, thinking ahead. "I'll pack us some sandwiches and we can all go to that glade you and Peanut discovered. We'll make a day of it!"

"Will Tristan come with us?"

Steve shook his head. "Probably not. He found some rare manuscript in the library and hasn't budged much from it in the last couple of days. When I came down for breakfast, he was already in there. Barely looked up long enough to say good morning."

"I hope he can make it."

"Don't worry, squirt. I'll ask him."

Surprising them all, Tristan joined the festivities, even lobbing a tattered tennis ball around a few times for the overjoyed Peanut.

"This location is very picturesque," Tristan noted, glancing around. "Reminds me of Lentari."

"Do you miss it?" Sarah asked.

"I do not have family, Lady Sarah. The Kri'yans are my

family, and if I can serve them best by being here, then I am quite content to stay as long as needed."

"That's not what I asked."

Tristan's mouth turned upward in a smile.

"Peanut, I would not —"

There was a loud splash, followed closely by nervous laughter.

"It is not my fault!" Mikal exclaimed, laughing as the drenched corgi emerged from the pond and vigorously shook herself off. Water droplets went flying everywhere. The boy made a move to grab the wet dog, but Peanut had other ideas. She sprinted around the boy, barking joyously before she caught sight of the water again and dove back in, spraying water everywhere.

Tristan nonchalantly moved his precious book out of harm's way, as though the prospect of averting impending water damage was something he did on a regular basis.

Sarah and Steve groaned, holding a rapid rock-paper-scissors session.

Steve sighed. "Oh, come on! Best two out of three!"

Sarah grinned, shaking her head. "Nope. Here's the towel. Have fun!"

Hours later, after they had returned from their picnic, husband and wife were enjoying some quiet time on the top floor while boy and tutor played a video game in the rec room.

"Are we still going to visit Annie tomorrow?"

Sarah nodded, walking into the luxurious master bathroom while simultaneously checking herself in the huge mirror. "That's the plan. She's totally excited to see all of us again."

"She's certainly handled the news quite well," Steve observed. "I'm impressed. I expected her to freak out when we told her what happened to us last year."

"What did you expect? She's a smart girl. I still think you didn't have to wave lit hands in front of her face."

"Hey, seeing is believing," Steve retorted. "I thought she looked a little skeptical and figured a small demonstration couldn't hurt."

"You scared the crap out of her, that's what you did."

"At any rate," Steve continued, disregarding Sarah's outburst, "Annie took the news well. She's quite fond of Mikal."

"It'll be nice to see her again."

"We get to bring Peanut, right? She's old enough now where she doesn't have any more accidents. Of course, it's only taken ten months or so. Besides, Mikal would be crushed without her."

"Mikal would be crushed or you'd be crushed?"

"She's Mikal's dog," Steve stated again for the umpteenth time.

"If all of us were standing in the room, Peanut would run to you first."

"Hmmph."

The following day, at precisely four in the afternoon, everyone gathered in the massive living room on the ground floor, ready to be transported to the home of Sarah's sister, Annie. One at a time, Sarah took each of their arms and teleported them over eight hundred miles southwest to Sacramento, California. There was a time, Sarah reflected, that numerous jumps of this magnitude would have depleted her resources. But since returning Steve's parents to Phoenix close to a year ago, she had been secretly building up her stamina, teleporting herself whenever she could. At last count, she could take upward of about ten to twelve jumps of varying distance before she started feeling the effects of her drained jhorun.

Annie's house had a split floor plan, with several guest rooms located in the southern wing of her home. The guest room that Steve and Sarah typically used whenever they visited was her teleportation point. Annie usually kept the door to this room closed for those occasions when Sarah teleported in as she was fairly certain not everyone would be as understanding as she was when it came to people appearing out of thin air.

Knocking politely on the closed door, they waited until Annie announced they should come on in. Sarah had just twisted the handle and pushed the door open when an over-enthusiastic Peanut barreled by Mikal, heading straight for the lady whom she knew was an extended member of her pack. This particular pack member, Peanut knew, had a free hand when it came to little morsels of food that *accidentally* found their way to the floor.

"Peanut! How're you doing, pretty girl?" Excited barks echoed down the hallway. "Does Peanut want a yummy treat? Here you go. Hi guys!" Annie said brightly, beaming at her sister and brother-in-law as they entered her living room.

Tristan gave her a small bow. "Lady Annie. A pleasure to see you again."

"Hello Tristan! Having a good day today?"

"Very pleasurable, indeed."

"Good day, Annie!"

Smiling warmly at the small boy before her, Annie gave the young prince a hug. "And how are you today, Mikal?"

"Very good, thanks!"

"I hear you're a big fan of video games now, is that right?"

Mikal grinned. His new favorite pastime was jamming to a good tune on the wildly popular Rock Group platform on Steve's online video game console. Long considering himself master of the guitar, Steve found himself being seriously challenged as the young prince proved himself to be a worthy adversary. Those nimble little fingers could seriously fly across the fret buttons!

"I enjoy the music games," Mikal answered, looking over at Steve. He raised an eyebrow. "There will come a time when you will rue the day you ever challenged me on *expert*."

"In your dreams, squirt."

"It just so happens that I rented a game system for the night, as well as a certain game."

Mikal's face lit up. "Really?"

Steve's expression mirrored the boy's. "Which one?"

"Rock Group, of course. I can't wait to see the two of you play it!"

"Fantastic!"

"Race you to the couch, kiddo!"

"So, Tristan," Annie said, after the dishes had been washed and the kitchen restored to order, "have you heard anything more about how things are going in R'Tal? Any more from that kingdom that's been causing problems?"

Tilting his head back, Tristan finished his goblet of sparkling cider. Like Annie, he had a fondness for the bubbling concoction. Gently placing the empty glass back on the table, he sighed.

"I have heard no news at all, and that troubles me greatly."

"Wouldn't that be good news?"

"Our network of spies typically informs us about troop movement, news of interest in Ylani, and so on. Of this, we have not had word of anything for nigh four months."

Steve and Sarah both leaned forward. This was news to them.

"No news, no nothing? What are they up to?"

"No one knows," Tristan confessed, "the lack of news is quite alarming. Our last check-in revealed nothing."

Sarah rose. "Would anyone care for something to drink? Mikal? Tristan? Steve, how about you?"

"I would like some water, please," Mikal called from the couch, busily hammering away at a fast paced 80's song. Tristan also asked for a glass.

"Who brought the neon lights?" Annie suddenly asked.

Steve, watching Mikal work his way through an 80s set list, glanced over at his sister-in-law.

"What was that?"

Annie pointed over to her darkened game room. Since there weren't any lights turned on in that room, it was very easy to see the green glow. "Something is giving off light over there. Is it a cell phone?"

Steve walked over to the pool table, staring down at the source of light. It was his Mythra sword. Tristan had persuaded him to bring it along. Come to think of it, the quiet tutor was always insisting he bring the mystical sword with him whenever he left the house. He'd have to inquire about that later.

The sword was sheathed, but the strap had come undone, and perhaps a quarter inch of the blade was exposed. Because of that, he could see that the green blade was glowing. As far as he could remember, the sword hadn't ever done that before! Then again, he rarely had the exquisite sword unsheathed.

As soon as Steve's hand closed around the hilt, he heard voices, voices that he knew no one else would be able to hear. Closing his eyes to concentrate on the faint murmurings in his head, Steve could pick out Rhenyon's voice shouting orders to his men. The sense of urgency was unmistakable. He could hear frantic shouts, the sounds of people struggling, but it was all so very faint! What was going on? Suddenly several phrases leapt out from the others:

...must get her back! ...attack upon royal blood unacceptable...

"Uh-oh. I think we have a problem," Steve whispered, more to himself than to anyone. Remaining motionless, he closed his eyes and continued to strain his senses, waiting to see if the voices said anything else.

Alarmed, Tristan stood. "What is it, Sir Steve?"

Steve opened his eyes and shot a look at Tristan, nodding his head in Mikal's direction.

"Lady Annie, would you be so kind as to take young Mikal and Peanut for a walk please?"

"O-kaaay. Come on, Mikal, grab Peanut. I have her leash."

Stomach rife with unease, Mikal nodded. The boy knew that when the grownups wanted to talk amongst themselves, it usually meant something bad had happened.

"What is it, Sir Steve?" Tristan repeated, after the front door closed behind Annie.

"I just heard Rhenyon's voice. He said something about having to get her back, and that an attack upon royal blood was unacceptable."

"Get her back?" Tristan repeated, starting to pace. "Wizards be damned. The only other way to force his majesty's hand, with his son out of harm's way, would be to target the queen. It sounds as though she's been abducted."

Sarah clapped her hands over her mouth. "We have to do something!"

"Our job is protecting the prince," Steve pointed out. "Don't you think the castle can handle this type of thing?"

"This is Mikal's mother we're talking about," Sarah insisted.

"I know she is. What do you suggest? That we head back to Lentari? We need to keep Mikal safe. That's the whole point of him being here." Steve looked at Tristan. "Don't you think that the king can deal with this without our help?"

Tristan was still pacing. "If the queen was truly taken hostage, then they might be able to force his majesty to acquiesce to their demands. And I can guarantee that they will not be pleasant."

"I just don't understand how someone would be able to infiltrate the castle's defenses!" Steve protested. "Rhenyon is Captain of the Royal Guard. How could anyone manage to get the queen out of his sight?"

"The fact remains that someone did. The queen is missing. Am I right to understand that this probably just happened?"

"I'd say so."

"Then we'd have the element of surprise," Sarah remarked. "A teleporter and a fire thrower to the rescue? Tristan, is that what you're thinking?"

"What about Mikal?" Steve wanted to know.

Sensing a commotion nearby, the trio glanced at the front door, which had just opened; the young corgi was struggling to pull Mikal back inside the house.

"What about me?" Mikal asked, returning from his brief walk with Annie. "What has happened? Tell me, please!"

Steve looked at Sarah. *Your call.*

Nodding, Sarah knelt down in front of the scared little boy.

"Okay, Mikal, here's the truth. We believe that your mother has been kidnapped. As near as we can determine, it just happened, perhaps a few minutes ago."

"How do you know?"

Steve held out Mythrin. "Rhenyon and I were given special swords crafted by the dwarves. Apparently, they can facilitate contact between the holders of the swords. I didn't even know they could do that, but nevertheless, I heard him. Up here," he added, tapping his head.

"Are you going to save my mother?"

"We're trying to figure out what to do."

Mikal shuddered, embracing Sarah. "Please, you must

save her!"

Peanut wriggled her way into their embrace, whining with apparent empathy. Since achieving adult size, Peanut had become twenty-seven pounds of solid muscle, and could, Steve was certain, squirm her way into an air-tight chamber.

Sarah looked down at the young boy in her arms, then over to her husband, who nodded. The look they shared had just decided their next course of action. Annie, noting the firm resolve that had just appeared over both her sister and her brother-in-law, raised a hand. Sarah glanced over.

"What is it?"

"I have a question. If the two of you return to Mikal's home world, then I would assume he'll be left here, right?"

"Both Mikal and Tristan stay put," Steve confirmed.

"In Coeur d'Alene?"

"Yes, they'll be safe there."

"By themselves? You're going to leave two foreigners in our world to fend for themselves for who knows how long?"

"What would you suggest?"

Without a word, Annie pulled out her cell and made a call.

"Mary, hi, it's Annie. Listen, I have a huge family emergency. I have to leave town for at least a week, maybe two. I have tons of PTO, so I should be covered. Are you okay with that? Great, I really appreciate it. Thank you so much."

Annie hung up the phone and looked at her surprised sister. "Let me pack some things. You get to call Mom."

Dumbfounded, Sarah could only nod. An hour later, everyone had assembled in the sitting room on the top floor of their manor, back in Idaho. Together, they faced the two massive carved doors.

"I've always wanted to see how this thing works," Annie confessed, staring at the huge relief spanning both doors.

Steve walked up, decked out in his protective leather armor. Deciding his ceremonial armor would be too cumbersome, he had instead elected to wear the much lighter leather armor given to him by the Council of Dwarves on the eve of their battle with the guur. His green-bladed sword,

Mythrin, was already strapped to his back, with the Nohrstaf nestled in its new holder that had been added to the sword's scabbard. Sarah appeared moments later, also choosing to wear the light armor she had received from the dwarves. She had given herself a good laugh as she had briefly visualized herself rescuing the queen in her dress-armor. Facing her husband, she pulled out both crystal keys, holding one in each hand.

"Which one? Purple or green?"

Strapping one of his magically enhanced gauntlets to his right arm, Steve glanced up. "Not the green one. Damn thing dumped us in the middle of the forest last time. The purple one should take us straight to the castle."

"Purple it is." She turned to her sister. "Here, take this." Quickly glancing at Tristan and Mikal to verify neither was watching her, she passed her sister the green key. "I don't want either of them to be tempted by this thing."

"How long do you think you will you be?" Annie asked, tucking the crystal key safely into her inside jacket pocket.

"We'll try to make it back as quickly as possible."

"You two be careful. Don't worry about us. I'll hold down the fort here."

"Thanks, Annie." Sarah gave her sister a hug. "We really owe you one."

Chapter 2 — Pursuit

The Great Hall was in chaos. Tables had been flung over; their contents strewn everywhere. Broken dishes, smashed goblets, and bits of food marred the formerly pristine marble floor. Soldiers could be seen darting to and fro, shouting out for their companions to hurry.

Steve turned to gaze at the portal behind him. His sister-in-law was still visible, standing behind Mikal. Annie had both of her hands on the boy's shoulders, as if to prevent him from leaping through the portal, which it looked as though he was ready to do. Tristan, restraining a very unhappy Peanut, moved a few paces closer.

"Find her. Protect her."

Steve nodded gravely. "Count on it."

The portal fuzzed out, replaced moments later by the carved representation of the castle.

"Where do we go from here?" Sarah gazed at the mess the Great Hall had become. "Shouldn't we go find the king?"

"Do you really want to take the time to track him down?"

Steve stepped out of the path of several running soldiers, pulling Sarah aside as well. No one had paid them the slightest bit of attention. "The longer we wait, the farther away they get. We need to get going."

"Where to?"

"Umm, let's go to the northern orchards and the dragon cave."

"Hang on, here we go."

Determined to keep his eyes open, the world around him winked out, only to be suddenly replaced by a very familiar mound of rocks. The incessant clamoring of activity had died away, leaving an eerie calm. Birds were singing. The surrounding trees were rustling in a light, gentle breeze. The waters of the northern moat stirred as Bredo the serpent searched for hapless victims.

"So how are we supposed to know which direction to go?" Sarah wondered aloud, looking around. "They could be anywhere by now."

"I doubt it. I think they would have high-tailed it back north."

"You're sure Ylani is to blame?"

"You think it could be someone else?"

Sarah shook her head. "Probably not. So, you think we need to head north?"

"Yes, I do." Steve knelt down, inspecting the ground. "Look! There appears to be a lot of activity all headed that way."

"Those tracks could be days old," Sarah pointed out. "No way of knowing if those are the ones we're looking for."

"True," Steve admitted, nodding his head. "But, there are a lot of tracks here. I think we should assume, since they're all heading north, that either they are the kidnappers themselves, or else it's people from R'Tal going after them."

Sarah peered ahead, singling out a copse of trees at least five miles distant. "How about we go to the other end of this clearing? See where the forest starts? I can put us right there."

Shading his eyes from the sun, Steve squinted into the distance. "Sounds good, let's go."

Moments later, they were staring at a section of the

ground nearly five miles away. Traversing up and down the edge of the forest, Sarah finally called out with some good news.

"Honey, over here!"

Steve hurried over, staring intently at the ground in front of his wife.

"What do you have?"

"Horse tracks. Lots of them."

"You're right," Steve said, squatting down to inspect the disturbed earth. "I'd say at least a dozen horses came through here, and from the looks of things, I'd say they were galloping full tilt."

"Galloping? How can you tell that? You're no tracker."

"I know I'm not. Never claimed to be. But check this out." Steve pointed to the deep gouges in the earth. "If a horse was simply walking, then it wouldn't have torn up the ground as much as this. But if it was running, then their hooves would be digging into the ground to give them as much purchase as possible. You follow?"

Sarah was slowly nodding her head. "Okay, I can buy that. Where'd you come up with that?"

"Would you believe I saw it in a movie?"

Sarah hesitated, shaking her head. "Actually, yes, I would."

Steve gazed at the impressive expanse of trees before them.

"How far can you teleport us at one time through that?"

"Distance doesn't matter," Sarah explained again to her husband. "As long as I can see where I'm going, I can take us as far as we need to.

"Crap, we're not going to be able to go that far then."

Sarah put her arms behind her, fists pressing in the small of her back, and gently leaned backwards. Stretching her muscles to see about relieving a pinched nerve (did she don her armor too fast?), Sarah felt her attention drawn to the distant treetops above them.

"You know what? I have an idea."

"What is it?"

"Stay here."

"Where are you go—"

Sarah vanished.

"—ing?" Steve drummed the fingers of his right hand along the hilt of Mythrin. Where'd she go? What was her idea? Had she seen something?

A shower of pine needles suddenly rained down upon him. Brushing the needles out of his hair, Steve glanced up. A steady trickle of needles appeared to be falling down from the enormous evergreen standing majestically a few feet away. Try as he might, his gaze couldn't penetrate the thick foliage of the tree. Eyes watering profusely, he blinked several more times, wiping out the debris that kept his vision blurred. Emerging from beneath the tree's canopy, Steve kept circling around, looking for the best vantage point. There! Something was moving around the top of the tree. Was that Sarah??

Suspended at least fifty feet up in the air, perched close to the trunk, Sarah fidgeted, trying to find the best toehold. Once she was certain the branch she was standing on wasn't going to start cracking beneath her, she peered around. As she had surmised, the view was much better from up here!

A sudden disturbance drew her attention slightly northwest. Way off in the distance, a huge flock of birds had suddenly erupted upward, vociferously announcing their displeasure. Even as far away as she was, Sarah could hear the faint squawks the flock was making. Had something spooked them? Noting the small mesa nearby, Sarah memorized the nearby environment. Certain she had an adequate image of the area in her mind, she returned to her husband's side.

"Were you up in that tree?"

Sarah nodded. "Fairly close to the top. I wanted to see where to go next. I found a good spot. Something spooked a flock of birds off that way. I want to see what it is."

"If we drop right in the middle of them," Steve warned, "then you had better —"

"Yes, I know. I'll find a safe spot to watch." Sarah watched as her husband opened his mouth to deliver an angry retort. "No, don't even say it. I won't leave you. What happens if you're overwhelmed? Or if you're hurt? I can stay hidden and teleport us out of there if the circumstances become too dangerous."

"I don't think —"

"Final offer. Either that or I stay put."

"Fine. Just find a really safe place out of the way, okay?"

Smiling, Sarah nodded. She hadn't been sure if he was going to object or not, but was rather pleased that he had agreed to let her stay.

"So, we're headed for a small mesa close to where I saw those birds. Ready?"

Igniting his hands, as if to verify that they would in fact still ignite, then giving them a quick flick to extinguish them, Steve nodded. "Ready when you are."

Gripping her husband's hand tightly, Sarah moved them northwest. The squawks of angry birds instantly assailed their ears. Whatever had riled them up had apparently done a wonderful job. Silently, Steve surveyed the area, noting the remnants of colorful plumage that were scattered about. The birds had clearly all chosen to retreat to the safety of the sky as quickly as they could.

Determining that no threats were in the immediate vicinity, Steve cautiously emerged from the safety of the trees. Squatting down to inspect the feather-strewn ground, he motioned Sarah over.

"Check it out. These look like hoof prints again. Think we're on the right trail?"

"I'd say so." Sarah started eyeing the trees again, looking for a suitable vantage point. Utilizing a rather robust-looking pine, Sarah was able to determine the next point they were going to jump to, a clearing on the bank of a narrow, swift moving river. The trees had thinned just enough for Sarah to acquire what she had started referring to as a 'safe zone', meaning she could picture enough of the surroundings for a safe jump.

Sarah held out her hand and waited for her husband to take it. Steve's face wore a quizzical expression as he stared around at the giant trees.

"What are you doing? Do you hear something?"

"No, but it feels like someone is watching us."

Alarmed, Sarah stepped closer to one of the enormous evergreens.

"They might have people hiding in the trees just waiting for the opportune time to attack us. Come on, let's get out of here."

"I think you're right. Let's go."

Steve jogged over to his wife, but just before he could reach her side he was abruptly yanked backwards, coming to a very sudden stop. Grunting painfully, he rubbed at the baldric strapped across his chest.

Sarah turned to him, concern apparent on her face. "What's the matter? Are you hurt? What's wrong with your chest?"

"It felt like someone just came up behind me and pulled me to a stop." He tugged at the baldric, hoping to loosen the sword belt so he could restore some circulation. "Oh man, that's going to leave a mark."

He grasped at his baldric and tried to loosen it. The belt was so tight that he couldn't even wiggle his fingers under it.

"What's the deal with this damn th— whoa!"

Whatever had pulled Steve to an abrupt stop was now pulling him backwards. Twin gouges appeared in the soft grass as Steve desperately dug in his heels in an attempt to slow his momentum.

Sarah jogged next to him as he was dragged backward. "Can you loosen the belt?"

"I'm trying! Damn thing is too tight!"

"I'm going to try and teleport the —"

Sarah trailed off as whatever what was pulling her husband let go. Steve windmilled his arms, but to no avail. He ended up falling flat on his back.

"Honey! Look!" Sarah bent down to retrieve an object from the ground.

Still sprawled on the ground, Steve twisted his head to see what it was. A sword? He painfully rose to his feet, rubbing his chest. A closer inspection of the sword had him forgetting his injuries.

"That's Rhenyon's sword!" Steve took the weapon and briefly unsheathed the striking blue blade. "What's it doing here? Rhenyon would never leave this behind."

"He must have lost it in a battle or something. Come on,

we *really* need to get going."

"Agreed." Swinging the sword over his left shoulder, Steve fastened the second baldric across his back.

As they progressed through the forest, stopping periodically for Sarah to determine the location of their next jump, Steve couldn't help but be amazed at the ease in which they were traversing through the countryside. He was pretty certain no one else in the kingdom was more equipped to deal with this kidnapping than the two of them. With Sarah's teleporting, and his own pyrotechnical abilities, Steve felt confident that they'd be able to successfully rescue the queen. He'd just have to keep an eye on Sarah. She'd made a lot of jumps, so —

"How are you feeling? How's your jhorun doing?"

Sarah turned. "I'm fine. Really. Not tired at all."

"Let me know the minute you start feeling any drain, okay?"

"I promise."

Three jumps later found them farther upstream, inspecting trees for Sarah to use, when they both straightened suddenly. Distant shouts could be heard, as well as the neighing of horses. Someone—or something—was headed their way, and they were moving rapidly.

"Quick, hide!" He pulled Sarah over to a large thicket of brush and squatted down low. With their backs against the trunk of a massive tree, they both felt fairly secure and hidden as the shouting came closer.

"Think it's the people we're looking for?" Steve whispered.

"Shhhhh!"

Moments later, a disheveled figure bolted out of the forest. His eyes darted around the area, looking for a suitable place to hide. However, three figures on horseback suddenly crashed through the brush right behind him. Within moments, they had their unfortunate prey surrounded. With his back to their hiding place, the prisoner sneered at his assailants.

"Think I am afraid of the likes of you? Face me on even terms if you can, cowards."

In the midst of the bushes, Steve and Sarah stiffened.

"That's Rhenyon!" Sarah hissed at her husband. "Do something!"

Steve's jhorun seethed in anger as he observed his friend being taunted by the horsemen. They clearly were trying to provoke the Lentarian into an attack so that they could claim self-defense when he 'mysteriously' turned up dead. If Rhenyon wanted a fair fight, then a fair fight he would get!

Gathering his jhorun, Steve concentrated. Focusing on the riders, his eyes slowly dropped until he was staring straight at the saddle girths. Three riderless horses coming right up. Careful not to harm the excited animals, Steve focused his jhorun to yet again produce his clever fire dot, and caressed it along each strap. Each belt snapped apart, with the surprised rider sliding off his mount's back.

Not ever seeing three saddles fail at the same time, Rhenyon stared at the riderless horses in surprise.

The fallen aggressors hastily got to their feet, drawing their swords as they did so. Annoyed and embarrassed, the leader checked on his two henchmen, only to discover they had started howling in pain and swatting at their swords. Hesitating only long enough to see about unbuckling their belts, both turned and ran as hard as they could in the opposite direction. The remaining rider was left speechless. His dumbstruck eyes swiveled to his opponents as realization dawned: he and his prey were now on equal ground.

"Give me a sword, coward. Let's settle this like men."

At that moment, one of the other former riders managed to successfully detach himself from his red-hot sword and arrived back on the scene. Grinning like an amateur burglar who had just discovered a hidden cache of gold, the grounded rider tossed his spare dagger to his companion. Smiling evilly, both men turned to face the Lentarian. Steve chose that moment to emerge from the base of the thicket. He ignited both hands and faced the two thunderstruck goons.

Rhenyon's mouth fell open as the last person he expected to see suddenly appeared at his side. He didn't know how Steve had known there had been trouble, nor did he know how he had managed to find his way here. He simply didn't care. He was just damn glad he was there.

"So, here's how this is gonna play," Steve began, eyeing both assailants. "The two of you are going to surrender. Now.

No questions, no negotiations, no nothing. If you want to keep living, decide now and save us both a lot of trouble. Oh, if you need a little bit of encouragement, let's see if this will help you decide."

Blasting out twin jets of flame, Steve created swirling tentacles of fire, which entwined themselves around the two trembling men. Just as suddenly, the ropes of fire snapped back into the outstretched hands of their creator. Steve eyed the two men.

"What's it gonna be?"

"We surrender."

"Excellent choice. Now," Steve pointed at the mercenary holding the small dagger, "you drop that and tie him up. And I do suggest you make it tight."

Retrieving a coil of rope from one of the fallen saddle bags, the first prisoner reluctantly tied up the second. Once Rhenyon had secured the first ruffian, he turned to his friend.

"Sir Steve! What the blazes are you doing here?"

"Heard the queen was kidnapped. We're here to lend a hand."

"We?"

Sarah emerged from her hiding place. "Hello, Rhenyon."

"Lady Sarah! So that explains how the two of you made it so far so fast! How did you learn the queen was taken from us?"

"From you, actually."

Rhenyon stopped rummaging through one of the fallen saddle bags and turned back to Steve.

"Sorry? Did you say that I told you? That is impossible. No one has contact with your world."

Steve nodded. "True, no one can contact us in our home world. Except for you, it seems."

"How —"

"We'll explain later. For now, we have to help the queen. Hon, do you think that you can send them all back to the castle?"

"She can send those two to the castle," Rhenyon corrected, pointing at the trussed-up men. "I am going with the two of you."

"Sarah can't teleport the three us at the same time, Rhenyon. I'm sorry. It would be easier —"

"Excuse me," Sarah interrupted, "can any of you actually teleport? No. Then let me be the judge of that."

Steve turned to his wife. "Can you take both of us with you at the same time?"

"I don't see why not. In fact, let's find out. Rhenyon, where's the king?"

"He will be secured in the Antechamber, so you will not —"

Rhenyon trailed off as Sarah leaned forward, grabbed the two prisoners by their ears, and vanished.

"She is a determined woman," Rhenyon muttered.

"You have no idea."

Sarah rejoined them thirty seconds later. "The king wasn't there, but there were plenty of soldiers more than happy to see to the accommodations of their newest guests."

Steve snorted. "They deserve everything they're gonna get."

"So, what now?"

"We press on. Rhenyon, any ideas on which way to go?"

Rhenyon started inspecting the trampled earth before them. "I have been following the tracks on foot, but I think that your method of pursuit will be much more efficient."

"How did you lose your horse?" Sarah wanted to know.

"Ambushed. Bloody cowards."

Steve unbuckled Mythron and presented it back to its rightful owner. "Did you drop something?"

Rhenyon's mouth dropped open for the second time. "I thought I lost this! How did you ever find it?"

Steve absentmindedly rubbed his chest. "It was easier than I thought. So, which way do we go?"

"I was tracking them north. We need to go *that way*," Rhenyon said, indicating the thickest, darkest part of the forest.

"In that case, I need to find a safe zone."

Sarah vanished.

"Safe zone?" Rhenyon repeated, glancing at Steve.

"Her term. She needs to see where she's going, so at the moment, she's probably up a tree."

"Impressive," Rhenyon said, nodding his head.

Their teleporter reappeared. "Got one. About five miles due north. There's a clearing there. I think we might have stayed there once before."

Sarah grabbed Rhenyon's right arm while taking her husband's left. Taking several deep breaths, she moved them all north.

Opening his eyes (why did he keep closing them?), Steve surveyed their surroundings. They were standing on a bare expanse of rock encompassing the entire clearing. It was as though the greenery had been gouged out, leaving nothing but solid rock below. He was disappointed. They weren't going to be able to find any tracks here.

"Perfect spot, Lady Sarah. You have a good eye!" Rhenyon knelt down and inspected various locations on the rocky ground. Standing, he moved over to the edge of trees, and thoroughly examined several low hanging branches.

"Perfect?" Steve snorted. "How so? There's nothing here to follow."

Rhenyon motioned them over. "See that area of rock? It has been chipped. There are scuff marks in no fewer than five places. And here—come see this." He led them to a nearby tree. "This branch has been bent back so far that it has cracked. And there's another just over there. They came through here, and they were in a hurry. We must overtake them."

"Do you think they'll find a place to camp, or do you think they will keep moving all night?" The prospect of traveling through the night didn't make him happy.

"They will find a place to camp. Even if they pressed on during the night, they still would not make it out of Lentari until mid-day tomorrow. However, their horses would die of exhaustion before then, so they must find a place to rest."

"If we can see exactly where they're going," Sarah began, "then I can drop the two of you directly in their path."

"That would be unwise," the captain warned. "We must know the nature of our adversaries. How many they number, how well they are armed, and so on."

* * *

Dusk was rapidly approaching, yet the kidnappers continued to press on. The mercenaries' only hope was to return to their kingdom as quickly as possible. They'd have been fools to believe that the Lentarians wouldn't launch a rescue party. Being careful not to let their trussed-up captive set foot on the ground, the captors expertly concealed all traces of their passage. They even reversed course several times to throw off anyone who might have managed to pick up their trail.

The leader of the motley group couldn't refrain from gloating. There simply wasn't any way someone could be following them. He fancied himself a tracker, and he knew how to conceal their presence. Not only would their trail be virtually impossible to track, but they were at least half a day's journey ahead of any pursuit. Their inside man saw to that. They had not only managed to lure the queen out into the open courtyard, but they had also managed to drop the portcullis to stem off several squadrons of soldiers that had assembled at an amazing pace. Only one soldier had managed to leap through before the heavy metal gate came crashing down. Whoever it was that was doggedly pursuing them clearly was an experienced tracker. After discovering their latest attempt to throw the tracker from their trail had failed, he had dispatched three men to deal with the problem.

The leader of the gang was already ticking off the ways he was going to spend the gold he earned once he delivered his prize.

* * *

They lost the trail several times, but Rhenyon always managed to point them back in the right direction. Steve was confident that the captain could somehow track a griffin in flight. However, whether it was due to the rapidly diminishing daylight, or their clearly exhausted tracker, they eventually lost all traces of their quarry.

"Nothing?" Steve asked, hours later.

Rhenyon angrily stood, throwing down a clump of grass in disgust.

"Not a thing. No tracks, no traces, nothing." Sighing heavily, Rhenyon leaned against the trunk of the large tree closest to him. "I have failed them," he said miserably. "The queen was taken right from under our noses."

Sarah appeared, having scouted the surrounding area from several different tree tops. She looked at Steve and sadly shook her head.

"Dammit!" Steve swore loudly. "If we can't find traces of them, then maybe they found a place to hole up for the night. Think that's possible?"

"Aye, that would be make sense. But where? This forest is huge, covering hundreds, if not thousands of leagues."

"Rhenyon, do you know if there are any caves in the area?"

The captain's tired, bloodshot eyes shifted over to Sarah's.

"None that I am aware of, milady."

"Well, what about —"

A sudden rustling of the wind sounded overhead. Rhenyon stiffened, all traces of fatigue disappearing instantly.

Steve glanced at the commander. "What're you —?"

Rhenyon silenced him instantly by raising a gloved hand. His other hand gravitated toward the hilt of his sword.

Steve stared up at the leaves of the closest tree. Had they both heard the same thing? He tensed. Was he worried about the blowing wind now? He truly needed to get some rest if … a soft thump sounded nearby, announcing the arrival of someone or something besides the three of them.

Sarah held her breath. She nervously eyed her husband, and then noted the tense body language of their Lentarian friend. Figuring now would be a good time to have a safe zone handy, she recalled the first jump she could think of, their former quarters deep inside castle R'Tal, and kept the image firmly ingrained in her head. Just in case.

Rhenyon turned to Sarah, silently indicating for her to stay put. He looked at Steve, then pointedly down at his hands. Steve nodded, the meaning coming through loud and clear. He was ready to barbecue whatever it was that had just arrived.

Twigs cracked and leaves crunched as the interloper headed in their direction. Steve glanced down at his hands, his jhorun clamoring to be released. It was more than ready to participate in the skirmish that was about to enfold. His clenched fists turned dark red.

Several loud squawks shattered the silence. Steve flinched, both hands igniting instantly. Rhenyon's sword appeared in his hand. More footsteps sounded as the being shuffled about. Then, the footsteps ventured closer still.

"I know you are there, humans. I offer my services."

"Who are you?" Rhenyon demanded, refusing to stand down. "Identify yourself."

Steve had stiffened as soon as he had heard the voice. High pitched, somewhat nasal in nature. It sounded like —

"Wait!" Steve leapt in front of the captain. Noticing that his hands were lit, he flicked them out. "You're a griffin, aren't you?"

"Were you expecting a dragon?"

"We weren't expecting anything," Steve answered. "Come on out where we can see you."

"You are the fire thrower, are you not?"

"Yeah, you could say that."

"Are you going to torch me?"

Steve snorted. "Wasn't planning on it, unless you attack us first."

The griffin emerged, ruffling its feathers, looking unabashedly at the humans. Its wings were still extended, as though it wasn't sure if it would be necessary to beat a hasty retreat. Its primary feathers were an earthy brown color similar to most griffins he had seen, yet, his secondary and tertiary feathers were bright red. Steve couldn't ever remember seeing a griffin with wings that color. Not to mention the fact that this was the smallest griffin he had ever seen. Perhaps a juvenile?

"Who are you, griffin? How did you find us?"

"I am Phane. Pheris is my sire."

"You're the son of the griffin liaison?"

"Aye. I was returning from visiting my sire when your queen was taken. I wanted to see where the small group of humans were fleeing to, so I followed. No one notices a juvenile griffin." Phane's feathers rustled irritably. "For the time being, those you have been pursuing have not moved. Humans are not nocturnal, so I believe them to be hibernating."

The three humans straightened up in unison.

"You know where they have taken our queen?" Rhenyon asked.

The young griffin nodded. "I do."

"How did you find us so easily?" Steve asked.

"Easily?" Phane shook his head. "It was no easy feat following the likes of the three of you Following just this one," Phane extended a wing and pointed it at Rhenyon, "was an easy task. But when you disappear and then reappear many leagues away, it is very difficult to track."

"So, where are they?" Steve demanded.

"How many men are there?" Rhenyon snapped.

"How is the queen?" Sarah wanted to know.

Phane sighed, ruffling his feathers yet again. His sire had warned them about the impetuousness of humans.

"They have chosen a bluff nearly five leagues from here, as the griffin flies," Phane explained. "It is situated on an outcropping of rock that is elevated, thus providing them excellent cover from the south, which happens to be the direction you would have to approach." Turning to Rhenyon, Phane continued. "There were fifteen human men and eighteen horses until three turned back to return south. I do not know what became of them," the griffin sadly admitted.

"They have been dealt with," Steve assured him.

"Have they any women with them?" Rhenyon asked.

Phane paused, thinking back to the many times he had studied the group of fleeing humans.

"I did not observe any human females."

"We're tracking the wrong people?" Steve groaned, rubbing his temples.

Rhenyon swore, forgetting Sarah was standing nearby. Sarah, however, suddenly stood.

"Phane, did you see anyone who was bound?"

"No, I did not."

"More horses than men. Hmm. The others are used for carrying supplies?"

"Aye, the other two are pack horses."

Steve held up a hand. "Wait a minute. You're off by one. Eighteen horses. Three left, to deal with Rhenyon, leaving fifteen. One horse for each man, leaving three. Two are pack horses, leaving one."

Phane clucked reprovingly. "I forgot him. Apologies. They have a child with them. The child rides the last horse."

Rhenyon paused. "A child? Or a small woman?"

"The child has not once dismounted the entire journey. I could not see his face as he was hooded at all times."

"That's the queen. It's got to be."

Steve turned to his wife. "How can you be so certain?"

"Because they do not let her walk," Rhenyon answered, causing Steve to look back. "If they do, they run the risk of her trying to escape by foot. She is wearing a hooded cloak because they probably have her gagged, and do not wish anyone to see the identity of their prisoner. The queen's face is well known by all her people."

"Well, let's go get those sons of —"

Sarah elbowed her husband in the stomach before he could finish the phrase.

The captain approached the young griffin. "Tell us how to find the camp."

"I will do better than that," the griffin stated boldly. "I will show you myself."

"Not necessary. Just tell us where they can be found."

"Can you see that well in the dark?" Phane asked, looking at each of them. "Unless you can, you will wander blindly about in this forest. If you wish to be successful, then you will need to approach by stealth. You cannot do that without my help."

"Let him be our guide, Rhenyon. We can definitely use the help."

"As you wish, griffin. Lead the way."

An hour later they arrived at the border of a small clearing. Directly north was the base of a sheer cliff wall, rising some hundred feet or so up into the air. Craning his head up, Steve could just make out the top of the bluff the kidnappers had camped on. If it wasn't for the faint light from their small campfire, Steve wouldn't have been able to tell if it was occupied or not. Crouching silently in the bushes, they observed the distant encampment. There simply wasn't any conceivable method to approach without divulging their presence. Sarah was going to have to teleport them in.

As Sarah was readying herself, trying to get a clear enough image of the surrounding area to qualify as a safe zone, a disturbance near the base of the cliff caught their attention. A large tree stump suddenly stood up, only to walk about ten feet away and then settle back down again.

"What the hell was that?" Steve hissed. "Since when do stumps get up and walk around?"

Rhenyon was silent, eyes narrowed, as he thoughtfully chewed his lower lip.

Steve turned to Phane. "Any idea what that was?" he whispered. "That clearly wasn't a tree stump."

Even in the darkness, Steve could tell the young griffin's eyes were wide open.

"Trolls."

"Trolls? As in live under a bridge, charge a toll, those types of trolls?"

The griffin was silent. Phane's keen eyes were now slowly scanning the surrounding forest.

"How many?" Rhenyon suddenly asked, slowly turning his head to gaze down at the griffin.

"By my count, at least four."

"Four what? Trolls? Is that bad?"

"The trolls were driven out centuries ago," Rhenyon answered, sounding tired. "Dimwitted creatures. Bloodthirsty. Wickedly strong."

"So," Steve began, rubbing his hands, "the question becomes, what are they doing here? Is this a coincidence, or have they somehow been coerced into helping these people flee Lentari?"

"I think it's obvious," Sarah said, "that whomever is in charge of this little abduction scheme has got some serious influence. If they can get trolls to do their bidding, then who knows what else they are capable of doing?"

"An angry troll is not a pleasant sight to behold," Rhenyon informed them. "I am mystified that someone found a way to overpower them."

"Great. Just peachy." Steve sighed, looking at his companions. "Do you think we can deal with that many trolls on our own?"

"There may be more protecting their camp up there." The captain's voice was soft, subdued. He turned to his companions. "If they have enlisted the aid of the trolls, then we have seriously underestimated our adversaries."

"What are you saying?" Steve asked. "We can't give up now!"

Sarah groaned. "Where can we find some allies of our own?"

Chapter 3 - Reinforcements

So, what are we gonna do?" Steve fidgeted in place, anxious to try his luck against those mobile tree trunks. "We can handle trolls. Can't be any worse than the guur, right?" Silence. "Am I right? We can't just sit here and do nothing!"

"Sir Steve is right," Rhenyon stated. "If we do nothing, then by dawn, they will have gone. We cannot let them take our queen into Ylani."

Sarah was silent as she sat, contemplating their choices.

"Look, we can't go blundering up there until we know what we face. Rhenyon said it best. We have to know the nature of our adversaries. We could be seriously outnumbered, or find something more dangerous than the trolls up on that bluff. Do we really want to chance it?"

"What do you suggest, milady?"

"Recon. We have to know what we're facing."

"You cannot see in the dark," Rhenyon said quietly, indicating for everyone to lower their voices. "Even if you were to situate yourself in one of the trees up there and observe, you have no way to relay what you see."

Growing more anxious by the minute, Steve turned to their griffin guide. "Phane, what would —"

But the young griffin was gone, having silently slipped away.

"What happened to him? Where'd he go?"

The captain peered around his companions, inspecting the area where he last saw the young griffin.

"He would not try to take them on himself, would he?"

"If he does, there goes our element of surprise."

Thirty minutes later, Phane finally returned, gliding in from the east. He touched down silently next to the fire thrower.

"Where have you —"

At that moment, a faint rustling of flapping wings could be heard. Nervously, the trio of humans eyed one another. What now? Another ally to the Ylani intruders?

A full-grown griffin suddenly materialized out of the darkness. It gave a slight bow and moved to the side, allowing room for the next griffin to land. One after the other, more griffins kept appearing, landing, bowing, and moving aside until a dozen adult griffins were silently standing about.

Sarah turned to Phane, who was beaming with pride.

"You did this, didn't you?"

Phane nodded his head. "You asked for some reinforcements, did you not? After I explained that the humans we were tracking were from the North, nearly all volunteered, but it was decided twelve would be more than adequate. Here they are!"

"Shh!" Sarah shushed. "Not so loud."

"Aye, sorry. What would you like us to do?"

Sarah looked to her husband, waiting to see what he'd say. At the same time, Steve was looking at Rhenyon, expecting him to start issuing instructions. The captain, however, was looking back at the fire thrower. Steve held up his hands.

"Hey, don't look at me. I defer to the one here who has the most experience at this type of thing. That would be you, pal."

Nodding appreciatively, Rhenyon turned to the griffins. "Up there on that bluff are at least a dozen human men.

There are also at least four trolls nearby." Several griffins squawked angrily. "Do not engage. I repeat, you will not engage. Observation only. What type of armament are they carrying? How many trolls are there in all? Learn all you can, but do not let yourself be discovered."

The few griffins that understood the human language softly squawked their orders to those that didn't. Avian heads started nodding as the instructions were relayed. Silently, the griffins took flight, disappearing into the darkness of the night sky.

Since she was normally sound asleep at this time of the night, Sarah naturally found herself becoming very groggy. Resting against the trunk of a massive tree, she tried to get a little rest. However, her mind refused to cooperate. All the jumbled thoughts in her head kept returning to one subject: the nature of her jhorun.

What about it? Was there something she'd overlooked? Again, she gave her mind permission to wander as it pleased, hoping an answer was forthcoming. Fortunately, it started to cooperate. A single question presented itself: did she really understand how her jhorun worked?

Sarah softly snorted. What an absurd question. She knew full well what her jhorun could do, and how to make it work. Why would that question surface? All she had to do was to visualize an object and instruct it where she wanted it moved to, and voila! It teleported instantly from one location to another. Teleportation. But--what if she didn't want the object to move instantly from one point to the other? Could she just...

It was like someone pressed her "sleep" button. Her thoughts suddenly quieted and she was out like a light.

Watching the sleeping human female sitting against the trunk of a massive evergreen, the young griffin remained nearby, fulfilling the promise he had made to the fire thrower. If any danger presented itself, he would alert her. In the meantime, the commander had been hard at work as he had sent out the adult griffins to map the surrounding area. If they were going to stage a rescue, then they needed to know all escape routes, the layout of the terrain, everything. The griffins were more than happy to comply. In their eyes, these humans they were spying on were of the same tribe that had attacked their cubs a year ago. The griffins had sensed an opportunity to avenge the wrongs done to them, and had leapt at the opportunity to administer a little retribution of their own.

* * *

From a vantage point nearly three hundred feet away, an alert Ylani scout had noticed an increasing amount of aerial activity centralized around a thick growth of trees somewhat southwest of where they were holding their prisoner. Coincidence? Seeing how they had yet to encounter any Lentarian retaliation thus far, the scout had strongly doubted it.

As silent as a shadow, the stealthy mercenary descended the small cliff using an ingenious system of hidden ropes and pulleys, all the while keeping an eye on the activity in the air. They hadn't managed to pull off the heist of the century only to fail now. This disturbance, minor or not, had to be investigated.

Approaching one of their sentinel trolls, he rapidly tapped the special obedience sequence onto the troll's hairy back, preparing the ugly brute for a possible attack. The inert troll swelled ominously, its breathing rapidly increasing, but remained motionless. It was ready to swing into action at the proper command.

Silently creeping through the forest, the scout kept angling toward the last area he had noticed movement. There! What was this? Griffins? Thanking his good fortune yet again for being blessed with nocturnal vision, the mercenary-for-hire watched with amazement as airborne griffins kept descending from the sky and disappearing into the trees, only to be replaced by others taking to the air. Were griffins usually this active at night? Were they participating in some type of hunt?

About ready to turn back toward their camp, his suspicions confirmed as harmless activity, the scout stiffened. He had just observed something that chilled his blood: Lentarians! Several of them, and they were deep in a hushed conversation. This had to be a rescue party—he *had* to warn the others!

Swiftly turning about, the spy took off like a shot, only to run full tilt into an immense stone wall. Where had it come from? Rubbing his throbbing head, his gaze traveled up. Way, way up. How could he have become so disoriented as to miss an obstacle of this size? Quizzically running his hand along the rough surface, his blood froze in his veins for a second time. Two green, reptilian eyes appeared and were staring down at him.

The scout stared in shock as his brain tried to process the information his eyes were reporting back to him. The wall was alive! A creature that large could only be—

A brief, trilled whistle sounded. It was the last act of a seriously unlucky spy.

Several hundred feet away, the alert troll lurched forward, having been called into action. Surprisingly silent for its bulk, the troll moved swiftly through the forest, following its nose. The scent of the human it was sworn to obey beckoned from the south. It had been instructed not to leave the area for any reason, but the scout had also ordered it to obey, so it would.

Farther and farther away it ran until it finally broke through the trees into a small clearing. The troll blinked stupidly, looking about with confusion. The scent originated from this area, yet there were no humans present. Scratching its skull with a meaty arm, dislodging several fleas in the process, the troll sniffed the air again. Its beady eyes were drawn to a large boulder near the center of the clearing. Lumbering over, the troll rolled the rock off to the side and gazed with mild interest at the gaping hole that had been uncovered. The scent of the human was strongest here. Confused, it poked several fingers into the opening, not knowing that the human he was searching for had recently been hammered into the ground.

An alarming scent manifested, one that the troll knew

and feared. Forgetting that it was supposed to obey its human masters, the troll gathered its strength and sprinted toward the safety of the trees, fear giving it a welcoming boost of speed.

It didn't make it.

* * *

"Did you feel that?" Rhenyon drew his sword.

The four griffins jerked up their heads, staring intently at the dark forest before them.

Steve moved next to the captain. "What is it? Did you hear something?"

"There was a thump and then the ground trembled beneath our feet." Rhenyon eyed his companions. "We are not alone."

"Think it's a troll?"

"I cannot say. If it were, I would think we would be able to smell it. I will go check it out."

Steve held up a hand. "No, you stay here. I'll go."

"You will not. I will go."

"You're needed here. If something happens to you, then we'd be in a world of hurt. I'll do it."

"And leave me to explain to Lady Sarah that something has happened to you? Methinks not. I will take my chances out there."

Off in the distance, another disturbance sounded, bringing both of them up short: a sickening crunch.

Both would-be rescuers glanced at each other. Rhenyon silently pointed to Phane, and then to the still sleeping Sarah. Phane nodded. He approached the sleeping human female and gently ran the tips of his primaries along Sarah's face. The caress was soft and gentle, and more than adequate to awaken her.

Thinking it was her husband, Sarah smiled, sleepily opening her eyes. Two avian eyes swam into focus. Eyes opening wide with alarm, Sarah rose to her feet.

"What's —"

Phane extended a wing, covering Sarah's mouth. Silently,

the griffin indicated where Rhenyon and Steve stood, both facing away from her. The captain had drawn his sword, and Steve appeared ready to ignite his hands.

"We meet again, human."

The voice was soft; feminine. It had drifted down from above, which didn't make any sense. Was the owner of the voice in the trees? It was far too dark for Steve to be able to see who, or what, it belonged to.

"Who's there?" Steve called out, as softly as he dared.

"A friend."

Wheels clicked. He'd heard that voice before!

"Pryllan? Is that you?"

"Indeed," came the reply.

"Who is Pryllan?" Rhenyon asked.

"Kahvel's mate."

Rhenyon reeled in shock. "A dragon? What is a dragon doing here?"

"I offer my assistance," Pryllan's voice answered from the darkness. "And I have already given it twice this night. You need to be more careful, human. Your camp was discovered by one of their scouts. He also had a mountain troll at his disposal."

Rhenyon swore softly. "Then we need to move. Now. If they know we are here, then it's only a matter of time before —"

"Be at ease, human soldier," the gentle voice spoke. "The captors know not they are being observed."

"You took care of the scout, dragon?"

"Aye, I did."

"And the troll?"

Pryllan's enormous silhouette finally materialized out of the darkness. She lowered her neck until her head was down at their eye-level.

"You owe me for that. I am still unable to remove that vile taste from my mouth."

"You ate it??"

"I did no such thing." The dragon bristled with annoyance, her folded wings rustling against her back. "No self-respecting dragon would dream of eating the likes of a troll." Pryllan's nostrils suddenly flared. She inhaled deeply, sampling the air. "There are griffins all about the area."

Rhenyon nodded. "We know. They have been giving us surveillance reports on the Ylanis."

"And what have you learned thus far?"

"After four hours, not as much as we would like," Rhenyon confessed. "The exact number of men is unknown. How well armed they are also is unknown. We did learn that there is one more troll protecting the camp itself, bringing the total to five."

"Four," Pryllan corrected, eyes glittering in the moonlight.

"Aye, right."

Sighing heavily, the graceful dragon again lowered her head, fixing the humans with a piercing gaze. "So, you still do not know the nature of your adversary, do you? This will not do." Her intense gaze shifted to Steve. "Sunrise is in just over an hour. There is still time. This is how you do aerial surveillance." With that, the dragon leaned forward and snatched the first human she could reach, which just happened to be Steve. Straightening, Pryllan cast her gaze skyward as she stretched her right foreleg up and behind her, depositing the thunderstruck human squarely on her back.

"But —"

"I would advise you to hang on."

"But —"

"Ready?"

"But —"

Reptilian muscles bunched together and then explosively launched them straight up. On her back, his knuckles white, as he gripped several spiky scales of the dragon's armor, Steve could only stare with amazement as he noticed Pryllan's wings had not opened until she cleared the treetops. That meant she had just leapt well over a hundred feet straight up! Once safely in the air, the dragon banked left, sending them into a gentle turn southward.

How exactly was he supposed to see anything from way up here? Steve blinked his eyes, trying to restore some moisture back into them. The air was whipping by so fast that it was hard enough just to keep his eyes open, let alone be of much help. It was pitch-black, and what little light the starry sky provided only further proved that this was, as much as he hated to admit it, a lousy idea.

Now miles away from the bluff, Pryllan's head turned on her supple neck to face her rider.

"What do you think, Steve?"

"It's fantastic!" The words were practically ripped out of his mouth by the howling wind. "You must fly all the time!"

"What I am about to do must remain our secret," the dragon cautioned. "Not to mention it is frowned upon for dragons to take on riders."

"Mum's the word!" Steve's voice called out from the dragon's massive back.

"You have my thanks," Pryllan said, gently. "And now, this is the reason I brought you with me."

A sudden warmth flooded Steve's body, spreading rapidly from the top of his head down to the bottom of his feet. Gone were all his aches and pains. Gone was the fatigue he had been feeling, his body energized as it had never been before. The howling of the wind faded away, his eyes clearing instantly. Everything sprang into focus, from every needle on every pine tree whizzing by, down to every nook and cranny of the daunting cliff wall his companions would still have to scale. What was this? There were a series of ropes tucked away in several cracks running the length of the rock wall. That must be how they were able to ascend the sheer cliff face so rapidly. Someone must have had this ready for them His gaze shifted as Pryllan gazed down, piercing the thick forest canopy to inspect the ground far below. Incredible! He watched as some type of small animal scampered out from its den to forage for food. The gaze suddenly shifted upward, where he was now watching one of the griffins in flight, slowly circling overhead.

"How are you doing this?" Steve practically yelled the question out, momentarily forgetting that with the absence of noise, it was no longer necessary to shout.

"A dragon can choose whether to share its sensory perceptions with others. We typically do not, and never with humans."

"Why are you making this exception for me?"

"You are different. I cannot explain."

"I truly, honestly, appreciate you sharing this with me. I didn't realize a dragon could share all of their senses."

"It is not a commonly known fact. And one that I would prefer you kept private, agreed?"

"Agreed."

"Now, let us observe those who wish to remain hidden."

The huge dragon banked right, leading them back toward the circling griffins.

"Won't they see us?"

"If they were to look up at the right time, possibly. Fortunately, the human eye will typically not see an object moving as fast as we are about to."

What was that supposed to mean?

Picking up his thought, Pryllan nodded. "You'll see."

It was as though someone flipped on the afterburners. The passing forest was suddenly rocketing by them, the added speed sending Steve sliding back several feet to jut up against the junction point of Pryllan's outstretched wings. Fortunately, handholds were everywhere along her back. One scale was raised up just a bit, serving as an adequate seat. With his butt pressed solidly up against another piece of armored plating, knuckles white, and face alive with wonder, Steve smiled. No matter how hard he tried, he couldn't wipe the childish grin from his face. This was awesome!

Sharing Pryllan's impressive visual abilities, Steve watched as her powerful gaze zeroed in on the small, quiet bluff where the Queen's abductors were hiding. As the dragon's gaze shifted from person to person, Steve started counting the people he could see. The gaze shifted to a small nondescript tent guarded by four men. Was it his imagination? Was he hearing someone sob? It had to be the queen! Clearly Pryllan's abilities extended to her auditory senses as well. The scene shifted to the circling griffins as Pryllan directed her senses elsewhere, seeking out the immobile trolls.

"Wait! Go back to that tent you were just looking at. I thought I heard the queen."

The dragon's gaze returned to the tiny canvas tent. Several men had moved off, but two still remained, guarding their sobbing prisoner.

"What are we looking for?" Pryllan inquired.

"There's enough room behind the tent for Sarah to acquire a safe zone. But there's a problem, though."

"What would that be?"

"Sarah has to see the location before she can teleport there. That means…" Steve trailed off.

"She would have to be on my back as well, is that what you are afraid of?"

"Yes."

"You may have noticed one additional human would make no difference to me."

"I know you can carry the weight. The problem would be with my wife. There's no way in hell I can convince her to ride on your back. The bribe necessary would be —"

Steve lost his train of thought as more and more people started moving about. Clearly the activity in the camp was increasing. What was happening? It was still dark out. Were they looking to get an early start? From the looks of things, the kidnappers were breaking camp.

"Back to the others! We need to warn them that they are preparing to move. Hurry!"

The powerful dragon banked south, returning them to the small clearing that served as their base. Standing up stiffly on Pryllan's back, Steve started working his way off the dragon's scaly back, sliding down the last ten feet off her right flank.

Sarah approached, her smile slowly melting into a concerned frown. After riding on the back of a dragon, her husband should have been all smiles. Had something happened?

Steve motioned Rhenyon and Sarah over.

"What did you see, Sir Steve?"

"Twelve men total, four keeping guard over a small tent," Steve responded instantly. "I heard … wait. Forget that. They're preparing to leave."

"Wizards be damned," Rhenyon cursed. "I had Lady Sarah relay a message to the king. He has not responded yet."

"He's probably trying to figure out what he can do on

such a short notice," Sarah suggested.

"Then, that means we need to stall them."

"How do you propose we do that?"

"I have an idea. I think I can buy you enough time until we hear from the king."

Sarah was perplexed. "Just what do you —"

"My dear, just trust me on this one. When you hear from the king, signal us."

"How am I supposed to do that?"

"Just jump up and down and wave your arms. We'll keep an eye on you."

"You can see me from up there?"

"I can't, but Pryllan can."

"Alright, will do."

"Pryllan, let's go."

Deftly plucking the human from the ground, the emerald green dragon placed her rider on her back yet again and launched them both back into the air.

"What are your plans?" the dragon inquired, once they were safely airborne.

"Can you do that flying-faster-than-crap bit again?"

Pryllan shared her wyverian senses once more and accelerated her velocity until the world was whizzing by.

"Look at their campfire," Steve instructed.

Their shared eyesight sought out the small bluff, singling out the crackling campfire. More mercenaries were huddled around the fire, warming themselves and their meal at the same time.

"What are we looking for?" the dragon asked.

"You'll see. Keep watching that fire. I'm going to try something."

Taking deep, steady breaths, Steve stared at the campfire that was miles away. Activating his jhorun, he cast it out at the distant fire, requesting all energy from that fire be drawn inward. With a smug grin on his face, he and Pryllan watched as the campfire shrank in size until it was nothing more than coals.

Those who were sitting around the fire were now gesturing angrily at one another. Apparently, they were blaming the person responsible for maintaining the fire. Nodules of flint were produced, and after repeated strikes from a worn specimen of iron pyrite, their campfire was blazing yet again.

While Pryllan circled overhead, Steve watched as the activity of the camp returned to normal. As more gathered around the fire, he snuffed the fire out again.

Again, heads swiveled to glare at the man who had just stowed his tinder kit. Dumbfounded, the clueless individual approached the coals, staring suspiciously at those still sitting around the hearth. Was someone playing a prank? Was one of his dimwitted companions extinguishing the fire when he wasn't looking? Harsh words were spoken as several men reached for their daggers. One man appeared, barking orders for people to sheath their knives. Was this their leader, then?

With the fire blazing once more, the tinder kit was again stowed, being shoved forcefully back into the pack that was leaning against a tree. Keeping a wary eye on his handiwork, the mercenary settled down against the trunk, muttering under his breath the entire time. Steve glanced over at the bag that now held the tinder kit. With a smile, he ignited the pack.

More shouts were heard as water was thrown on the burning bag. The owner of the tinder kit, confronted yet again with numerous scowls and threats, started backing away from the angry men. Steve laughed out loud as crude references were made regarding the unfortunate man's parentage. Glaring at the unlucky owner of the pack, the leader of the gang upended his leather canteen over their "second" campfire.

Enjoying this game, Steve eyed the canteen still in the hands of the leader. As soon as the man had turned his back on the scowling thief, the canteen became the next item to be engulfed in flames.

Casting dark looks at his fellow ruffians, the gang leader watched as his favorite canteen started to char. Dropping the leather bag before he received a nasty burn, the leader caught sight of the grinning thug. Eyes narrowed; more words were exchanged.

Grinning like a school kid, Steve ignited a small patch of the leader's tunic. More shouts. Yelling profusely, the gang leader dropped to the ground and rolled around in a desperate bid to extinguish the flames. With the fire finally put out, the leader glanced over at the still laughing hooligan. The glare he gave him was so cold that even the thug had started backpedaling. Clearly believing that these mysterious problems originated from the unlucky owner of the fire stones, the gang leader stalked over to a stump, tapped a sequence onto the surface, and then stood back to watch the fun.

The troll rose up, sniffing for its prey. Catching sight of the cowering human slowly retreating into the forest, the troll lurched forward, eager to claim its prize. With a cry of fright, the thug disappeared into the trees, with the troll hot on his heels.

"Very clever," Pryllan observed. "How soon before they discover someone else has been tampering with their fire?"

"Probably not too long," Steve admitted.

"Objective obtained, it would seem. Your lady is indicating we should return."

The camp on the cliff suddenly hushed as the flaps of the smallest tent were gently pushed aside. The hooded prisoner had poked out her head. The leader rushed over. It was clear the prisoner was to return to the tent. Soft words were spoken, only to be met with harsh words in return. The prisoner appeared to be extremely reluctant to return to the tent. Unfortunately, they received a back-handed slap that sent them reeling back into the tent. Two men returned to their positions, guarding the tent from unauthorized entry.

Steve had winced at the sheer brutality of the slap. He was livid. "They will pay for that. I promise you."

* * *

"What was the king's response?" Steve asked Rhenyon several minutes later as he slid off the dragon's back.

"I was unable to tell him precisely where we are due to my own uncertainty of our present location. Nevertheless, five full squadrons are en route to this general area, but will not make it here until much later. It would seem no aid will be coming our way anytime soon. My friends, we are on our own."

"So, help is on the way, only it won't reach us in time," Steve muttered. "This is just great."

"What if the king's men don't make it here in time?" Sarah said, looking at both her husband and the captain. "So what? Are you telling me you guys can't handle them?"

Rhenyon and Steve looked at each other, and then as one, looked up at the motionless dragon.

Rhenyon clapped his friend on the shoulder and motioned for the dragon to lower her head so she could be included in the hushed conversation.

"Here's what we are going to do…"

Chapter 4 - Liberation

The morning sky continued to brighten, the few remaining stars finally conceding defeat and winking out. The nocturnal residents of the forest relinquished control to their day-time counterparts, paving the way for bright colorful birds, small squirrel-like creatures, and loud buzzing insects to begin their orchestral accompaniment that heralded the dawn of a new day. Several of the squirrel creatures had stopped their foraging, their thick spotted tails twitching nervously, as they observed a group of humans who were frantically running to and fro. Only one tent was left standing on the bluff, and that was of a small canvas variety which housed their prized prisoner.

Several men methodically went through the small camp, erasing all traces that the bluff had ever been occupied. As the men worked to dismantle their hearth, the prisoner was retrieved and placed, hooded and gagged, back on the small horse. Harsh words were spoken as the reins were handed to one of the captors, the man unlucky enough to draw the short straw.

With the gear all packed and stowed, the group silently departed, with the sentinel trolls disappearing into the thick growth of trees that surrounded them. Not known for their agility or stealth, telltale signs of the trolls' presence sounded every few minutes as various grunts and snapping of twigs could be heard.

Thirty minutes later, the procession came to a halt as some type of disturbance could now be heard coming from up ahead. Angry squawks of rage pierced the air as numerous flapping wings were heard. The leader hesitated. What was going on? Cautiously poking his head around the corner to see what lay before them, he paused. Several griffins were fighting with each other as each tried to lay claim over the carcass of some dead animal. Well, let them have it.

Returning to the group, he informed everyone that they were going to give the battling griffins a wide berth. No sense in provoking an attack when what they wanted was secrecy. Heads nodded. No one wanted to face an angry griffin.

Backtracking to a fork in the trail that they had passed earlier, they headed slightly west as they quietly snuck by the battling griffins. Distant squawking filtered from above as other griffins came to watch the show. The leader cursed softly. The two fighting griffins were starting to attract the attention of even more of their kind. People were going to notice all the activity in the area sooner or later. Noticing a thick grove of trees up on the right, the mercenary slipped under the cover of dense foliage, motioning the others to join him as quickly as possible.

"What are we doing?" one man hissed.

"Blasted griffins are drawing too much attention to themselves," the leader explained. "We must get out of the area or else seek cover until things quiet down."

The captors groaned. "We have to wait for the griffins to shut up? Can we just shoot them down?"

"Nay. If you don't like it, Bezel, then you can seek out a means to navigate through this blasted forest yourself. If you find something, let us know, and we will gladly leave this cursed place."

The disgruntled thief disappeared into the trees. Several minutes later, he reemerged, indicating for the others to follow.

"We can make it through. The terrain is rough, but manageable. No one will find us through that."

The skeptical leader eyed their new guide. "Fine. We head north."

Navigating through the forest without having a path to follow was proving to be more of a chore than anyone had thought. The men were grumbling, casting dark looks at one another. The ground was rocky and uneven. Feet were fast becoming sore, muscles tiring quickly.

Their prisoner, however, couldn't help but smile at their misfortune. For the first time, the kidnappers refrained from placing the hood back over her head. She was still gagged, however, so she still wouldn't be able to shout for help. Sitting comfortably on her mount, her smile well hidden by the strip of fabric she was forced to bite down on, she delighted in seeing her captors stumble. Long giving up any hope of a rescue, the queen knew her only hope now lay with her husband and his ability to negotiate her release. She shuddered to think what price the Ylanis would demand.

The horse she was riding came to another sudden halt. What now? Leaning to the left so she could see around the person guiding her mount, she saw that an enormous tree had fallen and would be prolonging this delightful trip through the forest. There would be no navigating their way around this behemoth of a tree.

Curses flew unhindered amongst her captors. So far this morning, they had been having nothing but bad luck. First the quarrel with the griffins. Then this tree. The queen stiffened in her saddle. Two encounters, both happening directly in their path? Were these some type of diversionary tactics? If so, it was an odd way to go about rescuing someone. Alert now for the slightest sign of a rescue, the queen remained motionless and silent on her horse.

However, her captors were starting to show signs of apprehension as well. Was this the Lentarian response that they had been waiting for? Several men snorted, all thinking the same thought. This was the Lentarian retaliation for stealing their queen? Where were the archers? The knights? What about armed soldiers? All they could do was chop a tree down? Several men started to laugh. This couldn't be the Lentarians. Dolts that they were, even this was beneath them. This had to be just a fluke.

Mumbling to themselves, the group reversed their course yet again. As several men investigated the surrounding countryside, looking for ways around the fallen tree, the queen nonchalantly glanced down at the splintered trunk. She blinked, eyes opening wide. Were those teeth marks? It looked as though something actually felled the tree with a single bite. She shuddered.

With hopeful eyes scanning each tree, searching for any signs of help, the queen slowly hung her head. Hadn't she told herself to stop wishing for the impossible? Even she didn't know exactly where they were now, and she was the queen! How could she expect to be found in the middle of her country's largest forest? She closed her eyes, willing away her tears of frustration.

More shouts came from ahead. Suddenly men were running, all rushing to pull the stored gear out of various saddle bags. Confused, the queen turned to look behind her. Her captors were hastily making camp. Wood was tossed into a newly-created firepit. Within moments, a cheery fire was crackling away.

Confused, the queen twisted around on her saddle to see what the leader of this motley group was doing. What was going on? Had they lost their minds? Why would they be setting up camp out here in the open?

Minutes later, she was sitting silently on the ground in her canvas tent yet again. Struggling to hear what was being said outside, the queen held her breath. The men were clearly agitated about something. There! Someone had said something about hiding in plain sight. Was someone looking for them?

The flaps to her tent were flung aside as the gang leader came strolling in, carrying a makeshift chair and a bundle of rope. Leering at the queen, he set the chair up in the middle of the tent and started uncoiling the rope. The queen's head fell again. Without being told what to do, she voluntarily sat on the crude chair. Her arms and legs were quickly immobilized. He didn't even take the gag out. The queen's surprised eyes blinked. Who was out there that they thought she could signal?

After making certain his prisoner would be unable to escape or signal their presence to anyone, the thug hastily retreated from the tent, flinging the flaps closed behind him.

Willing away her tears, the queen closed her eyes. Would this never end? Her back ached; she was travel weary, and was tired of sitting. She fidgeted on the chair, trying to get comfortable. Suddenly, someone was touching her. She hadn't heard anyone re-enter her tent. Deeming them unworthy of any sort of response, she kept her eyes closed. Strong, firm hands lightly tugged her bonds, verifying that they were in place and holding. The brief flash of heat surprised her; she flinched, but at least managed to keep her eyes closed. She refused yet again to acknowledge the torment her captors were giving her. When no more badgering was forthcoming, she decided to open her eyes for a quick look. Sarah's kind eyes were smiling back at her. The queen could only stare at her in shock.

"Good morning, Your Majesty." Sarah gave a small curtsy.

Callé's eyes opened wide. Sarah leaned forward and untied her gag.

"Lady Sarah! What—how did you get here?" It was then that she noted she was no longer in the tent, and that her arms and legs were free. On shaky legs, she stood up. The ropes that had been immobilizing her slid down to the ground with a plop. Confused, she picked up one of the ends. It had been neatly sliced in two! A quick inspection of the ropes revealed burnt ends.

"Are you here with your husband? What is going on?" Callé looked about her. They were clearly still in the forest. Majestic evergreens surrounded her on all sides.

"Are you able to walk?" Sarah asked. "We need to get you someplace safe. There are trolls about and I personally don't want to run into any one of them."

The queen cautiously took a few steps, restoring circulation back to her legs, which she was horrified to learn had gone to sleep on her. She took a few hesitant steps toward the closest tree when she stumbled and would have taken a nasty fall had it not been for the griffin that materialized out of nowhere. Two shocked human eyes stared into two equally surprised avian ones as Callé held on to the griffin's neck. Once she was certain she would not take a tumble, she hastily released her death grip on the griffin.

"Your Majesty, may I present Phane, son of Pheris."

"Greetings, Your Majesty," Phane intoned, inclining his head.

Still too shocked at the absurdity of latching onto a griffin to break her fall, the queen gave a small nod of her head.

"They are going to discover that I am missing at any moment," Callé whispered, more to herself than to anyone.

"Then they are going to discover a pissed off fire thrower when they do."

"Sir Steve is in the tent? You must get him out of there, Lady Sarah! Those men have five trolls at their command."

"There are three left that I'm aware of."

The queen stared at her. "How were you able to defend yourself against a troll, let alone two?"

"They have their friends, we have ours."

"Regardless," the queen pleaded, "you need to get your husband to safety."

"I tried to argue with him, saying this was a foolish idea, but he wouldn't listen." Sarah looked at the queen. "He saw them slap you, up on that bluff. My husband can be somewhat stubborn when he chooses to be. He's looking to exact a little retribution."

"You knew I was there?"

"We have been tracking you for a while. Come on, we need to get somewhere safe."

Sarah took the queen's hand and vanished.

Moments later, Callé's eyes couldn't open any wider.

"Exactly what are we doing now?" the queen asked, hugging the tree trunk as tightly as she could. "Do you think this wise?"

Located some hundred feet or so up in the air, Sarah clutched the other side of the trunk.

"From here, I can see the camp those men set up. And I can see the tent. No one has gone back into it yet, which means they don't know you're missing. If something happens to Steve or Rhenyon, I can get them out of there. That's our role now. We're backup."

Callé's mouth dropped open.

"Rhenyon is here as well? How many men does he have with him?"

"Just him, I'm afraid."

At that moment, one man rose from where he was sitting at the hearth and looked back at the small tent. With a grunt he ambled off in that direction.

"Uh, oh," Sarah murmured, from her position up in the tree. Both she and the queen were silent as they watched the thug approach the tent. "Fireworks in three, two, one..."

The man disappeared inside the tent. For several tense moments nothing happened. Did Steve sneak out the back? Or did he —

WHOOOOOSH!!!

The small tent disappeared in a huge flash of fire. The thief emerged, screaming obscenities as he sprinted back to his companions, his backside burning. Another man emerged from the smoke and flames, unscathed. Steve walked nonchalantly toward the men who had sprung to their feet. Both of his hands were still lit, and even from this distance, Sarah could see that he had a pissed-off expression on his face.

Two men turned tail and ran for all they were worth, hoping to disappear into the thick underbrush of the forest. Turning to watch the men sprint for the trees, Steve scowled. His right hand blazed, his jhorun demanding to be released. A chaser formed, but oddly enough, refused to be thrown. Confused, Steve tried again, cocking his arm back to let the imaginary pitch fly. The chaser stuck like glue. A fleeting image of smacking his hand on the ground briefly flashed through his mind. Was he supposed to punch the ground?

Figuring it couldn't hurt to try, Steve knelt down and smacked the ground with the chaser still attached to his hand. The blazing orb melted into the earth and instantly streaked off toward its target, leaving a burning fire trail behind it. It rapidly accelerated toward the two fleeing men. One man turned, noting that the fire trail was rapidly approaching. Screaming more obscenities, each man decided to flee in a different direction. The chaser continued to snake toward its target, neatly forking off so that both men could be pursued. Both men disappeared into the forest. Suddenly realizing that his ground chaser would continue to pursue them throughout the thick growth of the forest, potentially putting hundreds, if not thousands of trees at risk, he held up a hand. The chaser halted, both fire trails just shy of entering the heavily wooded area.

Extinguish yourself, Steve ordered. It wasn't worth burning down the forest.

Both fire lines melted into the earth, leaving scorched trails upon the ground.

The shocked captors finally regained their senses after experiencing the surreal spectacle of seeing two men pursued by fire. With enthusiastic yells, everyone dove for their weapons. Swords were unsheathed, bows nocked with arrows. Several trilled whistles sounded as the trolls were called into action.

With a roar, several of the ugly brutes emerged from the trees, lumbering toward Steve as fast as they could. Unsure of what he should do next, he gazed at the two large creatures as they bore down on him. This couldn't be good. He released a jet of fire at the closest troll, causing the hideous creature to slam on the brakes. It lurched to the side, somehow managing to avoid singeing even so much as a single hair on its disgusting pelt.

Unhindered, the second troll had almost reached its human target. Roaring with anger, it dove at the motionless human, ready to rip the unfortunate biped limb from limb. Suddenly the troll vanished in mid leap, only to reappear moments later directly in the path of a massive tree. Not wasting any time, the troll wrapped its long limbs about the trunk and pulled, fully expecting the hapless biped to collapse to the ground. When the tree resisted being uprooted, the troll snorted with surprise. Not being the sharpest creature in existence, the troll grunted with effort as it attempted to wrestle the massive tree to the ground.

The first troll, after avoiding the blast of fire that had appeared directly before it, peered at the small human. Too stupid to realize that the human's hands were still ablaze, the troll resumed its advance toward its prey.

Several loud shrieks sounded from above, and within moments the sky was transformed into a whirlwind of activity. The griffins had all chosen that moment to attack, deftly swerving around one another as they assaulted the troll from the air. As dimwitted as the troll was, it knew it could handle one or two griffins. However, there were too many. It was time to abandon this foolish mission. Throwing its hairy arms up in an effort to protect its sensitive eyes, the troll lumbered toward the protection of the forest, disappearing into the dense foliage of the surrounding trees. The only sounds now were the flapping of wings and the occasional squawk from the griffins, along with the grunts of the tree-wrestling troll who could still be heard as it continued to try and pull the tree to the ground.

Flabbergasted, the former captors stared at one another. Where were the rest of the trolls? And where had the griffins come from?

"Arrows at the ready!" the leader barked out, aiming his own bow at one of the diving griffins.

"What are we shooting at?" one man asked.

"What do you think, dolt? The griffins!"

"What about him?"

"What about him who?"

"I think they are talking about me," Steve supplied helpfully, still standing quietly nearby. In one sweeping motion, Steve ignited all the wooden weapons he could see, watching with satisfaction as bowstrings snapped in rapid succession and the arrows crumbled to ash.

Undaunted, the closest mercenary drew his sword.

"You there, kill him! All others, take out those griffins!"

"Now you see me," Steve began, giving the agreed upon signal to his wife, "now you don't."

Steve vanished, joining Rhenyon who had been watching from the safety of the trees.

"How are we doing?" Steve inquired, snuffing out both hands, but electing to keep an eye on their circling allies.

With his bow strung, Rhenyon took aim at the next archer within range. Thus far, he had managed to incapacitate four of the mercenaries, all without moving an inch. "The griffins should be safe in the air. We can finish picking off his archers."

A volley of arrows suddenly appeared, streaking upward. One griffin squawked in pain as an arrow pierced its left wing. Able to use only the one wing, the wounded creature started spiraling out of control. From their vantage point, they could see a very hard landing approaching rapidly as the injured griffin descended ever closer to the valley floor. Suddenly, the griffin vanished, appearing moments later safe on the ground. Squawking in confusion, the griffin made eye contact with the human female in the treetops. Reverently, the griffin bowed to Sarah, who smiled and nodded back. Phane swerved close, wings flapping furiously as he fought to remain at eye level with the humans.

"What now? We cannot repel arrows!"

"Where'd the hell did they get more bows?" Steve angrily exclaimed. "I thought I burned them all. Okay. Here's what we do. Phane, tell the rest of the griffins to avoid getting too close to the ground. I'll throw a shield over the area where they are shooting. It should incinerate the arrows, but some might slip through, and I don't want any of you guys getting too close."

"Aye, will do!" The griffin flew off.

"That griffin is hurt!" Sarah was staring down at the wounded griffin who had just now regained its feet. "It's defenseless!"

"Send me down there," Steve instructed.

Sarah started to remove her medallion when she paused.

"I'll do it. If you go, then I'll have to help move you down there and move you back. This way I can go myself and you can be free to help the griffins."

"Not a chance."

Sarah patted his cheek. "That's so sweet, almost like you think you have a say in the matter. That griffin needs help, and I can give it. I'm going."

"Hey, I don't want anything to happen to you! I'm not about to—"

She will remain unharmed.

Steve glanced up, catching sight of the green dragon as it circled far overhead. He nodded.

"Just hurry, okay?"

Sarah smiled and nodded, vanishing moments later.

One of the men assigned to bringing down the attacking griffins cursed in disgust. He had finally run out of arrows. Still hadn't hit a thing, though. Glancing over at his companions who were firing arrows just as fast as they could, the archer threw down his empty quiver. Until he found some more, he was pretty much useless. Ready to ask his neighbor where he got his, a faint squawk sounded from somewhere nearby. The mercenary remembered that his neighbor had mentioned he had scored a hit on one of attacking griffins, the mercenary smiled to himself. The praise his companions would bestow upon him should he single-handedly dispatch a griffin, albeit a wounded one, was enough to spur him into action. The would-be hero took off, following the faint squawks his ears told him were nearby.

Quietly peering around the trunk of an enormous pine tree, the archer could hear the labored breathing of the agitated griffin. The giddy thug couldn't believe his luck. The griffin had its back to him! This was too easy! Wait, what was this? A woman was there, tending the griffin. This was going to be fun!

He never saw it coming. The blast of fire came spiraling out of nowhere, slamming into the surprised assassin with the force of a boulder thrown by a massive trebuchet. The jet of fire was so intense that several nearby boulders cracked in two before being reduced to gravel. Of the would-be assassin, nothing remained.

Far overhead, grunting with satisfaction, their airborne sentry watched as the last bits of ash fluttered away in the wind. Pryllan noted the grounded griffin was already flexing its newly healed wing. She nodded her head to both griffin and human, not knowing (or caring) that they would be unable to see her. She was ready to bank left, away from the battle, when she cocked her head. She could hear the unmistakable grunts of a troll. Thus far, the last of the unpleasant northern mountain-dwelling creatures had been eluding her. What she spotted drew her up short. There was the final troll, attempting to uproot one of the huge evergreens. Over and over, it pulled and pulled, grunting with frustration as the tree refused to budge. Pryllan quietly landed nearby and snorted with disgust. If ever a species deserved to be extinct, it was this one.

Steve focused on a section of space twenty feet above the firing archers and created a shimmering wall of heat. *No fire*, he ordered his jhorun. *Just blazing, intense heat. It's got to be hot and it must be invisible.* As a pleasant side effect, Steve noted, the heat shield that had materialized appeared to be baking the assailants below as all were covered in a fine sheen of sweat. Heat waves were radiating off his shield as Steve increased the temperature as much as he could. He didn't care. No more griffins would be harmed during the rescue of the queen, thank you very much.

"They are expending tremendous numbers of arrows trying to shoot down the griffins." Rhenyon remarked to the queen. "I do not understand. They should have exhausted their supply by now."

"I don't understand it, either," Steve remarked, increasing the intensity of the left side of his shield as several archers targeted two of the circling griffins. "I watched those arrows burn as I torched all the bows, too. Everyone down there has a bow, with a quiver full of arrows. It's almost as if —"

He singled out three archers in his range of vision and set all three bows, with their quivers, on fire. Steve heard shouts of surprise as the torched bows and arrows were flung away. All three archers crouched down, and then resurfaced moments later with new bows and fully loaded quivers.

"What the hell? They have spares for their spares?"

"There is some other force at work here," Rhenyon spat, eyeing the men with disgust. "Where is the dragon?"

"Dispatching the trolls for us." Steve scanned the skies, looking for the telltale green dragon that was circling about somewhere overhead. "Why are we going through this? Wouldn't it be easier to just scare everyone off, or else finish them off? Why risk ourselves here?"

"Those men kidnapped the queen," Rhenyon spat out, glaring at the mercenaries who were valiantly trying to fend off the constant griffin attacks. "We need to know who they are, who hired them, what their intentions are, and so on."

"What about those two people we sent back to the castle? Isn't two enough?"

"The more the merrier. They will pay, I assure you." Tapping his fingers on the hilt of his sword, Rhenyon suddenly straightened. "They might not ever exhaust their supplies, but we can certainly make it difficult for them." Rhenyon unslung the bow he had procured from one of his three previous attackers. The remaining archers had protected themselves well, hiding behind large boulders and trees. They would have to reposition themselves as well if they wanted to get a clear shot. "Do you have a bow? If so, follow my lead."

"Sorry, I don't. What I have is … no, wait! I think I do." Reaching behind his back to grasp Mythrin's scabbard, Steve felt along the leather sheath until he felt the newly redesigned Nohrstaf holder. With a grunt, he pulled the unremarkable-looking weapon free. The small club rested in his hands for a few moments before becoming a bow that matched Rhenyon's. Most puzzling, however, was the fact that there didn't appear to be any string to fit an arrow to, yet the bow was bent as though a stout piece of whipcord held it firmly in place.

Ready to release an arrow, Rhenyon glanced over, saw the oddity of Steve's bow, and eased his grip on the arrow.

"Where is the string? How are you to fire an arrow if

your bow does not have a string to hold it?"

"Beats the hell out of me." Experimentally, Steve traced his fingers along the imaginary line where the string should be. A faint, shimmering line materialized briefly, disappearing moments later.

"Did you see that?" Rhenyon moved closer to the bow, peering intently at the space where the silvery line had appeared. He put two fingers together and pretended an arrow was already notched, pulling back as though he was ready to fire the arrow.

The shimmering line appeared again, and this time an arrow composed of what appeared to be silver light appeared. Satisfied, Rhenyon returned his attention back to his own bow. "There's your answer, then. Just pull the string and an arrow appears."

"But what am I —"

"Shardwyn gave you that, did he not?"

Steve nodded.

"Then you should have expected it to behave in an unusual way. Now. Follow me. Quietly. We need a better vantage point."

Moving locations several times, they both finally situated themselves a fair distance away, with several of the firing archers within their line of sight.

"Aim for the man in the middle," Rhenyon instructed. "Non-fatal." His bow twanged, the arrow appearing in the leg of one of the men. With a howl, the archer went down.

Shaking his head, Steve placed two fingers in the area where an arrow should be. The silver string appeared. Pulling the string back, the silver arrow also reappeared. He grunted with effort as his arms started to tremble. He targeted the man in the middle of the group. Steve looked at the man's right leg. The Nohrstaf-bow grew warm. Adjusting his aim to the torso, the bow grew cold, almost icy. Nodding his head as he realized how the unique weapon's targeting system worked, Steve again took aim at the man's right leg. The bow responded by growing warm once more. His arm recoiled just a bit as the string was released.

The silver arrow streaked unerringly toward its target,

sinking deeply into the man's right thigh. Howling in pain, the archer dropped his bow and stared stupidly at the shining silver arrow protruding from his leg. As he moved to grasp the still quivering shaft, the wounded man gasped in horror as the arrow slowly dissolved, leaving an oozing wound on his leg.

"Excellent shot, Sir Steve."

Demonstrating why he held the rank of Captain of the Royal Guard, Rhenyon skillfully incapacitated three other men before Steve could even sight his next target. The gang leader then barked more orders at the archers who were still hastily firing arrows up into the sky. The men fell back, muttering angrily amongst themselves.

Rhenyon stiffened. The remaining men were now assembling something from various components that were pulled out of their storage packs. A large wooden bow was bolted to a much larger piece of wood, held in place by a brace on either side. The ungainly tripod-looking device was rapidly fortified as several men continued to work on its construction. Whipcord was produced, and was stretched between the ends, fastening onto the clasp of the stock. A wicked, barbed spear was then placed into the groove of the weapon.

"Didn't see that coming," Steve observed, nervously looking at Rhenyon. "Now what? We can't let them fire whatever that thing is. Is it a crossbow?"

"Aye. They are targeting the griffins. Come, they have to be stopped!"

Both Rhenyon and Steve fired arrow after arrow at the men, but unfortunately none landed. The men rotated the hastily assembled crossbow, ducking behind the weapon as arrow after arrow sought to hinder their progress. Aiming directly at the heart of the circling griffins, the men chortled with glee. With that many of them in such close proximity, a kill was certain, perhaps even more than one!

TWANG!

The barbed projectile was released, speeding straight toward the oblivious griffins. Before the oversized arrow could reach its target, however, it was deftly plucked from the sky by a huge creature that had just materialized out of thin air.

Breaking the giant arrow in half, then in half again, and finally in half one more time, Pryllan flung the splinters of wood back at the speechless humans. Adding her own roar of anger to the angry squawks of the griffins, the dragon spat a steady stream of fire at the cowering archers.

They were barely able to drag the large wooden crossbow out of the way, thus preventing it from being fried to a crisp by the angry dragon. However, two fireballs thrown by the angry fire thrower collided head-on with the large weapon, causing the crossbow to instantly erupt into flames. Within moments, the string had snapped and the wood was reduced to charred husks.

"We need to retreat!" one man cried out. "We cannot face a dragon!"

"Hold your ground, cowards! No dragon has perfect armor! We can take that flying lizard out if we can find a weakness, some missing scales, anything!"

"If you would like to see if the dragon will hold still long enough for us to inspect its armor, you go right ahead," one man snarled, scowling at their leader. "No one here is a good enough shot to be able to hit something like that, and that is only if the dragon is standing still. Nay, we need to retreat! No prize is worth this!"

"He will suck out your very soul when he learns of your cowardice," the leader hissed back, pulling back his lips in a snarl. "So go ahead. Leave. Some things are worse than death. There will be no coming back from where he will send you."

Horrified, eyes as big as dinner plates, the thug picked up his bow and started blindly firing arrows at the circling griffins. Fortunately, the dragon had moved off, providing cover from high above. Her sleek, serpentine form began slow, methodical fly-bys of the surrounding forest.

Realizing their prospects were beginning to dim, the gang leader came to a rapid decision. Desperate times definitely called for desperate measures. The queen was clearly hiding nearby, nearly three quarters of his men were incapacitated, and those infernal griffins were preventing his remaining men from executing a proper search of the surrounding forest. To top off matters, the inexplicable appearance of a winged dragon had rattled the nerves of everyone. How had they pulled that off, anyway? His large, shaking hands fumbled with the small, leather pouch fastened to his belt. Hesitant fingers extracted the carved ebony figurine within and placed it reverently on the ground before him.

Cautiously backing away from the grossly misshapen statuette, the desperate gang leader invoked the spell and then watched, horrified, as the thing on the ground began to swell in size. Muted groans came from the creature as it sprouted hair all over its muscled body. It writhed in pain as tightly knotted muscles continued to increase in size. Twenty seconds later, the snarling drakyr took its first breath. Two glowing red eyes latched on to the trembling leader. Twice the size of a normal human, a huge, clawed foot took its first step toward its invoker.

Cursing himself for agreeing to take possession of this evil talisman, the leader cowered under the drakyr's intense gaze. The Ylani wizard had insisted he take it, as a precaution to such circumstances he now found himself faced with. However, it still didn't change the fact that the thing before him represented every nightmare he'd ever had since he was a boy.

"Ideennntiifffyyy…" the creature hissed, spraying flecks of spittle everywhere.

"Uh, uh, Taran," the trembling man whispered.

The two red eyes narrowed. That name had been programmed into its creation. "Obbjjjeeccttiivvee."

"Uh, reacquisition of the missing Lentarian queen."

"Diiirrrreeccttiiivvveeee."

Becoming bolder by the second, Taran pointed a finger at the fire thrower, who was busy burning as many of their weapons as possible.

"Kill *him*!" he shrieked.

The drakyr's thick skull swung around to gaze at the human not thirty feet from it. It let out a roar as it lumbered across the ground, flinging anything in its path out of its way, which included several humans who crumpled into heaps after being slammed mercilessly into the thick tree trunks.

"What the mother freakin' *hell* is that?" Steve watched in abject horror as a creature covered in thick black fur came swiftly toward him. It was about eight feet tall, had three clawed fingers on each hand, which in turn were on oddly twisted muscular arms. Fangs reminiscent of a saber-tooth tiger projected out of the creature's maw. Its two red eyes had singled out its next prey, and it was hungry.

Summoning his jhorun for an intense defensive blast, he fired everything he had at the creature. The blast hit the drakyr square on the chest. However, instead of inflicting a mortal wound, or causing any damage, the creature just howled its frustration. Inexplicably, a jet of fire shot out of its gaping mouth, angling straight toward him.

Shock registered on Steve's face, just before he was able to throw his hands up and blast out his own jet of fire. The two streams hit head-on, causing an explosive reaction that blew both creature and human off their feet. Rubbing his sore tailbone, Steve was the first to get to his feet.

"Okay, that can't be good. Sarah!" Steve called, giving the signal for his wife. "Time to go!"

Moments later, he joined the rest of his team up in the treetops.

"What the hell was that?" Steve demanded of the queen. "That thing spit fire at me! Did you see it?"

Sarah nodded. "It was rather hard to miss."

"I have never seen the likes of that before," Callé answered, "and would not shed a tear if I never saw one again."

There was a roar of anger as the drakyr realized it had lost its prey. Several jets of fire appeared as, in its fury it attacked the next available target it could see, namely the griffins.

"It's not gonna stop, is it?" Steve asked, not really expecting an answer.

That demon has been summoned by some of the darkest magic I have ever had the misfortune of seeing. They are usually called into existence to serve a single purpose. We do not have to guess what its purpose is in this case. It must be vanquished.

What do you think, Pryllan, Steve thought back. *Can you take it out?*

Only if it was foolish enough to venture out into the open. However, I do not believe it to be a foolish creature. It will not leave the cover of the trees.

What if we lured it out?

"What's going on?" Sarah asked. "What are you doing?"

"I'm trying to remember what this area looked like from the air. Hang on a sec."

There is a small valley less than two leagues from your present location. If you can get it to follow you there, then I will destroy it.

I will let everyone here know. Watch for us.

"Okay, I think I remember seeing a small valley not far from here when I was flying with Pryllan earlier," Steve fibbed, trying to disguise the fact that he shared a mental connection with the huge dragon. "I'll bet if we could lure that thing out in the open, Pryllan would be able to take it out."

Sarah was shaking her head. "Lure it out? And how do you propose we do that? I don't want to go anywhere near that thing. It scares me."

"I concur with Lady Sarah," the queen agreed. "If that creature is down there, I will remain here."

"We have to deal with this thing," Steve argued. "You said it was invoked, right? Invoked to do what? I'm pretty sure we can figure out what it was created to do. As long as you live, Your Majesty, it will continue to hunt you. We have to do this."

Callé sighed. "All this trouble because of me. Very well. What would you have me do?"

"First things first. Sarah, I need you to bring Rhenyon here."

"We're up in a tree!"

"Fine, then put him in the next tree over. And we'll need Phane, too."

Down below, the drakyr snarled its frustration at the swirling griffins over its head. It had yet to make a kill and it was famished. Unable to feast on its primary prey, it needed to find sustenance elsewhere. As far as the drakyr was concerned, anyone other than the invoker was fair game. Red, inhuman eyes swiveled to observe several injured humans as they scrambled madly backwards, trying to flee. While not the preferred meal, these should do nicely.

Taking a deep breath to fuel the blast of flames necessary to expeditiously dispatch these ungainly bipeds, the drakyr opened its fanged mouth. Before the blast could be administered, several griffins swooped in out of nowhere, raking their claws down its chest. Black blood matted its fur as it glared angrily at the winged creatures flying around above it. The demon blasted off several jets of fire in an attempt to bring the elusive creatures down, however the griffins kept spiraling merrily out of harm's reach.

The winds shifted, bringing in new scents from the north. The creature paused. It had just caught a whiff of a scent that had its blood boiling. Brushing off the griffins as one would do with an annoying gnat, the drakyr moved off, following its nose north.

"Is it moving?"

Rhenyon peered down through the foliage. The dark brute had just moved off, disappearing into the thick growth of the trees. "Aye, Lady Sarah, it just disappeared over that ridge."

"Alright, I'll go get Steve. Be right back."

Sarah vanished, reappearing moments later with her husband.

"Are we all ready to go?"

"It's him," Callé exclaimed, pointing down to a lone figure walking about, inspecting the carnage below.

"Who?"

"Taran. He was in charge of the others."

Steve stiffened, clearly wanting a confrontation. Rhenyon was also staring silently down at the lone figure.

"Hon, no, you can't. We have to keep that thing moving." Sarah looked over at Rhenyon, smacking him lightly on the arm. "You, too. We don't have time for this."

Sharing a look with Rhenyon, Steve nodded his head. There had to be something he could do to repay the trouble that this individual had bestowed upon all of them. But what? As if in response to his unasked question, both of his hands suddenly ignited. Looking down at his flaming hands as though they belonged to someone else, Steve raised an eyebrow. What now? His jhorun was intensifying, tingling like mad.

"What are you doing?" Sarah hissed. "Put those out!"

"Sorry! I don't know why they just ignited like that."

Giving both hands a snap, as one would do to fling off excess water, he watched with amazement as tentacles of fire erupted from both hands and sped down to the hapless thug below. The fiery strands interlaced themselves all about the frightened mercenary, creating a formidable cage from which there would be no escape.

"Hmmm, I didn't know you could do that." Sarah observed, impressed.

"That makes two of us."

"Ah. Let's go."

Moving steadily through the forest, the drakyr paused. The scent, which was becoming more and more faint, had finally disappeared. Deciding it was best to return to the area in which it had been created, it turned about.

"Hey, ugly! I've seen roadkill that looks better than you!"

While the drakyr was unable to understand the meaning of what was said, the gist of the message came through loud and clear: an insult. The angry red eyes swiveled to glare at the human who had just appeared over the next hill. It roared its anger and spewed out another jet of fire. The human scrambled back, disappearing from sight. Running as fast as it could, the drakyr arrived at the crest of the next hill and sniffed the air. Yes, the scent of fresh meat was still close. The prey would not be able to hide from this particular predator, Steve knew, not when there was nowhere to hide. Striding forward slowly, constantly sniffing the air to determine which way to go, a second taunt reached the drakyr's ears.

"You run like a sissy! If you were my kid, I'd put your ugly ass up for adoption!"

As before, Steve disappeared down the hill while the

angry demon lumbered closer. Once again it discovered the human missing. Venting its frustration, two massive burly arms smashed down on the closest boulder, which shattered instantly, having been reduced to gravel by the colossal blow.

In this manner, with Steve doing the taunting, and Sarah moving him safely out of the way, they were able to keep the dim-witted Nightmare On Legs heading north, toward the small valley.

Finding herself a good vantage point on the opposite side of the vale Pryllan had described, Sarah teleported both Rhenyon and the queen from the treetop she had just vacated. Ever since rescuing Callé, Rhenyon had pointedly refused to leave her side.

"What now?" Callé asked.

"Steve will position himself directly out in the open," Rhenyon answered. "When that thing leaves the cover of the trees, then the dragon will appear and eliminate it for us."

"What if it doesn't go for Steve out there in the open?" Sarah wanted to know.

"Then I shall join him out there," Callé stated.

"Methinks not, milady," Rhenyon snapped. "You will not place yourself in any more danger."

"I will decide what I will and will not do," the queen coolly declared, her tone quite firm. "It exists because of me. If I can help rid the world of it, then I will."

The drakyr finally approached the forest edge, gazing out at the open expanse in front of it. There, standing directly in the center of the valley, was the human that continued to taunt it. The creature cocked its head. The infernal biped continued to release a tirade of jeers, then held up one arm with a single digit extended. The drakyr snarled, its blood boiling again as it seethed in anger. Instincts warned it not to leave the safety of the forest, yet the pull of nearby prey kept it staring longingly out at the center of the small valley. Suddenly the biped moved out of the way, revealing a second smaller biped. Its nostrils flared. This was the primary objective!

Roaring with rage, it emerged from the forest, racing as fast as it could toward the two defenseless humans. The smaller one was cowering in fright. The drakyr could taste the fear emanating from her. The larger biped continued to extend its arm with the digit exposed. Was the biped displaying some type of defense mechanism? Clearly an inferior creature, it would be dispatched quickly.

"Are you ready, Your Majesty?"

Clinging to Steve's arm, the queen could only nod as the ghoulish form of the drakyr drew closer. Remaining motionless, they waited. It was a hundred feet away. Now seventy. Once it was fifty feet away, Steve moved directly in front of the queen, blocking her from the demon's sight. Looking at the distant trees, he gave the signal. Callé vanished.

Clutching a mimet in each fist, Steve concentrated, focusing every ounce of his jhorun into his hands.

Pryllan—hurry!

His hands began to sting as both turned an ugly red. The demon was almost upon him, which caused both hands to sting so badly that Steve could easily believe they were on fire. This was going to be one hell of a blast!

Raising both hands, Steve let loose his jhorun and watched streams of pure fire jet from his outstretched palms. Twin blasts of fire streaked straight toward the lumbering drakyr.

The demon dove to the ground, clearly expecting the jets of fire to pass harmlessly over its head. Watching from a safe distance, Steve grinned as he watched the jets of fire curve in mid-air to streak downwards, striking the creature squarely on the back. Much to his dismay, the drakyr was back on its feet in record time and released its own blast.

The two jets struck each other head-on. The explosion knocked each of them backward by several feet. Bracing himself, Steve doubled his efforts, visualizing both jets of fire going right down the creature's throat. Activating one of the mimets, he felt the surge of additional power merge with his own, increasing the temperature of his flames.

Snarling with rage, the drakyr increased its attacks as well, focusing on volume instead of temperature. Up until now, it had been operating under the assumption that it would get to feed on this biped once it had been dispatched, but that was proving to be more difficult that it had planned on. The prey had not succumbed to the flames, instead, spewing its own flames right back at it. Pumping as much fire as it was able, it decided that it didn't need to feed on this human after all, with the desire to kill now outweighing the desire to feed.

Shuddering under the intensity of the blasts, Steve was now forced to take a few steps backwards. Sweating profusely, he continued to let the blasts hammer at him. Where was that blasted dragon? Was this not out in the open enough for her? Activating the second mimet, Steve sent a brutal blast of energy back toward the growling demon, this time forcing *it* to take a few steps back. It was then that Steve noticed his reinforcements had finally put in an appearance.

Taking several steps backward to regain its balance, the demon bumped up against some type of obstacle. However, when it turned, it was startled to discover the still form of a dragon sitting right beside it. Before surprise could register, the dragon raised a mighty forearm.

Determined to vanquish this demon as quickly as possible, Pryllan smashed her closed claw down, expecting the creature to be hammered into the earth like it did with the human spy from the previous night. Unbeknownst to the dragon, or the demon, however, the section of valley floor they were all standing on just happened to be a solid slab of sedimentary rock, formed ages ago when the valley used to be a large lake. When tons of pressure was applied from above, and an immovable object existed below, it wasn't surprising to learn that whatever was caught in the middle would be rendered into goo.

The demon practically exploded.

Bereft of the resisting jet of fire, Steve was blown off his feet. Pryllan, in the meantime, looked down at her forearm in disgust. Her once glossy scales were now covered in thick black gelatinous goo. Extending her neck even further, she noticed that the black slime was also covering many of her scales down her chest.

"I think you got 'em," Steve observed, lying flat on his back, staring over at the dragon.

Rhenyon, Callé, and Sarah emerged from their hiding place amongst the trees and were at the forest edge, staring at the center of the valley. The demon had been permanently vanquished; they all came running up to the dragon.

"Look at her! Poor thing, she has monster guts all over her."

Callé and Sarah timidly approached the slimed dragon, while Rhenyon angled over to give Steve an arm up.

"Are you uninjured, Sir Steve?"

"Yeah, I'm fine." Steve started brushing off the little bits of grass and leaves that had stuck to his tunic. "Well, that was unpleasant."

Together, they approached Pryllan, who was still inspecting her soiled scales.

"Are you okay, Pryllan?"

"Do not approach. The creature's entrails appear to be everywhere."

"Pryllan, you're pretty much fireproof, aren't you?" Sarah suddenly asked.

"Aye."

Sarah turned to her husband. "Why don't you clean her up? She helped us out, that's the least we can do."

"Clean her? With what?"

"Fire, silly. Burn that stuff off of her."

Quizzically, Steve turned to the green dragon. "Would that work?"

Pryllan paused, surprised that she hadn't thought of that simple idea herself. "Aye, I believe it would. You have my thanks."

Using jets of flame as he would water from a garden hose, he doused the motionless dragon in blasts of fire, erasing all traces of the unsightly goo. As a cleaning medium, it worked quite well; the smell, however, was not one he wished to remember. Burnt, smashed demon was not pleasing to the senses. Once the dragon's scales had been returned to their full glossy shine, Pryllan rose.

"You did well, Steve. You did not back down when the

demon approached, nor did you flee when it attacked. I will leave you now. You can return to R'Tal on your own."

"We'll take it from here," Steve confirmed. "We owe you big, my friend. Thanks for everything."

"You are welcome. I stand by my earlier observation. Remember your vow."

Pryllan departed in her trademark fashion, leaping straight up. Reaching the apex of her jump, she extended her wings and disappeared into the clouds.

"What did she mean by that?" Sarah asked.

"Time to head back to the castle, right?" Steve asked, a little too quickly.

"Not yet," Rhenyon said, gesturing back at the forest. "We need to collect that Taran fellow and any others we can find. He has much to answer for."

Retracing their steps back into the woods, Sarah sidled up to her husband. "What did Pryllan mean when she said 'remember your vow'"?

"I'll tell you later."

"Promise?"

Steve grinned. "Aye, I do!"

When they finally returned to the spot where the fire cage had been created, they were shocked to discover their prisoner dead on the ground, the restrictive strands of fire still in place. A small, black dagger had been thrust into his heart.

"He committed suicide? Why would he do that?"

"What if it wasn't suicide?" Sarah asked, looking about. "Did you guys miss someone? It certainly looks like someone wanted to shut this guy up."

"Where are all the people that we took out with the arrows?" Steve wanted to know.

Bewildered by the absence of all his prospective prisoners, Rhenyon studied the ground before them.

"The tracks do not make sense. You can see from the marks here, and here, that they were barely able to walk, yet only made it a few feet before all traces disappear."

"Well, where did they go then?" Steve asked, looking around.

"They might have teleported," Sarah observed. "That would explain why there aren't that many tracks."

"But who teleported them?" Rhenyon asked. "People who hire themselves out to be mercenaries typically do not have strong jhorun."

"Well, something happened to them, 'cause they aren't here."

"Damn," Rhenyon swore. "I had hoped to interrogate that Taran fellow."

"Probably a good thing for him, then," Steve observed, eyeing the still blazing fire net. *Extinguish yourself*, Steve ordered. The fire prison disappeared with a poof. Rhenyon squatted down, holding a finger to Taran's neck. Shaking his head, he rose.

"Serves him right."

"Hey, look on the bright side," Steve said companionably, slapping Rhenyon on the back. "We rescued the queen and still managed to send a couple of new friends back to the castle for you to get to know better. What are you complaining about?"

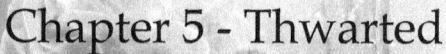

Chapter 5 - Thwarted

W ell? Where is she? Have you brought her?"
"With regret, sire, we have not."

"You told me the queen accepted our invitation, did you not?"

The scrawny messenger hesitated. "I am very sorry to say she declined at the last moment, sire."

With a curse, the portly king rose from his gilded throne, struggling to extricate his considerable bulk from the confining chair. His black piggish eyes glared angrily at his golden throne as it yet again clung to his enormous backside. With a loud thump, the chair fell back to the ground.

"What happened? Why did she change her mind?"

Swallowing nervously, the gaunt man with the hooked nose bowed low, too scared to make eye contact with the king.

"Forgive me, sire. I do not know. I am just your humble messenger."

The king sighed. Good help was so hard to find these

days. Glaring at the trembling man before him, he briefly considered incarcerating the witless fool. Fortunately for Hooked Nose, King Ewam had more important things to do.

"Send that Taran fellow to me immediately."

"My most abject apologies, sire, but Taran did not return. The welcoming party was ambushed before they could return. Taran did not survive."

The king's eyes narrowed as he studied Hooked Nose.

"Fetch Warrick immediately."

"At once, sire." The aide bolted out of the room, eager to put as much distance as possible between himself and the angry monarch.

The king paced irritably about the throne room, scattering the frantic aides who were unfortunate enough to fall within his way. How many envoys had he dispatched in the past several years? Three? Four? All had suffered some inexplicable setback resulting in failure. This was the first time he'd heard of where innocent Ylanis had perished. An attack upon one of his men could only be interpreted as a direct attack against him. Did they honestly think the people of Ylani would not scream for retaliation? Of course they would, which was why this didn't make sense.

The castle staff, having long been accustomed to the short temper of their king, wisely avoided their muttering monarch. Whenever his majesty descended into one of his darker moods, it was best to avoid attention. Therefore, the throne room bustled with activity.

A door slammed in the distance, drawing the king up short. With a grunt, he strode purposely down the hall, approaching the far recesses of the vaulted chamber. A thin, middle aged man wearing robes entirely of cobalt blue had entered and was now heading toward the rapidly approaching king. The man in blue bowed his head.

"Your Majesty. You sent for me?"

"Indeed, I did, Warrick. You have some explaining to do. My personal chambers. Now."

Without waiting to see if his advisor was following, King Ewam strode over to an ornate door recessed into the wall behind his throne. Once the door had been securely closed behind them, the king whirled angrily on the trembling man.

"So, what was it this time? Flock of attacking griffins? Renegade goblin clan? Perhaps the ogres?"

"Indeed, the envoy was attacked, Your Majesty."

"I presume. Attacked by whom?"

"As far as we can tell, it was the Lentarians."

"The Lentarians, you say. You have proof, do you not?"

"Aye, there is proof, sire. If you will come with me, I will show you."

"Where?"

"The barracks, sire."

Leading the frowning king from the small chamber, Warrick led him past the frantic activity of the throne room, past the meeting hall, and out into the castle foyer. Maids, serving girls, and soldiers alike all hastened to clear a path for the angry king as he strode to the castle's eastern wing.

In less than a minute, Ewam was making no effort to suppress his scowl. The king deliberately cut his pace by half, thus forcing Warrick to slow as well. The most powerful man in Ylani was not about to present himself wheezing like a dog in front of his own soldiers. King Ewam grew even angrier when, after five minutes of painful walking, his indefatigable subordinate failed to pick up the (non)subtle cues that he was out of breath. He finally dropped his pace to a very slow walk.

Long accustomed to the king's temper, Warrick rolled his eyes, being careful to face the opposite direction while doing so. He pretended to study the passing tapestries, which allowed him to be overtaken by the winded king. King Ewam irritably huffed past him, but came to an abrupt stop as the corridor dead-ended. His eyes narrowed as he looked pointedly at the door on the left, then the one on the right. The king didn't have a clue as to which one to take.

Warrick interpreted the king's hesitation as a desire for royal protocol to be followed, so he leapt around him to open the left door. King Ewam swept into the entryway, looking first right, then moving off to the left.

"This had better be good," the king growled, wiping beads of sweat from his brow. "If you have made me come all this way for naught, you will have a most unrestful night tonight. Catch my meaning?"

Several feet behind the grumbling king, Warrick rolled his eyes for the second time. "Yes, sire. You will not be disappointed."

Finally reaching the end of the corridor, King Ewam banged the door open and emerged into the main common room of the barracks. Several off-duty soldiers leapt to attention, remnants of their meals sent soaring across the room. One lieutenant who had been enjoying a pipe also leapt to his feet.

"Sire!"

The king eyed the soldier's uniform, noting the distinctive marks on his shoulder that denoted an officer. One gold bar and two silver bars. What rank was that, anyway? Corporal? Lieutenant? Captain? Once more his advisor came to his aid.

"Lieutenant, you may present to the king the items you discovered from the failed mission to Lentari."

"Sir, at once." The man gestured to two others who were standing in the doorway leading up to the main barracks. The two men ducked back inside, reappearing moments later carrying a large bundle between them.

"Place it here," the lieutenant ordered, indicating the floor before them. The bundle was dropped unceremoniously at their feet. Casting a dark look at his two helpers, the lieutenant squatted down to open the bundle. Carefully untying the leather cord holding remnants of a small canvas tent together, a collection of items was revealed to the eyes of the king. Several feathered arrows were presented first.

"Arrows equipped with the feathers of a purple kyte," Warrick exclaimed, leaning over the king's shoulder. "Purple kytes are native to Lentari."

"Native, yes," the king nodded, rotating the arrows in his pudgy hands, "but not uncommon in Ylani either." The arrows were dropped back onto the canvas. "This tells me nothing."

The officer picked up a piece of torn fabric, presenting it reverently to the king. "A torn piece of Lentarian uniform, clearly showing the royal insignia."

The king studied the small piece of tunic. With a grunt, he brought it closer to his face, scrutinizing it closely. With a curse, the torn fabric joined the arrows back on the canvas.

"The insignia clearly shows a thundercloud over castle R'Tal."

"It does, aye," the officer confirmed, retrieving the uniform scrap.

The king rolled his eyes, his mood continuing to darken.

"That is the royal insignia of Kri'Fallum, not Entu, who has not held the throne for more than a decade. What you have there is a piece of an old Lentarian uniform that no soldier would wear without insulting their present king. Warrick, I grow tired of this charade. Either show me hard proof or I am sending the both of you down to the dungeon for trying to pin this debacle on someone else."

Not wanting to spend any time whatsoever in the dank dungeon far below them, the lieutenant dropped to his knees and brushed aside bits of junk and debris as he searched for something, anything, to appease the king. With an exclamation of triumph, the soldier grabbed an object from the pile and stood. Holding it reverently, he presented a golden dagger, hilt-first, to the king. Red smears still coated parts of the blade.

"This," the lieutenant began, "was pulled from the chest of Taran after his body was discovered by our spies."

The king took the dagger, studying the exquisite craftsmanship of the hilt.

"Look there," the lieutenant said, pointing to an insignia depicting the castle at R'Tal with a griffin standing in front, one paw raised. "That, if I am not mistaken, is the present royal seal of Lentari. And, I believe the other, smaller symbol, is the personal seal of the captain of the royal guards."

The king's eyes snapped to the lieutenants. "Are you telling me that this belongs to —"

"Rhenyon. Aye sir, I am."

"Rhenyon killed Taran," Warrick murmured, shock in his voice. "The implications of that are —"

"I know what the implications are," the king snapped, still studying the bloody dagger. "I must think about this."

"What is there to think about?" Warrick spat. "You have the evidence right there in your hand. You must act now!"

The king's gaze had dropped to the dagger in his hand, but at this, his eyes slowly raised until it was locked on his advisor's.

"Lieutenant," the king began, still staring at Warrick, "take our insistent friend here into custody. Apparently, he needs to cool off, and I can think of no better way to do that than an overnight stay in the dungeon. Take him away."

The lieutenant snapped to attention. "Yes, sire!"

"You would do well to remember, Warrick," the king advised, as the muttering counselor was guided out of the barracks, "where your place is. You do not ever, *ever*, order the king about. Those accommodations can be made permanent. Remember that."

The king's eyes followed his aide as he was forcefully led from the room. As the door started to swing closed, he clearly heard a long, drawn-out sigh.

"Another blasted night in the dungeon. Not again."

* * *

With an exasperated sigh, King Ewam sank down upon his heavily fortified oak chair. One glance at his paper-strewn desk had him wincing. For too long had he been cultivating this failed relationship with their southern neighbor. For too long had he been obsessed with searching for the strongest jhorun in his country.

The king rose and began to pace. What do they feel they need to hide? Are the rumors true? Is the jhorun that the Lentarians possess that much stronger than their own? The secret of unparalleled jhorun would be his, of that he was certain. His own jhorun, the ability to conjure a few clouds, paled in comparison to those rumored to be found down in Kri'Entu's kingdom.

Ewam stopped at an immense tapestry-sized map that hung on the wall behind his desk. With another sigh, he aimed his oversized rear-end back into his chair, spinning around to gaze admiringly at all the wondrous accomplishments he figured he was solely responsible for. There, along the southeastern border, for example. Until he exerted his influence, weren't those small villages suffering at the hand of the nearby goblin horde? He himself had ordered his troops to drive off the repugnant creatures once and for all. Sure, the losses had been significant. But as a result of his thoughtfulness, the three villages had thanked him by sending twenty of their finest horses.

His eyes roamed west, stopping at the newly completed road that now connected the southern village of Bristol with the rest of the kingdom. Before his involvement, citizens of that northern village would have had to travel many leagues west, almost halfway to their seafaring neighbors, before finding the Northern Pass, the main thoroughfare heading through the mountains and consequently to the capital. Wasn't he the one that pushed through the proposal to secure the necessary manpower to get the job done? Sure, it had taken every last man in Bristol, and was even necessary to pull men from the nearby seaport of Arlan to get the massive task finished in under three years, but hadn't he provided everyone with jobs? Besides, it wasn't his fault that common laborers didn't earn as much as a skilled blacksmith.

Looking at the main seaport village on the far western shore, he nodded his head. He had personally commissioned five new seaworthy vessels in the past five years, each capable of journeying to such distant lands as Lyros, land of exquisite spice and untold riches. In another ten years, the king reasoned, the village should have made enough to pay back the treasury for the huge sum of money it took to fabricate those ships. With interest, of course.

Farther to the north, his eyes rested on the expanse of mountainous rock that stretched between the village of Barod and its closest neighbor, Myrn. The citizens of Barod had been clamoring for years to have some type of passageway west that would allow them to open up trade with their neighbors there. Separating the two villages, however, were many leagues of heavily wooded terrain, complete with steep slopes and rolling hills. Tapping his fingers on his desk, he spent the next ten minutes determining how much it would deplete his treasury to undertake such a task. However, no matter how he calculated the numbers, once he applied it to the funds he knew were available for improvements, he came up with the same answer: insufficient funds.

Scowling, King Ewam glanced back at Arlan. If two ships were dispatched to Lyros, then the bounty returned would certainly finance this latest undertaking. Smiling with satisfaction, the king wrote out the order and dispatched a messenger to the far western shores. Whether or not the Arlan residents would want to take such a perilous journey hadn't even crossed his mind. The king's attention was already leagues away.

Several hours later, a curt knock sounded on his private door. The king, who had fallen asleep at his desk yet again, jerked awake, his crown tumbling off his brow. The small coronet tumbled noisily onto his desk, flipping around in circles before Ewam slapped a hand on it to silence its movements.

"One minute," the king called, straightening his robes, attempting to cover the distinctive damp spot that appeared on his silk shirt. There must be something he was allergic to in here, he thought angrily. Breathing through his mouth had caused a rather copious amount of drool to trickle down the front of his chest. One last check to make certain every trace was covered, he sat up straight in his chair, giving every appearance he was hard at work and had been so for quite some time.

"Enter."

A young aide nervously poked her head into his office.

"Your Majesty, there are reports of yet another troll attack in Myrn."

"Another one? What the blazes is going on up there? Have I not told those people numerous times to not provoke the trolls?"

Hearing his exasperated tone of voice, the aide trembled. She was going to be spending the night in the dungeon. She just knew it.

"We have had peace with the trolls for over twenty years. Now, in the last six months, there have been five attacks.

Why?"

The female aide blinked her eyes at the king. Did he really expect a lowly aide to have an answer to that?

"Uh…"

Waving his hand dismissively, the king rose and strode out of his office, nearly bowling over the motionless girl who still stood petrified in the doorway.

"I will get to the bottom of this," King Ewam muttered, casting about the throne room for a suitable messenger. "I want you to fetch General Reitus at once."

A small, thin boy of perhaps sixteen years jumped to attention and bowed, before he bolted out of the room.

"Now then," the king said, rubbing his hands together, "I will need…" he glanced behind him to see if the young girl was still standing motionless in the doorway to his office, which she was. "Good. Still there. Find the liaison to Myrn and have him report to my office. That will be all."

The girl nodded her head before darting off. She didn't know who she was looking for, but then again, it didn't matter. If the king ordered, you obeyed.

* * *

"Just what the ruddy hell is going on up there?" The king asked half an hour later, as he tipped back his goblet to take a healthy swig of ale. "This makes the fifth time your village has been attacked this year, has it not?"

The nervous, thin man bowed deeply in front of him. "Indeed, Your Majesty."

"I want to know why," the Ylani general stated, pacing behind the nervous man. "No other village has reported being attacked. Do you not find that odd, Your Majesty?"

"Listen, Mr., umm," the king scratched his beard. What had he said his name was?

"Leyton, sire."

"Right. Listen, Mr. Leyton, the trolls have not posed a problem for us for several decades. Now they are attacking. I agree with General Reitus. I want to know why. Why now? What is provoking them? If I find out your village is responsible, directly or indirectly, then you will all be punished, that I promise you. I do not tolerate anyone threatening the peace that I have worked so hard to achieve."

"They are trolls, sire!" the liaison complained. "Do they need a reason? Can you not drive them off? We have been asking for years for the removal of all mountain trolls."

"Answer the question, peasant."

"You avoided answering my question, Mr. Leyton." The king glared at the general as the two of them both spoke at the same time. "I will not ask again. What is provoking them? What do you know about it?"

"Just rumors, sir."

The king sat back in his chair and stared at the thin man before him. The king was briefly reminded of a cornered rat wishing to flee. Reitus continued to pace. Ten seconds of silence passed as the representative of Myrn stared at his shoes before looking up to see the king's angry eyes staring straight into his own. The nervous man took a breath.

"Several of our sentries have reported seeing small bands of men stealing away into the night several times last month."

"Allow me to venture a guess. The trolls would then attack afterward."

Leyton sadly shook his head. "Usually the following night."

"Would it not stand to reason, then, that these men are stirring up trouble? Where is the constable? Why has he not dealt with these troublemakers himself?"

"The constable is a weak man," Leyton grumbled. "He lacks the support and confidence of the people. No one is comfortable confessing anything to him."

King Ewam angrily shook his head. Someone he personally appointed had become too cowardly to see to the safety of his own people?

"Station."

Leyton turned to look behind him, fully expecting to see someone else besides the pacing general. There wasn't.

"I know you are there. Come here."

Silence.

"You will enter now or you will find your new lodgings

several floors below us. Do I make myself clear?"

The door hastily opened, the eavesdropper nervously stepping inside. The red-faced girl bowed low, refusing to meet the king's eyes. Luckily, Ewam was busy scribbling out a new set of orders. Hastily imprinting his seal upon the scroll, he handed it to the girl. "Use an official messenger. They are to see to it that this reaches the eyes of the Myrn Constable."

"At once, sire." The girl all but sprinted from the room.

"Back to the matters at hand," the king continued, returning his attention back to the man before him, as though catching people eavesdropping on him was a daily occurrence. "The constable will be replaced. Now, tell me everything you know about these 'nocturnal activities'."

"I was only privy to the excursions once," the liaison began, nervously shuffling his feet. "I could not sleep one night, so I went into another room to read. I had just found a candle when, before I could light it, five men exited a house several doors down."

"What were they wearing?" General Reitus interrupted.

"They were all in black," Leyton reported.

"Were they carrying anything? Did they take any horses?"

"Several had swords, but aside from that, I could not see anything else."

"No horses?" Reitus repeated.

"None that I could see."

"How long were they gone?"

"I do not know, sir."

Reitus sighed, muttering quietly to himself.

King Ewam shook his head, rolling his eyes yet again. Was everyone typically this slow? Strange how he hadn't ever noticed that before.

"How long did you read?" the king asked.

"Perhaps three hours."

"Then they were gone for at least three hours," General Reitus remarked, nodding his head as though he himself had been responsible for coaxing that tidbit out of the simpleton before him.

While the general mumbled and muttered to himself, trying to divine what else might be gleaned from the sparse amount of information Leyton had provided, King Ewam studied the man he had appointed to the highest military position. While first appearances would lead one to believe the general to be a man well past his prime, incapable of the intense, physical demands his post required, the king knew the general was not one to be underestimated. Beneath that calm façade of a middle-aged gentleman lay the athletic prowess belonging to someone at least three decades his junior. The general could hold his own on the battlefield, his energy and stamina admired by all. However, upstairs, he could be a little slow on the uptake.

"Three hours is more than enough time to make it well up into the hills," Leyton observed, eyeing both the general and the king. "I wish I could tell you what they were doing, but I just do not know."

"Could you recognize anyone?" King Ewam wanted to know.

"They wore hoods. I was unable to see any faces."

"Well, then, what can you tell us?" General Reitus asked, his frustration evident to all.

"We will not get anything more from him. You are dismissed."

Leyton nodded, bowing to both king and general. Without hesitation, he turned and exited the room as fast as his legs would take him.

"What do you think, general?" The king returned to his desk and sat down, spinning around yet again to peruse the tapestry map. "Myrn is situated in the middle of the forest, up against the base of the mountains there. Three hours is more than adequate to venture into the forest, seek out the trolls, and cause mischief."

"The forest covers many leagues. Trolls are known to be all throughout the mountains." General Reitus tapped the area around the small icon denoting Myrn on the map. "If the trolls do not want to share, then I say we force them to or they can vacate the area. Willingly or not."

"Then how do you explain Barod?" the king asked, pointing to its respective icon. "Same forest, same mountains, yet no reports of any attacks whatsoever. No, I want you to find out what is happening there and you will do so tomorrow. Dispatch as many men as you see fit. These attacks will stop. And if you discover that townsfolk from Myrn are responsible, then have them brought here. Understood?"

"Aye, sire, consider it done."

Once the general had departed to give the orders, the king's tired eyes fell back to his desk, resting on the blood-spattered blade of Captain Rhenyon's jeweled dagger. Turning the blade over, he studied the exquisite gold markings adorning the hilt. There, as Warrick had mentioned, was the great seal of Lentari. And there, on the other side, was the smaller mark consisting of a large tree with a set of crisscrossing swords in the middle. This, he presumed, must be Rhenyon's crest.

His instincts were telling him that something wasn't right with this scenario. Why would the Lentarian captain of the guard, a man well known for his skill with a blade, leave behind such a noticeable weapon as this? If he wanted that Taran fellow dead, then he could have done the deed with any number of weapons. Why use his personal dagger?

Well, assuming Rhenyon didn't kill Taran, then who did? How did they get his personal dagger? Clearly the Lentarian captain must have been in the area. How else would his dagger have wound up there? Obviously, his peace envoy met up with a contingent of Lentarian soldiers. Could the Lentarians have been behind this attack? Or maybe a Lentarian might be trying to frame one of their own?

King Ewam's eyes flicked over to a portrait of his own parents. The last time the King of Ylani and the King of Lentari had actually sat down together was when his father was king. Even then, tension was high as his father had demanded to know yet again how the Lentarians could possess jhorun so much stronger than their own. He remembered his father demanding tests of the water, food, even the very air, for any trace of foreign materials. Naturally, the results were negative. The Lentarian King, Fallun, had been more than cooperative, insisting time and time again that they weren't keeping any secrets from their northern brethren. And naturally, Ewam's father, Othen, had refuted the results, declaring the tests flawed. There just *had* to be some reason why their jhorun was so much inferior to that of the Lentarians.

As a small boy, Ewam was teased mercilessly when it was revealed his jhorun involved summoning small unimpressive cirrus clouds high in the sky. No matter how much he had concentrated, he was unable to produce anything more than a few light wispy clouds. Had he been able to produce some thunderclouds, or possibly generate a few lightning bolts out of his conjurations, then that would have been respectable. Instead, however, his jhorun had remained at the level of a five-year old child. Not a fact that the proud king wanted spread around.

When on that fateful day an unsuccessful hunting party had returned from a ten day absence, and they were standing before the king explaining how they became lost, one hunter had forever changed the life of his king. The hunting team had all decided to venture off in different directions for a few hours to see if they could have any better luck when one man had stumbled across a long deserted campsite, complete with a desiccated corpse. Rifling through the belongings that had been half-buried in the soft dirt for over a century, the hunter discovered a small spherical object that he had dutifully turned over to the king. Ewam's father, seeing no value to the sphere, had given it to his son for his tenth birthday.

Only by sheer luck did he stumble upon the secret of the sphere. A month had passed, finding the future king staring angrily up at the sky for the hundredth time. While holding his favorite good-luck charm, he had yet again been tormented by his peers. Watching the gang of boys laughing hysterically as they ran away, Ewam had wished yet again for the ability to generate a true thunderstorm, one that was capable of washing away those mean-spirited boys in a huge flood of water. Much to his amazement, his charm had grown warm. Huge, dark cumulus clouds appeared, blotting out the sun over the entire village. Within moments, torrential rain was falling, threatening to wash several houses away. The gang of boys were screaming with terror as lightning flashed all about them, thunder booming so loud that the very foundations of the neighboring houses were shaking.

Smiling, Ewam had looked down at the marble. His

charm had turned out to be the best good-luck charm he could have been given.

Over the years, thanks to his charm, he had become respected, even feared. The strapping prince had the power to summon a small hurricane and lay waste to entire hordes of enemies if so desired. However, by his thirtieth birthday, the strength of his charm had faded to a mere shade of its former power. Fortunately, even the sliver of power the charm offered still made his own natural jhorun pale in comparison. Therefore, his next course of action became clear: find a new charm.

He always knew that someone had to have made the sphere. Somebody must have more of the charms. Once he had become king, he had dispatched expedition after expedition to the area where the original hunting party was said to have been encamped, yet to no avail. The campsite of that ancient traveler had either vanished or been swallowed up by the forest once and for all. Where was the traveler from? Was he Ylani? Maybe a Lentarian? Once again, the Fates gave him a perfect birthday present.

On his fortieth birthday, word came from one of their spies planted in the Lentarian capital, R'Tal, that a traveler had appeared, possessing a charm resembling the king's. Ewam was ecstatic! His soul craved that new charm, desiring the power he once had at his disposal. After paying a hefty bribe, his spy successfully stole the charm away from the hapless trader and returned to Ylani with all haste.

That was ten years ago. The sphere's power had diminished once more, no doubt from his constant tapping of the charm's power to portray as his own. Now, however, he was fast running out of excuses for why he hadn't conjured up a thunderstorm in more than a year. Rumors had begun to spread like wildfire. He must find another charm, and fast. Clearly the common denominator here was Lentari. Since the people there were constantly displaying incredible levels of jhorun, that meant they had access to a fresh supply of the charms, didn't it? He must discover the source of those spheres!

However, the Lentarian king must have been tipped off

to his plans. Every spy stationed in Lentari had reported that no such charms were in use. Most disturbing was the lack of visual confirmation. No one had even reported seeing one of the charms, let alone observing one in use. Besides, trying to keep the importance of the charms from his men, and from Warrick, had been difficult enough. The last thing he needed was to have someone else figure out what the charms' secret nature was and covet it for themselves.

Not for the first time did the idea creep into the king's head that maybe Lentari was trying to provoke an attack. Perhaps Kri'Entu wanted to keep the secret of the charms to himself. They must think that with their more powerful jhorun, they would have the advantage. Well, he didn't care how strong an adversary they faced. If the Lentarians wanted a reaction, then they would not be disappointed.

A loud knocking shattered his reverie, and much to his surprise, the door burst open. A middle-aged woman hurried into the room.

"My Lord, please forgive me. It's your grandson. His malady is worsening!"

"Take me to Aerlin. Now!"

His breaths were coming faster, his wheezing louder. However, he didn't care. All he was concentrating on now was doing his best to keep up with the running girl. He cursed. How was he expected to maintain this velocity for more than a few minutes? By the time he reached the top floor of the North Wing, he was going to need a medic for himself.

Banging into the room he had commissioned as an infirmary, several women, including his daughter, all jumped with surprise. A young boy of about seven, bathed in sweat, thrashed about on his bed, oblivious to everything. The king, also bathed in sweat, hurried to the bedside and looked down at the frail boy.

"How is he?"

"Nothing is helping, Father. Nothing!"

Noting the exasperation in his daughter's voice, the king looked angrily at the three medics in the room. "This is your specialty. You need to do something!"

"The malady is resisting everything we try," one medic,

too exhausted to care if the king took offense, snapped. "We have administered forskolin root, which aids the immune system in fighting diseases. No response. We have tried swallowwort, which helps strengthen the lungs. Unchanged. We have tried —"

"I do not wish to hear of failures," the king spat out, glaring at the tired medic. "Have you administered anything that has helped at all?"

The three medics went into a huddle as they conferred quietly with one another. Their spokesman finally broke away from the other two and faced the king.

"Only when we brewed a tea made from the leaves of the hyssop plant was the prince able to get some rest."

"Why have you not given more of this plant?"

"His tea is there," the medic reported, indicating the steaming bowl of liquid by the bed. "We have just given him another bowl. The fragrance from the simmering tea also appears to have a soothing effect while he sleeps. Seeing how he needs his rest, I have placed orders to have a bowl of steaming hyssop tea placed bedside at all times."

The king was nodding his head in approval. "Good. Has anything helped him to regain his strength?"

Sadly, the three medics shook their heads. "We work day and night, Your Majesty. We will not fail this boy."

"Send out word yet again," the king ordered, addressing one of his aides, "to any and all healers who have any skill, no matter how minor. They are to report to the castle at once. Understood?"

The aide bowed. "Aye, sir."

King Ewam leaned over the bed, gently touching his grandson's hand. "Hang in there, Aerlin."

The prince's weak eyes opened, shifting slightly to his grandfather's. The boy smiled.

Exhausted and frustrated, the king returned to his private office. The bustle of the throne room didn't appeal to him today. What he wanted was quiet. Solitude.

Someone knocked on the door.

The king sighed. He just wasn't going to get it today. "Enter."

This time, a girl in her early twenties appeared. How many aides did he have, anyway? "Sire, the constable from Bristol is here for the census."

One of the king's recent additions to Ylani laws had been a requirement for all villages to periodically census their residents and report their findings to the king himself.

"Already? Blast. Very well, send him in."

For the next two hours the king sat behind his personal desk and listened as the constable droned on and on, flipping through page after page of his census report. Birth rates were strong. Unemployment was down. Crime was slightly up, but within tolerances. It wasn't until the constable began summing up the variety of jhorun present, another new law that the king had imposed, that Ewam started to pay attention.

"Bird calls, holding breath underwater, knife sharpener, wood finder," the constable ticked off, eyes traveling down the long list of names.

"How long underwater?" the king suddenly asked. If it was substantial, that might prove to be useful.

"Two minutes, sire."

The king huffed out his irritation. Holding one's breath for two minutes wasn't that spectacular.

"Continue."

As the constable continued reading from the list of jhorun found in Bristol, the king sat back with disgust. Useless! All utterly useless! Not one remarkable jhorun in the whole lot. He had a sneaking suspicion that when he received similar reports from other villages, the results would mirror these.

Pitiful. Bird calls! His people could make bird calls! And someone could hold their breath a little longer than most people. So what? What did he care about such inconsequential jhorun? Were any of these jhorun going to be able to save his grandson? No mention of an herbalist. Not one mention of a healer. Nothing.

King Ewam's eyes found the map of his kingdom again, but what he focused on was due south. Lentari. Clearly their jhorun was more powerful. Their king was a wyverie. Their queen had a jhorun purported to be the equivalent of a truth serum. Someone there *must* have a strong enough jhorun to eradicate his grandson's malady.

Why did they keep distancing themselves? Did they truly believe their kingdom was that superior to his? Why would they refuse to help him? How many times had he pleaded for help only to be denied? Four times? Five? It was intolerable!

"We are done here," the king stated, holding out a hand for the report.

"As you wish, sire." The constable handed the papers to the king before being dismissed.

"Station!"

An aide poked her head into his office. "Sire?"

"Send for General Reitus immediately."

"At once, sire." The aide vanished.

The king sat behind his desk, tapping his fingers. "Station!"

A young boy knocked on the open door. "Sire, you called?"

"Fetch Warrick from the dungeon."

"Yes, sire." The boy disappeared.

His senior advisor arrived first.

"You sent for me, sire?"

"I did. You mentioned that you had several other ideas on how to discover what jhoruns exist in Lentari?"

"Aye, sire. There is —"

"I do not care. I need to know. Whatever you have to do, do it."

The thin man smiled, bowing low. "You will have that information."

Warrick exited the king's office just as General Reitus came strolling in.

"Sire?"

"I have wasted enough time with trying to peacefully ask for help." King Ewam rose from his chair. "My grandson does not have much time left. I will not stand by and let him die."

The general nodded, whether in understanding, or in sympathy, Ewam didn't know. Either way, the elderly soldier remained silent.

"Alert your troops. If I have to take drastic measures, I

want you ready."

Reitus nodded. "Your Majesty, we *will* be ready."

Chapter 6 — Predicament

Do you have any idea how much trouble you have caused, young man?"

"I am sorry, Tristan. Really. Please do not be mad at me!"

An arm shot out and spun the boy in the opposite direction.

"Mikal, you swiped the key from my pocket! How did you even know that I had it?"

The boy mumbled something so softly that no one heard him.

"Again, Mikal, so we can all hear you."

Mikal refused to look Annie in the eye. "I saw Sarah give it to you."

Another arm spun him around to face the other direction.

"Mikal, you are not supposed to be here. *We* are not supposed to be here!"

The boy stared at his feet. "I was not going to go through. I just wanted to know if I could."

"Who do you think you're fooling with that?" Annie

demanded. "If you weren't planning on using it, then you wouldn't have pick-pocketed that key from my jacket!"

"Peanut bolted through. I had to get her!"

"Don't try to change the subject with me, squirt. My one job was to keep you safe while Steve and Sarah are gone."

The boy continued to stare at the ground, shuffling his feet. "I did not mean to make such a mess of things. I had to get Peanut."

Annie stared around at the unfamiliar forest. "We need to find something that will work for a leash. We can't let her wander aimlessly around here and I don't think you are going to want to carry her everywhere. She'll get too heavy for you."

Putting the wriggling dog down on the ground, Mikal looked around. He pointed to a thin, nearby tree.

"That's a bralen tree. Its branches are very flexible. Can you hold Peanut for a moment?"

Annie squatted down and hooked several fingers in the corgi's collar.

"Got her. What're you doing?"

Mikal had walked over to the willowy tree and selected a thin branch. Giving a sharp tug to the tree limb, he started peeling off the smaller branches. Once all the tiny shoots had been removed, he inspected his newly created leash. While not ideal, it would suffice. Looping one end of the branch through the dog's collar, he tied the end into a knot, tugging firmly to verify its strength.

"So where are we? Why didn't we show up in the castle? Where is everyone?"

"I am not sure where we are," Mikal admitted, looking around. "The forest is huge, and all the trees look the same to me."

Annie turned to Tristan, who was still scowling at the boy. "You've mentioned before that there is more than one portal here. Where's the closest one? If it's as dangerous as everyone says it is for Mikal to be here, we need to get out of here as quickly as possible."

"Agreed, Lady Annie." Tristan was silent as he listened to the faint sounds emanating from all around them. "It would appear that there is a waterfall in the area. This correlates with what the Nohrin reported upon their first arrival."

"Okay, you may know them as the Nohrin," Annie began, "but to me, they're my sister and my brother-in-law. Can you just refer to them by their names?"

"In your world, yes, they are your family. Here," Tristan gestured to the forest around them, "they are the famous Nohrin, protectors of the prince. And now, thanks to young Mikal here, that honor has been bestowed unto us until we can either return home or else find the Nohrin."

"Give me back the key," Annie demanded, holding her hand out to the prince.

Mikal looked at her, surprise registering on his face. He blinked his eyes a few times.

"Give Lady Annie the key," Tristan reiterated.

Those shocked eyes swiveled over to his tutor's. Annie suddenly let out a loud groan.

"Oh, dear God, you don't have the key, do you?"

The boy began to systematically pat down his pockets. With a laugh, he pulled the crystal key out of his pants pocket.

"Just kidding! Do you have any idea how many times I have heard the story of how they forgot to retrieve the key after using the portal?" Mikal asked, sheepishly offering the green key back to Annie. "I was only borrowing this."

Scowling, Annie took the key and slipped it into her own pocket. She turned to Tristan. "Okay, we're in Lentari. We need to get someplace safe. Where do we go?"

"It was said that if the Nohrin, namely Steve and Sarah," Tristan hastily corrected, "were to have traveled in the opposite direction upon their first arrival here, they would have encountered Avin in less than a day. So, we head west."

"Do they have a portal there that we can use to go home?"

"There is a portal there," Tristan confirmed, "but I do not believe that key will work."

This caused Annie to come to an abrupt stop.

"What? Say that again? We have the key. We're going to a portal. Why wouldn't it work?"

"Because," Tristan explained, "each key is tuned to each portal. There are different keys that activate their respective portals. That one," he indicated the key Annie had pulled out to stare at, "is tuned to the portal in your world, but the source portal is the castle portal."

Annie rolled her eyes, shaking her head. Perfect. Just perfect. It figures. Wait a moment.

"Then how do you explain," she began, "that this key, which apparently is activated from the castle portal, dropped us in the middle of the forest? Why didn't it take us back to the castle?"

"I do not have an answer for you," Tristan shook his head. "You would have to talk to the maker of the keys, the Strathos, for an answer."

"My sister has mentioned a dwarf key maker. Is that who you're talking about?"

"Aye," the soldier agreed, nodding. "Maelnar."

"If I ever do see him, remind me to have him fix this thing then."

Masking his smile, Tristan bowed. "I will, Lady Annie."

* * *

"You really have nothing to complain about, you know."

"Are you kidding? I am not able to exhibit it! Why would you think I would like that?"

"Sarah can't manifest hers, either," Annie returned, "yet you have told me, repeatedly, that you have always liked the concept of teleportation. Explain that then."

"What she does is cool," the boy muttered, straining yet again to not lose his grip on his makeshift leash as Peanut continued to explore the passing countryside. "She can move things about, including herself."

"And you can enhance others, right?"

Mikal sighed. Whatever, or whoever, was responsible for doling out jhoruns to the people of Lentari truly did have a sense of humor he thought yet again. How was it fair that one of his childhood friends, who had the ability to project an illusory bug, could have a cooler jhorun than his own? Sure, with his help, he could give others temporary enhancement where, for example, instead of being able to create a temporary bug for a couple of minutes, the bug would exist for close to an hour. His parents had told him, over and over, that they were very proud of his abilities. He sighed again.

"Yes, I can enhance others."

"Have you ever enhanced Steve's jhorun?"

"His jhorun is very strong. I do not think he would wish for a stronger jhorun."

"How does it work?" Annie asked.

"How does what work?"

"If you want to enhance someone's jhorun, what do you have to do? I mean, do you have to physically touch the person?"

The boy nodded, comprehending Annie's question. He was silent as he thought about how to best demonstrate what he could do. Tristan increased his pace until he was walking side-by-side.

"You may demonstrate on me, if you like."

Mikal gazed up at his tutor walking next to him. Yes, that would work.

"Show Annie the knives you can summon," he instructed.

Tristan held out both hands, daggers instantly appearing in both of them.

"Summon the biggest knife that you can."

Without breaking stride, the soldier dropped both knives on the ground. Thinking several sticks had been dropped down to her level, Peanut hesitated long enough to determine the new objects had a funny scent to them and were to be left alone. A dagger with a six-inch blade then appeared in Tristan's outstretched hand. He presented it hilt-first to Mikal.

Startled, Annie looked behind them to see both fallen daggers lying on the ground where Tristan had carelessly dropped them.

"Um, do you really want to leave those things there? What if they fell into the wrong hands? Like, oh, I don't know, a child's?"

"Those daggers will cease to exist in about a quarter hour. It matters not who possesses them, nor where they have been taken. They will simply be no more. Therefore, it is perfectly safe."

"Oh."

Tristan indicated the knife Mikal was holding. "That weapon is the largest I can conjure on my own. No matter how hard I concentrate, that is the best that I can do."

Tucking several loose strands of hair behind her ear, Annie looked at the gleaming weapon. "Okay, now what?"

Mikal laid his hand briefly over Tristan's, momentarily closing his eyes. Annie had stopped walking, more interested in watching the demonstration of the boy's abilities than in where she was going. Was anything happening? She was expecting a flash of light, or maybe a jerking movement from Tristan. Nothing. After a few moments, Mikal opened his eyes and stepped back.

"Try it now."

A hailstorm of falling weapons fell all about them, causing all present to jump in surprise. Peanut darted between Mikal's legs.

"Jesus!" Annie slowly looked about them. They were now standing in a neat circle of swords sunk half-way up to their hilts. The weapons were still quivering slightly from their fall from who-knows-where.

"And you think your jhorun is lame? Are you serious?"

Despite himself, Mikal was impressed. He watched as Tristan knelt down to inspect one of the swords that had just fallen. "That is the most that have ever appeared! Cool!"

"Be that as it may, young sir," Tristan cautioned, "you must be careful. They could have struck someone. You do not want to harm Peanut, do you?" Mikal vehemently shook his head no. "She could have been struck by one of the swords. You must think about how your actions could affect those around you. As for myself, I ask that you warn me first if you increase my jhorun by that much, understood?"

"I understand. Sorry, Annie." The boy squatted down to give Peanut an affectionate hug. "I am sorry, Peanut." The young corgi was quite forgiving, planting doggie kisses over every inch of his face that she could reach.

Annie squatted down to try and pull one of the swords from the ground. It didn't budge.

Tristan stepped to her side.

"May I?"

One eyebrow raised; Annie nodded. "If you think you can pull it out, then be my —"

Tristan grasped the hilt of the sword and smoothly drew it out, presenting it hilt-first to the skeptical woman. Standing in the middle of the forest, holding the newly conjured sword, Annie stared in wonder at their companion. She kept forgetting that, while he didn't look it, a dedicated and well-trained soldier hid beneath Tristan's quiet demeanor. Clearly, he was more physically fit than she gave him credit for. She yet again tried to guess his age.

Subtly studying his physique as he turned away to walk next to the boy, Annie shook her head. It was his hair that was throwing off her estimates. He didn't have any. Whether he chose to keep his head shaved, or had thinning hair and didn't want his self-esteem to suffer, she couldn't say. She finally revised her latest guess from early 40s to late 30s. Maybe mid-30s. If he was in his 40s, then he was the strongest 40-year-old that she had ever seen. Clearly those baggy clothes he was always wearing was disguising a—

She shook her head in bewilderment. Where had that thought come from? Shaking her head and laughing at herself, Annie hurried to catch up with the other two.

"What about those swords? You aren't going to leave them like that, are you?"

"They will vanish eventually, Lady Annie."

"But how long will it take? You said it can typically take up to fifteen minutes for anything you conjure to vanish. But that's when you haven't been enhanced."

Tristan stopped and turned back toward Annie. "If it pleases you, I will deal with them."

"It would please me if you make them go away."

"As you wish, Lady Annie."

The soldier's eyes flicked over to the circle of swords, including the one Annie was still holding. Just as suddenly as they appeared, they vanished, leaving a perfect circle of holes in the ground and Annie empty-handed.

"Thank you."

"Anytime, milady."

* * *

"Are we there yet?"

Annie snorted, merriment dancing behind her eyes.

"What's the matter, Mikal?" she teased. "Too used to having Sarah zip you around, huh?"

Mikal cast a dark look at the lady who had become an aunt to him. An unintelligible murmur escaped his lips.

"We have perhaps another thirty minutes before we reach Avin," Tristan reported, giving the young boy an encouraging smile. "You are doing excellent. Keep up the pace. I would prefer it if we reach the village before nightfall. How is Peanut faring?"

"She is tiring, but I think she will be okay."

"What are we going to do once we get there?" Annie asked. "Is there a hotel or something we can stay at?"

"None like you are used to," Tristan said, staring hard at the trees bordering them on their right. "Avin has several inns that will suffice. Leave our accommodations to me. I will take care of it."

His gaze returned again to the passing countryside, slowly scanning the nearby trees.

"What is it?" Annie whispered, coming up behind him. "You have been staring at the trees now for the last twenty minutes. What's going on?"

"We are being followed, Lady Annie," Tristan said quietly.

"Someone is following us from inside the forest? Who?"

"Outlaws."

"Oh, you have *got* to be kidding me."

As if on cue, five men leapt stealthily out of the trees to surround them. All were thin, grubby, and probably in their early twenties.

The first thing Annie noted was the smell. Body odor. Bad body odor. None of the men before her appeared to have taken a bath in at least several weeks. All were dressed in rags, and all, unfortunately, were armed with wicked, homemade daggers. Annie had a feeling that no amount of money would appease these people. They wanted blood. Cautiously, she and Mikal stepped closer to Tristan.

"We come in peace," Tristan said, slowly circling around, forcing Annie and Mikal to move with him. "We do not want any trouble."

"You are outnumbered, traveler. Perhaps you have noticed that." The thief gestured to Mikal and Annie. "Turn out your pockets. All of you."

"Just do as they say," Tristan said, his eyes never breaking contact with the leader. "We will be alright."

Mikal reached inside his pockets to pull them out. A couple of candy wrappers fell out, and two American quarters. One of the thieves snatched the coins off the ground. The outlaw's eyes traveled to Annie.

"I'm sorry," Annie began, feeling inside her pants pockets. "These pants aren't really designed to have me pull out my pockets. There's nothing in them, I promise. I don't even have my —"

Annie screamed as the head mugger leapt forward to determine for himself that she didn't have anything in her pockets. Detecting the sudden aggressive movement, Peanut instantly began to bark. Mikal had his hands full as the young dog strained on her leash to leap in front of the member of her pack whom she had detected was now in peril. However, before the malodorous individual could touch Annie, a knife had appeared in Tristan's hand. The mugger was fast, but the well-trained soldier was faster. Much faster.

Even before the outlaw had realized what was happening, he had been forcefully knocked to the ground. Right about then, several of his men began howling in pain. As he stupidly looked at his companions, his eyes noted the daggers sticking out of the right legs of three of his men. How in the world did that happen?

"Kill him! Kill them all! Now!"

Clutching Mikal tightly, Annie yanked the leash away from him and pulled Peanut toward her so that she could hook several fingers in her collar. They watched in awe as Tristan swiftly and silently moved amongst the outlaws. A fist pummeled one man's jaw, sending him straight into unconsciousness. All three of the wounded outlaws wisely chose to limp away, disappearing as rapidly as they could into the forest.

One of the two remaining uninjured outlaws, the only one left standing at the moment, pulled out a second knife and advanced on the soldier. Rapidly sizing up his opponent, Tristan slowly backed away. Figuring he had the advantage, the outlaw grinned menacingly as he started waving his daggers around. Inexplicably, his victim stopped retreating. A knife appeared in each of his outstretched hands. The smile melted away.

"Consider your options carefully," Tristan whispered, eyeing his opponent dangerously. "Pursue this and you will suffer. That I promise you."

The outlaw hesitated. His victim clearly knew his way around a blade. Did he chance a fair fight or should he wait for backup? Just then, their leader reappeared, rubbing his sore jaw. Glaring at the strangely dressed peasant, he pulled out a second dagger as well. This whole mission had been blown. It was time to cut their losses and be done with this. The outlaws shared a look and smiled, clinking their blades together. Four blades against two. This should be child's play.

Tristan held his ground as the two outlaws edged ever closer. Watching both of the men for the subtle cues that even they didn't realize they were giving off, Tristan knew not only when they were going to attack, but also how. Both men lunged suddenly, hoping he would be caught unaware. A quick step to his left and a flick of his wrist had one of the outlaws grabbing his arm, cursing and swearing. Enraged, the second outlaw nimbly jumped to the right and was barely able to block the lunge directed at his abdomen.

From a safe distance, Annie, still clutching the trembling boy and the madly barking dog, watched as Tristan battled with both outlaws. One clearly was an inferior fighter as he was constantly hopping about, howling in pain, numerous cuts appearing all over his arms and chest. She gasped with shock as the crack sounded. Tristan had seized the opportunity to even the playing field, and sent a vicious jab at the man still howling and dancing about. The blow landed, knocking the outlaw out cold.

The first outlaw was back on his feet. With a yell of

outrage, he vigorously attacked the peasant. Inexplicably, the peasant feinted and parried with the skill of a master swordsman. Only the king's soldiers had such skill. Wizards be damned! Was that who he was facing? A soldier in disguise?

The yells of outrage switched to yells of frustration. The outlaw was now desperately fighting for the upper hand, trying to force his opponent back enough to beat a hasty retreat. Unfortunately, his "victim" continued to advance, pushing the outlaw further away from the woman and boy. If he tried to retreat now, he would most certainly be cut down by the much more skilled fighter. What could he do?

That momentary lapse of concentration was all Tristan needed. The outlaw's right hand was knocked down by a vicious jab, the homemade knife striking the ground by his feet. Alarmed, the outlaw glanced down. He never saw the backwards thrust of Tristan's elbow. Contact was made and it was lights out.

"My god, Tristan, are you okay?" Annie had finally released her death grip on the young prince, handing the leash back to him as well. "That was far and away the scariest thing I have ever seen."

Tristan bowed. "I am fine, Lady Annie. These men were unskilled in the ways of hand-to-hand combat. Let us be off. There might be others nearby."

Grabbing Mikal's hand, Annie followed Tristan as he guided them far away from the scene of the battle. It was close to a half hour before Tristan finally spoke.

"The last man recognized me as a king's soldier. I could see it in his eyes."

"Okay, what does that mean?"

"Think about it. A lone soldier, escorting a woman and child through the country."

"Okay," Annie admitted, "it looks suspicious."

"Aye, it does. We must assume that they will figure out young Mikal here has returned to Lentari. More than enough reason to make haste to Avin."

* * *

"We must be getting close, right? You did say that Avin was only an hour or two from the waterfall?"

"As the seasoned traveler travels, aye."

"What does that mean?" Mikal asked. He didn't know about the grown-ups, but he was tired of walking. He wanted to rest. And, he wanted something to eat. Peanut, however, was having the time of her life bounding through the tall grass lining the road. Small mammals scampered away, seeking refuge from the creature that kept sticking her nose into every nook and cranny.

Annie smiled. "It means we are traveling slower than the normal person does. So it might take a bit longer."

Tristan nodded.

"Why did you just wince?"

"No reason, milady."

Annie reached over and grabbed the back of Tristan's tunic, gently pulling him to a stop.

"Don't give me that. Have you been hurt?"

"Nothing serious."

"You're injured? Why didn't you say something? How bad is it?"

"A minor wound, I can assure —"

"Let me be the judge of that. Pull up your shirt. Now."

Reluctantly, Tristan pulled up his tunic to reveal a two-inch-long bleeding laceration just below his ribcage.

"Omigod, Tristan! You should have said something! We need to clean that up before it gets infected!"

"It was a clean cut. It will be fine."

"Did you not see those disgusting knives they were holding? We need to clean that out."

Mikal tugged on Annie's arm, pointing back the way they came.

"We passed a small brook just a little bit ago."

"We did? I didn't see anything."

"Nor did I, but I did hear Peanut drinking. And, she had a wet muzzle for a while afterwards."

"Perfect. Tristan, I need you to tear your undershirt into several pieces for me."

Too bemused by the situation to offer any resistance, the

soldier complied, handing the pieces of cloth over.

"I'll be right back.

"Please stay in sight, Lady Annie."

Annie turned, beaming one of her smiles. "I will, don't worry."

As she started walking back down the path, staring intently at the ground, Mikal sidled up to his tutor.

"I think she likes you."

"What makes you say that?"

"Did you not see the way she was smiling at you?"

"She was just being nice. That is all."

Mikal shook his head. "You have not been watching her. Every time she looks at you, she smiles."

Gingerly prodding the wound on his chest, Tristan looked over at the boy. "You should not be staring at her, young sir. It is considered rude."

"Still," Mikal insisted, hooking a thumb in Annie's direction, "I think you truly like her. Want me to find out if she likes you back?"

"You will do no such thing."

"Why not? It will be our secret. Do you not think I can find out without making it sound suspicious?"

"No, I do not," Tristan confirmed.

"So, then, you *are* interested!"

"I did not say that."

Off in the distance, Annie had finally discovered the source of water that Peanut had drunk from. The two of them watched as she squatted down next to the bubbling brook, dipping several of the shirt fragments into the cool, clear water.

"I cannot help but wonder," Tristan commented, as the two of them watched Sarah's sister, "about Lady Annie. When the Nohrin first arrived here in Lentari, they discovered that they had jhorun. I wonder if Lady Annie will also develop her own jhorun. She is from their world."

"I would think so." The boy watched as Annie began walking back toward them. "I wonder what it would be. I think it will be something strong. Sarah has a strong jhorun, and Annie is her sister."

Tristan nodded his head thoughtfully. "She exudes such energy, such charm. I am sure when her jhorun does manifest itself, it will be … what? Why are you looking at me like that?"

"I am going to ask her if she likes you back."

"Mikal, you will hold your tongue. Is that understood?"

The young prince snickered.

Wanting to change the subject, Tristan stretched his back. "If she does develop a jhorun, it will probably do so in a few days or more. That's how long it took for the Nohrin to develop theirs."

"What do you think she will be able to do?" Mikal asked.

The soldier turned to the boy.

"I wish I knew."

"I think it would be cool if she could have the ability to control illusions. Like, maybe making something look like something else entirely."

Tristan nodded.

"What about levitation? I think being able to fly would be super cool!"

Tristan nodded again.

"I know! She could conjure food! Sarah can do that."

"Lady Sarah teleports provisions from one place to another. She cannot conjure foodstuff out of nothing."

"Then, would that not be cool if she could do that?"

"It would be useful," Tristan admitted. "However, I do not think that is what her jhorun will be."

Mikal blinked a few times. "How can you be certain?"

"Just a feeling. Lady Annie is a nurturer."

"A what?"

"A nurturer."

"What is that?"

"A nurturer," Tristan explained, "is one who cares for the well-being of others. A caretaker."

"You mean she helps others?"

"It is more than that. She is concerned about all those around her. Why do you think she volunteered to look after the two of us when she learned Sir Steve and Lady Sarah had to return here? She cares about us."

The boy was silent as he digested that.

Annie rejoined them moments later.

"Okay, hold still. This is going to probably sting a little. I'm sorry, it can't be helped."

The soldier stood motionless as his wound was gently tended. Annie carefully wiped the excess blood away, revealing the severity of the laceration. As she gently cleansed the wound, she winced as she felt Tristan's body flinch.

"Sorry."

"Think nothing of it."

"Doesn't that hurt?"

"Yes."

"Then why aren't you yelling?"

"I am yelling. Internally."

"Tristan, this looks really bad. We really need to have this seen by a doctor. Your cut is bigger than I thought."

"Fear not, Lady Annie. As soon as we reach Avin, I will consult the services of a healer."

Ninety minutes later, Annie was scowling.

"You call this a town? There's hardly anything here!"

"What is the matter?"

Annie gestured at the quiet town. "Avin. I thought it'd be bigger."

"You were expecting a village the size of Sacramento?"

Annie and Tristan, with Mikal and Peanut standing in front, observed the small community that was Avin. Descending into the depression that the town was nestled in, Annie counted no fewer than fifty or so cottages on their way into the square. Figuring the same number of houses were on the other side of the center, with more scattered about, Annie guesstimated it to be home to at least three hundred people.

As they walked down the main street, Annie couldn't help but admire the quaint shops with small stands set up outside their storefronts, proudly displaying their wares. One had fresh produce. Another sold barbecued meat of some sort. Peanut hesitated long enough to gaze up at the elderly shop owner and wag her short stump of a tail. With a smile, the friendly shopkeeper tossed a small chunk of meat down to her. It lasted about two seconds before the young dog was licking her chops, tail wagging happily.

"Is the inn nearby?"

"I believe there are several. There is one over there," Tristan pointed to a two-story cottage that looked no different than the other houses they had passed on the way in to town.

"Shouldn't we be heading that way, then?"

"I know you are tired. Please, bear with me. Our objective is to get to the castle. I will rest easier when we are safe within its walls. Right now, we must find the office of the Constable."

While Annie and Mikal chose a large boulder to rest upon, Tristan disappeared into the closest shop to ask for directions.

"At least men here have no problem asking for directions."

Mikal gave her a quizzical look.

"Ask me about it later, kiddo."

Tristan emerged, gesturing further down the street.

"We are looking for a large stone house with two arched doors."

Peanut tugged at her leash. Enticing smells were beckoning her farther west.

"Come on, Peanut. We are looking for a big house with two doors. Think you can find it, pretty girl?"

Several enthusiastic barks sounded in response.

Ten minutes later, they were standing before a large two-story stone building with matching twin doorways.

"Wait here, I will find out if the constable is here."

Finding another large boulder to rest upon, Annie gratefully sank down onto the hard surface, thankful to give her aching feet a break. Mikal, on the other hand, let Peanut explore the surrounding area.

"Don't venture too far," she ordered.

"We will not go far," Mikal promised.

Sitting on a rock before the constable's office, Annie stared around in wonder. Here she was, in a village in another world, waiting for word on how to be transported to a castle. A castle! Definitely not what she thought she'd be doing when she started this day.

She recalled stretching out on one of the numerous chaise lounges scattered around the mansion's perimeter. She had chosen one close to her sister's beloved gardens as this was where Mikal was playing frisbee with Peanut. She hadn't remembered dozing off, but when she awoke, everything was quiet. Too quiet. Instantly rising up, she began searching for the boy, assuming he was simply playing hide and seek with the dog. Not finding him anywhere outside, she enlisted the help of his tutor, who was in the library yet again.

"Tristan, have you seen Mikal? I can't find him anywhere."

"Do you hear Peanut?"

Standing motionless, both of them listened intently. Nothing. One could have heard a pin drop.

"I don't —"

At that moment, the very distinctive click of doggie toe nails on hard wood sounded from one floor above. The top floor.

"Oh, son of a bitch." Annie's hands flew to her inside jacket pocket. Empty. She patted the pockets on her jeans. Empty as well. The green key that had been placed into her possession had vanished.

"The key is gone! He's using the portal!"

"Wizards be damned! Hurry, hurry! He must not be allowed to use it!"

Both adults sprinted from the library, tearing up the staircase in time to see Peanut bolt through the fully-activated portal. Mikal, calling for Peanut to return, darted after him.

Executing twin leaps that would make a Hollywood stuntman proud, Annie and Tristan leapt through the portal just before it fuzzed out.

Now, here she was in a foreign world, in a foreign village, suffering from a realization that the roles had been reversed. Tristan and Mikal were no longer the foreigners, she was. She was in their world. And somewhere in this world, presumably in the castle, were her sister and brother-in-law. She sighed. They were not going to be happy to see her.

Tristan emerged from the stone edifice. Glancing around, he spotted Annie sitting on the rock a short distance away. He hurried over to her.

"We have a problem."

"No vacancies?"

"I am not familiar with that word."

"It was a joke. It means no room at the inn."

"I have not been at the inn, so I do not know the answer to that."

Annie sighed, rolling her eyes. "What's the problem?"

"We will not be able to make it to R'Tal tonight."

"The castle? Why not?"

"The portal key has been stolen."

"And they don't have a spare? Of course, they don't have a spare," Annie said, answering herself as she threw up her hands. "If spares to the keys were available, then Sarah and Steve wouldn't have had such a problem when they first arrived here. Alright, so what do we do?"

"Each portal has two keys that will operate it," Tristan clarified. "One located here in the village, and the other in the castle. Until the portal at the castle is activated with Avin's key, the castle will have no idea that contact has been cut off."

"That can't be good. So, what are we going to do?"

"I will explain on the way. Let us find the inn. Where is Mikal?"

"Just over there, letting Peanut sniff around."

"Fetch him at once. I do not trust this."

"Don't trust what?"

"The key was stolen only a few hours ago. I believe somebody knows we are here and is trying to prevent us from reaching the safety of the castle."

"Aren't there any phones here? There's got to be some way to send word, right?"

"Aye, that is the other thing that concerns me. Every village has a supply of trained kytes that can deliver messages."

"Trained kites? Are you serious?"

"A kyte is a small bird, Lady Annie."

"Oh, like carrier pigeons. I get it. What about them?"

"When the constable discovered the theft of the key, he went to report it to the king, only he discovered the kyte pens empty, the doors purposely left open. Someone had released them back into the wild. Do you not understand? We have no way of contacting anyone now, let alone the castle."

"You think the theft of the key and the release of the

birds are related?"

"Undoubtedly."

"To prevent us from making contact with anyone?"

"Aye."

"But how could anyone possibly know we're here?" Annie demanded, tucking several loose strands of her long brunette hair behind her ear. "Us being here is just a fluke. This simply has to be a coincidence."

"I do not believe in coincidences, Lady Annie."

"Okay, now you're starting to freak me out."

"Where is Mikal?" Tristan asked again, glancing around. "Mikal!"

No answer. Annie gave it a try.

"Mikal!!"

Deciding to try a different technique that would definitely get the boy's attention, Annie called for their furry companion.

"Peanut!"

From around the side of the building that was a few doors down from them, they heard their canine companion joyfully start barking.

"Peanut!" Annie called again, making her voice as high and enthusiastic as possible. "Where's my pretty girl? Come here, Peanut! That's a good girl!"

The young corgi came barreling around the corner, running full tilt into Annie's open arms, physically dragging her handler with her.

"That is one strong dog," Mikal remarked, disentangling himself from the leash that had been wrapped securely about his arm.

"Didn't you hear us calling you?" Annie scolded, giving Peanut another friendly pat.

"I am sorry, I did not. I was talking with some people just over there."

Tristan stiffened. "What other people?"

"Just a couple of villagers who were curious about Peanut. There are no dogs like her here."

"That's all they wanted?" Annie asked, alarmed.

"Aye. Did I do something wrong?"

"We think someone may know that you have returned here."

"We are no longer safe. We are heading to the inn," Tristan informed them. "The one we want should be a little further down. Largest structure here. Come."

"Someone knows I am here?" the boy asked, looking up at Tristan, then over to Annie. "How would they know that? We have not been in Lentari for a long time, and only returned earlier today."

"Nonetheless, someone knows. The portal has been disabled, and the village kytes have been released."

"Who would do that?" Mikal wanted to know.

"Someone that wants to get their hands on you."

At the intersection of a smaller street, they came upon another inn. This one was a huge three-story structure that appeared to be composed of both timber and stone. The thickly thatched roof contained three enormous chimneys, all belching dark smoke. The ground floor windows were all open wide to allow as much fresh, cool air in as possible, while chasing out the scents of cooking, smoke, and the like. The big, double doors were wide open.

"That?" Annie sputtered, staring at the large building a hundred feet away. "That's where you want to stay? It looks like a barn! We had better not have to share a bathroom with anyone else."

"I told you earlier that it will be different from what you are used to."

"Still, it's a place to rest," Annie admitted. "I'm all for putting my feet up for a while. After you."

Taking the young corgi's leash himself, Tristan guided everyone into the large inn. Lady Annie was going to be very surprised to learn that the rooms found at these inns typically had but one bed. Mouth turned upward with the beginnings of a smile, he stepped up to the counter and signaled the proprietor for service.

Chapter 7 - Decision

So, what happened to all those people we shot in the leg?" Steve wondered aloud again. "Did they hop back to Ylani?"

"No footprints," Rhenyon reminded him. Again. "But they did have help. I want to know from whom, or what."

"And by that, you think some wizard was helping them?"

"You saw it with your own eyes. Constant supply of weapons. Quivers that never went empty. Vanishing when the battle was over. I can think of no other explanation."

Steve was nodding. "If someone that powerful was helping them, it would explain what happened to that guy I snared with my net, 'cause I still don't think he committed suicide."

"Nor do I, Sir Steve. I believe he was silenced for fear of a loose tongue."

The castle's western entrance finally came into view. The group stopped dead. The huge drawbridge was closed, yet it was hours before sunset. Even the portcullis had been lowered.

"I don't think I've ever seen the drawbridge closed up like that. At least not while it was still light out," Sarah observed. "Even the northern gates were closed. What now?"

The group of four humans, with the young griffin circling overhead, paused as they beheld the majestic castle. Not only was the drawbridge closed, every window had also been sealed shut. The streets typically lined with vendors, carts, and horses were all deathly quiet and mysteriously empty.

"They are under full alert," the queen said, eyeing the hushed castle.

"Can't you just teleport us in?" Steve asked, turning to his wife.

"Yes, I could. Very easily. But do you want to? Look at that castle!" She gestured to the formidable palace sitting quietly in the distance. "What do you think would happen to us if we suddenly popped into existence in front of a group of soldiers? We'd be lucky if we weren't hacked to pieces."

"Lady Sarah is right," Rhenyon said, gazing speculatively at the castle. "We must not appear in their midst without announcing our presence. My soldiers would not waste time with questions."

"What do we do?" Steve wanted to know. "Is there a doorbell or something we can use?"

Rhenyon looked up, watching the young griffin in flight. He waved his arm, gesturing for Phane to join them. Landing moments later, the griffin approached.

"What do you see in there?" Rhenyon asked.

"Nothing. No people, no horses, no activity."

"The guards are there," the captain murmured, more to himself than to anyone. "They have concealed themselves. I am sure by now we have been spotted. Word of our presence must have been reported."

Ny'Callé observed her home, noting the sealed windows and lack of activity. "They fear another attack. No wonder all have taken refuge inside. We must let them know who we are."

"Well," Steve said, scratching his head, "I have an idea."

Rhenyon grinned, knowing full well what his friend had in mind.

"Let us move out of the way," he cautioned, gently pushing everyone away from the fire thrower.

At a distance of several hundred feet from the closed drawbridge, Steve raised his right forearm straight up. Silent for a few seconds as he contemplated what he was about to do, he let loose two fireballs, watching as they raced up into the air. With a smile on his face, he then fired off a curved arc of fire, ordering his jhorun to maintain the shape as it traveled upward. Slowing the fireballs until they were hovering several hundred feet or so up in the air, he let the flaming arc catch up. Once it was in place, he let it hang there, burning merrily away. Smiling, he turned to his wife.

"What do you think? Think they'll see it?"

Shaking her head, Sarah stared up at the big smiley face grinning down from above.

"I'm sure they'll notice it."

W-H-A-M!

The castle drawbridge fell to the ground with a bone jarring thud. Soldiers were streaming outside, all running straight for them.

"Yep," Sarah confirmed, eyeing the throngs of people headed their way. "I'm quite confident they will."

Steve's smile melted away. "Are they happy to see us or are they planning on attacking us?"

Rhenyon stepped around him to stand in front of their group. He unsheathed Mythron and held it up, hoping that the unusual blue blade would be instantly recognized. It was. The advancing soldiers skidded to a stop, staring at the unique weapon. Several men in front were pushed aside.

"Captain?"

Rhenyon nodded, slipping the blue blade back into its scabbard.

"Lieutenant Pheron."

"Where the ruddy hell have you been, Captain? We have been—" Pheron's eyes widened as his gaze locked on the woman standing quietly beside him.

"Your Majesty! Thank the wizards you are safe! What happened to you? How did you escape?"

"Hello, Lieutenant," the queen smiled at the tall soldier.

"I had some help. Perhaps you might recognize them?"

Pheron's eyes flicked back to the two people standing behind the queen. A man and a woman. He had not recognized them at first so had paid them no heed. As he studied the man's familiar face, Steve helpfully held up a hand and ignited it.

"Sir Steve! Lady Sarah!" Pheron nodded, smiling. "I should have known."

"Should have known what, Lieutenant?" Rhenyon wanted to know.

"Several soldiers reported seeing a woman and two bound men appearing out of thin air. The woman said the men were involved with the queen's kidnapping. The lady vanished while the two men were taken into custody."

Sarah smiled. "Yes, that was me."

Armored knights appeared out of nowhere, clanking noisily as they surrounded the small group.

"Where is the king?" the queen asked, hoping to catch sight of her husband.

"His Majesty has been secured in the Antechamber," Pheron reported. "When we received word that a band of intruders were outside the castle, we decided to secure first and inquire later."

"Excellent, Lieutenant," Rhenyon nodded, inspecting the troops before him. "Exactly what I would have done. However, now that you know it is us, kindly tell your men to stand down."

"Aye, sir." Pheron spun in place, facing the men standing at attention. "Stand down. These are not intruders. Her Majesty has been returned to us. Flanking positions. We will escort her safely back inside the castle. If you will follow me, Captain."

"Proceed, Lieutenant. We will be right behind you."

The procession slowly made its way inside the castle. The armored knights fell in behind.

"One side! Out of my way!!"

The throng of well-wishers parted right down the middle as Kri'Entu came hurrying out of the castle interior, pushing aside peasants and soldiers alike.

"Where is she?"

Callé hurried by the curious onlookers and leapt into her husband's arms, weeping uncontrollably, and not caring who might be witnessing her emotional outburst.

"I thought I had lost you," the king choked out, holding on to his beloved wife. "I feared the worst. How did you ever manage to escape?"

With tears flowing freely down her face, the queen turned to smile at Rhenyon. "I had help."

The king's eyes focused on the soldier standing quietly at attention just to the right of his wife. "Captain, I do not know how you managed to accomplish this heroic feat, but rest assured, I will never forget it."

Rhenyon smiled, bowing low. "I cannot take sole responsibility, Your Majesty. If not for some much-needed assistance, I would still be tracking the queen."

Bowing again, the captain moved off to the right, revealing a man and woman. Smiling, the couple also gave a small bow.

Kri'Entu stared at the Nohrin, words escaping him. Ny'Callé stepped forward, still holding her husband's hand. "I do not know how they knew I needed help, but they did, appearing when Rhenyon needed them most. Without their help, I would still be a prisoner."

"I do not know how to thank you," the king repeated, staring first at Sarah, then at Steve. "Where is Mikal?"

"Safe in our world, with Tristan," Steve answered. "Sarah's sister is also with them. Also, for the record, we had some help, too."

"Who?"

"Phane."

A surprised squawk sounded from nearby. An adult griffin appeared and bowed before the king.

"Your Majesty, please pardon my interruption."

The king nodded, indicating for the griffin liaison to proceed. Pheris turned to the fire thrower.

"Pleased I am, to see Her Majesty safe. But did I hear you correctly? Did you say that my cub played a part in the rescue?"

Smiling, Steve nodded, stepping out of the way to reveal a very surprised, wide-eyed, adolescent griffin. "Phane is to be commended. He was flying home when the abduction took place, and elected to follow the kidnappers until they camped for the night. He found us and guided us to them."

Pheris looked at his offspring, pride emanating from every feather. "Well done, young one."

Uncomfortable being at the center of attention, if only for a moment, Phane nervously rustled his wings.

Kri'Entu addressed Sarah. "Your sister waits with Tristan and my son? Please give her my thanks when you see her next, Lady Sarah."

"I will, Your Majesty."

"Would you please accompany us to the Antechamber?"

All present hesitated. Whom did he want to see? Steve figured it was the captain, Rhenyon assumed it was the Nohrin, Phane just knew it was him. Catching sight of her rescuers, the queen smiled and tugged on her husband's arm, bringing him to a gentle stop. Kri'Entu smiled.

"Sorry, that was not very clear. Captain, Steve, and Lady Sarah, please come with us. Pheris," the king turned to the griffin liaison, "I just want to say that I thank the day human and griffin became allies. You honor us with your courage and your bravery. Please convey my thanks to your son."

Honored, the griffin bowed. "It is we who are honored, Your Majesty. And I will."

As the small group exited the throne room, Phane began emitting excited squawks and screeches as he relayed to his sire all that had happened.

Closing the door to the Antechamber securely behind them, the king indicated for everyone to take a seat in the semi-circular arrangement of plush chairs. Sinking heavily down into his, the king removed his crown and placed it on a small table next to his chair. Running his hands through his graying hair, and then leaning back, sighed deeply.

"First off, Rhenyon," the king began, surprising everyone with his uncharacteristic lack of formality, "you just earned your third gold bar. I would like to extend my, no, *we* would like to extend our sincerest congratulations. Commander."

Rhenyon's eyebrows shot up and froze there. Staring open-mouthed at the king, the newly appointed commander swiveled his head to meet the gaze of the queen. Recovering from the shock of his sudden promotion, Rhenyon formally rose.

"It has been my honor to serve, Your Majesties."

"It is we who are honored, Captain. *Commander*," Ny'Callé quickly corrected, blushing. "Forgive me."

"Congrats, buddy!" Steve slapped Rhenyon heartily on the back.

"It couldn't happen to a more deserving person," Sarah added, smiling at their friend.

"As for the two of you," the king began, staring hard at his son's bodyguards, "how exactly did you know that Callé had been taken from us?"

"From Rhenyon, actually," Steve answered.

"You mentioned that before," Rhenyon remarked, sinking back down into his chair. "How, exactly, did I inform you what had happened to the queen?"

"Well, we had just gone to visit Annie, that's Sarah's sister, when Mythrin started glowing. I should have known something was up, 'cause whenever we go somewhere, Tristan insists I bring it along. That was your doing, I take it?"

The king nodded.

"Anyway," Steve continued, "I hadn't ever noticed it glowing before. As soon as I picked it up, I heard Rhenyon's voice, saying something about an attack upon royal blood and having to get her back. We just put two and two together."

"If you do not mind my asking," Rhenyon began, addressing the king, "did you know the swords could facilitate contact between the worlds? Is that why you told Tristan to make sure Sir Steve always had his sword with him?"

Kri'Entu was smiling. Turning to face his new commander, the king nodded. "Maelnar informed me that the holders of the Mythra triad should keep their weapons close at all times. He did not specify why." With a smile, he added, "I put two and two together."

"So, you had Tristan make sure I had it with me whenever possible," Steve said, nodding. "Makes sense."

"Once we learned what had happened, my sister volunteered to stay with Tristan and Mikal. She didn't like the idea of the two of them, since they are foreigners to our world, staying by themselves."

"Very considerate of her," Entu observed. "She has our eternal thanks."

"I'll be sure to let her know," Sarah promised.

"The question arises, then, of how to thank the two of you for the services you have performed for us."

Steve held up a hand. "There really isn't any need, Your Majesty. We were only trying to —"

"Nevertheless," the king interrupted, dismissing Steve's objection, "the two of you shall be awarded with ..." he trailed off as he tapped his fingers on the arm of his chair. He turned to his wife. "What can we bestow upon them? There are no medals for non-Lentarians."

"You are the king," Callé said, simply. "Make something up."

"Very well." The king was silent for a moment. "Commander, you shall be witness to this."

Rhenyon nodded, smiling.

"It is my honor to inform that you will be the first two inductees into the Order of the Mythra Triad, highest honor we can bestow upon non-Lentarians."

Bemused, Steve smiled. "That sounds really cool. Thanks!"

"The medals will have to be crafted. Fear not, I will inform you when they are done and can bestow them unto you with a proper ceremony."

"A ceremony?" Sarah nervously looked at her husband. She didn't like being at the center of attention, either.

"So we can properly thank you for all you have done for us," Callé told her, still clasping her husband's hand.

The king was looking at his wife when he suddenly frowned. She was looking pale, which wasn't unusual considering the trauma she had just undergone. However, something didn't feel right. That familiar pull that he had grown so accustomed to was mysteriously absent.

"You know, I really did not try to do anything to save you.

Do you realize that?"

Callé turned to regard her husband. What an odd thing to say!

"That is not true and you know it, dear."

"Aye, I do know it, and it was *not* true."

Sarah gasped, sitting up straight.

"What is it?" Steve asked, alarmed.

"Wizards be damned!!" Rhenyon spat out, leaping to his feet.

The queen's eyes had gone wide open.

"Okay, what did I miss here?" Steve asked, getting irritated. "What's going on?"

"The king just lied in front of the queen," Sarah explained.

"He was just teasing her. I'm sure he didn't mean it."

"Nobody can lie in front of me," the queen whispered, tears beginning to stream down her face.

"Hell," Steve muttered as he finally realized what everyone else already knew: the queen's jhorun had been stolen!

"How is that possible?" Rhenyon demanded, beginning to pace as he was accustomed to do when deeply disturbed. "She was in the custody of hired mercenaries the entire time. They never reached Ylani!"

The king leaned forward to clasp both of his wife's hands. "What can you remember? Were you approached by anyone other than your captors?"

"No. I was tied up and blindfolded nearly the entire time I was taken."

"Nearly?" Rhenyon repeated, sitting back into his chair. "When were you not immobilized?"

Callé was silent as she recalled her long ordeal as prisoner.

"It was so beautiful," she began, taking a deep breath. "I remember thinking that I should go for a walk after we had our midday meal."

"That's right," Kri'Entu nodded, recalling yesterday afternoon. "You have no idea how much I regret not accompanying you. I seem to remember you barely touched your food."

"Something must have been bothering me, as nothing really tasted good."

Steve held up a hand. "Wait. Your food tasted bad?"

"Aye."

"All your food or only certain portions?"

The queen was silent as she thought about the lunch she ate the previous day.

"It did not start off tasting bad, but after a few minutes, I lost my appetite."

Steve glanced at his wife. "Think it's food poisoning?"

Sarah was nodding. "Sure does sounds like it."

"You believe the queen was poisoned?" Rhenyon asked, dumbfounded.

"I think she was drugged, not poisoned," Sarah clarified.

"What makes you say that, Lady Sarah?"

"An Agatha Christie movie we both saw last year."

King, queen, and commander all had blank expressions on their faces.

"Sorry, think of it as a series of popular stories from our world that have been re-enacted," Steve explained, "like a play, so that others can follow along without having to read the book."

Callé nodded. "Traveling entertainers sometimes perform skits for amusement," she explained to her husband. The king nodded.

"Anyway," Steve continued, taking a deep breath, "this particular story had a scene where one person was drugged, and then had a meal, only nothing tasted good. It was discovered later that a drug of some type had been slipped into his beer. Or ale, whichever you prefer."

"I am no specialist in herbology," Rhenyon said, "but I do know some about potions and their after-effects. They can throw one's palate into disarray."

The king's face turned stony. "Someone drugged the queen? In our own castle? Contact the kitchen staff and find out who was on duty yesterday."

"Consider it done, sire." Commander Rhenyon motioned one of the chamber guards over and relayed his instructions. The young soldier darted away, en route to the kitchens.

"What happened next?" Entu gently asked, still holding his wife's hand.

"I was dizzy, and thought a walk outside in the fresh air would help. Several men were there, men I did not recognize, yet I did not hesitate when they asked me to ride with them. I could not help myself. Before I knew what was happening, I was sitting on their horse and was being led to the West Gate."

"Where were the guards?" the king demanded, turning angrily to Rhenyon. "How was it that a set of complete strangers could simply lead the queen out of the castle on horseback?"

"All my men were busy dealing with fires that had broken out amongst several street vendors. In a matter of moments, they had the queen at the outer garrison."

"How did they make it out of the castle, then?" the king inquired, still angry about the apparent ease in which his wife had been taken.

"I can only assume that it was a well-planned mission, sire. They had men in all the right places. They refrained from running to the gates, thus avoiding attention. They had enough of a lead that they made it out the West Gate — despite our two squadrons of quickly mobilized soldiers — before the portcullis dropped. I barely made it through."

"They could have ambushed you, and you could have been killed," the queen whispered, wide-eyed at the thought. "All because of me."

"What else can you remember?"

"Once we made it to the forest," the queen continued, "we rendezvoused with the rest of their men and made for the mountains. I did not regain my senses until we finally stopped for the night, which was on a cliff. They assembled a hasty meal, of which I did not partake. They were angry. They taunted, but I refused to acknowledge them." The words were coming faster now as Callé recollected more of the previous night's occurrences. "Someone said something about the water —"

"So, you did not eat any of their food?" Rhenyon clarified.

"None. I did not trust it. In fact, the only thing I did do was risk a drink of water. I was terribly thirsty."

"Water. That's it?" Steve leaned back in his chair.

"Aye. Only water. But…" Callé hesitated.

"But what?" Entu wanted to know. Steve, Sarah, and the commander leaned forward in their seats.

"It was odd."

"What was?"

"The cup they used."

"One moment, if you please." The king rose, summoned a page, and whispered a fast set of instructions to the young man. Without a word, the servant vanished into the far recesses of the room. Sounds of a door opening and closing were heard moments later.

"Is everything alright, Your Majesty?" Rhenyon asked.

"Aye, I want Shardwyn's input on this."

"Do you think that the glass she drank from somehow snagged her jhorun?" Steve whistled. "If so, then we need to find it and smash it into a million pieces. If I see it, I'll do it."

The king smiled briefly at the fire thrower. "Appreciated. If given the chance, I hope you will not hesitate in doing just that."

"You can count on it," Steve confirmed.

They all heard a door open behind them and a shrill voice suddenly sounded from the darkness.

"I am going just as fast as I am able to, young sir. Stop pushing me so! Would you care to have ass ears to match that personality of yours?"

Steve snorted, trying to mask his laughter. Rhenyon grinned, having to look away as well. The king rose from his seat again.

"Ah, Shardwyn. I do thank you for coming on such short notice."

The tall, thin gray-haired man approached the sitting area and gave a small bow before he turned to his escort and scowled.

"Your man saw to that. Jus' had to ask politely. Glad to see you back safely, milady."

The king decided now was the time to be direct. "The queen drank from some type of glass and as a result, her jhorun has been taken from her."

The castle wizard gasped and looked in horror over at the

queen, who was sullenly staring at the thick rug on the floor.

"So, that is why they took her, is that it? To steal her jhorun so that you would order the return of your son? Have you sent for him yet?"

Thunderstruck, Rhenyon, Steve, Sarah, and Callé all turned to the king.

"Wizards be damned, this was all just a ploy so that you would have your son returned?" Rhenyon was up and pacing once more.

"I should have foreseen this," Kri'Entu muttered, massaging his temples. "Why did I not see this coming?"

"There's no way you could have known what was going to happen, Your Majesty," Sarah said, softly. "Clearly, whoever arranged the kidnapping knows Mikal can restore missing jhoruns."

Pulling a chair over, Shardwyn joined the impromptu meeting. "I do not believe any potion exists that can steal a jhorun, so therefore it must be the vessel which held the water. Tell me about this glass, Your Majesty."

"I do not remember much about it, I am sorry."

"First impressions have a way of staying with you much longer than anyone would believe," the wizard said. "If the right questions are asked, then you would be surprised at how much you can remember."

"She is ready," the king declared. "Ask away."

The queen turned to stare at her husband. "You might ask if I am, in fact, ready. In truth I am not, but I also want to apprehend those responsible for doing this to me. Shardwyn, go ahead."

"This cup," Shardwyn began, leaning back into his chair and closing his eyes, "describe it. Was it glass? Stone? Metal?"

"Metal," the queen answered, closing her eyes as well in an effort to help remember the traumatic events from the previous day.

"Did it have a stem? Handle? How wide was the mouth of the cup?"

Callé was silent as she thought about the shape of the vessel.

"Wide base, like you would find with our fine glasses. It

had a stem, but not as delicate."

"Thicker?"

The queen nodded. "Aye. No handles. The mouth was larger, about the size of the goblet I saw on Entu's desk earlier."

Everyone turned to look at the water goblet on the king's desk.

"Adornments? Any symbols? Crests? Jewels? Was it maybe gold or silver?"

"Silver," Callé said instantly. "No, wait, not silver but not gold. A little darker than silver."

"Pewter?" Steve helpfully suggested.

Callé smiled, nodding. "Aye, pewter. And I do remember seeing a mark on it."

"There was a mark?" Entu eagerly leaned forward. "Was it —"

Shardwyn held up a hand. "Your Majesty, I must have the queen describe it in her own words, in her own way."

Leaning back in his chair, the king nodded. "Understood. Proceed."

"Did you see this mark?" Shardwyn asked, eyes still closed.

"I had just picked up the goblet, and while I was drinking, my fingers felt what I thought was an inscription on the other side. I rotated the goblet and saw two lightning bolts. Is that significant?"

"A wizard's mark is very unique," Shardwyn answered, deep in thought. "Are you sure that was the mark you saw?"

"Aye, I am sure of it."

"Do you recognize this mark?" Entu asked Shardwyn.

"Dual lightning bolts," the wizard muttered, thinking hard, "etched onto the surface. Hmm…"

Kri'Entu recognized the wizard's silence as being in the affirmative. "It would seem that if you do not know this wizard outright, then you have seen this mark before. Am I right?"

"Correct," Shardwyn admitted, finally opening his eyes. "I am trying to remember where I have seen it. I know I have. Blasted memory. Getting older does nothing but pickle the mind."

Sarah stifled a giggle. The queen smiled fleetingly.

"Fear not, Your Majesty, it will come to me."

"So, you are certain that this goblet was enchanted?"

"Undoubtedly, sire. Look at the facts. Her Majesty does not remember seeing any wizard, did not partake of any food, and drank only a little water from a pewter goblet with the mark of a sorcerer on it. She is returned to us without her jhorun. I do not think it gets any clearer than that."

"We should ask the others who had their jhoruns taken from them," Rhenyon suggested. "We should ask them if they remember drinking from such a goblet as the one you have described."

"Excellent notion, Commander," Kri'Entu nodded. "Tristan is unavailable. There were two others, I believe. Find them. Ask them."

Rhenyon motioned another guard over, and within moments, that soldier was hurrying out of the chamber.

"As soon as I know, you will know," Rhenyon vowed.

"If they do, then what does that tell us?" Sarah asked. "That this Ylani wizard has created some type of goblet that steals the jhorun from whoever drinks from it? I think that's really creepy."

"It would appear so, milady," Shardwyn said. "I would love to study this goblet further. So, whoever finds it first is to bring it straight back to me without fail!"

"No offense, Shardwyn," Steve spoke up, drawing everyone's attention to himself, "but if I so much as see this thing, or anything else that I think could be it, I'm gonna melt it down to scrap metal."

"Your Majesty," Shardwyn began, turning his imploring eyes onto the king, "if I am given a chance to study it, I might be able to learn how the jhorun was taken and therefore return it to the original owner. Would that not be a wise idea?"

"If Sir Steve has the opportunity," Rhenyon said, deciding to add his opinion, "I must agree that it should be destroyed. Immediately."

"Do you not want to learn how to counteract the power this wizard apparently has?" Shardwyn pressed. "If we destroy his means to steal jhorun, what is to prevent him from creating another goblet? Nay, we must learn how to reverse the damage it causes."

"Which brings us to my son," Entu said, staring straight at the wizard. "Mikal can easily return the queen's jhorun, which makes it apparent why she was abducted in the first place. They know Mikal is out of reach. They want him returned."

"Why make it so obvious?"

Everyone turned to Sarah.

"It's clear everyone knows what Mikal is capable of doing. My question is, let's just say this Ylani wizard knows Mikal is safely out of his reach. If it's jhorun he wants, then he could very easily keep abducting other people. Everyone would assume that they are just missing, right? Or if the person turns up dead, you'd never know if that person's jhorun was stolen, right?"

Silence.

"Why, then? Why be so blatant about kidnapping a member of the royal family and taking that person's jhorun?"

"What's on your mind, my dear?" Steve asked, turning to his wife. "Think there's something else to this?"

Sarah nodded. "I do. Something doesn't add up. It just doesn't make sense that they want to take him so that this other wizard can freely take jhoruns."

Rhenyon was nodding. "I agree. If that were the case, then why try to abduct the prince? Why not just kill him? I think Lady Sarah is right. They want him for something else."

"But what?" Callé asked helplessly. "His jhorun is the enhancement of others. Why would they want that?"

Sarah shook her head. "What if that isn't the true nature of his jhorun?"

Both king and queen stared at the teleporter.

"I mean, how do you know his jhorun is enhancement?" Sarah persisted. "Do you have someone you take him to who can determine what it is, or do you have to wait for something to happen?"

The queen nodded. "Typically, by age five, a Lentarian child will have demonstrated his abilities. Then the parents would know what the nature of their child's jhorun."

"So, there isn't someone responsible for officially

identifying a person's jhorun?" Sarah wanted to know.

"No," the king said, shaking his head, "there is not. Why do you ask, Lady Sarah? Do you think that Mikal's abilities have been misidentified?"

"Not necessarily misidentified," Sarah said, "but possibly misunderstood."

"It is possible," the queen said, slowly, "but what would it be then? If not enhancement, how would you explain what Mikal can do?"

Sarah shrugged, looking at the others. "I really haven't seen Mikal use his abilities, so I cannot say for certain. But I'll bet the answer is there."

"I'll bet you're right," Steve spoke up, smiling at his wife. "It would explain why everyone is so damn interested in him."

"Be that as it may," the king interjected, "whether Mikal has some unknown abilities or not, we do know that he can restore missing jhorun. Therefore, he must be —"

"No," Callé interrupted, "do not even suggest it. I do not care what happens to me. Mikal must be kept safe. He will remain safe in the Nohrin's world."

"No," Kri'Entu overruled. "I will not have you suffer without your jhorun. Mikal will return just long enough to verify your jhorun has been restored."

Callé furiously turned to her husband. "No, Entu, I forbid it! I will not place our son in mortal danger, not even for myself. He must remain safe!"

"We will take all precautions," Entu declared, giving his wife a gentle look. "I realize you do not agree with me, and I hereby accept your anger. However, I will *not* see you suffer. This will be done." Taking his wife's hand, he gently added, "I am sorry, my love. I hope one day you will forgive me."

"Your son will be safe, Your Majesty," Rhenyon insisted, rising out of his chair. "All of my men will be on high alert."

"No one is gonna touch him," Steve promised. "I'll personally deep fry anyone's sorry ass who tries."

Callé nodded. "You have my thanks. Both of you."

* * *

Later that night, Steve and Sarah found themselves back in the guest quarters they had previously stayed in during their first visit.

"It's like nothing has changed," Steve remarked, walking around the room.

"Nothing has. Check this out. All of our clothes are still here."

Sarah was standing before the closet. All of her gowns were hanging right where she had left them. Steve's clothes were also there.

"What do you want to bet," he began, running a finger over the numerous hanging dresses, "that no one has stayed in this room since we were here."

"Seems like wasted space, if you ask me."

"The queen clearly wasn't keen on the idea of Mikal coming back here."

Sarah turned, facing her husband. "Would you? Defeats the purpose of having him stay with us. He's safe in our world. Nobody can touch him. I would have to agree with the queen. He shouldn't be returned."

"Not to start an argument here," Steve began, sitting down on the bed. "But I would have to agree with the king. If something happened to you, then you'd better believe that I would do whatever I could to make sure you're okay."

"Even at the expense of our child? Provided we had one, that is."

"If I knew he would be safe, then yeah. I would. Do you really think they are going to try something when he does make it back?"

Sarah shrugged. "I don't know. I don't even know how they'd know he was back."

"Well, think about it," Steve said, removing various pieces of leather armor and dropping them on the floor. "As I understand it, ol' DW —"

"DW?" Sarah interrupted. "What's that?"

"Sorry. Stands for Dark Wizard. If DW notices that his newly stolen truth jhorun has vanished, he's gonna know that the one person who can steal them back has returned home."

"True," Sarah was nodding. "But seriously, how fast

could he possibly find out? I mean, he's in another country. That would suggest there are Ylani spies here in the castle that would know about Mikal's return and get word to your DW person."

"The king has vowed that Mikal's return will be kept strictly secret. No one but us, Rhenyon, and the Kri'yans will know."

"Rhenyon still thinks that somehow they'll find out," Sarah remarked, pulling her own shoes off.

"Well, I think he's right, we have to be ready for that contingency."

"I just wish we could have gotten him tonight."

"Me, too. But the king decided to maintain the illusion that all was well with the queen. That's why he decided to go through with the award ceremony for Rhenyon. We'll go home first thing tomorrow morning to escort him back here. He'll do his thing for his mom, then we can all go back home."

Sleep didn't come easily for Sarah. Once again, too many things were going through her mind. Was it going to be just as simple as that? Return home to get Mikal, have him restore his mother's jhorun, and then they could return home? Or were they going to be ambushed when they tried to cross back over with Mikal?

Tired of battling her overactive mind, Sarah chose to lie next to her husband, closing her eyes. If she stopped trying to silence her thoughts, then maybe they would just silence themselves. It had worked before, so she'd give it a few moments and see if her brain would shut up.

No such luck. Her swirling thoughts continued to jump from one subject to another. Was Mikal going to be safe? Could they expect an ambush when he was returned? Was she really going to get any sleep tonight with Steve snoring as loud as he was? Was she right about Mikal's jhorun?

Mentally throwing up her hands in defeat, she waited to see what else her imagination was going to throw her way. Surprisingly enough, her thoughts suddenly coalesced into one, namely the nature of her own jhorun.

This again? She thought crossly. What about her jhorun's

blasted nature should she wonder about? The notion of trying an experiment briefly flashed in her mind. An experiment? Here? Now? No, thank you very much. Such things could wait for morning.

An hour later, after tossing and turning on the bed like a rotisserie chicken, she finally acceded to the whims of her imagination. *Fine. They want to experiment, then let's experiment.* Besides, she reasoned, if she accidentally woke her husband, he'd never remember. Invoking her memory, she tried to think of something nearby she could move. Not teleport, but actually move. There, on the table by the sofa, by the light of the flickering candle, was her ever-present tube of lip balm. She had applied a thin layer to her lips moments before turning in for the night.

No vanishing, she ordered her jhorun. *No disappearing. I want it to stay completely visible. Move it from the table over to me.*

The small tube zipped across the room and smacked into the side of her husband's head before rolling down his body, coming to a rest against her side. Sarah clapped her hands over her mouth to keep from laughing out loud or letting out a triumphant shout. She clearly had to be able to see what she was doing when trying that form of her jhorun. She couldn't wait to show her husband!

Steve, after being thumped on the side of his head by the balm, had naturally assumed he was snoring and his wife was poking him to make him roll over. With a grunt, he complied.

Chapter 8 — Divided

"How long will it take to retrieve Mikal?"

"Not long, Your Majesty. All we have to do is find him. The house is big. More than likely, he'll be outside playing with Peanut."

Kri'Entu paused in his descent down the grand staircase. He turned to his son's female bodyguard.

"What is a 'peanut'?"

"In this case, Peanut is the name of a dog. She is his constant companion. At least when Steve isn't around."

Both the king and queen gave their son's bodyguards an appraising stare.

"You gave him a dog?" Callé asked, a smile slowly spreading on her face as she pictured her son frolicking with a dog in another world. "Did you hear that, dear? Mikal has a dog."

"You both have shown Mikal more kindness than we could have ever hoped for. We are thankful."

Everyone resumed their trek down the stairs.

"We weren't too sure how you guys would react to us giving him a pet," Steve remarked, looking around the Great Hall. "I will say, though, he has handled the responsibility of owning a dog very well. Do you have many dogs here?"

"A few. Most run in wild packs."

"They haven't been domesticated here, then?" Sarah asked.

"Some are kept as pets. Most are ignored."

Following the king and queen into the smaller portal chamber, Sarah pulled out her key.

"Want me to go with you?" Steve asked his wife.

"No, I don't think that's necessary, do you? I won't be gone long. Probably only a minute or two."

"What if Annie has taken them to a movie or something?"

"Then I can call her cell to find out where she is."

"Mmm, good one."

Inserting the purple key into the keyhole, Sarah activated the portal and watched as the image of their upstairs sitting room formed. Giving her husband a quick kiss goodbye, she disappeared down the stairs, calling for her sister. A few moments later, the portal fuzzed out, returning to the carved representation of the castle they were presently in.

"Has he been much trouble?" Callé suddenly asked.

Kri'Entu made no indication he had heard his wife's question, but Steve noted that the king's head was now cocked in their direction.

"None whatsoever. He's a bright kid who loves to play outside. He doesn't even give Tristan any trouble. I can't say I was that attentive when I was in school."

"The two of you are to be commended," Kri'Entu said, taking his wife's hand. "It has been a tremendous relief to know he is in such capable hands."

The newly appointed commander poked his head into the room.

"Pardon my interruption," Rhenyon began, giving a small bow to the king and queen.

"Yes, Commander," the king waved him over. "What is it?"

"I thought you would like to know. Five squadrons now

surround the castle. Three more have been stationed at strategic points throughout the castle interior. An additional three squadrons also patrol the outer garrison."

"Excellent, Commander."

"Eleven squadrons. That's a lot of men," Steve observed.

"We are taking no chances, Sir Steve."

"Can't say that I blame you."

"If they went to this much trouble to guarantee Mikal's return," the king stated, his tone becoming grim, "then it only stands to reason that they will try to take him the moment he arrives. We must be ready."

"How will they know when he returns?"

"We have spies in Ylani," the king answered, meeting Steve's gaze. "We have to believe Ylani has spies of their own, too. Even if they do not, we must assume that they will somehow find out."

Several people began shouting nearby, startling all of them. Kri'Entu grabbed Rhenyon by the arm and pulled him toward the throne room with the queen following quietly. Wanting desperately to know what was happening, but not wanting Sarah to arrive to an empty room, Steve elected to stay behind. Adopting Rhenyon's custom when he was disturbed, he paced. How long did it take to find a small boy, anyway? Then again, he admitted, the mansion was huge. It might take Sarah a while to ascertain his whereabouts.

The amount of activity in the adjacent room suddenly doubled. More shouting, more scurrying, more people running about. What was going on? Was this the ambush the king had been fearing? Stopping in the doorway to see for himself what was happening, Steve observed the king, Rhenyon, and several others wildly gesturing around a large table. There was some type of parchment spread out on its surface. Someone said Capily and tapped the paper. It had to be a map.

The familiar humming manifested once more. Turning, Steve watched as the portal returned to life. An image of Sarah appeared, standing with her hands on her hips and wearing a worried expression on her face.

"What's the matter?" he asked, as his wife strode through

the portal to join him. "Where's Mikal?"

"No one is home. I tried calling Annie's cell. I followed the rings until I found it out by the garden. The cars are there, too."

"Are you sure they haven't taken a hike or anything?"

"Annie wouldn't leave without her cell. I found several books open in the library, plus a glass of what I assume used to be iced tea out by a chaise lounge in the garden. Not to mention I couldn't find the key anywhere. That's why it took me so long. I think they used it."

Steve placed a hand over each temple and rubbed. "Aww, man. This isn't good."

"You're telling me. They've been praising us for how well we're doing, and now we appear to have lost him."

"Nobody home, no key," Steve was ticking off different points on his left hand, "and all signs indicate that they left abruptly. They're here somewhere, aren't they?"

"What are we going to do? His parents have to be told." Sarah looked around. "Where'd everyone go?"

"In the throne room. Something is going on. Must be what the king has been fearing. Lots of shouting and lots of activity."

"Why aren't you in there?"

"Well, for starters, I'd be in the way. And second, I was waiting for you."

Sarah took his hand and pulled him toward the commotion. "You need to tell them."

Steve took a deep breath. "Fine, I'll do it."

She fell into step behind her husband as he threaded his way to the center of the room, angling for the table where the king was still deep in conversation with several others. Callé, standing off to the side, caught sight of the Nohrin. Her smile melted away as she noticed that her son wasn't with them. She hurried to their side.

"What has happened? Where is Mikal?"

"He wasn't there," Steve reported, deciding now wasn't the time to beat around the bush. "The key is missing as well."

"And Tristan?"

"Also missing. So is Sarah's sister."

The queen's eyes widened in shock, darting quickly over to her husband. "Mikal has returned. Tristan and your sister must have followed. It has to be. What would possess him to sneak back here? Why risk it?"

"He knew you were in trouble," Sarah said to the queen. "He probably thought he could help."

"He should not have returned. He is in danger. Where do you think they are now?"

"If they used the green key, then they would have been dumped in the middle of the forest like we were."

"Hush, not another word. Let me get Entu."

Callé hurried over to the table and tapped her husband's shoulder. Startled, Kri'Entu turned to see his wife. Bending down so that she could whisper in his ear, he stiffened. Eyes opened wide, he glanced up at the Nohrin. Excusing himself, he snagged Rhenyon by the arm and ushered everyone into the Antechamber.

"You are dismissed," the king said, addressing the motionless guards. The three soldiers gave a curt bow before exiting the chamber.

"Mikal is already here? When? How did this happen?"

"We don't know," Steve answered. "It was recent, we do know that much. No one was at the house, so that means Annie and Tristan are here, too."

"This explains a lot, Your Majesty."

Kri'Entu turned to regard his newly-appointed commander. "You think these events are related?"

Rhenyon nodded. "I do."

"What's related?" Steve asked, looking from king to commander. "What's going on?"

"Reports are coming in that three of our villages are under attack. And, just moments ago, we received word a large fire has broken out in Avin."

"They know," Sarah whispered, more to herself than to anyone.

"Aye, that is my thought, too," Rhenyon agreed.

"They're trying to draw your forces away from the castle, aren't they?" Steve asked.

Wearily, the king nodded. "Aye. And I have no choice." Kri'Entu looked at his trusted friend. "Commander, you are to go to Capily with three squadrons. Protect the village. Whom do you suggest I send to Donlari?"

"Lieutenant Pheron," Rhenyon instantly answered. "He is loyal to the crown. Send Lieutenant Rhein to Avin."

"Excellent choice. Have Lieutenants Pheron and Rhein report to the portal chamber. Several squadrons will accompany each of them. I need one more man to lead the Verdayn excursion. Whom do you recommend, commander?"

"Send me to Avin," Steve interrupted, surprising everyone. "Send Rhein to Verdayn. No one is better equipped to put out a fire than I am, and I can guarantee I'll put it out faster." Blank stares met his gaze. "Trust me, time is not on our side right now. The sooner I put it out, the sooner I can help look for Mikal. If they used that green key, it means they were dumped fairly close to Avin. Isn't that what you once told me?"

Both Kri'Entu and Rhenyon were silent as they considered Steve's proposal.

"Look, I don't need any squadrons. Save your manpower."

"And if you are attacked?"

Steve snorted. "What moron in their right mind would attack a fire thrower?"

"Your assistance is very much appreciated. Very well. Sir Steve will go to Avin to deal with the fire. Lieutenant Rhein will go to Verdayn."

"Send me, too," Sarah added, taking her husband's hand. "Not to stay, just so that I can get familiarized. Once I am, then I'll come back here and then you can send me to Capily. I've already been to Donlari. Come to think of it, I haven't been to Verdayn, either."

"You want to see all the villages?" Kri'Entu looked briefly at Rhenyon. "Now is not the time for sightseeing, Lady Sarah. May I ask why?"

"Safe zones," Sarah explained. "As soon as I am familiar with the area, then I won't need a portal to get from here to there. Plus, I can take several people with me at the same time. But until I see the area, I can't do anything."

"I am unwilling to send you into the thick of danger, milady."

"Appreciated, I'm sure, but I can help out. Please! You have to let me do this!"

The king's eyes swiveled over to Steve's. "Are you all right with this?"

"Sarah can definitely take care of herself," he answered, giving his wife a fleeting smile. "Besides, if she sees trouble, she can get herself to safety without a portal. As soon as I get the fires out in Avin, I can have her teleport me to Capily or Donlari, or wherever I'm needed."

The king nodded, thinking fast. "Aye, we could use the help. We must find my son. Very well. Commander, assemble your men. You have ten minutes. Meet us in the portal chamber."

"Aye, sir." Rhenyon gave a quick bow and vanished into the crowd of people bustling about.

"Steve, do you know what this means?"

"What?"

"Back in your armor, my dear."

"Damn."

Ten minutes later, well over a hundred soldiers were crowded into the portal chamber as Kri'Entu pulled out a velvet case with several crystal keys. Extracting a light blue one, he activated the portal and stood back as a picture of rolling surf appeared through the window of a large room.

"Good luck to you, Commander."

"My thanks, Your Majesty."

"Take this, just in case." Kri'Entu handed the blue key to Rhenyon, who fashioned a makeshift necklace out of a piece of leather cord. Sliding the key around his neck, he tucked it safely inside his tunic.

"Report back as soon as you are able."

"Acknowledged."

Rhenyon led his squads of soldiers into the portal and vanished from sight as they silently slipped out of the constable's office.

"Might as well get this one over with." Sarah stepped through the portal and stared hard at the room she was in, taking a few moments to gaze outside at the endless western sea. "This is Capily, right?"

The king nodded. "Aye. How long do you need to create your safe zone?"

Sarah turned, looking back through the portal. "No time at all. I just want to get a few different locations in case I need to use them."

"While the village is under siege by who knows what?" Steve sputtered. "No way. Do that later. Get back here." At that moment, the portal faded out. "Oh, son of a b-"

Sarah popped back into existence a split second later.

"Fine, I'll just use that room as my reference point then."

"Lieutenant Pheron, you are next."

Kri'Entu pulled out a brown key and inserted it into the portal. The office of Donlari's constable was in a large building with sparse furnishings. The image that appeared showed a darkened house, with several people huddled together, staring out the window. An elderly man dressed in a dark brown tunic with matching trousers turned to stare at the portal.

"Thank the Wizards! Your Majesty, we are under attack and our key was stolen! You must—"

Kri'Entu held a finger to his lips to silence the constable. He handed the brown key to Pheron as he stepped through. Also tying the key to a leather strap, the lieutenant mimicked his commander, tucking the key safely out of sight beneath his leather armor. As he stepped into the room, he motioned his men to follow and indicated for those already in the room to remain silent. The portal faded out.

"Lieutenant Rhein, are you ready?" The king withdrew a burgundy key and handed it to Rhein as the scene in the portal shifted again. "Return as soon as you are able."

Rhein nodded. "Understood, sir."

Stepping through the portal into a darkened office, the lieutenant slipped out of sight, his men following silently behind. Sarah stepped through, taking in as much of the sparse office as possible.

"Not much here," she observed. Walking over to the window opposite the portal, she looked outside, admiring the heavily forested surroundings. "Very pretty. Okay, I can remember this. Reminds me of Placerville."

"Just make sure you keep the two separate. Don't want to shoot for Verdayn and get Placerville instead," Steve joked.

"Not much chance of that."

"Ok, that should be en—"

The portal faded out.

"—ough," Steve finished. He sighed.

Sarah appeared moments later.

"Okay, that leaves us with Avin. Be careful, Sir Steve," Kri'Entu cautioned. "Whoever started those fires is more than likely still in the area. Lady Sarah, remain only long enough to create your safe zone then come straight back here immediately, understood? Without our village portal keys, you are now our sole method of communication and teleportation within the villages."

Sarah nodded. "Understood."

A dark blue key was produced. Activating the portal once more, a darkened hall met their eyes, with twin matching entry doors facing north. Kri'Entu handed Steve the blue key as both husband and wife stepped through. Slipping the key into his trouser pocket, they turned to look behind them, watching as the grim-faced king disappeared. Planting the image of the room solidly in her memory, Sarah took her husband's hand.

"Be careful, okay?"

"And you. I'll put this out as fast as I can. I'm not thinking it'll take that long."

"And if whoever started the fires is still in the area?"

"Well, you know what they say. If you play with matches, then you're gonna get burned."

Shaking her head, Sarah kissed her husband. "I love you, honey. You watch your back, okay?"

"Will do. And I love you more!"

Sarah smiled, vanishing moments later.

Pushing open one of the twin doors, Steve stepped outside. Sure enough, the first thing he noted was the scent of wood burning, reminding him of a campfire. However, people weren't typically yelling and screaming around them.

Rushing out into the street, he followed the general flow of people until he came upon three small cottages that were completely engulfed in flames. A large three-story structure was nearby. He was surprised it hadn't caught fire yet.

A fire train had been created, with townsfolk helplessly tossing small buckets of water onto the roaring flames. Empty buckets were then passed back down the line to be refilled moments later. Even though bucket after bucket of water was tossed onto the raging inferno, they might as well have been trying to put out the fire with tea cups. The size and strength of the fire was just too great.

Looking around to better familiarize himself with the surrounding environment, Steve pondered how to put out a fire this big. If he pulled all the energy inward, as he typically did, then that would mean the energy of the fire would then be within him, right? A campfire was one thing. However, this was one mother of a fire! Could he handle that much energy at one time? Where was the closest source of water, anyway?

Steve's eyes traced the line of people back to a small well in the town square. That would never do. If something bad happened, he was going to need a larger water source than that. Not to mention there were trees everywhere. Maybe this wasn't such a hot idea after all, no pun intended.

The barking of a dog caught his attention. Damned if that didn't sound just like —

His blood ran cold. "Oh, shit."

The blaze had already consumed three small cottages, and had just spread to a nearby fourth. Tristan wearily continued to fling bucket after bucket of water on the flames, all to no avail. The fire was simply too hot. Unless they could—

Without warning, the crackling fire abruptly froze in place. The rapidly expanding flames on the rooftop of the fourth cottage had curiously stopped their advancement as well. Tristan stared at the oddly unmoving flames, wondering what was happening, when the motionless tongues of fire suddenly exploded skyward. The speechless soldier watched in awe as some invisible vortex sucked the flames from the burning buildings high up into the sky, coalescing into a huge mass of writhing fiery tentacles. In complete silence, the entire town watched as more and more of the fire was sucked off the burning cottages. The jets of flame that were twisting and turning in midair suddenly decided to rocket back toward the ground. In fact, Tristan noted, if all the transfixed people didn't seek cover, then they were going to be severely burned!

"Look out! It's coming back!"

Inexplicably, the descending mass of fiery tentacles twisted again, swerving around buildings and bystanders until it slammed into one man standing by himself a ways off. Flames continued to be pulled off the four burning buildings until nothing but smoking ruins remained. Tristan grabbed a nearby blanket from one of the sleepy residents and went to the burning man's aid, only to be unable to approach; he was just too hot. Tristan sadly watched as the man became completely engulfed. There was nothing anyone could do for him. He shook his head. That was one brave soul. No horrible yelling, no frantic rolling on the ground, just a calm resolve as he accepted his fate. In fact, Tristan squinted his eyes to double-check, it looked like the burning man had just scratched his head! What was going on? His eyes widened even further as the flickering flames began diminishing, as though they were being absorbed into the villager's body. A few moments later, the totally unscathed man began brushing his clothes off and checked for burn marks.

"Well, that wasn't too bad."

"Sir Steve!"

"Tristan! Do I really need to ask just what the hell you're doing here?"

"My most abject apologies, Sir Steve. It was not my intent to return."

"Let me guess. Mikal snuck through, and you followed."

The normally reserved soldier blinked his eyes with surprise. "As a matter of fact, that is absolutely correct, Sir Steve."

"Is Annie here, too?"

"Aye. And Peanut."

"Yeah, I thought I heard her. Where are they?"

"I left them just outside the inn. We were inside when the fires broke out."

Tristan guided him over to the inn where many of the tenants were still milling about. Peanut, catching sight of her pack's alpha male, wriggled free from Mikal's grasp and tore across the plaza. Her joyful barks caused many onlookers to glance in their direction as the young corgi leapt into her kneeling master's arms.

"Peanut, pretty girl, what are you doing here?" The young dog squirmed with ecstasy, pleased with the amount of attention she was getting. Annie and Mikal joined him moments later.

"Steve!" Mikal was out of breath, practically jumping up and down with excitement. "We saw the whole thing! That was super cool!"

Annie gave him a brief hug. "We are sure glad to see you! I knew you could mess with fire, but I never imagined you could put out a burning house, let alone three."

"Four," Mikal corrected, proudly looking up at his bodyguard.

Steve smiled briefly as he leveled a gaze at Annie and Tristan. "You guys are currently the subject of a countrywide manhunt, did you know that?"

"You knew we were here?" Tristan asked, amazed. "How did you find us so fast? It is good that you showed up when you did. The inn would have been the next to go."

"We didn't know you were here in this village specifically," Steve clarified. "We heard about the fires and I volunteered to put 'em out."

"The portal is down and the key has been stolen. All of the village kytes have been released. How did you know?"

"Easy. The king told us."

"How did the king know?"

"Not a clue."

"So how did you know that we were here?" Annie asked.

"Sarah returned home to get Mikal. No one was there. How long have you been here?"

"Since yesterday afternoon," Annie answered. "Bet you

want to know what we're doing here, huh?"

"The thought had crossed my mind."

"Mikal, care to tell him?"

The boy stared at his feet, shifting his weight from one leg to the other. "Peanut bolted through the portal. I had to get her!"

"I see," Steve said, squatting down. "So, let me get this straight. Peanut activated the portal by herself, then leapt through on her own accord, is that right?"

Mikal scuffed his feet on the ground. "Not exactly."

When no more explanations were forthcoming, Steve hooked a finger under the boy's chin and gently lifted his head up.

"Why did you steal the key?"

"I had to help my mother!"

"That's what we're doing, sport. In fact, we've already rescued her."

"The queen is safe?" Tristan interrupted. "Is she unharmed?"

Steve straightened, meeting Tristan's gaze. "We, uh, we need Mikal. That's why Sarah went back to the house."

Tristan stiffened. "Are you certain?"

"Positive. Long story short, that's why his mom was taken."

"Wizards be damned," the soldier softly muttered.

"Oh, it gets better, I'm afraid. They know he's back."

Tristan's solemn gaze fell upon the charred remains of the burnt cottages.

"I suspected as much. I did not want to believe it."

"I don't think they knew specifically where you were," Steve clarified. "Every village has been attacked. There is trouble in Capily, which Rhenyon is taking care of, and there's trouble in Donlari, where Pheron has been dispatched."

"And Verdayn?"

"Rhein is handling that one."

"How many squadrons of soldiers were dispatched to each village?"

"Umm, at least two I think."

"They are dividing his forces," Tristan said, more to

himself than to anyone. "If the other villages have been attacked, then the castle will be next."

"Then we need to get back to the castle. Is everyone ready to go?"

"The portal key has been stolen, Sir Steve."

"Someone stole your key? Who?"

"A clarification. We have the portal key we used to get here. However, the town's portal key is missing."

"Definitely sounds like they wanted to cut off access to this village from the castle," Steve remarked. "No problem, we can just use ours."

Tristan pointed at the key Annie had pulled out of her pocket.

"That key will not take us back to the castle."

"Damn things are more trouble than they're worth," Steve grumbled. "Okay, fine, so we need Avin's key, is that it?"

"Correct. It has been stolen."

Steve's mouth turned upward in a grin. He pulled the blue portal key out of his pocket and tossed it gently up into the air.

"Lucky for me," Steve said, still tossing the key around, "I have the spare."

"Is that the king's personal portal key?"

Steve nodded.

"He must have suspected that is what the invaders were after."

"Did you guys stay at that inn?" Steve asked, pointing at the three-story house directly behind them.

"Yes, we did," Annie answered, her brow furrowing as she looked back at Tristan. "I've been giving Tristan some helpful feedback to pass along to the head of the tourism board here. They've got their work cut out for them."

Steve chuckled, grinning at his sister-in-law.

"Hotel accommodations here aren't exactly what we're used to. You get a bed and a little fireplace in case it gets cold."

"Yeah, only one bed."

"Really?" Steve eyed both Tristan and Annie. "So, did you

guys, you know, umm…?"

Annie smacked him on the arm. Hard.

* * *

Finding a chair well out of the way, Sarah sat and waited. Reports were already coming back from Capily. Rhenyon and his soldiers had completely surprised the band of invaders, appearing just as they had stormed the constable's office. Clearly their intent was to acquire each village's portal key, thus severing contact with the outside world. Sarah could only imagine their surprise as they thought for certain the building was empty and fifty armed soldiers came pouring out.

Only a few of the invaders had resisted. All the others elected to retreat to their ship. It was clear, though, that the notion of retreat hadn't been discussed, because it was every man for himself as they raced back to the small boat on the beach. The problem became evident as the first person who reached the boat commandeered it for himself, pushing it into the water long before anyone else had a chance to board. The rest of the invaders, shouting numerous curses at the fortunate individual in the boat, eventually surrendered.

Pheron and his men made short work of the small band of outlaws who were terrorizing the river village of Donlari. The ruffians were busy pillaging a small group of cottages when they discovered themselves completely surrounded by an angry contingent of armed Lentarian soldiers. They surrendered without a fight.

Verdayn proved to be a little more problematic, however.

"Lieutenant Rhein is in trouble," Kri'Entu announced to his staff, startling Sarah. "The invaders he and his men are facing are not amateurs, but skilled warriors. For now, they are holding their ground. In case I am not here, send whoever arrives back first straight to Verdayn as reinforcements."

"How, Your Majesty?" one advisor asked. "The portal key is with the lieutenant."

"Damn," the king swore, sighing heavily. His eyes alighted on Sarah. "How many can you teleport at one time?"

"The most I've done is four," Sarah answered.

"Four. How many trips with four can you do?"

"I have a couple of mimets to recharge my jhorun if I need to. I think I can do maybe ten jumps with that many people with me."

"Be ready, Lady Sarah."

"What about Steve?"

"What about Sir Steve?" the king inquired.

"Have we heard anything from Avin? Did he get the fires out?"

The king blinked as he realized no one had given him any reports on the small mountain village.

"There has been no word on Avin," Kri'Entu admitted.

"It's been at least thirty minutes. That should be more than enough time for him to put out a couple of fires."

"Has he ever put out a fire larger than a campfire?"

"Ummm, no," she admitted.

"He has the key. If he encounters difficulty, he could always return back here."

"Maybe I should go check on him."

"Your safe zone is in the constable's office. What if the office is on fire? What then?"

Sarah hesitated. She didn't want to appear smack in the middle of a roaring fire.

"Ummm, good question." Sarah shrugged. "However, I don't think it can be avoided. I'm going to have to risk it. I need to know that Steve's okay."

"What the hell?"

Sarah whirled around. That was her husband's voice! Both Sarah and the king hurried to the doorway to peer into the portal chamber. Steve strolled out, blue portal key in hand.

Kri'Entu gave a sigh of relief.

"Glad to see you safe, Sir Steve. Odd that I did not hear the portal chimes."

"I didn't use the portal."

"You did not use the portal?"

"How did you get back then?"

Both Sarah and the king smiled briefly at one another as each spoke at the same time.

"I assumed Sarah got me, which is very cool and

something I didn't even know she could do. We can get into that later. Sarah, Your Majesty, Mikal is in Avin, in the constable's office."

"What?! Is he safe?"

"Tristan, Annie, and Mikal are all safe. Peanut, too. I was just about to activate the portal when all of a sudden, I was here."

"I'd really like to know how I did that," Sarah remarked, giving her husband a hug. "Be right back. I'm going to go get everyone."

Kri'Entu gestured to the key in Steve's hand. "Use the key, Lady Sarah. Save your jhorun."

Sarah smiled, taking the blue key from her husband's outstretched hand. "Thanks. Don't mind if I do. Be right back."

"Find me as soon as you return," the king instructed. "We need to secure Mikal in the Antechamber. We will have your sister join him there."

"Will do, Your Majesty."

Smiling at her husband, Sarah ducked back into the portal chamber. Moments later they all heard the soft, musical humming of the activated portal.

"So, how're we doing?" Steve asked the king.

"Capily is secure," Entu reported, anxiously watching the portal room for signs of his son. "As is Donlari. We are having problems in Verdayn still. Were you able to extinguish the fires in Avin? How bad were they?"

"Got 'em all out. Three cottages were destroyed. The rooftop of a fourth cottage had just caught fire when I arrived."

"Where?"

"I wish I could tell you specifically," Steve said, thinking back to the layout of the village. "All I can tell you is that the torched houses were close to a really big one."

"Three stories?" the king asked.

"Yeah, three stories. Two, maybe three chimneys."

"That is one of the inns. I know exactly where you are referring to."

"That's where Tristan, Annie, and Mikal stayed last night."

Kri'Entu nodded. Suddenly his head jerked up, eyes automatically snapping over to the portal chamber. He had just heard voices coming from the smaller room. The excited barks of a dog also met his ears. Kri'Entu smiled. It had been mentioned that his son's dog had also made the journey from the other world.

"Peanut, get back here! Right now!"

Steve grinned. Peanut had just made her entrance into the room, her makeshift leash trailing behind her as she beheld a whole slew of new scents. Her short tail wagging happily, she began exploring the large throne room, pausing a few moments before each new human she encountered. Sarah and Annie appeared moments later, followed closely by Tristan. A very nervous little boy poked his head around the corner to look for his father.

"Tristan!"

Mikal jumped with surprise. His father had materialized right in front of him.

"Sire." Tristan bowed.

"Secure Mikal in the Antechamber at once. Stay with him."

"At once, Your Majesty. Mikal, come. Fetch Peanut."

Sarah and Annie approached.

"Your Majesty, may I present my sister, Annie. Annie, this is Kri'Entu, King of Lentari."

Not sure if a curtsy was expected, or if she should bow, Annie gave a weak smile. "Hello."

"Lady Annie, I am delighted to make your acquaintance." Kri'Entu smiled, looking around the busy throne room. "You are not catching us at our best."

"All of this because Mikal is back?"

"Aye."

"I'll fill you in later," Sarah promised her sister. "For now, they need you to wait with Mikal in the Antechamber. Think of it as a safe room."

"Where is it?"

Kri'Entu grabbed the closest soldier. "Escort Lady Annie to the Antechamber."

The soldier nodded. "Aye, Your Majesty."

"We'll join you as soon as we can."

As Annie left the throne room, the king approached again.

"Lady Sarah. Sir Steve."

"Yes?"

Steve arrived at his wife's side. "Yes?"

The king faced the fire thrower. "I must ask your help one more time. All of the other teams are securing their respective villages. As a result, none have returned yet. If I dispatch any more men, it will leave this castle more vulnerable than it already is, and that I will not do."

"I understand. What can I do?"

"Have Lady Sarah take you to Verdayn. Lieutenant Rhein could use some help."

Steve interlaced his fingers together and stretched his arms, cracking his knuckles.

"You got it. Sarah, I'd like to order a one-way ticket to Verdayn, please."

Smiling, Sarah nodded. "You be careful."

"You betcha."

* * *

Rhein cursed under his breath. Things were not going as smoothly as he had anticipated. These outlaws were well armed, had full quivers, and demonstrated extreme proficiency with their bows. Not only did they not flee when two fully armed squadrons of soldiers appeared, the ruffians, instead, had managed to incapacitate a third of his men with their well-placed shots. Inexplicably, the arrows found their way between pieces of armor, suggesting someone was quite familiar with Lentarian armor. Refusing to abandon his fallen companions, Rhein had ordered makeshift shelters to be constructed as quickly as possible. Several wagons were commandeered and then tipped on their sides, providing cover from the relentless barrage of streaking arrows.

"Give up the key, Lentarian, and you just might live through this!"

Rhein gritted his teeth. The constant verbal onslaught

was just as relentless as the steady stream of projectiles.

"You were lucky to have captured the town key," Rhein called back, putting a healthy sneer in his own voice. "It will be a cold day in hell before you get this one. Fear not, both keys will be back in our possession before this day is over!"

"Your men are pinned down. You have your wounded to look after. Surrender now and we will spare your measly lives. Keep me waiting much longer, scum, and you will not find my offer as generous."

"Generous, my eye," one soldier muttered, noting the low number of arrows in his quiver.

"What will it be?"

"We will never surrender!" another soldier shouted. Others followed suit, adding their own curses.

Their attackers started up a chant of their own: "Burn 'em out! Burn 'em out!"

The chant spread like, well, wildfire. The outlaws knew they had the advantage. It was time to end this and claim the second key that had miraculously fallen within their grasp. Thinking of the rewards he would earn should he present two portal keys to the same town, the gang leader chortled with glee. This was the best the Lentarians could do? Pathetic.

Several arrows were lit. Archers fit them to their strings, pulled back, and released. Three flaming arrows plunked into the tipped-over carts. It would be only a matter of moments before the flimsy wooden barriers would burn to the ground, removing their cover. They just had to wait.

The burning arrows petered out, leaving small scorch marks. The ongoing chant lessened. The wagons hadn't ignited! Four more arrows were lit, appearing moments later next to their unlit counterparts. As before, the wood started to burn, but quickly died out. Now the chanting had stopped altogether. What was going on?

Someone, somewhere, started shouting. Now several were. Soon yells were heard all around them. The outlaws were flinging their bows down, watching as their burning weapons were rapidly reduced to ash. Then the shouts became screams of pain as anything comprised of metal began glowing red. Swords were flung to the ground, armor hastily unfastened and cast aside. The outlaws were looking about in confusion. Was this some new type of weapon?

"Hi guys! Got room for one more at this party?"

There was a sudden silence as the attackers stared at one another. A lone man had appeared in their midst, grinning away as he inspected the surroundings. Who was this?

"He must be Lentarian! Get him!"

Five thugs approached the lone man walking calmly toward them. This was just too easy!

"Not a good idea, guys." Steve ignited both hands and watched with satisfaction as the encroaching outlaws hesitated. He waited a moment, wanting to see what they would do. No one moved. "This is the part where you guys run like hell."

The outlaws remained motionless. Time for some incentive. Taking aim at his assailants, he blasted off two jets of fire. Everyone in his path dove for the ground.

"It's the fire thrower! Run!"

Encourage them to flee the village.

Pryllan? Steve thought, looking up into the air. *Is that you?*

Aye. Force them to depart the village. I guarantee it will be the last thing they do.

What is your interest with these men?

They are the humans responsible for decimating two flocks of bolgers that my brethren and I feed on.

They stole your food?

In a manner of speaking, aye. Many of my brethren feel it is the village's fault. I have convinced them that the invading marauders are responsible. However, due to the agreement we have with the human king, we will not attack humans while they remain in the village. Get them to flee, the dragon urged again.

Steve smiled as he imagined several dragons lying in ambush.

Leave it to me. By the way, it's nice hearing from you!

And you as well.

The outlaws were cautiously approaching. They clearly must have thought his brief conversation with Pryllan was a sign of weakness, or a perhaps a momentary lack of courage.

Either way, they weren't going to let an opportunity slip by. If the fire thrower would remain motionless for just a few moments more…

Meanwhile, lost deep in thought as he imagined his dragon friends confronting these outlaws, Steve smiled. If only he could see the looks on their faces when… Detecting movement, his eyes returned to ground level and noted the advancing men. Raising both arms, he blasted a huge wall of flames at the thugs. They scattered. Steve raised both arms straight up and blasted out fiery tentacles. Twisting and turning, the tentacles lashed out in all directions before finally snapping back into their creator's open palms.

"Now listen up! This goes for everyone! I am gonna tell you right now, if I so much as see one of you jackasses in this village, then you're gonna get fried. Literally. Try to take a shot at me, and not only will it not land on me, I'll send a chaser your way. One of these guys." He ignited a chaser and held it high with his right hand. "Clear out. Now. You have five seconds to decide."

About fifty feet up an embankment, Steve caught sight of one outlaw as he cautiously peered around the tree he was hiding behind. Steve met the man's eyes. With a curse, the outlaw darted back behind the tree.

"Okay, you want to test me. Fine. Let's see how you like this." Steve threw the chaser at the man behind the tree.

The ball of fire streaked unerringly toward its target, slowing its pace only enough to swerve around several trees in its way. The swirling ball of fire was halted mere inches from its intended target.

"You're pushing your luck!" Steve called out in his loudest voice. "You want to stay where you are? Fine. Don't say I didn't warn you."

Still running on adrenaline from the massive amount of jhorun he had absorbed from the Avin fires, Steve created several dozen more chasers, all floating eerily in the air directly above his head.

"That's at least one for each of you! Last chance!" Looking up at his chasers, Steve instructed them to start circling. That did it.

"Fall back! Retreat! Back to the forest!"

Pryllan, get ready. Here they come!

You have our thanks, Steve. We are ready.

Just to make sure they didn't leave anyone behind, Steve had the chasers play a little follow-the-leader, weaving the long train of fireballs amongst the trees, zipping them by any potential hiding places. Once he was assured that all had fled the area, Steve called the chasers back. One by one, they flew back into his outstretched palm, vanishing from sight.

Rhein and his men finally emerged from their makeshift shelters.

"Sir Steve! Damn glad to see you!"

"Hello Rhein. Are you guys alright?"

"We have wounded. We must return to the castle as soon as possible." Rhein removed the portal key from around his neck and handed it to Steve. "Can you get the portal ready? We will meet you in the constable's office."

"Got it."

Steve?

Walking back up the street, Steve hesitated. He cocked his head. *Yes? I'm here.*

One of these humans had a crystal key in their possession. Do you know anything about it?

Steve smiled, nodding. *I do. That's Verdayn's portal key. It was stolen from their constable's office.*

I will hold on to it for you.

As always, my thanks, Pryllan.

You are welcome, my friend.

* * *

"Am I glad to see you!" Sarah rushed into his arms, giving him a huge bear hug. "Are you okay?"

"Never better."

"Is Rhein okay?"

"His men were hit pretty hard. About a dozen or so were badly wounded. I'm told all are going to make it just fine, though."

"Excellent. Was he glad to see you?"

"You have no idea. They were pinned down. With a little persuasion, the bad guys left."

Rhenyon arrived, followed closely by Kri'Entu.

"Sir Steve, you are uninjured?"

"I'm fine, Rhenyon, thanks. You okay?"

"Most assuredly. Were you able to take any prisoners?"

"Ummm, no, I wasn't."

The king sighed. "If the invaders slipped away, then they will more than likely return with a much larger force. Commander, we have to start planning for —"

"Hang on," Steve interrupted. "That particular group of men will not bother anyone anymore, Your Majesty."

"But you just said you did not take any prisoners. Did you dispatch them instead?"

Sarah's eyes opened wide.

"I did not. Not a one, actually."

"How can you be certain they will not return?" Rhenyon asked, confused.

"Ummm…"

"Honey, what are you not telling us?"

Steve looked at his wife, then at the king. How much should he tell them? He trusted everyone present; however, he also did not want to break the oath he had made with Pryllan. He made eye contact with Rhenyon and nodded his head toward the door.

Curious about what he was about to hear, Rhenyon complied, sealing the four of them inside the portal chamber.

"What is it?" Kri'Entu asked, alarmed.

"No need for concern," Steve assured him. "This is an important secret and I don't want this information publicly known. I trust everyone here, implicitly, so I need to ask that each of you also honor this secret as well, okay?"

Kri'Entu nodded. "Consider it done."

Rhenyon nodded as well. "Agreed."

"You know I will," Sarah said, taking his hand.

"There were no invaders who survived in Verdayn," Steve clarified. "They were, um, dispatched as soon as they left the village."

The king stared at him. "By whom?"

"The dragons."

Kri'Entu's eyebrows shot up. "Dragons! Are you certain?"

Rhenyon was incredulous. "Were dragons in the village?"

"No, but they were waiting just outside. You see, I seem to have some type of mental connection with Pryllan, Kahvel's mate. She's been in telepathic contact."

"Telepathy. That explains a few things," Sarah remarked, nodding her head. "Back there, when we were rescuing the queen, when you went silent for a bit, you were talking to Pryllan, weren't you?"

"Yes, I was," Steve admitted. "She contacted me in Verdayn and said that these attackers were the same humans who had decimated their food supply. Sounds like the rest were driven off."

"Telepathic dragons. I had no idea."

"It's something I don't think the dragons want to become common knowledge," Steve added.

"Their secret will remain safe," the king vowed.

"Thanks. I appreciate it. Anyway, Pryllan told me that the rest of the dragons believed the people of Verdayn were responsible for the loss of their food."

The king uttered a string of curses under his breath. All his hard work to ensure peace with the dragons had just flown right out the window.

Correctly guessing what the king was thinking, Steve gave him a friendly pat on the shoulder. "Hey, not to worry. Pryllan convinced them that fault lies with the invaders and not the villagers. They chose to wait just outside the village perimeter for the prime opportunity, which apparently, I gave them."

"And you forced the attackers to flee, thus herding them into the clutches of the dragons."

"Yep."

Rhenyon was nodding. "Serves them right."

"Oh, that reminds me. Pryllan has Verdayn's key. She's holding on to it for me."

"Excellent, Sir Steve. Very well done."

Steve bowed, grinning like a school kid.

* * *

Hours later, Steve, Sarah, and Annie found themselves seated at a table in the Great Hall. Peanut was sitting a few feet away, watching all the people walk by. With the tension level of the castle finally returning to normal, Steve and Sarah decided to introduce Annie to her first Lentarian meal.

"So, what is this? Looks like a big Hot Pocket."

Steve snorted, spraying water across his plate.

"It's called a phedra," Sarah explained to her sister. "It has meat, cheese, and some veggies in it."

"Spicy?"

"No. Even Steve will eat them."

Surprised, Annie raised an eyebrow in his direction. "Really? No further explanations are necessary."

"Hardy har har."

"I still can't believe the castle wasn't attacked," Sarah remarked, cutting into her own pastry. "I thought that was the whole plan."

"It was, Lady Sarah."

They all turned to see Tristan smiling at them.

"We have room for one more. Have a seat."

Annie scooted over so Tristan could sit down.

"So, what happened?" Steve wanted to know. "Where was the attack? Did I miss it?"

"What happened," Tristan explained, "was that they were counting on the castle being unprotected, or at least with a minimal contingent of armed personnel. By the time they arrived, however, Commander Rhenyon had returned, as well as Lieutenant Pheron. They seriously underestimated us. This time. I do not think they will again should there be a next time."

"So, they did attack? I didn't hear anything."

"We saw them at the edge of the forest. All they did was stare at the castle. I think they were waiting for the most opportune time to attack, and when it became apparent that the castle was too well guarded, they finally deduced their mission had failed."

"Where's Mikal?" Annie asked.

Tristan turned to her. "He is visiting his mother. He has tried restoring her jhorun."

"Tried?"

"He says he has done the same thing for her that he did for me, but so far, it does not appear that the queen's jhorun has regenerated. We have to wait for some signs of it to appear before we know that it has been fully restored."

"How long will that take?"

"Unknown, Sir Steve. As soon as Mikal restored mine, I was able to conjure a small dagger for a few moments. It takes a while to heal."

"Oh, I get it," Sarah said, nodding her head. "You can tell when your jhorun is working because you can see when you conjure a dagger. The queen can't manifest hers at all. It very well might already be healing but it's probably just hard to tell."

"Agreed, Lady Sarah. Now we must wait. Lady Annie, may I ask you a question?"

Having taken a large bite out of her phedra, Annie covered her mouth and looked at the Lentarian she had come to regard as a close friend. Swallowing hastily, she tried to clear her mouth. "Of course."

"Did you use any ointment when you soaked those pieces of cloth back at that stream?"

"Ointment?" Annie shook her head. "I don't have any ointment. Why? Haven't you seen a doctor yet?"

"The reason I ask, Lady Annie," Tristan raised his shirt, "is that I apparently do not need to."

Annie sucked in her breath as she looked at the laceration she had just cleaned yesterday. A thin, pink line, resembling nothing more than a minor cat scratch, met her eyes.

"What happened to it? I thought you were going to have to get stitches or something."

Tristan lowered his shirt and smiled cryptically at her.

"Welcome to Lentari, Lady Annie."

Chapter 9 — Apprehension

"There is no other option," King Ewam was saying. "Frankly, I am tired of wasting my time. We will cease these fruitless endeavors with our southern neighbors."

"What are your intentions, sire?" one of his senior advisors asked.

"My grandson worsens. I do not know how much longer he can hold on. Clearly no one in Ylani is capable of curing him and the Lentarians have ignored all of our pleas."

"Is it war, then? Over one small boy?"

"Who speaks?"

At that moment a pin dropping would have sounded like a thunderclap.

"WHO SPEAKS?"

Several of those present around the table fidgeted in place.

"Do not make me ask again."

A heavyset man dressed entirely in scarlet stood.

"I am truly sorry to be the one to voice this," he began.

"Listen, Phallus," the king began angrily, taking a deep breath.

"It's Talus, sire," the man said, his face reddening.

"Talus. Whatever. I will not let my grandson suffer any longer. It's time for action!"

"At the expense of how many?"

"You would prefer to watch my grandson slip away?"

"I am appalled that our healers have been unable to do anything for the boy," Talus said slowly, choosing his words with care. "But if you choose to go to war over the apparent lack of empathy from our brothers to the south, then you doom hundreds, perhaps thousands of good Ylanis."

"What would you have me do? The level of jhorun necessary to rid Aerlin of this damned malady exists in Lentari. It must!"

A brief knock on the door had all present turning to stare at the young girl standing in the doorway.

"Forgive me, sire, but you have given instructions that all communiqués from Nestor be delivered to you personally."

"Yes, yes, give it here."

Eager to deliver her message and depart just as hastily as possible, the girl all but ran to the king's side. Ewam snatched the message and broke the wax seal. His eyes skimmed the brief communication.

"Hah! What say you to this?" the king tossed the paper onto the table before them. "Lentari has forged a new alliance."

One of the more recently elected advisors leaned forward.

"Begging your pardon, sire, but who is Nestor?"

"Code name for our spy network in Lentari."

"Nestor?" The tone of disdain was unmistakable.

The king was silent as he scowled at his newest advisor.

"My apologies," the adviser bowed his head. "It is not important. Please, sire, do continue."

"As I was saying," King Ewam continued, still frowning at the insubordinate man, "a new alliance now exists in Lentari."

"With whom?" one advisor wanted to know.

"The griffins. Although I cannot fathom why they would want to ally themselves with such creatures."

Warrick's familiar voice spoke up. "Then I am afraid the news continues to worsen."

This got the king's attention. "What news? Why have you not reported it earlier?"

"I just learned of it myself. When you mentioned a new Lentarian ally I just assumed that our news was the same."

"You have news of another alliance? Not with the griffins?"

"Aye, I do, Your Majesty. And it is not with the griffins."

"With whom?"

"We have just received reports that the Lord of the Dragons has forged an alliance with Lentari as well."

Several men cursed with disgust. The king, however, paled.

"They can count the dragons as allies now?"

Warrick nodded.

"I do not care if they have the allegiance of every living creature there," General Reitus spat. "If they think they can invade us without a fight, then they are sorely mistaken. Every village is willing to send men to … That reminds me. I have one other bit of news."

At that moment, a serving girl entered, offering mugs of water or ale to whomever wished it. Not one drop of water was poured.

"What is it, general?"

"It would seem that some of our men have been disappearing."

"Disappearing?"

"Aye."

"Soldiers? Villagers? How many?"

General Reitus consulted his notes. "Villagers. At least twenty from Arlan, thirty from both Barod and Bristol, at least ten from —"

King Ewam was on his feet, sputtering with rage.

"What?! Ylani citizens are being abducted from their homes?" His angry black eyes glared at the small group of men huddled around the table. "Warrick, what say you to this news? Do all the constables not send you reports on a monthly basis? Are you not the recipient of those reports?

Why have you not said anything earlier?"

"Sire, this is the first I have heard of this. None of the constables have indicated anything to me."

"General, when did you receive this news? Was it today? From whom?"

"I found out only earlier today, Your Majesty. This was a special report from Myrn, reporting that another five men had been reported missing. The report clearly stated 'another', so I had the Archives searched, checking constable reports for the last two years. They —"

"You accessed my files?" Warrick demanded, adopting what he hoped was his most intimidating stance as he attempted a fierce scowl. "There's nothing in any of them to even suggest such a problem."

"I had to check. And you might want to pay a visit to the infirmary to have your throat checked out."

"Wait." The king tapped his fingers on the surface of the table. "A report from earlier today says that men are missing, yet the monthly status reports say otherwise. Clearly someone is lying."

"Or," Reitus murmured, more to himself than to anyone, "the constable reports are flawed, and the message from Myrn is legitimate. Or," he added again, before the whining advisor he detested could get a word in edgewise, "the reports are legitimate, but doctored before they reach *him*." The general rolled his eyes as he said this, hooking a thumb in Warrick's direction.

King Ewam glanced over at Warrick.

"Do the constables give you those reports directly? Or are they delivered by messenger?"

"A few use their own personal messengers," Warrick answered, "while most others use kytes."

"So, you do not know if they might have been tampered with?"

"I have never had reason to believe otherwise."

"When all of this is over, we are giving the census system an overhaul," King Ewam muttered under his breath.

"Are we to do nothing about this then?"

"Of course not. Track down the village representatives

to authenticate the veracity of these claims. I want to hear it from their own mouths that they are indeed missing some of their citizens."

Warrick bowed low. "Consider it done, sire."

"So what do you think it means, sire?" General Reitus asked as he stroked the stubble of his beard. "New allegiances for Lentari? Our villages are missing men? They must be preparing for an attack."

"Using our own men against us? Methinks not, General. Nevertheless, put all villages on high alert. If some unknown force is secretly absconding with our men, I want to know about it."

General Reitus gave a curt bow. "It will be done, sire."

"Maybe we should look into invoking some of our own ancient alliances."

The voice was soft and quiet, yet might as well have been shouted. The room silenced instantly.

In the process of taking a healthy swig of ale, the king froze. He slowly lowered his tankard until it clanked noisily onto the table. "What was that?"

"For the good of the kingdom, we should invoke our ancient alliances."

"Aye, that's what I thought you said. What would the likes of you know about the ancient alliances?"

The normally silent councilman gave the king a thin smile.

"More than you might think, sire. I know which creatures have given their allegiance to the crown."

"By all means, enlighten us."

The advisor smiled again.

"Trolls."

Many of those present gasped in unison.

"You cannot possibly think that —"

"Malwerns," the advisor continued, smoothly cutting off the objections.

There were several nervous chuckles.

"Therons."

The chuckles vanished.

"Therons are our allies?" one man asked incredulously.

"They were, many centuries ago."

"Let me get this straight," King Ewam said, sarcasm practically dripping from every word. "You would suggest we send an emissary to the trolls and inform them that their ancestors pledged their support to our ancestors and therefore they need to be ready to fight for us?"

"Why not, sire? If the Lentarians are forming new alliances, then the prudent thing to do would be for us to rekindle our alliances as well."

"With the trolls? Are you daft?"

"I mention it only as a last resort, sire."

The king sat back in his chair.

"Just because the alliance exists does not mean it will be honored. I will not condone the ancient allegiances, but I will not put too much credence with their authenticity. General, in the event they are needed, prepare your men. That is all for now. Warrick, remain behind."

Everyone rose from the table. The mutterings began even before the last person departed the room. Warrick sat motionless in his chair.

As soon as they were alone, the king approached. Placing both hands on the table before them, King Ewam leaned down so that his face was inches from that of his advisor's.

"You mentioned the other day you had other means to inform me what jhoruns the Lentarians have, do you remember?"

The thin man swallowed nervously.

"Aye, sire."

"Then do it. Time to get creative, Warrick. I will expect a progress report by the end of the week."

Faster and faster he walked, hastily pushing by servants and soldiers alike. Knowing his close association with the king, the thin nervous man was given a wide berth by all in his path. Walking arrogantly down the hastily cleared aisles, Warrick progressed further into the dungeons. The deeper he descended, the less populated each level became. Finally descending into the lowest subterranean level of the castle, he scowled with irritation as he spied a pair of guards lazily patrolling the corridors directly in front of him.

There was a time, he recalled, when no one bothered to inspect this insignificant, seldom used part of the dungeon. Located roughly two hundred feet directly beneath the throne room, it was as far away from the outside world as possible. What did it mean? Did the king suspect something? Impossible. No one but he even knew of the Master's existence, let alone the secret location to his lair. That could only mean that the king was edging ever closer to senility. All the more reason to rid the kingdom of his Supreme Fatness.

Ducking into a nondescript cell just as the soldiers reached the end of the corridor and turned around, Warrick hastily activated the false door and slipped inside, gently pushing the wall back into place as the guards passed by.

Blinking unseeing eyes in the total darkness, he retrieved a torch from its holder that he knew was just inside the door. Muttering an incantation under his breath, he watched with satisfaction as the torch sprang to life. Thanks to his numerous midnight sessions with the Master, not only was his jhorun increasing in strength, but he had also been learning helpful new enchantments. Warrick looked with pride at his lit torch, much like a new father would with his newborn child.

The Master had untold power, he thought yet again. How fortunate this powerful wizard had consented to become his apprentice! Well, Warrick thought ruefully, more like an assistant. Still, his original pathetically weak jhorun had been replaced with a much more efficient ability. His mastery over new skills was increasing at a steady pace. Not once did it enter his consciousness that he should be ashamed to think so poorly of his natural jhorun. Who cared about finding hidden springs of water, anyway? Had it been helpful to his parents on their farm? Well, sure, but he was never destined to be a farmer.

Much greater things lay in store for him. Why else would fate have paired him up with an outcast wizard bent on destroying all ties with Lentari? And, thanks to the genius of his Master, his new ability was working wonders on the dimwitted king.

"Stupid fool," Warrick mumbled to himself, shaking his

head. As the Master had predicted, it had been quite easy to plant subliminal instructions into the king's head. Nothing blatant, the Master had warned, only small, subtle requests would work. For now. A stronger degree of control was forthcoming, the Master had promised.

Descending the final steps of the steep stone staircase, Warrick came to a halt outside a thick wooden door as a loud crash sounded from the other side. Hand hovering inches away from the handle, he paused as a string of curses that would have caused a malwern to blush with shame sounded from within the sealed chamber.

He gave a deep sigh. The Master was clearly not in a good mood, and the news he had to impart was not going to improve the situation. Steeling himself, he pushed open the door, ducking reflexively as an object came whistling by his ear, smashing into the heavy wood door just as it clanged shut.

"What are you doing here?" the all too familiar voice hissed out. "I have not sent for you."

Warrick bowed low, second guessing his decision yet again to share the news from Ewam's impromptu meeting.

"My apologies. I come with news."

"What could you possibly know that you think I do not?"

"The king has learned of the missing villagers."

The Master whirled to face him, his deep crimson robes flaring about his feet. "Indeed."

"I cannot fathom how this happened."

The Master said nothing as he regarded his assistant with flat, expressionless eyes. Warrick nervously fidgeted from one leg to the other. Thirty seconds passed before the Master finally responded.

"Whether or not King Witless knows that some of his people are missing is completely irrelevant." His cold, green eyes locked onto Warrick's. "I would not advise you to lie to me again, are we clear? If you miss one of those wretched reports because you were too busy unsuccessfully trying to woo a serving wench, then just say so."

The lit torch slipped out of the trembling man's hand and clanged loudly on the floor. By the time the torch had rolled to the Master's feet, Warrick had finally regained the ability to speak.

"I, uh …"

With a flick of a wrist, the torch re-lit itself and rose up smoothly from the floor. Warrick gaped with astonishment as it hovered directly in front of him, waiting patiently to be reclaimed.

"How did you —"

"Do you have any other news to impart or is that it?"

"Uh …"

"You were not going to tell me anything of a, oh, I do not know, perhaps a wyverian nature with regards to Lentari?"

"How—"

"Dragons are of no importance. Griffins are of no importance."

"Then what is, Master?"

"My one chance to snatch that brat has ended in failure! I never should have trusted that spineless dolt with such an important task. Clearly Taran did not have the courage to invoke the talisman I sent along should they have encountered trouble."

"Uh …"

"What?"

"The demon was invoked."

"Impossible. If it was invoked, then that brat would be sitting before me."

"It was vanquished, Master."

The wizard was silent as he digested this latest bit of information. His drakyr had been vanquished? How was that possible? By whom?

Interpreting his silence as a request for more info, Warrick stumbled on.

"I do not know how it was vanquished, only that the prince's bodyguard was directly responsible."

"You are referring to the Nohrin, are you not?"

"You know about the Nohrin?"

"Mythical bodyguards do not concern me. Nor should they you."

"Clearly you misjudged the Nohrin," Warrick insisted.

"They did defeat the demon."

"Inconsequential."

Warrick could only stare at his mentor. Did he not understand that this was the famous Nohrin from the Bakkian? The levels of jhorun that the Nohrin possess was said to rival that of the strongest wizards!

"If he is truly a Nohrin, as the Bakkian suggests, should we not make him the next target? We lost the prince. We should not lose the opportunity to steal a jhorun as powerful as his. He is a fire thrower! Did you know that?"

"The Bakkian." The sneer in his voice was unmistakable. "I do not hold credence in ancient drivel. If those fools want to believe in archaic nonsense, then let them. As for the fire thrower, he is irrelevant. Only the boy matters."

"Do you not realize," Warrick tried again, "how much the fire thrower's jhorun would fetch? Use the Chalix! Together we can—"

"Enough prattling. Close your mouth and listen."

Inexplicably, Warrick's mouth snapped closed of its own volition. No matter how he tried, he couldn't pry open his lips to vent his frustrations. With a sigh, he realized that he was going to have to wait this one out.

"You do not understand the severity of the situation. Therefore, let me explain it to you in the manner that someone with your intelligence is sure to follow."

The fiercely intense wizard began slowly pacing about his lair while the spellbound Warrick could only watch and listen.

"I do not care about bodyguards," the Master began, glaring hard at his assistant. "Whether there is one man or an entire legion of soldiers protecting the boy, he will be mine. Nothing else matters. If I have to use every ounce of my power, I will have him. I— you want to say something? So be it. Speak."

With control of his mouth returned to him, Warrick took a breath.

"What is so special about this boy? Where does this fascination come from?"

"That boy," the Master said slowly, "is the key to Ewam's removal from the throne."

"The boy can rid us of King Ewam? How? Is he some secret illegitimate prince of Ylani, destined to usurp the throne?"

The look on the Master's face spoke volumes. Perhaps it was time to rethink his decision about using this moron as an assistant.

"That boy will never be king. Of Lentari, Ylani, or any other kingdom. His role here, however, is vital. With his help, I will fashion the strongest army ever known to man. Lentari's demise will be inevitable."

"Just to be clear, we are talking about Kri'Entu's son, are we not? How can he do that? Why would he?"

The last vestige of patience finally trickled away. He took a breath, thinking briefly on what would be the easiest and most painful way to enact radical rearrangements of the human body.

"Forgive me, Master," Warrick added hastily, recognizing the danger signs brewing in his teacher. "I want to better serve you, and I thought I could render more assistance if I could fathom *why* you needed this boy as much as you do."

"If I feel inclined to share the details of my plans, then I will do so. Until such time, and I guarantee it will not be anytime soon, if you so much as breathe word of this to anyone, your tongue will drop out of your mouth before you can even utter a single word. Is that understood?"

Warrick's face reddened. "Completely, Master."

"For now, I have a task for you."

"Anything, Master."

"Interrogate the survivors. Learn everything there is to know about the failed abduction. I must know how my drakyr was vanquished. If this fire thrower was truly responsible, I want to know. Is that understood?"

"Completely, Master."

"Do not fail me, Warrick. If you cannot persuade them to talk, then I will, and you will share their fate. Do we understand one another?"

"Completely, Master."

Chapter 10 — Infiltration

You're shitting me, right?"

Tristan's mouth quivered. "I am not, Lady Annie."

"There's no way."

"Your sister and her husband both developed jhoruns upon their arrival. Why should you be any different?"

Annie shook her head. "It just isn't possible. I can't have a magic power. There's got to be some explanation for it, that's all. Maybe there was something in that water?"

"I think it's cool, Seester!" Steve said jovially. "The power to heal. That's a handy jhorun."

She turned to her brother-in-law. "You actually think that I have some rapid healing power?"

"Why not?" her sister asked, taking a sip of tara juice from her glass. "We both developed jhoruns, why shouldn't you? Steve's right. Your jhorun is very handy. Very powerful."

Annie was still shaking her head.

"Lady Annie," Tristan knelt down in front of her chair, looking her straight in her eyes. "If I can prove this to you, will you believe me?"

"How are you going to do that?"

"Sir Steve," Tristan called, glancing behind him. "I require your assistance."

"You do? What do you need?"

Tristan extended his right arm behind him, palm facing down.

"You need an arm up?"

Sarah's eyes widened as she realized what Tristan wanted to do. "Are you serious? You want Steve to give you a burn? I don't think this is a good idea. There's got to be a better way."

Steve frowned. "You're taking a lot on faith, pal."

"Just a minor burn, please. If this is what it will take to prove my point, then it will be worth it. If I am wrong, then I will live with my injury."

Shaking his head, Steve ignited his left hand. Eyeing the flickering orange flames, he decreased the temp as much as he was able to. The orange flames turned blue.

"That's as low as I can get it. The problem is, I don't think I can grab your hand and keep mine lit," Steve warned, eyeing Tristan's outstretched arm. "I don't want to burn you, and if I don't want to, then I more than likely won't."

With a sigh, Tristan sat back on his heels, glanced briefly behind him once more to judge Steve's proximity, then lurched backward to grab his hand. He let out a small cry of pain as contact was made. Fortunately, Steve's hand quickly reverted back to normal as his sense of camaraderie kicked in. He truly did not want to be the source of anyone's pain. Meanwhile, Sarah had rushed forward to inspect Tristan's reddening hand, ready to administer a drop from the small vial nestled in her medallion.

"It's a first-degree burn. Looks painful, like it's ready to blister. Tristan, are you okay?"

Tristan nodded, turning questioningly to look at Annie, who had been staring wide-eyed at the spectacle before her.

"You just burned yourself to prove a point? What's the matter with you?"

"If you please, Lady Annie, can you try to heal this?"

"How? How am I supposed to do that? Don't you think

that if I could, then I would?"

Coming to her sister's aid, Sarah stepped forward. "For me, I had to concentrate. I had to focus. Think about his hand. Obviously, you don't want to see him burned. If you truly have a healing jhorun, and since you used your hands last time, then more than likely your jhorun manifests itself through your hands. See if you can feel any prickly sensations, like your hands are going numb."

"My hands are going to go numb?"

"Not numb," Steve added, "but like they fell asleep and then woke up. You know those little tingly feelings you get?"

Annie nodded.

"It's rather like that. It was exactly the same for the two of us."

Skeptical, Annie looked down at her hands. She raised an eyebrow. This wasn't going to work. No matter how hard she tried, she just couldn't believe her hands had some magical healing power.

Steve sighed. "Just humor us, would you?"

Annie rolled her eyes. "Fine."

Closing her eyes, she thought about what she had been asked to do. How was she supposed to magically heal someone when she truly believed that she couldn't? Her sister had said that all she had to do was to think about what she wanted to accomplish. Opening her eyes, she looked again at Tristan's burnt hand. He had deliberately let himself be burned in order to prove his point. Even though he wasn't displaying any discomfort, a burn that nasty-looking couldn't feel good. She had been troubled when she had seen him wounded before. It shouldn't be any different this time, she reasoned. She didn't want him feeling any pain, especially on her behalf. It wasn't too difficult to believe she was experiencing the shock of seeing Tristan's first wound, or reliving the terror she felt as she realized there were no cell phones to dial 911, or that there weren't any hospitals around. She could—

Annie hesitated. Her fingers were starting to feel like they were falling asleep. No, she corrected, not asleep. Steve was right. It felt as though her hands had been asleep and were starting to awaken. The warm, tingling sensations quickly spread from finger to finger until it felt as though both hands were gently pulsating.

"Okay, this is really weird. Either I'm psyching myself out or I think I'm experiencing those tingle things."

"You got the tingles? That quickly? Damn!" Steve was amazed. "That's impressive!"

"So, if that's what these things are, what do I do with them? And what do I have to do to make them go away?"

"Well, once your jhorun does what you tell it to, then they usually will go away on their own."

"I just tell it what I want it to do? That's it?"

"In a nutshell, yes."

Annie stared at Tristan's injured hand. Tentatively, she reached out to touch the burnt skin. *I want this burn to heal*, she hesitantly instructed her hands, feeling foolish. However, her imagination must still be playing tricks on her because it appeared as though the spot she had just touched had become a little less red. Still skeptical, she touched another spot on his hand, this time maintaining contact. Counting to ten, she moved her finger off and leaned forward to inspect the burnt skin. She gasped in shock. The skin had lost the angry red color and had reverted back to its normal state.

His theory confirmed, Tristan smiled.

"You better wipe that smug grin off your face there, buddy."

"My apologies, Lady Annie."

As though she was polishing a piece of fine china, she took Tristan's injured hand in her own and lightly ran her fingertips over his damaged skin. Several minutes later, all traces of the injury were gone. Astonished, Annie stared down at the hand she was holding. Suddenly realizing how it must appear to the others, to be caught tenderly holding Tristan's hand, she blushed, hastily returning her hands to her lap.

"Yeah, well, okay. Didn't see that coming."

Sarah tucked her medallion away as she inspected Tristan's hand.

"Nicely done. No traces of a burn anywhere."

"I really did that. I healed his hand! I don't get it. Why

was I given a jhorun? I'm not part of that prophecy thing."

"Maybe you are," Steve added, grinning at her.

"The Bakkian references only two Nohrin," Tristan answered helpfully. "Not three."

"That was a joke, man."

"Oh. My apologies."

"Don't sweat it. Any new developments with the queen?" Steve wanted to know.

"With regret, no. Nothing yet." Tristan sighed. "Mikal is sitting with her now. He has not left her side and I doubt he will until some signs of her jhorun manifests."

"Understandable."

"Hopefully it won't be too much longer," Sarah added. "The sooner we can get Mikal to safety, the sooner we can all relax."

"Agreed, milady," a voice called from behind.

They all turned as Rhenyon walked up to their table. Not wanting his commander to think he was neglecting his duties, Tristan rose.

"Good day to all of you. I must be off. Commander."

Rhenyon nodded in his direction.

"Lieutenant."

Sarah gestured to the empty seat next to Annie. "Join us."

"I have some information for you," Rhenyon began. "Those two Ylanis that you transported back here?"

"I remember them," Sarah said, nodding her head.

"They are from Myrn."

Steve leaned forward. "From where?"

"Myrn. It is a small village in northern Ylani."

"Okay. How does that help us?"

"It gives us a place to start."

"A place to start what?" Sarah asked.

"We need to learn why Ylani is so interested in young Mikal."

"What do you suggest?" Steve wanted to know.

"That an undercover team be sent to Myrn to see what can be learned."

Steve nodded his head. "Makes sense. Who are you going to send? I assume you will head the team. Pheron? Maybe Rhein?"

"The team must be kept small so as to avoid attention. Aye, I will lead the team, and I would like the two of you to accompany me."

Sarah choked on her juice. "Us? What in the world for? You must have all kinds of trained men that would be a much better choice."

"I have trained men, aye," Rhenyon admitted, "but none are teleporters, and certainly none are fire throwers."

Steve looked at his wife. "I'm not keen on putting her in danger, Rhenyon."

"Hence her jhorun. If she encounters trouble, she can return here. She can even return all of us to safety should the situation call for it."

"So, I'll handle the protection, and she'll see to our safety, is that it?"

"I am fully prepared to use my own men, but I believe this mission would be accomplished much faster and much safer if it was just the three of us instead of an entire contingent of my men."

Steve sat up straight in his chair. "Wait. Just the three of us? That's it? No squadrons, no backup, no nothing?"

"He did mention he didn't want to attract attention," Sarah reminded her husband while she smiled at the commander.

"You're going along with this?"

"Three people would certainly attract less attention than a group of soldiers. Besides, you don't have to worry about me."

"You're not worried about getting hurt?"

"With you two?" Sarah was silent as she thought about it. She smiled. "No, I'm really not."

"Isn't this part of your job description?" Annie suddenly chimed in. "I mean, you're Mikal's protectors, right?"

Steve turned to regard the person sitting across from him.

"What does that have to do with being Mikal's bodyguards?"

"Well, I mean, clearly he's in danger still. If you can eliminate this threat against him, then you'd be protecting him, wouldn't you?"

"Not helping, Seester."

Rhenyon grinned. He looked at the woman sitting next to him, as if noticing her for the first time.

"I do not believe we have been introduced, milady."

"Oh, sorry. Rhenyon, this is Annie, Sarah's sister. Annie, this is Rhenyon, newly appointed Commander of the Royal Guards."

Rhenyon rose to his feet. "A pleasure to make your acquaintance, Lady Annie."

Annie smiled meekly. "Nice to meet you, too."

"So, will you accompany me to Myrn?"

"Before I agree to that, I need your word on something," Steve said, turning back to his wife. "At the first signs of danger, I need you to agree to take yourself out of harm's way, okay?"

"Fine, if the situation calls for it," Sarah said slowly, choosing her words with care, "then I will get out of the way."

"What about Mikal?"

"Kre'Mikal has taken up residence in the Antechamber," Rhenyon answered. "And there is a full squadron of my men protecting the Queen's personal chamber. Everyone is safe."

Running out of excuses, Steve finally nodded. He sighed heavily.

"When do you want to go? Better yet, how far away is it? How are we going to get there?"

"I plan to depart tomorrow morning. As for how long it will take us to get there, that is up to Lady Sarah."

"Don't expect me to teleport there," Sarah warned, frowning. "I haven't seen it. I can't teleport to a place I haven't seen before."

"If you knew what it looked like, could you take us there?"

"Without having been there? That's a good question. I don't know. I'd have to be able to visualize it very clearly in my mind. Do you have a picture of this village?"

"More like a drawing."

"A drawing? I don't think that'll work, Rhenyon. I'm sorry."

"I understand. In that case, we can—"

Steve held up a hand.

"Wait. It couldn't hurt to try, could it? Sarah, if you look at this picture, can you try to see if you can visualize something in your head? If not, no biggie, we'll get there the old-fashioned way. But if there's a chance, it'd be worth it, don't you think?"

Sarah shrugged. "I can try, but I seriously doubt it'll work."

"Very well." Rhenyon rose to his feet. "Come with me."

Steve and Sarah stood up. Rhenyon looked back at the brunette woman still sitting quietly.

"Lady Annie, you are welcome to join us."

Thirty minutes later they were all crowded around one of the research tables, examining a charcoal sketch of a small mountainous village.

"It's a very good drawing," Sarah admitted. She leaned over the table in the Royal Archives and studied the sketch, her fingers lightly tracing the outlines of the mountains and the trees. "However, it's just a sketch. There isn't any color, no textures, nothing to relate to."

Everyone was silent as they watched Sarah walk around the table to observe the drawing from different angles. Without realizing it, her eyes closed.

"This doesn't really show the river that well," she murmured, still slowly circling the table.

Annie cocked her head as she leaned over the table to stare at the drawing. "I don't remember seeing a river on that thing."

Steve walked over to the table to check for himself. "Because there isn't."

"Yes, there is," Sarah contradicted, coming to a stop. Eyes still closed, she gently traced an invisible line on the parchment. "It weaves through the trees here and here. The riverbank hides it from view by these houses here."

Steve leaned over the table to inspect the imaginary river his wife's hand had indicated was there. Looking up, he studied her face.

"You do know that your eyes are closed, right?"

"Hmmm?"

"Your eyes. They're closed. What are you seeing right now?"

"A small village in the woods. There are mountains in all directions. I can see the river."

"I thought you said that this wasn't going to work."

"I would have bet a million dollars that it wouldn't. But, as soon as I saw that sketch, I was looking at the real-life scene in my head. How spooky is that?"

"Not spooky, but awesome! Now we don't have to worry about how long it'll take to get there."

"You're looking at the real-life version of this picture in your head?" Annie asked.

"Yes."

"That's amazing."

"No more amazing than you being able to heal nasty burns on a person's hand."

"So how are you able to see a live picture in your head?" Annie wanted to know. "I thought your jhorun was teleportation."

"It is, and I have no idea."

"Do you think you can teleport there, Lady Sarah?" Rhenyon inquired.

"Easily."

"Excellent. We leave at dawn."

* * *

Sunlight was streaming through the branches of the evergreens, scattering sunbeams all about the glen they were standing in. A well-traveled road hugged the riverbank as it angled toward the quiet village nestled in the middle of a small valley. Heavily forested mountains ringed the valley from all directions.

"The road is paved? How nice!"

"Looks like cobblestones." Steve knelt down to inspect the smooth rocks lining the road. Try as he might, he couldn't pry any rocks loose, even those that looked as though they were movable.

"Have you ever been here before?" Sarah asked Rhenyon.

"I have not, milady."

"But you've been to Ylani before, right?" Steve asked

their companion.

"I have been to their castle on several occasions," Rhenyon confirmed.

"So where do we start?"

Rhenyon pointed at the village.

"We should see if we can find a tavern. Our story will be that we are peasants. Sarah will be my sister, and you can be her husband."

"There's a stretch," Steve remarked, grinning at his friend.

"Under no circumstances are you to use your jhorun," Rhenyon instructed again, looking pointedly at Steve. "The slightest misstep here will instantly reveal our identities."

"So, what are we supposed to be, anyway?" Steve asked.

"Farmers."

"We're farmers, huh?" Steve commented, looking down at himself. "We look like the Three Stooges."

"We're supposed to be dressed alike," Sarah said. "Weren't you paying attention to what Rhenyon said earlier?"

The three of them were all dressed in peasant garb consisting of heavily worn dark brown tunics and trousers. Not wanting to be chilled in the early morning air, Sarah had elected to don a light parka. She felt the fabric again. Very lightweight material, yet it was doing a remarkable job of keeping her warm.

Steve clapped his hands. "So, we're hicks. Peachy. Let's go find us a bar."

"Tavern," Rhenyon corrected.

"Whatever."

At the threshold of the village gate, a lone guard ambled out of a tiny sentry post.

"Good day, travelers. What business do you have here?"

"We are thirsty. There a tavern 'round 'ere?" Rhenyon asked slowly, as though he had just been asked a complex riddle.

"Very well, welcome. The tavern can be found just down there, second building on your right."

"Thanks," Steve answered automatically.

"My pleasure. Enjoy yourselves."

As they made their way toward the local pub, Steve

increased his pace until he was walking side-by-side with Rhenyon and his wife.

"Seems like an awfully jovial guy, don't you think?"

"I was thinking the same thing," Sarah said in a hushed tone. "I don't know what I was expecting, but that wasn't it."

"Hush," Rhenyon said in a low voice. "We are here. Follow my lead."

However, Steve made it to the door first. Long accustomed to waiting for his wife to enter first, Steve pulled open the door just as several patrons were departing. Not thinking anything about it, he waited patiently as an elderly couple stepped out into the bright sunshine.

"My thanks, young sir." Both patrons smiled warmly at the kind man holding open the door.

"Anytime."

Rhenyon entered first, followed closely by Sarah. Bringing up the rear, Steve let the door swing shut behind him, looking around as he did so. The room they were standing in had about ten large tables scattered about, with only two presently occupied. A roaring fire was blazing away in the hearth while what looked like a group of friends were sitting on stools next to the counter running the length of the back wall. Following Rhenyon and his wife, they selected a table fairly close to the blazing fire. Steve glanced at the fire, noting with amusement that the flames flickered, momentarily increasing in volume.

"These people seem nice," Sarah observed. "I thought Ylani hated Lentari."

"As did I," Rhenyon admitted, watching the four people on the stools laugh and slap each other on the back.

"Feels like we're missing something here," Steve added, watching the serving girl approach their table.

"Good day to you," the girl said, smiling at each of them. "What can I bring you?"

Not knowing what was available, or what to order without drawing attention to either of them, husband and wife let Rhenyon place their orders. Steve could only hope it was edible. With the order placed, the girl retreated, reappearing moments later with three mugs of torpa juice. Steve eyed the bright green liquid, turning nonchalantly to observe his wife.

Whatever it was, she seemed to like it. Taking a deep breath, he took a sip. He smacked his lips. Not bad. Tasted like kiwis. While not his favorite, it would do. He took another sip.

"So what now?" he asked, turning to look at their team leader.

"Be silent. Listen."

"To what?"

Sarah put her hand over his.

"Listen to those people over at the bar," she whispered, nodding in the direction of the counter.

Surreptitiously watching the group of friends, Steve could just make out the tail end of their conversation.

"… so much better without him, don' you think?"

"You only say that 'cause the two of you did not get along."

"Be that as it may, you cannot say that you have not enjoyed spending more time here."

One man was nodding. "True. What if he went to Lentari?"

"Then he becomes their problem."

"Did you hear that Burlin also went missin'?" another man piped up.

"Someone else I will not miss. Whom do you think I should thank for this?" one friend joked, causing the rest of his group to burst out laughing.

Steve shrugged. "A couple of people have turned up missing. So what?"

"I think it's more than that," Sarah whispered, still watching the group.

"My uncle says the farming in Lentari is much better. He has moved his entire family there."

"Are you thinking about joining them?" one friend incredulously asked the other.

"Maybe."

"Interesting," Rhenyon murmured under his breath.

"What?" Steve softly asked.

"I have fought in enough battles to know when one approaches. You can feel it in the air. I feel nothing here."

"Maybe they don't know what has been going on," Sarah whispered.

Rhenyon and Steve both looked over at her.

"How could they not know, Lady Sarah?"

"Think about it, Rhenyon. Everyone we've met here so far has been polite, nice, with no signs of animosity anywhere. Almost like the townspeople don't know that Ylani and Lentari are at odds with one another."

"What about the missing people?" Steve whispered, glancing pointedly at the group of people still laughing amongst themselves at the counter.

"Missing people," Sarah repeated, lowering her voice so that it could only be heard at their table, "and villagers that clearly aren't missed. I think someone needs to go talk to them."

Husband and wife turned to regard their Lentarian friend.

"Agreed, I will go." Rhenyon rose from the table and, with his mug in his hand, approached the counter.

The small group of friends turned to behold the newcomer.

"Greetings! Are you passing through?"

"Aye, just gettin' a bite to eat before I collect some supplies."

"Ah, a farmer then."

"Aye. I hope you do not mind me asking, but I could not help overhearing your previous comment. Your friend went missing?"

"He is no friend to us or anyone else in Myrn," another man huffed out, turning his attention to Rhenyon. "Good riddance if you ask me."

"Well, why would we want the opinion from the likes of you?"

The man grinned at his companion and gulped more ale.

"This man is a troublemaker then?" Rhenyon asked carefully.

There were a chorus of 'ayes.'

"Has anyone else turned up missing?" Rhenyon thoughtfully stroked his beard. "Makes me yearn for my farm."

"Think you will be safe in your farm? I hear that missing villagers have been reported as far away as Arlan. No village is safe," the man muttered darkly.

"Every village has been hit? Just men, or is it women and children, too?"

"Nay, just the men. They say if you do anything foolish that will land yourself in the dungeon, in any dungeon, then you might as well sign your death warrant."

"Prisoners? Was this person that you were talking about earlier a prisoner?"

"Aye, captured one day and vanished the next."

"What do the constables say?"

"The constables are all weak. They only whine to the king. Do you think the king does anything about it?"

"You think the king is not concerned?" Rhenyon asked.

"What do you think, friend?"

"I would like to believe our king is taking precautions to see to the welfare of his citizens."

At this, the four men fell silent. The individual that Rhenyon had been speaking to suddenly squinted his eyes and stared hard at him.

"Where did you say your farm was?"

"About two days journey from here, due west," Rhenyon responded readily, figuring sooner or later someone would want a few more details about their cover story.

"Long way to go for supplies," one man commented.

"I prefer my privacy."

At that moment, the friendly sentry guard from earlier entered, eager for an ale after an uneventful shift. His superior, enjoying the fact that he was able to have a drink while on duty, accompanied him.

"Two ales," the sentry ordered, watching as the small group of people at the counter hastily broke apart. Figuring his superior would have a second drink after this one was finished, the guard deliberately chose a table close to the counter. Nodding his head in approval, the officer sat, watching as the sentry remained at the counter waiting for their drink order to be filled. One other man, unmistakably a peasant, remained at the counter. Tilting his mug back, the peasant finished his drink before thunking it back down on the counter and staggering away. Finishing his own drink,

Rhenyon turned around and met the officer's eyes. Both gasped as each recognized the other.

"Jalen!"

The fugitive Lentarian soldier leapt to his feet, his ale flying off the upturned table. "Rhenyon?! Guards! We have an intruder! Spy!"

Pounding footsteps sounded from outside as soldiers hastily rushed toward the tavern.

Rhenyon thrust his elbow backward, catching the startled sentry across his right cheek. The sentry flew backwards, smashing into the counter. Rhenyon looked past the traitor to catch Sarah's eye.

"Take him to the castle! Hurry!"

Jalen looked behind him and recognized the famous Nohrin. "Wizards be damned! Where the hell are the guards?! There are intruders here! Spies!"

Sarah rose sputtering, looking down at her husband. "Umm…"

"Don't you think now would be a good time for all of us to all just zap back to the castle?" Steve asked worriedly, eyeing the door. It'd only be a matter of moments before reinforcements would rush through.

"No! Lady Sarah, you must hurry! Get him to the castle!"

Jalen sneered. "If you think any of you will make it out of here alive, then —"

"Rhenyon, forget it. I'm not going to ditch you guys here. Not going to happen."

"We should all go!" Steve insisted again, ready to ignite his hands.

"No, this is perfect," Rhenyon said, shaking his head. "Lady Sarah, follow us then, but from a distance. Just hurry!"

Not really sure of what Rhenyon had in mind, and flat-out unwilling to desert her husband, Sarah teleported herself behind the still sputtering traitor. Darting in to grab Jalen's ear, she teleported them straight to castle R'Tal's throne room. Depositing the cursing Jalen at the feet of the thunderstruck king, Sarah gave a quick curtsy.

"Present for you, compliments of Rhenyon. Gotta go!"

Sarah teleported back just in time to see Rhenyon and her

husband escorted from the tavern.

"I sure hope you know what the hell you're doing, pal," Steve muttered under his breath as he glared at Rhenyon's back. Bound and manacled, they were led away.

Chapter 11 — Incarcerated

"This is not a good idea."

Rhenyon smiled. "Aye, probably not."

"Didn't we overhear those guys telling us to avoid the dungeon?"

"Indeed. This is perfect."

"If you say so. Don't forget, people have been disappearing from here."

"Keep your voice down."

"I just want to make sure Sarah is okay. We told her to follow us."

"So?"

"I hope she stays hidden."

"Even if she's seen, she can remove herself from danger. Now be silent!"

"What's your plan for getting us out of here?" Steve asked in a hushed tone.

"Well —"

"You do have a plan, right?"

Rhenyon nodded. "I will, aye."

"You will? Just what the hell— "

A sudden disturbance from outside their cell silenced them both instantly. Keys rattled as someone wrestled with the heavy iron door and its equally stubborn lock.

"Do not make eye contact," Rhenyon whispered. "Do not give them any reason to notice you."

The rusty door was finally flung open. Two guards entered, dragging a struggling prisoner between them.

"You are making a mistake! Please! Do not do this! I did not take anything! I swear it on my father's grave!"

Everyone tensed as the next cell over was unlocked and the prisoner flung inside. Laughing heartily, the guards slammed the door, re-locking the cell. Tugging the metal bars to verify the prisoner was secure, the two men departed, slamming the outer door behind them. Metal scraped over metal as a heavy iron bar was put in place over the outer door, effectively preventing any unauthorized entry.

"What do we do now?" Steve whispered to Rhenyon. "He could have been planted in here to spy on us. Probably wouldn't take much to sound the alarm."

"I will handle this," Rhenyon whispered back, standing up and giving Steve a friendly pat on his shoulder.

"Friend, who are you?"

"It's a mistake, just a mistake. Has to be. I will wake up safe and sound in my bed. Just a dream…"

Hoping to play on the sympathies of the prison's newest member, Rhenyon tried again.

"We, too, are being held unjustly. What is your story, friend?"

The blubbering from the next cell abated.

"Who's that? Who's there?"

"We are farmers."

"F-farmers?"

"Aye. We were in the wrong place at the wrong time. Some miscreant mistakenly identified us as spies. And now, here we are."

"They say that I s-s-stole food! I am to lose my hand tomorrow at sunrise." The speaker broke out in sobs again.

Very softly, he added, "I am so sorry, my beloved Rhae. I tried. I really tried."

"Man alive, sounds like you really pissed someone off," Steve commented. "You're going to lose your hand? What did you do?"

"My wife's sister was taken from us. It was my duty to protect her. She's only a girl! It devastated my poor Rhae." The man sniffed loudly and brushed the back of his arm across his face. "Who are you? Where did you come from?"

"My name is —"

"I am called Zia," a soft voice answered.

Steve and Rhenyon both froze. They eyed each other. Someone else was in the next cell? And their name was Zia? Steve knew that was the name of one of Sarah's Internet aliases!

"Sarah?" Steve softly called out. "Is that you?"

"Expecting someone else?"

"What the hell are you doing in there? How did you find us?"

"I got tired of waiting. Besides, I was told I could follow."

"Zia, who are they?" the unknown prisoner asked. "Do you know each other?"

"My brother and my husband are in the next cell. You might have heard my brother," Sarah said, perfectly mimicking Rhenyon's accent. "We were branded as spies by a guard at a local tavern here, when we're clearly not. My husband and I are farmers. Everyone in my family is." Sarah sighed loudly. "I do not know what my fate will be."

"That is unfortunate, miss. With regret, I am in no position to help you."

"Do you know where your wife's sister was taken?" Steve asked from the next cell.

"Who is that? Who speaks?"

"That was my husband, Jay." Sarah had decided against giving out their real names. "My brother is with him."

"What is his name?"

"My brother's name? Ummm, his name is, umm…" Uh, oh. She had to come up with a name for Rhenyon and had to do so fast. "Max. Maximillian."

Rhenyon snorted softly. "Maximillian?" he whispered, looking quizzically at the fire thrower.

Steve shrugged. "Don't ask me. I think Max was the name of a dog she had when she was little."

Another snort.

"What's your name?" Sarah gently asked the sobbing newcomer.

"H-Harlen."

"Harlen, we're pleased to make your acquaintance."

The only response she received was several sniffles.

"They say you stole something? What?"

"They—they claim I stole several loaves of bread. I did not! I swear it!"

"What about your wife's sister? What happened to her?"

"She's just a girl," Harlen sobbed. "She was my responsibility. I could not protect her."

"Why was she taken?" Steve asked.

"No one knows! Rhae said there were no explanations, no accusations, nothing! Soldiers came into my home while I was at work and whisked her away!"

The pitiful man continued to sob.

"Oh, the hell with this." Sarah grabbed Harlen's left wrist and teleported them both to the adjoining cell.

Harlen's eyes flew open. "What manner of wizardry is this? Where did the two of you come from?"

"We're actually in the next cell," Sarah explained. "I just brought us here."

Harlen's eyes widened. "A teleporter!"

"Aye. We must keep that our little secret, agreed?"

"Then why do you not teleport out of here?"

Sarah smiled briefly at Rhenyon before turning back to their new friend. "Recon."

"You are here because you want to spy on someone? That makes no sense at all! Why would you stay?"

"Harlen, let me ask you something." Steve interrupted, pausing a moment while he thought about what he wanted to say. "What are your feelings toward Lentari?"

"Lentari? The kingdom on our southern border? It is very scenic."

"Ummm, have you and your wife ever been there?"

"Aye, on several occasions. The castle in R'Tal holds a floral festival every spring that Rhae and Nala both enjoy attending. I sometimes accompany them."

"Your wife and her sister travel each year to Lentari so they can check out flowers?"

Sarah elbowed her husband hard in the ribs. "What woman doesn't love flowers? If we were here at that time, you know very well we'd attend."

"Just get him out of here." Rhenyon rolled his eyes. It was hard enough to keep the Nohrin quiet. Now there was a distraught prisoner to contend with. Sooner or later, he knew someone was going to take notice.

"Where do I take him?" Sarah asked, letting her accent drop. Harlen didn't notice. "I can't show up in the middle of that tavern now. You said I should refrain from doing anything that would attract attention, right?"

"What's on the other side of this wall?" Steve asked, knocking several knuckles against the stone wall. "Couldn't you just drop him on the other side?"

"This is just a simple stone building," Sarah explained. "It's not underground or anything. I don't know what's directly behind us. What, were you blindfolded when you guys were brought in here?"

"No. I wasn't paying attention."

"We are in the village penitentiary," Rhenyon observed. "Therefore, there probably will be no other structures nearby."

"There aren't," Sarah confirmed.

"How thick do you think these stones are?"

"Why?" Steve wanted to know.

"You might be able to cut a small hole in the wall, enough for your new friend here to wiggle through."

"Just teleport him outside, to a location you're familiar with."

"I probably could," Sarah agreed, nodding her head. "But how do you know we wouldn't appear in front of a group of soldiers on patrol? Or teleport in front of some villagers?" Now she shook her head. "I could take him directly behind the wall in a heartbeat, only I don't know what it looks like. For all I know there are obstacles out there. Rocks, trees, etc. I can't take that chance."

"Can't you visualize what's out there?"

"I've already done that. It's dark. I can't see anything."

"So, how'd you get in?"

"I told you, I followed from a distance. I made sure I kept you guys in sight at all times. Sometimes I'd hide behind a door, other times I'd teleport in right behind the guards." She rapped the stone a few times with her knuckles. "Do you think you could even burn through solid stone? That's bound to attract attention, don't you think?"

Deciding the best way to be rid of their newest cellmate was to help him escape, Rhenyon walked to the perimeter wall and stared out the barred window. He rapped his knuckles a few times on one of the bars.

"Do you think you could melt enough bars so we could squeeze through?"

"I don't know, man, that iron is pretty solid."

"Ah. So you cannot melt a simple iron bar. My apologies. I had assumed that you could. No matter. We will —"

Sarah stifled a giggle and looked at her husband, who was scowling at the commander.

"Okay, step aside. I'll handle this."

"Think you can handle it, my love?"

"Don't lose yourself in the part," Steve grumbled.

Sarah laughed as she turned to Harlen.

"If we get you out of here, do you have a safe place to go?"

Harlen vigorously nodded his head. "Aye, I can hide in my shop until I am forgotten."

"What kind of shop do you have?" Steve asked, interested in what set of skills someone like this could possibly possess.

"Blacksmith."

Steve perked up. "Really? What do you make there? Shields? Swords?"

"Hon, really? Not now."

Smiling sheepishly at his wife, Steve grinned. "Sorry."

"Do you live in the village?"

"Aye. My shop is next to the Quad."

"Next to the what?"

"The Quad. It is what we call the Four Trees."

At a loss, Steve looked at Rhenyon, who shrugged. He didn't know anything about a special group of trees, either.

Harlen looked at his right hand before looking anxiously back at thick iron bars blocking their means of escape, hoping against hope that his newfound friends would have some way to prevent him from losing any appendages. In all his years of blacksmithing, he had not once encountered a one-handed smith.

Steve approached the window, tugging on several of the bars.

"How should I do this?"

"Do not use blasts of fire," Rhenyon advised. "We must not attract any attention."

"Remember when you heated up those cauldrons at Thacken Lodge?"

Steve turned to his wife. He nodded.

"Yeah, I do. Okay, you guys had better take cover."

Nodding, Sarah took Rhenyon's arm with her left and Harlen's arm with her right. They vanished, reappearing moments later in Harlen's original cell.

"Zia," Rhenyon said, almost forgetting that she had adopted another name, "if you please, stand guard out in the corridor. Alert us if anyone approaches."

Sarah nodded. "Will do." She vanished, appearing moments later outside the cell. She walked over to the barred window to look through the outer door.

"Everyone ready?"

"Ready here," Rhenyon called back

Steve stared at one of the bars, willing his jhorun to heat the iron to its melting point. Within a few seconds, the iron bar was glowing red. However, it did not melt. Willing his jhorun to increase the heat as much as he could, Steve ordered the bar to melt, soften, anything! Nothing. It was glowing red, but that was about it. He risked a glance over his shoulder, forgetting that the others were hiding in the other cell.

"It didn't melt. I'm going to try again."

He turned his attention back to the bar which had started to revert to black as it cooled. It rapidly reheated, the bar obediently switching back to red. Unfortunately, it still did not melt.

"Can you touch the metal when it's that hot?" Rhenyon inquired. "If the metal is soft enough, you might be able to bend it out of shape."

"Yeah, sure, let me try."

Steve approached the red bar and tentatively poked a finger at it. He smiled. He still couldn't feel a thing. Gripping the red bar tightly in with both hands, he tugged, fully expecting the bar to break free. It didn't.

Grunting, Steve braced both of his legs against the stone wall and heaved. The red-hot iron was still refusing to budge.

"No luck! I mean I can touch the bar, but it still won't budge."

"Try heating and pulling at the same time," Sarah suggested.

"It's not going to work."

"Would you please try?"

Annoyed, Steve gripped the bar again and sent a blast of heat into it, giving a violent tug as he did so. Suddenly he was holding the bar of iron in his hand. How had his wife known that would happen?

"Ummm, I got it."

Sarah and the others reappeared.

"So it worked?"

Steve hefted the bar in front of her.

"Obviously. How did you know that would work?"

"It dawned on me that maybe physical contact, and not visual contact, would work better. Didn't you tell me when you were making the dragon sword last year that you were able to heat it in your hand in just a couple of seconds?"

Steve nodded. "Okay, I do remember that."

"You will need to remove these two bars as well, Sir Steve, if a person is to escape this cell."

Curious about Sarah's revelation, he grabbed the top of the next bar and repeated the process. Sure enough, the top bar melted through and popped free of the metal frame. He slid his hand down the bar to the bottom and sent another blast. The bar came free.

With the three bars removed from the window, they now had an opening large enough for a human to squeeze through.

"Harlen, get going."

His future brightening considerably, their formerly distraught cellmate stared at the window. "How is this possible?"

"It's best if you do not ask too many questions," Rhenyon advised. "I would also suggest you keep as silent as possible about what you have seen, is that understood?"

Not questioning the authoritative tone coming from the Lentarian commander, Harlen nodded at once. "Aye, sir."

"Off you go." Rhenyon gestured to the opening. "Move."

Steve cupped his hands together and gave Harlen a leg up.

"Stay hidden as long as you can," Sarah called.

He was already off, having silently disappeared into the trees.

"We've got company!" Sarah suddenly whispered, waving her arms to attract Rhenyon's attention.

Metal scraped over metal as the heavy bar was removed from the outer cell door.

"Lady Sarah, get back in the cell!"

"Hon, get yourself out of here!"

"I'm not going to desert you."

"Move me back to the other cell. Hide here, in this one," Rhenyon instructed, as various keys were inserted into the locked door. "There should be a prisoner in there. We don't want to arouse suspicion."

"If they make a stink, or ask you anything, you are to get yourself out of here, okay?"

"If I go, we all go. Final offer."

"Fine. Whatever. Just hurry!"

Sarah returned Rhenyon to her husband's cell before jumping back to her own, throwing the hood from her parka over her head in the process. Steve and Rhenyon hastily stretched a piece of burlap across the window to conceal Harlen's escape hole. Steve then kicked the iron bars under the decrepit mattress.

The correct key was finally inserted and the lock grudgingly yielded to the repeated attempts at gaining entry. Three men entered. Two were the same two guards who had escorted Harlen in, but the third was unknown. He was short and thin, and was wearing bright blue robes.

Steve snorted. It definitely was not a good look for the guy.

"These are the two spies?" the thin man asked, turning to look at the soldier on his right.

"Aye."

The man's gaze fell upon Steve. He stared a moment before his eyes shifted to Rhenyon's.

"Who are you? What kingdom are you from?"

"We are not spies, m' lord," Rhenyon blurted out, his IQ appearing to have shed a hundred points. "I don' know what that feller's problem is."

"If you are not spies, then who are you? What is your name, peasant?"

"My name is Maximillimum," Rhenyon said slowly, his tongue tripping over the name Sarah had assigned him. "Me and m' brother are farmers."

Their interrogator's eyes shifted momentarily to Steve's before returning to Rhenyon's.

"You expect me to believe that you are simple farmers? Why would you be accused of being spies, then? What were you doing?"

"We were jus' havin' a drink," Rhenyon whined, doing a remarkable job of sounding intoxicated. "Tha's all."

"Who accused the two of you?"

Rhenyon gave a half-hearted shrug. "Some soldier. I don' know who."

"What is your brother's name?"

Rhenyon turned to look behind him. Nodding, Steve also decided to play the part of a dimwitted imbecile.

"Howdy. I'm Jay. What's your name, pal?"

Lips wrinkling in disgust, the newcomer turned back to the guards.

"You call these two spies?"

"What's your name?" Steve asked again. "I am Jay. This here's m' brother, Max."

Scowling with irritation, the thin man turned back to the prisoners. The one who had asked for his name had such a goofy, harmless expression on his face that he responded automatically.

"Warrick."

"Pleased t' meetcha, pal." Steve slurred, extending his right arm.

Having no desire to touch the filthy, moronic idiot, Warrick turned angrily to the guards once more.

"Find out who identified these buffoons as spies and have them report here. Immediately."

"Sir," the guard on the left hesitantly raised his hand.

"What?"

"It was Lieutenant Jalen, sir."

"He is your commanding officer?"

"Aye."

"Fetch him at once."

One of the guards took off, leaving the remaining guard uncomfortably shuffling from foot to foot.

"How long will it take to bring Lieutenant Jalen here?" Warrick asked impatiently.

"It will be just a few more moments, sir. He only has to check the tavern."

Deciding a formal reprimand was in order, Warrick gave a thin smile in return.

"Ummm, sir? Could you step out here for a moment?"

Surprised, both Warrick and the guard turned to stare at the soldier on the other side of the door. In spite of himself, Warrick was impressed. That was quick!

"You may escort the lieutenant in."

"He is presently missing, sire."

"Lieutenant Jalen is missing?" Warrick frowned. One of their officers allegedly identifies several spies and then vanishes? Maybe there was some credibility to these claims after all. He needed to send off a message of his own.

"Find him. For your sake, as quickly as possible."

The guard paled. "At once, sir."

Warrick departed, leaving the two guards staring nervously at one another.

"Grab any other men you can find," one soldier informed the other. "Search the taverns from top to bottom. Find the lieutenant!"

The guard nodded. Both men hurriedly left the prison, slamming and securing the door behind them.

"Now what do we do?" Steve asked, turning to Rhenyon. "Don't you think it's time to go?"

"You may be right. Milady, join us, if you please."

Sarah appeared, pushing back her hood.

"Are we finally getting out of here?"

"I see no reason to stay longer. I do not think we can learn anything else here, so —"

Rhenyon trailed off as Sarah's eyes rolled back in her head and she toppled forward. Steve caught her before she collapsed. Both he and Rhenyon gently lowered her to a sitting position.

"Milady! Are you alright?"

"Sweetie! What's going on? Are you okay?"

Sarah smiled weakly as both spoke at the same time.

"I'm okay. I just got very dizzy. It felt just like it did when I teleported for the first time but ten times worse. It's almost as if —"

Her eyes widened in shock. She stared first at her husband, then at Rhenyon.

"We were just teleported!"

"What? No we weren't." Steve pointed at the ragged piece of burlap still covering part of the barred window. "We haven't moved. Look, there's your proof. That thing is still blocking Harlen's escape hole."

Sarah shook her head. "No, I swear it. We've been teleported."

Curious, Rhenyon strode over to the wall and lifted a corner of the burlap scrap to peer behind it. With a shout of surprise, he yanked the fabric off the window. Steve sucked in his breath. The bars that he had cut through were whole again! Sarah was right. They were now in an entirely different prison!

"What the hell? Where are we now?" Steve wondered aloud, staring around. "This place certainly looks the same."

"It's like the entire contents of the other place were moved into an identical one," Sarah surmised. "None of you felt the jump?"

Rhenyon shook his head. "I did not feel a thing, milady."

"Same here," Steve added.

"I wonder where —"

Rhenyon threw both hands up in twin 'wait' gestures. "Someone is coming! Quickly, help me cover the window! Lady Sarah, back in your cell!"

"It was back in that village. Where exactly am I supposed to go?"

"Check to see if there's another one you can hide in! Hurry!"

Sarah vanished, appearing outside of the cell moments later. She looked in on the space on the left.

"This one is empty," she whispered to the two of them. "I'll hide in this one. Did you know there are at least ten more cells out here? There weren't that many before."

Throwing the hood back over her head, she teleported inside the chamber, backing far away from the door.

The main prison door banged open. Three new guards appeared. Surprisingly, they started unlocking cells, beckoning for all occupants to come out into the open. Steve and Rhenyon's was next, then Sarah's. Cautiously eyeing her husband, she looked around. There must have been a dozen people besides herself now nervously milling about.

"The lot of you, listen up!" One of the guards banged his sword several times on the bars. "Anyone not interested in getting a second chance at your freedom may return to your cells."

Nobody moved.

"Excellent. You have been brought here because each of you have been sentenced to either spend your entire life in the dungeon, or else have been given death sentences. You all have been pardoned. That is, if you would like to earn your freedom. What say you?"

There were a chorus of "ayes."

"Excellent. Follow me. You will have a chance to pledge your allegiance to your benefactor."

"Who is our benefactor?" one man asked in a tremulous voice.

"A very powerful wizard."

Several gasped. "A wizard? Why would a wizard take pity on the likes of us?"

"What does he want in return?" Another prisoner asked. "What will he ask of us?"

"Does it matter? Is your freedom not worth it?"

"Since when does a wizard have the power to grant a pardon?" another man asked. "Would that not be up to the king?"

If the guard heard the question, he chose to ignore it. Instead, they were led deeper into the dungeons, with two silent guards bringing up the rear. Finally descending the last flight of stairs, they discovered a heavy wooden door, open wide to welcome the new recruits.

Warrick appeared, smiling profusely.

"Welcome, welcome. Do come in."

"Said the spider to the fly," Steve muttered softly under his breath as the dozen or so men shuffled hesitantly into the large chamber. The three of them cautiously brought up the rear. Warrick hastily closed the thick door behind them.

"Are you our benefactor?" one man asked.

"Not me, no sir." Warrick smiled, having gone through this same routine many times before. "He will be with us in just a few moments."

"Where are we?"

"Deep underground, in his workshop."

An extremely heavyset man pointed to a wall which had racks and racks of small crystal vials on them.

"What are all of those fer?"

"You will find out," Warrick promised, smiling.

"Is he really a wizard?" Steve asked, playing the part of a scared prisoner perfectly.

"Ah, I remember you. The witless brother. Jay, was it not? Aye, he is a wizard."

"The most powerful in the entire kingdom, I can assure you."

All present jumped at the loud voice. Everyone looked around, trying to spot its owner. However, no one else was visible.

"Do you see anyone?" one man asked another.

"He's a wizard," his friend explained. "He could be anywhere!"

"Indeed I can, and you would do well to remember that."

"Why are you hiding, then?"

"Who speaks?"

A tall, broad-shouldered man stepped forward. "I did."

"What is your name, peasant?"

"Burlin."

Steve felt a jolt of recognition. This was one of the missing people from Myrn!

A slight chill crept into the disembodied voice.

"I prefer to observe these mundane proceedings from a distance."

Burlin snorted with amusement.

"So you hide like a coward? Some wizard."

The temperature in the chamber dropped twenty degrees. Literally. Being naturally resistant to the cold, Steve watched with amusement as his breath came out in thick jets of fog. Growing colder by the second, Sarah scooted closer to her husband.

"Insolent pig," the voice snarled. "You *dare* call me coward?"

Acclimatized to the colder temperatures of his mountainous village, the brawny villager was unimpressed.

"Is that the best you can do? You are path-"

He never finished his sentence. Burlin stiffened with surprise, and then moved no more. A blue crystalline hue spread slowly across his skin as he froze solid, lips raised upward in a sneer. Wanting to make it clear that they were not to be associated with this unlucky citizen of Myrn, the group of prisoners gave the sparkling crystal statue a wide berth.

"Any more objections?" the voice nonchalantly inquired.

Nobody spoke a word.

"Excellent, we may proceed."

"What do you want of us?" one man cried out, the same

one as before.

A lone figure appeared out of the shadows. Slowly and deliberately, the wizard pushed back his hood, reveling in the utter silence of his captive audience. The striking blond-haired young man smugly appraised his newest recruits. His piercing blue eyes scanned the distraught faces before him, searching for any further signs of insolence. He smiled. Nothing but fearful looks met his eyes. Perfect.

"You ask what I want of you? Simple." The wizard smiled once more. "Loyalty. You work for me now. Follow my orders. I need dependable men to carry out my plans."

"And what plans are those?"

"What do you think, miscreant? Domination."

"Domination? Over who?"

The wizard smiled. "Ylani. Lentari. They are just the beginning. Ylani will declare war upon its southern neighbors at any moment. Lentari is more than capable of defending itself, so when the two of them are completely engrossed with one another, my army will then take control of both kingdoms."

Virtually everyone present snorted with derision. "One army?" one man scoffed. "Two kingdoms? You are dreamin.' Why would we willingly become traitors?"

"If your freedom is not an adequate reason for your allegiance, then how about this? A more powerful jhorun."

"Impossible. Our jhoruns cannot be exchanged."

The blonde wizard turned to his assistant. "Warrick, inform our guests what jhorun you were born with."

"I had the ability to find tiny pockets of water underground."

Several men laughed.

"Not something I was proud of," Warrick confessed, smiling conspiratorially at the small group of prisoners.

"What is your jhorun now?" their spokesman wanted to know.

"I can implant minor commands into other people's minds," Warrick proudly declared.

Many of the prisoners nodded their heads. That was a very powerful jhorun to have.

"Prove it," their spokesman demanded.

"Very well. A moment, if you please." Warrick turned to retrieve the props he had used for all the other demonstrations. Taking the bundle of clothes down from a shelf at the back of the room, Warrick handed the package to his volunteer. As the skeptical prisoner took the bundle, the desire to change his clothing was implanted into his head.

"Where can I —?"

"Right over there," Warrick interrupted, pointing to a screen set up for this very purpose. "You may change right over there."

Nodding appreciatively, the volunteer disappeared behind the screen, reappearing a few moments later. Everyone, including the three Lentarian spies, burst out laughing. The former prisoner was now decked out in a frilly pink dress. Tugging the hem of the garment down so that it fell evenly across his knobby knees, the unwitting assistant scowled at his companions.

"What are you laughing at? What's so funny?"

Removing the suggestion he had implanted, Warrick smiled as the prisoner looked down in horror at his attire.

"What the blazes am I doin' in a dress?"

Dumbfounded, the prisoners stared at the smug wizard.

"You promise you will give us stronger jhoruns?"

"Once you have demonstrated your loyalty, aye."

"What type of jhorun can you give us?"

The blonde wizard gestured to the racks behind him. Hundreds of tiny crystal vials glinted in the flickering torchlight.

"As you can see, I have quite a few to choose from. Only the most dedicated and loyal of my followers can earn the privilege of having their jhoruns replaced."

Steve gazed at the tiny vials. "Each of those has a jhorun in it?"

"Each and every one," the wizard confirmed.

"How is that possible?" one man asked.

"The Chalix," Warrick proudly answered.

The wizard's cold blue eyes flashed with annoyance. This was *his* moment in the spotlight. He should be the one to reveal his greatest achievement. Scowling at his witless sidekick, he turned back to his audience.

"Serve me well," the wizard instructed, "and I will let you pick your next jhorun from among those."

"What's a chalix?" Rhenyon asked, slurring his voice once more.

The strange man walked over to his extensive rack of vials and produced a tiny key. He unlocked the bureau's secret inner compartment and withdrew a heavy felt bag. Once the pouch's drawstring was untied, the bag fell away to reveal a nondescript pewter goblet. The wizard smiled as he clutched his prized possession tightly in his fist. A few moments later, the cup was held up high, as though this was the deepest, darkest secret known to man.

Even from where he was standing, Steve could see the distinctive mark etched upon its surface: twin lightning bolts.

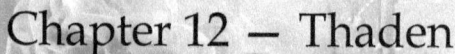

Chapter 12 — Thaden

That's it!" Steve hissed under his breath. "It has to be! Time to melt that sucker down!"

"No, you can't!" Sarah whispered back, taking both of his hands in hers. "This isn't the right time."

"Lady Sarah is right," Rhenyon softly murmured. "We do anything now and we will attract unwanted attention. We must bide our time."

"We don't know if, or when, we'll get another shot at this. We need to destroy that thing!"

"We do, aye, but not yet. Observe."

Stumbling blindly to the front of the new recruits, Rhenyon pointed at the goblet.

"What is that fer? It is naught but a cup."

Keeping his smile plastered on his face, Warrick nodded. "Ah, but it looks like a cup. In reality, this is a very powerful talisman."

"And tha' little bit o' metal can steal someone's jhorun, is that it?"

Master and apprentice both nodded, the same smug expression on each of their faces.

"How does it work?" someone else asked. "You take a drink of some potion and poof, no more jhorun?"

"A single sip of any liquid," the wizard crooned softly, gently caressing the surface of the Chalix, "and your jhorun is absorbed by this goblet to be harvested at a later date."

"I don' understand," Rhenyon slurred, spraying tiny drops of spittle in Warrick's direction. "Wha' happens to you then? If your jhorun is in one of them little bottles, can you get it back by just breakin' 'em open again?"

"If the vial is improperly opened," Warrick explained, "then the jhorun contained within will be lost forever. To properly exchange your jhorun with one of these, you must first have your original jhorun stripped away. You cannot have two jhoruns at the same time. Once the old is removed, only then you would be ready for your replacement. Any other questions?"

"Jeez, pal," Steve added, nodding his head in the wizard's direction, "You must be the most powerful wizard alive! Well, except for Shardwyn."

"Do not ever speak of that charlatan in my presence!" The young wizard was on his feet in a flash, all but frothing with rage. "His power pales in comparison to mine!"

"I didn't mean nuthin'," Steve stammered, doing a remarkable job of appearing contrite. "Ol' Shardwyn is known far and wide as being the most powerful. Between the two of us, I think you have nothing t' worry 'bout."

Mollified, the blonde wizard settled back into his chair. Clearly the prisoner was feeling foolish. His face and his hands had turned dark red.

"Don't overdo it," Sarah whispered to her husband.

"Just trying to get into the spirit of this," Steve whispered back.

"What's the matter wit' that Lentarian wizard?" Rhenyon asked, clearly not finished in provoking their benefactor. "What do you have against him?"

"That old fool still believes jhorun cannot be tampered with," the wizard spat out. "I proved him wrong. I proved everyone wrong."

"Shardwyn could gift you wit' a jhorun if he desired it, right? I 'eard he did it before."

The young wizard's gaze locked onto the commander.

"Sheer luck. Has he been able to recreate his previous success? Of course not. I personally captured several Lentarian spies and returned them without their jhorun just to see if any progress had been made. Of course, none had."

"The two of them are related," Sarah whispered in her husband's ear. "I just know it. I'll bet they're father and son."

"How do you know so much about the Lentarian wizard?" Rhenyon suddenly asked, having overheard Sarah's observation. "Are you kin? You look like kin."

The blonde man said nothing.

"So, you are kin. Is he your father, then?"

"Aye, he is," Warrick proudly answered.

"I did not know Shard-- I mean, that other wizard—had any offspring," one man exclaimed to another.

"I am not surprised that my father does not talk about me. I am Thaden, his only son. I was expelled from the kingdom of my birth by my father's own hand."

"That insensitive dolt," Steve muttered, loudly enough for everyone to hear.

For a brief moment, a smile manifested on the wizard's face before being replaced by his trademark frown.

"So you are Lentarian?" someone asked.

"Only by birth. My loyalty to the crown died the day my own kingdom betrayed me. The Kri'yans believed every poisonous word my father uttered. He was incapable of recognizing the importance of my work."

"What type of work?" Steve asked, genuinely curious.

"The exploration of the true nature of jhorun," Thaden answered, gazing affectionately at his racks of vials. "I have researched and cataloged hundreds."

"As you can plainly see before you," Warrick added, gesturing to the racks of multicolored ampules.

"How often do you acquire new ones?" Rhenyon asked, curious in spite of himself.

Thaden walked over to the racks and carefully selected a

golden vial. Turning to face his audience, he held the amber-colored container between two fingers.

"This is one of my favorites," the wizard announced. "I harvested this just yesterday." He smiled maliciously. "Let me ask you something. Has anyone noticed if the Lentarian queen has been acting peculiar lately?"

The newly freed prisoners shuffled uncomfortably from foot to foot. They looked amongst their fellows to see if anyone had anything to say. Rhenyon, Steve, and Sarah, however, had all given a slight jerk. Fortunately, Thaden was sharing a conspiratorial smile with his assistant.

"I was in R'Tal just yesterday," Rhenyon said slowly, briefly surprised that he wasn't fabricating any lies. "I saw the queen. She did not appear to have fallen ill."

"Then she is masking her condition well. This is her jhorun," Thaden gloated, twirling the ampule between his thumb and forefinger. He briefly unsealed the vial and gently inhaled before resealing the crystal vessel. "A very powerful manifestation of veracity, if I am not mistaken."

"But the queen still has her jhorun!" Steve protested, eyes locked on the small vial.

"Methinks not. Not while I hold this. Besides," Thaden gestured dismissively, "by now her son has returned to see to his mother's jhorun."

"The little boy prince is not in the kingdom," another man piped up. "He was sent away nigh a year ago to live with his protectors. It is said they come from another world."

"Rest assured, the boy *has* returned."

The wizard spoke with such finality that all heads swiveled in his direction, waiting for an explanation. When none was forthcoming, Rhenyon gave a small cough.

"What interest could you possibly have in the likes of a small boy such as he?" one man asked, cowering moments later when the wizard's full attention fell upon him. "I mean, er, he's just a boy!"

"That boy is more important than even he realizes."

While his master tried to staunch the unending flow of questions without revealing any confidential information, Warrick rested a hip on one of the racks of vials, anxiously waiting to be dismissed for the day. He was eagerly looking forward to an ale or two, hoping it would calm his nerves. Smiling with anticipation, he fidgeted on the rack, causing several vials to softly clink together. Thaden threw a disapproving frown in his direction. With a scowl, the wizard returned his attention to his audience.

Standing near the back of the group, Steve continued to fume as he glared at the golden vial. He risked a look over at his wife, who was slowly gazing about the room. Rhenyon, too, was staring hard at the vial containing the queen's jhorun. He didn't look very happy, either. Steve's gaze returned to the pewter goblet, watching intently as it was returned to its holding place nestled in the heart of the largest rack of vials.

Clink.

Steve's attention returned to the dude in blue. The wizard had just scowled again. An idea was starting to form. Clearly Shardwyn's son didn't like anyone messing with his beloved vials. Tired of standing idly by while this arrogant schmuck gloated over the queen's misfortune, Steve decided it was time to see just what kind of a pest he could make of himself. Bringing his levels of jhorun up to full strength, his eyes slowly dropped until he was staring at Warrick's right foot.

No fire, no smoke.

Within moments Warrick was fidgeting even more, uncertain why his foot was suddenly hot. More vials clinked together, rewarding him with yet another scowl from his master.

Doing his best not to smile, Steve applied the same amount of heat to the other foot while keeping the first one at the same temp. Beads of sweat were forming on the skinny dude's brow. Excellent. Steve's eyes moved to Warrick's belt. There was a small dagger just visible on his waist.

Within moments, the surface temperature of the knife had increased to a point where it could be felt through several layers of clothing.

No turning it red. We must not attract attention.

The dagger obediently stayed the same color, giving no indication it was now hot enough to administer a burn if touched.

Nervously shifting from foot to foot, Warrick could not get comfortable. He had broken out in a sweat, his feet were hot, and as a result, he had shifted uneasily against one of the master's racks of stored jhorun. After the vials had clinked twice more, Thaden turned. The wizard regarded him coldly.

"Problem?"

"My apologies. I am fine."

Thaden turned to his new henchmen.

Clink.

The young wizard turned back to his apprentice, his patience rapidly dwindling.

"Really?"

"My most humble apologies."

"Be still. And silent."

"Of course."

Clink.

"I do not recall ever being this warm in here."

"Because it is not. Be silent."

Steve grinned, moving behind Rhenyon to conceal his smile. He waited a few more minutes before peering cautiously around his companions. Sweating profusely, the dude in blue was now acting like he had ants in his pants. Perfect. What else could he do?

Steve looked back at all the colorful crystal vials. So every one of those things represented someone's jhorun? This was unacceptable. He had to do something! Look at all of them! How many jhoruns had this guy stolen? How many lives had Thaden personally destroyed because of this obsession of his? He had to be stopped!

"Don't even think about it," Sarah softly warned, squeezing her husband's hand tightly.

"What? I wasn't gonna do anything."

"Bull. I know that look. You can't."

"Why not?"

"Would you want someone to steal your jhorun and then destroy it? We might be able to locate their original owners."

He froze. Dammit. That made sense. If there was a chance, albeit a very slim one, they really should see if they could track down and locate the owners of all these jhoruns.

If his powerful elemental jhorun were to be taken from him, he'd sure as hell want it back, too. He sighed. Fine. Destroying the racks of vials was out.

"What do you think? Think you can snag all of them?" Steve asked, turning to look at the multiple racks of vials.

Sarah regarded the vials, head swiveling slowly as she inspected the racks. Slowly she nodded. "You're really going to do this, aren't you?"

"I have to. I owe it to Mikal's parents."

Sarah sighed. "I hope you know what you're doing. As for them," she looked pointedly at the vials and smiled at her husband, "where should I put them?"

"We need a safe place where they won't be trampled."

"I can put them in our room back at the castle. Would that work?"

"Perfect. Be ready," Steve warned his wife while simultaneously nudging Rhenyon in the ribs.

"For what?" Rhenyon whispered back.

"We're taking the jhorun. All of it. My guess is Twinkletoes there ain't gonna like it too much."

Rhenyon's head swiveled to give Sarah an appraising stare. "You can teleport all of them at the same time?"

"I believe so," Sarah answered, turning to regard the hundreds of vials again. "There are a lot of them, but they're small. I might have to do it in a couple of batches."

"If you do, then you're gonna have to make it quick."

"Ya think?"

"Here, take these."

Steve passed two of his power crystals to his wife.

"Just in case."

"Thanks. Ready when you are."

Rhenyon shook his head.

"Do you think it wise to confront this wizard?"

Steve turned to his friend. "We can take him."

"He's a wizard," Rhenyon insisted.

"Trust me, pal, we can take him. Besides," Steve persisted, "if things go south, then Sarah can jump us out of here."

"I still think it unwise, but I am ready."

"Okay, here we go. One distraction coming right up."

Steve glanced over at a shelf lined with books and then back at the fire in the hearth. That should do nicely. Focusing his jhorun on the blazing fire, he sent a brutal dose of heat to one of the burning logs. The added boost instantly broke the log apart, the exposed sap crackling merrily. He created a small spark inside the fire and jumped it over to the shelf.

"Watch out, fool!" Thaden cried, giving Warrick a not-so-subtle kick in the pants. "Put that out!"

Snatching a leather canteen from the surface of one of the work tables, Warrick moved to extinguish the glowing spark. Uh, oh. The spark had just caught the closest book on fire.

"Take it off the shelf before anything else catches fire," Thaden instructed. "Be quick about it!"

Warrick hastily snatched the burning book from the shelf before any others could catch fire. He blinked. Right before his very eyes another book had caught flame. Pulling the second tome off the shelf, he moved to toss it into the hearth when another book caught. Then another. And another.

"Master! The books are all burning! I cannot stop them!"

The wizard impatiently gestured with his right hand. A powerful gust of frigid air materialized out of nowhere and lashed at the burning shelf. The burning books were unaffected. Thaden blinked in confusion as he again directed the blast of air at the shelf of books. Again, the flames refused to be extinguished. He slowly faced his new recruits, his eyes narrowing.

"Fire thrower! I know you are here! Show yourself, coward!"

"You call me a coward, you pathetic, sniveling, wannabe excuse of a wizard?"

"I am the strongest wizard you will ever encounter! And the last! No one can escape my wrath!"

"I'm shaking in my boots. Hey, here's something for you. Turn around and tell me if you notice anything wrong with this picture."

Thaden turned and gasped with shock. His vials! His beloved collection of jhorun was gone. Every last one! Nothing but empty shelves met his eyes.

"What manner of trickery is this?" Thaden cried, staring in shock at the empty racks. "This is impossible! You cannot have stolen my vials! What manner of illusion is this?"

Steve stepped out from behind the group of terrified men and locked eyes on the wizard.

Thaden stared for a moment and then laughed out loud. It sounded forced.

"You are the fire thrower? I expected more. No matter. You have been a pathetic thorn in my side long enough and it is time to have it extricated. Mercilessly."

"Figured it out yet, dumbass?"

Thaden quizzically cocked his head. "Figured what out?"

"That your precious jhorun is gone. You think I've hidden it? Hah! You're a bigger moron than I gave you credit for."

Thaden bristled with anger. "Do you actually think you will make it out of here alive?"

"Alive and kicking," Steve confirmed, still glaring at the wizard. "Think you can freeze me solid? Think again. Oh, as long as we're officially dropping all pretenses, I have something for you, compliments of the queen."

"And that would be —?"

Twin jets of fire rocketed straight toward the wizard, forcing him to dive for cover behind one of his own work tables.

Seeing red, Steve took stock of the various implements in the wizard's lair. Hands ignited, he shot a glance behind him at the terrified group of ex-prisoners.

"Beat it. Don't stop, just keep running. Go find your king and beg his forgiveness."

Without the merest whisper of complaint, the group of prisoners bolted from the chamber, clambering up the stairs two at a time in a frantic bid to distance themselves from the battling wizard and fire thrower. The last man up the stairs paused long enough to slam the heavy door shut behind them.

In the short amount of time that Steve had issued his warning, Thaden had summoned up the strongest blast of magically enhanced, super-cooled air that he could manage, and flung it straight at the fire thrower.

"Watch out!" Rhenyon called from behind an overturned table.

"Steve!" Sarah screamed out. "Look out!"

A mini iceberg instantly formed in the exact spot where Steve had been standing.

"So, who else do I have the pleasure of eliminating?" Thaden cackled, slowly emerging from behind an overturned table. "Did I hear a woman's voice? Would you be the other Nohrin then?"

"Say nothing, milady," Rhenyon whispered to Sarah, physically pushing her behind him.

"You have until I find you to return my vials to me, teleporter," Thaden called out. "If you do not, then your fate will be that of the fire thrower."

The crack echoed like gunfire in the enclosed chamber. Thaden whirled around to stare at the huge block of ice. Jagged chunks were cleaving off and falling to the ground. The wizard continued to stare in shock as he watched the massive block of ice rapidly shrink right before his eyes. In just a few seconds, the remaining slab broke apart and fell away.

"Is that the best you can do?"

Several cabinets across the room burst into flame. Steve took a few steps toward the shocked wizard.

"You probably learned that one from your dad, huh?"

The shelf of books that had been previously extinguished reignited.

"Didn't work on me when your dad tried and it sure as hell won't work when a little peon like you would try, either."

Thaden's personal desk erupted into flames.

Diving behind his swiftly charring desk, Thaden yanked out several drawers, frantically dumping their contents onto the ground. Snatching a miniature sword from the debris, Thaden murmured an incantation and flung the tiny weapon at Steve.

The toy sword rapidly grew in size until a five foot long, two-handed broadsword was flying straight at him. Steve ducked, but then realized he didn't have to as the sword abruptly vanished, reappearing moments later sunk deep into a wooden support beam a few feet away.

Uttering a string of curses, Thaden scanned the room,

searching for the teleporter. He spotted her hiding behind a pillar next to another peasant. He recalled a spell that could temporarily impart a state of paralysis to everyone in a twenty-foot radius. He began to chant.

The fireball appeared out of nowhere and slammed into the table he was crouching behind, breaking his concentration. The blast had missed his head by only a fraction of an inch. Cursing, Thaden tipped over an adjacent table and crouched behind it, only to have a second chaser slam into it, reducing that table to charred splinters. About ready to bolt for the nearest cover, the young wizard caught sight of a familiar object sitting unobtrusively on the floor. With a shout of triumph, he grabbed the small leather pouch and pulled out an oddly misshapen figurine.

Watching intently from behind her pillar, Sarah gasped with shock as she recognized the object that would rapidly become another drakyr. She did not want to battle with another demon, thank you very much. Sarah teleported the pouch—and the figure—out of Thaden's grasp, drawing a squawk of outrage from the wizard. She hastily dropped the figurine back into the pouch and tied it securely. She passed the pouch to Rhenyon.

"Here, you take this thing. I want nothing to do with it."

"What is it?"

"One of those demon things. Thaden was trying to invoke another one."

"Wizards be damned!" He took the pouch and dropped it into one of his outer pockets. "Remind me to give this to Shardwyn when we see him next. Do not let me forget about it. I do not want to carry this around, either."

"Will do."

Several small explosions drew their attention back to the battle between wizard and fire thrower. Thaden was sprinting across his own work area with a large, fiery orb in hot pursuit. Steve grinned as Thaden dove behind several fallen shelves, narrowly avoiding being struck by his chaser. Damn, almost got him that time.

"I gotta tell you, I'm having a blast. How about you?"

"You will rue the day we ever met!" Thaden angrily

retorted, desperately searching for something else in his arsenal that might incapacitate the fire thrower.

CLANG!!! The metallic impact echoed loudly throughout the chamber.

Curious, Steve slowly moved toward the overturned table that Thaden had been crouching behind. A large shield was still rocking from side to side, a significant dent visible near the center. Cautiously peeking around the table, Steve snorted with laughter as Thaden was just now regaining his feet and nursing a bloody nose. Startled, he looked back at his wife. Sarah grinned back at him, giving her husband a smug *yep, that was me* look. His wonderful wife had just used her jhorun to take a shot at the wizard. He made a mental note to try and avoid having any arguments with her in the future. He knew he would end up losing.

"Nice shot!" Steve called out.

"Thanks!"

"How's that feel, sport? Nose a little tender? Maybe you'd like us to—" Steve hesitated. He could now hear a soft buzzing noise growing steadily louder. Covering his ears had no effect. Now what was the wizard trying?

"What's the matter with him?" Sarah whispered from across the room, watching as her husband covered his ears for the second time.

"It has to be the assistant," Rhenyon scowled, his eyes darting about the room, searching for Warrick. "I will wager he's trying to implant a suggestion into Steve's mind. Wait here, milady. I have to help Sir Steve. Promise me you will remain here."

"I promise. Go help him!"

Steve shook his head. A major headache was brewing. "Really? Giving me a headache is what you're resorting to now?"

Ignoring the fire thrower's continued taunts, Thaden hissed with frustration.

"Why is he not surrendering?" Thaden crouched down lower behind an overturned table. "Just get him to turn around! Think you can make him do that one simple task?"

Gritting his teeth as he concentrated with all his might,

Warrick planted the desire to face the other direction. The fire thrower hesitated, shook his head, and moved off. In the wrong direction.

"Why is it not working, master?" Warrick whined. "I am giving him the order to turn around and he will not!"

"Be silent! He must have some type of enchantment about him that is immune to subliminal command. You will have to create a diversion."

"Whatever for, master? You can create a much better diversion than I!"

"I have to retrieve my goblet," Thaden whispered, eyeing the one intact non-burning rack. "I cannot let it be destroyed."

"Can you not summon the cup from here? Must we venture into the open?"

"That rack has been enchanted against teleportation. Even I cannot teleport it out until the compartment is opened."

The spreading fire hit a cabinet of various chemicals. A series of rapid-fire explosions broke out as several highly flammable potions caught fire.

"Quickly now! Create a diversion!"

"What would you have me do? I cannot face the fire thrower! My commands do not work on him!"

"Then make for the door!" Thaden hissed. "Think you can handle that? Draw his attention away from me! Go now or so help me I will give you an udder from a bolger!"

Thaden pushed him into the center of the room. Warrick stared in shock as the witless brother from before, Jay, stood about ten meters away. This was the fire thrower? Clearly, he hadn't recognized him. After only a few seconds of shocked silence, Warrick bolted for the door while Steve held out his right arm, slowly rotating it until his palm was facing up. Another large fiery orb appeared.

As Warrick continued to scramble toward the passageway leading up, he risked a glance backwards. The fire thrower was pursuing, moving further and further away from his master. Excellent! Expecting to be pelted with a fireball at any moment, Warrick fumbled with the bulky latch, finally pulling the massive door open. He briefly thought he might be able to manage an escape when something slammed into him from his left, knocking the wind clean out of him. Hitting the stone floor with a bone-jarring thud, Warrick was shocked to discover that he had forgotten about the first brother. Before he could even fathom what was happening, his arms and legs were immobilized.

"Untie me at once!" Warrick demanded, implanting the suggestion at the same time.

Rhenyon hesitated, and then moved to untie the ropes binding Warrick's hands together. Suddenly Rhenyon's vision blurred as some type of liquid was splashed into his face. He smacked his lips. Ale!

"Still with me?" Sarah asked, dropping the mug on the ground. "You'll hate yourself if you let him go. Trust me."

Rhenyon snorted. "I would do no such thing."

"Then why are you untying his hands?"

Shocked, Rhenyon stared at his hands as they were indeed in the process of untying the prisoner's ropes.

"Lady Sarah, you have my thanks. Watch me closely. If I start to do something else I normally would not do, you have my full permission to do whatever it takes to snap me out of it."

"You got it. Just remember that you asked for it."

"Agreed. Try anything like that again, fool," he angrily hissed to Warrick, "and I personally guarantee you will not live through it. Do we understand one another?"

Warrick's terrified eyes blinked several times. He nodded slowly.

A sudden movement drew Sarah's attention back to the room with all the burning furniture. Thaden had his back to them, facing the one rack that wasn't burning.

"Hon! Behind you!"

Still holding the chaser, Steve twisted and threw the fireball at the same time. The flaming orb streaked straight toward the wizard's back. Thaden risked a glance over his shoulder and cursed. He only had a moment before the speeding fireball would strike its target. Fortunately, he only needed one.

The chaser slammed into the racks and exploded,

decimating all three sets of wooden shelves. When the smoke cleared, Steve cursed with disgust.

"He took the damn cup. Look! It's empty. Dammit! Even that dude in blue is gone."

A loud clamoring began outside the chamber and grew steadily louder. Apparently, the residents of the castle had finally noticed that all was not well was down in their dungeon. The clanking of heavily armed soldiers could be heard descending the stairs as fast as they could.

"Hon, you need to get us out of here!"

The first group of soldiers burst into the chamber just as Sarah snatched Steve's arm, and then Rhenyon's, and ducked out of sight. The world tilted sideways as the scene shifted. Now they were standing in a dark hallway lit with only a few flickering torches on the walls. A row of at least twenty cells stretched away into the distance before being swallowed by the darkness.

"Ok, so where are we now? I don't remember this place."

Sarah blinked as she looked around. She hadn't realized how tired she was. Teleporting over two hundred vials at the same time was more draining than she had originally thought possible.

"Son of a biscuit eater." She frowned. This was not where she wanted to go. "Looks like another dungeon."

"Well, this has to be a place you've been to before, right?"

"Ordinarily I'd agree, however, does this look familiar to you?" Sarah fumbled in her pocket searching for one of the power crystals. If she didn't recharge soon, she was going to fall asleep.

Steve and Rhenyon both looked around.

"We have not been here before, milady."

"I think I know why. I haven't had a chance to recharge my jhorun yet. Blindly jumping with two additional people, after moving all those vials, is apparently beyond me."

"Are those things in our room now?" Steve wanted to know.

"They should be safe and sound in Castle R'Tal," Sarah confirmed, sighing heavily. Her exhausted jhorun was starting to shut down, ready to take a nap. She was more than inclined to let it.

Steve passed her a charged mimet. "Use this."

"I still have the two you gave me earlier. I'll use one of them. Provided I can find them."

There. Her jhorun restored, Sarah looked around. "Okay, let's get out of here. I want to —"

"Who—who's there?" a voice softly called out.

All three of them froze. Rhenyon recovered first.

"Who speaks? Where are you?"

A disheveled girl of about fifteen appeared at the bars of a cell about twenty feet away.

Sarah hurried over to the girl. The poor thing was filthy. Under all that grime she was probably very pretty.

"Let me guess. You're Nala, aren't you?"

The girl gasped with shock.

"How do you know my name?"

"Because I'm that good. Come on, we're going to get you out of here."

The girl received another shock as the stranger vanished right before her eyes only to reappear moments later standing right next to her! With the strange woman holding her arm, the cell bars vanished.

"What happened? Where—"

"Trust me, don't ask. Ready? Keep quiet. We're leaving. Right now."

Taking Rhenyon's arm in her left, the terrified girl's in her right, and with Steve leaning in and grasping her hands, the four of them vanished, appearing moments later in a small cell with a barred window that was missing several bars. Apparently, the tarp covering evidence of their tampering had fallen.

"Beautiful," Steve observed, squatting down to retrieve the piece of burlap. "We're back in Myrn."

Sarah rose up on her tiptoes to look through the window.

"Okay, Nala, think you can take it from here? Can you make it home on your own?"

The shocked girl stared the window. "You want me to leave through that? And then what am I supposed to do?"

"What do you mean what are you supposed to do?" Steve

asked, annoyed. "You go home, that's what. I'd lay low for a while, too. That's what Harlen said he was gonna do."

"You know Harlen?" the girl asked, hopeful.

"Yep. We helped him escape, too. Now listen. Can you make it home or not?"

The girl's eyes filled. She shook her head.

Oh, give me a break, Steve thought angrily, turning to the others. "Now what? We can't leave her here."

"We find his shop and drop her off there," Sarah suggested. "Come on, we need to go!"

Steve sighed. "Okay, okay, fine." He knocked his knuckles against the stone wall. "Can you take us to the other side of this?"

"For the same reason as before, no. I'm not going to take that chance."

Exasperated, Rhenyon dragged several of the crates over to the window. In just a few seconds he had pulled himself out of the cell.

"You cut through those bars?" Nala asked, bewildered. "How could you do that?"

Steve briefly ignited his hands and smiled at the girl. "Because I'm that good, too. Okay, your turn. Get going."

Sarah followed, with Steve bringing up the rear. Once the four of them were standing on the other side, Sarah looked back into the cell. Using her jhorun, she lifted the burlap back into place, blocking their escape once more. It was inevitable that the heavy fabric would again fall to the floor, but by that time they should be far away from this place.

"Okay, how the hell did you do that?"

"Tell you when we make it back."

"So how're we supposed to find this guy?"

"We must find the Quad, remember?" Rhenyon said, looking around the dense forest. "Once we find the town center, we must then look for a group of four distinct trees, and then look for a blacksmith shop. It should be his."

Smiling, Nala turned to the commander. "Aye, that's right. How did you know? Have you been there before?"

The three adults turned to the girl.

"You just said that you didn't know how to find your way."

"Well, I cannot tell you how to get there from right here," the girl clarified, rolling her eyes, "but once I am in town, I can find Har's shop. I am sure of it."

Shaking her head, Sarah smiled. "Stay here. I'm going to check that tavern and see if anyone is there." She vanished moments later.

"I would love that jhorun," Nala remarked, sighing wistfully.

"Who wouldn't?" Steve muttered.

The girl turned to the strange man. "Are you really a fire thrower?"

"Yep."

"And she was your wife?"

"Yep."

"Ah."

Steve finally turned to the girl. "Ah? What's that supposed to mean?"

Nala had already turned to Rhenyon. "And are you—"

"Married, aye."

Nala sighed. Sarah appeared moments later.

"The tavern is a no go. It's crawling with soldiers. They are searching everywhere. You guys, I think they are looking for us. We have got to get out of here. Please? Let's get going. I found some place else we can go."

Five minutes later they were peering cautiously through the trees at the outskirts of the village. The sun had already set, but there were still people milling about. Steve guessed it would be too dark to see in about fifteen minutes.

"So where do you think—"

"Bet we're looking for that." Sarah pointed off to the left. "Come on. That's got to be the Quad."

About fifty feet away, situated next to a row of shops, were four gnarled birch-type trees that had all twisted together and then grown upward as one unique trunk. Not ten feet away was a tidy shop with a small wooden sign hanging out front with a picture of an anvil on it.

"Oh, look," Nala observed, smiling. "There it is."

Another commotion sounded nearby. More soldiers were entering the village and fanning out.

"Hurry!" Sarah grabbed her husband's hand and pulled him up to the door of the blacksmith. Taking a couple of moments to familiarize herself with the layout of the workshop by peering through the front window, she cast a quick glance around to make sure no one was watching. With the coast clear, she hooked her right arm back through Rhenyon's, grabbed Nala's with her left, and waited for her husband to take her hand. Once inside the shop, Sarah softly called out to their new friend.

"Harlen, are you here?"

A timid voice answered from the darkness.

"Who's there?"

"It's me, Zia."

Harlen's ashen face appeared out of the shadows.

"Zia! I thought you might be soldiers. Glad I am to see you out of that dastardly —"

Harlen trailed off as he noticed his wife's sister standing quietly nearby.

"Nala! Thank the powers that be, you are safe! How did you ever manage to—"

"Harlen," Sarah interrupted, snapping her fingers to get his attention, "we can't stay. We have to leave. Right now. Nala, are you going to be okay?"

"She will be fine," Harlen assured them, moving to put his arm around the young girl, but then whipping it away as his nose finally reported in with its own status report.

"Okay, you can take it from here."

"What's the rush?"

Someone knocked on the front door. After a few moments, the knocks increased in frequency until they thought the door would be knocked off its hinges.

"Tenants of the blacksmith shop, are you in there? Open up in the name of the king!"

"Everyone be silent!" Harlen whispered, noting with alarm that the fire thrower had ignited his hands. "All the windows are shuttered. From the outside we appear to be closed."

"Well, if we are—"

Rhenyon surged forward to clap a hand over the girl's

mouth, cutting her off instantly.

"Nala!" Harlen hissed furiously. "Shh!"

Whoever was at the door pounded a few more times then moved off to the next shop.

Rhenyon used his free hand to yank Harlen over to where he was standing with the witless girl. Taking the blacksmith's hand in his own, the commander took his left hand off of Nala's mouth only to replace it with Harlen's.

"Keep her silent. We must be off."

"We're getting out of here. Now. Everyone ready?"

"If I didn't know better, I'd say they were following us."

Sarah angrily turned to her husband.

"Just now figured that out?"

"But how? How are they—"

Sarah shushed him as the shopkeeper vanished into the far recesses of his shop, dragging the struggling girl with him. They all heard a door open and close in the distance.

Before the guards outside could smash their way inside, Sarah lunged forward, grabbing both Steve and Rhenyon's hands. Once more, the world tilted sideways and the three of them lost their balance before slamming into a solid, immovable object.

"Ow! Son of a—" Steve trailed off as the three of them slowly got to their feet. "Ummm …"

Rhenyon rose painfully to his feet.

"Where is this? Where are we now, Lady Sarah?"

Sarah had clapped her hands over her mouth.

Alarmed, Rhenyon unsheathed his sword, the striking blue blade sparkled in the bright sunlight. "Where are we?"

Steve walked over to the closest window and peered outside at the beginnings of an enormous Victorian garden.

"We're home. Our home," he clarified, looking with amazement at his wife. "You just teleported the three of us back to our world!"

"This is your world?" Rhenyon asked, joining Steve at the window. "How is that possible?"

The two men turned to give Sarah an appraising stare.

"Very impressive, milady."

"Nice going, my dear!"

"Don't praise me yet. Anyone have a spare key to get back?" Their smiles slowly melted away.

"I do not carry a key to your portal," Rhenyon quickly pointed out.

"Mine is back in our quarters," Steve added.

"I don't have mine, either," Sarah confirmed.

"Hey, you got us here. Can't you just take us back!"

"How? I've been trying to teleport something from our world to Lentari and back again ever since I first teleported that key a year ago. I haven't had any luck."

"Use a power crystal, milady," Rhenyon suggested, pointing at Steve. "Recharge and see if you can find a way to return us. You might have to send just one of us to retrieve your key so that we can use the portal to return to the castle."

"How does that help me?" Sarah asked crossly, rubbing her temples. She was getting a headache. "Whether it's one person or three, it doesn't matter. I just can't visualize where I'm going, so I can't …"

Sarah trailed off as she suddenly realized why she was unsuccessful in transporting between worlds. She hadn't been able to bring up a mental picture of her intended destination. She closed her eyes. There, see? She tried to visualize the Antechamber, yet no pictures formed. She knew full well what the room looked like, of course, but for some reason, she just could not summon a picture of that room. Whenever she jumped somewhere, she always had to be able to visualize the location in her head. Something was blocking her. But what?

"Why are you frowning?" Steve asked. "What's wrong?"

"I just figured out why I can't teleport to Lentari from here, or vice versa. I can't picture the scene in my head."

"Why not? You been there many times now."

"No kidding. Hadn't thought of that. Thanks."

Steve remained silent, biting his tongue. No sense in poking the bear. If his wife said she couldn't picture something in her head, then she couldn't.

"Is something blocking your visions, milady?" Rhenyon asked, concerned.

"It's like I can't concentrate," Sarah said slowly, becoming angrier as she thought about the reason why she couldn't teleport. Here they were, in their world, when they really needed to get themselves back to Lentari. Clearly, she was capable of doing it, but her mind kept wandering every time she asked it to picture a destination.

Realizing that she was indeed tired from the unexpected jump from Lentari, she retrieved the last charged mimet from her pocket and restored her jhorun. The tingles manifested instantly. Apparently her jhorun didn't like being balked, either. Stomping over to the closest chair, Sarah plopped down and closed her eyes.

Giving Steve a gentle nudge in his ribs, Rhenyon nodded in Sarah's direction. Steve slowly drew his thumb and forefinger across his lips, giving his friend the universally recognized 'zip your lips' gesture. Rhenyon nodded. It would seem they were supposed to wait for something to happen.

"Whatever is blocking her is seriously pissing her off," Steve whispered to the commander.

"I noticed."

"Give her a moment to figure it out."

"Think she will?"

"Will what?"

"Ascertain why she is unable to teleport."

"Without a doubt. She's a smart girl. Check it out. Her eyes are closed. That means she's doing some serious concentrating. I know she can do this. After all, we're here, aren't we? We just have to wait and see."

Ten minutes later, as he and Rhenyon fidgeted from leg to leg, Sarah suddenly smiled. Her eyes were still closed, but at least she looked happy about it.

"Figure something out?" Steve asked, using as gentle of a voice as he could muster.

"I think I've got it," Sarah reported.

"Do you think you can get us back now?"

"Yes. If I focus every scrap of attention I have, and if you two can keep quiet, then I'm able to conjure an image of Lentari. Let's try it now. When I'm ready, I'll hold my hand out."

Steve nodded.

Sarah smiled again. An image of a large, bustling inn appeared. A burly, heavyset man was behind the counter joking amiably with several patrons. It was Thacken! This had to be Donlari! Well, not her first choice, but it would do.

"I've got it. Let's go."

Her husband timidly approached, followed closely by Rhenyon. Steve carefully took his wife's left hand. Keeping her eyes closed, Sarah held out her right. However, when no one took it, her head turned in that direction.

"Who's not holding on? Come on! If I lose this image, I'm going to be uber pissed."

Rhenyon shot a nervous glance at Steve and mouthed, *is it safe?*

Steve grinned and nodded his head.

Rhenyon leaned forward and took her hand. "When you are ready, Lady Sarah."

"Why are you two acting so nervous?"

"No reason. Just afraid for our lives," Steve muttered under his breath.

Sarah swung her right hand at her husband, momentarily forgetting she was holding Rhenyon's. The combined force from the two of them knocked Steve clean on his butt. Doing his best not to smirk too much, Rhenyon offered their fallen companion an arm up.

"My apologies, Sir Steve."

"Yeah, yeah, don't sweat it. Let's go."

The great room in Thacken Lodge was filled to capacity. Virtually every table in the inn was jammed full of peasants and soldiers, all joking and laughing amongst themselves. Bolli was in her element. With a smile on her face, she took orders for ale, sheppar pie, more ale, water, and a myriad of other minor requests.

Belying the laws of nature, Bolli stacked plate after plate onto her two best serving girls before loading up herself. She prided her sense of balance, so much so that she and her girls were able to deliver a dozen meals all at the same time to the large table full of very appreciative soldiers.

Smiling graciously, Bolli turned and gasped with shock as three people appeared out of thin air and stumbled to the ground.

"Man, those landings really stink."

"Hey, you try to jump that far and let's just see if you can do it any better."

Bolli smiled with delight as she recognized the first stranger who regained his feet. She looked at the woman he was helping up. Then her eyes fell upon the man rising stiffly to his feet as well. His face was very well known. But not as much as the other two!

"Steve, Sarah! Welcome back to our lodge!"

"You remember us?" Sarah asked, bewildered.

"Remember you? You are the famous Nohrin! To think, we had the Nohrin stay a night right here in our own little inn!"

Stretching his sore back, Steve turned to the smiling innkeeper.

"Nice to see a friendly face. How have you been, Bolli?"

Sarah turned to Rhenyon, alarm clearly written on her face.

"We really need to go. I don't want them to find us."

Rhenyon leaned close. "Ylani soldiers? We are quite safe from them, I assure you."

"Think I'm the only teleporter? They were following us throughout Ylani. Who's to say they can't follow us here?"

Rhenyon slowly nodded. "Agreed, milady."

Noting a disturbance from across the room, Thacken ambled out from behind the counter. Pushing aside all the staring soldiers who were curiously snapping to attention, the brawny proprietor gave a shout of recognition.

"Steve! Sarah! How the ruddy hell are you? Listen up everyone! Our lodge's two most famous occupants have returned for a visit! Behold the Nohrin!"

Cheers went up as everyone present rose to their feet for a better look.

"Really, this isn't necessary," Steve began, but was cut off as Thacken took his hand and raised it high into the air.

"The Nohrin were discovered right here in our inn!"

"Only because I discovered them," Rhenyon muttered as he pushed his way through to the front of the group.

"People, I must take the Nohrin from you. We are on important business for the king. Lady Sarah, if you will kindly take us back to the castle?"

"Thacken, Bolli, it was good to see you guys. We'll come back for a visit when things aren't so hectic, okay?"

"We will keep you to your word, Steve. Go protect the prince!"

"You got it."

Steve turned to his wife as she handed the two spent mimets back to her husband and exchanged them for the charged crystal he offered. She recharged her jhorun back to full strength (again), and took each of their arms. Easily bringing up an image inside the massive fortress, she teleported the three of them back to their quarters inside Castle R'Tal.

Steve whistled. "Wow. Now that's an impressive sight."

Looking around their room, Rhenyon gasped with astonishment at the hundreds of vials that were now sitting on the bed, the chairs, scattered across the floor, etc.

"Now can we get to the Antechamber? Please? I want to be rid of this thing."

Steve turned to his wife.

"What thing? What's the matter? What's with all the urgency?"

"I'll tell you as soon as we get there. Please? We have to hurry!"

Stopping only to retrieve the golden ampule that he had spotted as soon as they arrived in the Nohrin's personal quarters, Rhenyon followed husband and wife as they ran from the room.

"One side! Emergency! Make way!" the commander called out in his most authoritative voice. He had a really good idea what was bothering Lady Sarah.

"Commander! I did not know you made it back already. May I have a word?"

Without stopping, Rhenyon turned to look behind him. There was his first lieutenant, Pheron.

"Lieutenant! There's no time. Find the king and tell him we are en route to the Antechamber. Hurry! Send for Shardwyn, too!"

"At once, sir!"

Ten minutes later, all three burst into the protected chamber, gasping for breath, and scaring ten years of life right off the king.

"Commander? Steve, Sarah! When did you return? What is the matter?"

"What the *hell* is going on?" Steve asked, bending over to catch his breath.

"Two squadrons, secure the Antechamber!" Rhenyon snapped out, barely winded. He turned to the king. "Sire, I recommend you raise the drawbridge and lower the portcullis. Secure the castle!"

"Do as he says!" Kri'Entu barked out as the flabbergasted soldiers eyed one another. "Secure the castle, immediately!"

Rhenyon turned to Sarah. "So *that's* how they were able to follow us. He is able to track it."

Sarah nodded.

"What are you two talking about?" Steve wanted to know.

"Milady, however did you manage to get it?"

Still gasping for breath, Sarah smiled as she withdrew the pewter goblet from beneath her parka.

Steve wheezed out a triumphant shout. "Omigod, that's awesome! I totally thought he took it and ran. Man alive, that dude is gonna be pissed!"

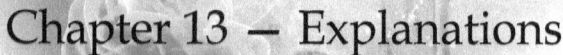

Chapter 13 — Explanations

Kri'Entu stared at the pewter goblet. "Is that—?"

Rhenyon nodded. "Aye, it is. Sire, I think it wise if Shardwyn joined us. I have sent Lieutenant Pheron to find him, but you might be able to locate him quicker. We have disturbing news that he needs to hear."

"Understood." The king motioned one of his staff over. "Have Shardwyn report to me at once."

The guard bowed low and exited the chamber.

"How disturbing?" Kri'Entu inquired, turning back to face the commander.

"The dark wizard is none other than his son."

The king whistled. "I knew he recognized that mark."

"My thoughts exactly, sire."

"Don't be too hard on him," Sarah implored, drawing the king's eyes to her own. "It's probably embarrassing for him and he was taking the time to confirm his suspicions."

"Understood, Lady Sarah. Nevertheless, he should have informed us."

"Sire," Rhenyon added, reaching into his tunic, "I am afraid the news continues to worsen. I believe this belongs to the queen." He handed the gold-colored vial to the king.

Kri'Entu studied the vial meticulously before handing it back.

"This is the queen's? Methinks not." The king handed it back. "I have never seen it before."

"Aye, you have," Rhenyon contradicted, pushing the vial back into the king's hands. "*That* is the queen's jhorun."

The king gasped as he stared at the small crystal vial.

"Are you certain?"

"You betcha," Steve confirmed, nodding his head. "That S.O.B. said it was his favorite jhorun he had collected thus far. Speaking of which, there are now over two hundred of those things up in our room. We swiped 'em all."

"If what Rhenyon says is true," Sarah added, nervously looking at the pewter goblet, "and Thaden was, in fact, tracking us by that thing, then he has to know where we are by now. We should bring those vials down here. I really don't want him to somehow get his hands on them again."

"Agreed, milady. Sire, Lady Sarah is correct. In the Nohrin's quarters are hundreds more of these vials, each containing someone's jhorun. We need to have them safely moved here as soon as possible."

"I concur, commander. See to it."

Rhenyon turned to gesture at the shadows along the far wall. One guard materialized out of the darkness and hurried over.

"Commander."

"Gather as many men as you need. In the Nohrin's quarters, you will find hundreds of these vials. Bring them all here, on the double. And be careful."

"I could just teleport them here," Sarah suggested.

"It drained you last time," Steve observed. "Let them get 'em."

Kri'Entu was nodding. "Aye, save your strength, Lady Sarah."

The sentry hurried off, commandeering several more guards just outside the Antechamber.

"Let me see if I understand you properly, Commander," the king said, slowly approaching the three of them. "Inside this vial is the manifestation of a person's jhorun?" Rhenyon nodded. "And," the king continued, "in their chamber are many more of these, clearly indicating he had been collecting the jhorun for an extended period of time?"

"He will want them back," Rhenyon observed, his left hand resting on Mythron's hilt. "He said so himself before we destroyed his lair."

"Perhaps you should oversee the transportation of the vials, commander," the king suggested softly.

Rhenyon's face turned grim, the hidden meaning of the suggestion coming through loud and clear. He nodded.

"Understood."

Once he had departed, Sarah finally sank down into one of the plush chairs, sighing heavily as she did.

"Are you alright, Lady Sarah?" Kri'Entu asked, also taking a seat. He motioned Steve to do the same.

"I've had to restore my jhorun several times, but I still feel drained. Jeez, what a trip."

"How did you manage to snag that thing?" Steve asked, hooking a thumb at the pewter goblet sitting on the small table before them.

"I took it as soon as he put it back in its holder."

"But I overheard him saying that the holder was supposed to be enchanted against teleportation?"

"That's what the dwarves said about all their enchantments, too, yet I still made it through."

"I, too, would like to know how you accomplished that," the king thoughtfully added.

"I'm so tired of having more questions than answers," Steve griped, standing up and beginning to pace. "For instance, why is it we can use our jhoruns where they aren't supposed to work? Why are we able to use mimets that have been charged by others? Why can our jhoruns —"

A door opened and closed in the recesses of the Antechamber. Shardwyn appeared, smiling at the Nohrin. He tipped his head to the king.

"Greetings o' rescuers of the Queen!" Oblivious to the

neutral stares he received from both Steve and Sarah, the wizard turned to the king. "You sent for me, sire?"

"I did, aye." Kri'Entu gestured at one of the empty chairs. "Have a seat, Shardwyn."

"Mmm, I believe I will. What can I do for…?" Shardwyn froze into a half-sitting position and gasped with shock as his eyes fell upon the small table. "It cannot be."

"You'd better believe it is," Steve added, sitting back down onto his chair, tapping his fingers absentmindedly.

"However did you get your hands on it?"

"It wasn't easy. Your son really didn't want to part with it."

Shardwyn hesitated, arms outstretched and ready to pick up the goblet. He sighed and sank down heavily onto his chair.

"Did you know your son was responsible for creating that?" Kri'Entu asked, indicating the cup.

The wizard sighed again and ran a hand through his hair.

"I had suspected, Your Majesty. I did not want to believe. Thaden has had a difficult life. This really should not surprise me."

Kri'Entu scowled. "You should have informed us you suspected your son. Withholding information such as that could have cost lives, Shardwyn."

The wizard refused to meet the king's eyes. Slowly, he nodded. "It was wrong of me to not share my suspicions. I beg your forgiveness."

"Fear not. We will give you a chance to redeem yourself."

"I will do whatever it takes to regain your trust. To regain everyone's trust."

With a smile, the king turned to Steve. He nodded in the wizard's direction. *Here's your chance. Take it.*

A smile formed. Steve nodded in comprehension.

"Perhaps you can clear a few things up for us."

The wizard smiled as he turned to the Nohrin.

"Ask away! I shall be more than happy to answer anything you wish to know!"

"Remember that you said that. Okay, first question. Why do our jhoruns work in our world when Tristan's does not?"

The smile melted away.

"Why can I teleport through the dwarves' barrier and apparently defeat the enchantments your son put in place to prevent teleportation?" Sarah asked, warming up. "Even he couldn't teleport the goblet out of its holder until the compartment it was resting in was opened. I know, he said so himself."

The wizard was silent as his eyes flicked between husband and wife.

"Why can the two of us use mimets that have been charged by other people when you told me specifically that it was impossible?"

"How was I able to teleport the first key from our world here last year?"

"Why is Thaden so fascinated with Mikal? He's not ever going to let this go. We heard that, too."

"Why is it I can look at a simple drawing and then I'm able to visualize the locale perfectly in my head, making it possible for me to teleport someplace I've never been to?"

With a satisfactory smile on his face, Kri'Entu leaned back in his chair.

Shardwyn took a deep breath.

"Good questions, they all are. I wish I could answer each and every one, but sadly, I cannot."

"What can you answer?" the king wanted to know.

Solemnly, Shardwyn leaned forward to pick up the goblet. Reverently, he turned it this way and that, all the while mumbling to himself before he finally looked up.

"Did he say how the goblet works?"

"Actually," Steve said, "he did. Didn't say much about it, but what he did say was that you only had to take a sip of any liquid from that cup and then the drinker's jhorun would be absorbed into the goblet itself, to be collected at a later date."

"Remarkable. Did he say anything else?"

"Well," Steve scratched his head. "I don't think you want to hear this, but he called you a charlatan. Said he knew about you giving my grandparents jhorun."

"As well he should. I told him."

"Said you got lucky and that you haven't been able to,

to… how did he phrase it, Sarah?"

"That he was 'unable to recreate his past success' I think," she answered.

"He said that, did he?"

"Yeah," Steve confirmed. "He said he purposely kidnapped several Lentarian citizens and stripped their jhorun from them just to see if you had been able to recreate whatever you did last time."

"Well, he is right," Shardwyn confirmed with a sigh. "I have not been able to tune a jorii that perfectly with a human since that night."

Kri'Entu sighed. He should have known the clever wizard would have found a way to tamper with the powerful jhorun enhancer. Thankfully, the kingdom's horde of power spheres was safely tucked away in the Nohrin's world so no one could ever be tempted to use one for their own personal gain.

"You used a jorii to give my grandparents a jhorun?" Steve asked, surprised.

"Aye," Shardwyn nodded. "By sheer happenstance I discovered that a jorii has a very specific type of energy signature, very similar to that of a human. I was able to adjust the jorii to match the energies of a person, and the result of the pairing was the creation of a jhorun, albeit a minor one."

"So why couldn't you perform the same experiment again when Tristan's jhorun was taken from him?" Steve asked.

"I tried, m' boy, believe me, I tried. I recreated everything from ambient temperature in my workshop down to the exact outfit I was wearing. Nothing. My son is right. I did get lucky. And until I can determine what I am doing wrong, then I am no better than he."

"I'm not interested in your pity party right now," Sarah snapped, rubbing her temples. A headache was forming and was threatening to go nuclear. She briefly considered trying her luck at teleporting a bottle of aspirin from Coeur d'Alene. "We want answers, Shardwyn. Did you know," Sarah sat up straighter in her chair, "that we just came back from our world? I jumped the three of us straight from Ylani to our home world! Not only that, none of us had a key, so I had to jump us from our house straight back here, *without a portal*."

"But that is impossible," the wizard breathed, the shock apparent on his wrinkled face.

"Yeah, I know it's supposed to be impossible," Steve interjected angrily. "That's what everyone keeps saying, yet she can clearly do it."

Kri'Entu cleared his throat, drawing everyone's attention to himself. "Shardwyn, I believe it is time, as the lady has indicated, for some explanations. What can you tell us about Lady Sarah's remarkable jhorun? How is it possible to teleport between worlds when you told me yourself that it was impossible?"

"By all reckoning, it should be impossible," Shardwyn insisted again. "I do not know, Your Majesty."

"Is there someone who would?" Sarah asked.

All eyes now shifted to the teleporters.

"Shardwyn, we keep pressing for information, and you keep saying you do not know. Who might have the answers we're looking for?"

The wizard was silent as he searched his memory for anyone else besides the person that had just sprang to mind.

The king leaned forward. "Well?"

Shardwyn mumbled his response.

Steve blinked. "What was that?"

The wizard stiffened. "The Strathos, celebrated key maker of the Kla Guur".

"The Strathos? Why have I heard that name before?" Steve turned to his wife. "Wasn't that another name for Maelnar?"

Sarah nodded. She looked back at the wizard. Why was he scowling?

"He often goes by that name, aye," Shardwyn confirmed, but then he slowly shook his head. "You will not have much luck persuading him to talk, however. He is one of the most tight-lipped dwarves I have ever had the misfortune of dealing with."

Confused, Sarah shared a look with her husband. "Tight-lipped? Maelnar? Are we talking about the same dwarf here?" She turned back to the wizard. "Does he have a son named Breslin?"

"Aye, he has six offspring. Five daughters and one son."

"Pssht," Sarah scoffed. "I can have him here in ten minutes. *And* I can guarantee he'll talk with us."

"I am sorry, milady," Shardwyn began. "We do not have a direct line of communication with the dwarves. It will take some time for a message to reach him, especially if he's in one of their subterranean cities, which I suspect he is."

"I need paper and a pen."

Bemused, the king himself walked over to his desk to retrieve the supplies Sarah had requested.

"What are you going to tell him?" Steve wanted to know.

"I'm going to politely ask him for some information Shardwyn has indicated he has. For example …" Sarah trailed off as she thought about what to write. With a smile, she composed her question, folded the paper, and sealed it inside the envelope that Kri'Entu had offered her.

Sarah closed her eyes and brought up an image of the council chamber in Borahgg, deep inside the Bohani Mountains. There was the scene, complete with the ornate table that she had admired last year. That would do. She deposited the letter directly on the table.

"Let's give them a minute or so to respond."

The door opened, admitting Rhenyon. He hurried to Steve's side and gave him a questioning look.

"Sarah sent a message to Maelnar. We're waiting for an answer."

"Ah."

The entire company, save one, sat with a smug smile while they awaited the key maker's response. Shardwyn's shocked eyes darted from Sarah's and back to the king's.

"Maelnar is a very important dwarf, milady. Do not be surprised if he is otherwise occupied."

"Somehow, I think he won't ignore me."

When the appropriate amount of time had elapsed, Sarah retrieved the envelope. Unfolding the paper inside, she silently read the response. She nodded, pleased.

"What? Sarah, what does it say?"

She held up the paper. "Curious as to what I asked?"

Steve nodded. "Well, yeah! Obviously!"

"Good. Hold that thought. I'll go get him and you can ask him yourself. Be right back." Sarah vanished.

"Maelnar is coming? Here??" Surprised, Shardwyn looked to see the king's reaction

Kri'Entu was sitting on a corner of his desk, hands clasped together in his lap with a smile on his face. The king nodded.

"Can Lady Sarah teleport all the way to Borahgg?"

Still smiling at the wizard, Steve nodded.

"Borahgg's a piece of cake. Didn't you hear her earlier? She jumped all the way from Ylani to our world, then from our world to here."

"With the two of us accompanying her," Rhenyon reminded them.

Steve snapped his fingers. "Right! Good point."

Sarah appeared in that moment, holding the arm of a very familiar dwarf.

"Now that is the way to travel, lass," Maelnar nodded, grinning his approval. "I did not feel a thing."

Releasing his grip on Sarah's arm, the elderly dwarf turned to the king. He bowed low.

"Kri'Entu. It has been many years, lad. You honor me by seeing me on such short notice."

Kri'Entu returned the bow. "Think nothing of it, master dwarf. It is we who are honored. You are welcome here as long as you wish to stay."

Steve and Rhenyon had both risen to their feet and approached their friend.

"Hey there, Maelnar," Steve remarked, genuinely glad to see the dwarf. "How's it going?"

Maelnar grinned as Steve approached. He gave the fire thrower a short bow. "Sir Steve, glad to see you again. Likewise, Captain."

"He's actually a commander now," Sarah supplied helpfully.

"Is he indeed? My apologies, Commander."

Rhenyon nodded in return.

Someone cleared their throat. Maelnar turned to regard the tall thin man behind the king.

"Wizard."

Shardwyn gave the tiniest of nods. "Dwarf."

"What's with you two?" Sarah asked, looking from the scowling wizard to the equally scowling dwarf. "Are you guys holding a grudge or something?"

"Your wizard there will still not admit he misidentified the Nohrin over thirty years ago."

Shardwyn scowled again, belying his normal jovial nature. "I still say they could have been, dwarf."

"Are you referring to my grandparents?" Steve asked, watching the wizard closely.

"Aye. The prophecy said that the Nohrin had to be two foreigners. The Scribes met that requirement," Shardwyn insisted.

"And how, exactly, could that have been changed, wizard?" the dwarf asked, moving to stand directly before the tall human. "They had been here for over thirty years with no signs of their own jhorun developing naturally. They were therefore *not* the Nohrin. You cannot deny that, lad."

The stubborn old man crossed his arms. "They could have been. We just did not give them enough time."

"Shardwyn," Steve interjected, as softly as he could, "We got our jhoruns within days of our arrival. Days. It just wasn't meant to be. Sarah and I have talked long and hard on this particular subject. Always the 'what if' scenario. Well, you know what? Let it go. We're here. They aren't. Let's move on, okay? Besides, Mikal wasn't even around at that time, so it couldn't have been them."

"Sir Steve is correct." Kri'Entu rose from his position on the desk to clap a hand on Shardwyn's shoulder. "Now is not the time to harbor a grudge. No one thinks differently of you. Let us all be seated. Hmm, it would appear we need another chair."

Also noticing they were one chair short, Rhenyon rose, intent on retrieving the plush chair he had spotted in the far corner of the chamber. Sarah laid a hand on his arm, drawing him up short.

"Allow me."

Bemused, Rhenyon sat back down while Sarah looked

over at the chair. Suddenly the recliner spun around to face their direction and then slid forward effortlessly to neatly join the rest. Nodding his thanks, Maelnar hopped up into the chair, slightly sinking down onto the plush cushion. The king was staring at her.

"I did not know you possessed telekinetic abilities, milady."

"Neither did I until I tried. Just another question I'm hoping to have answered. Well, not really a question," Sarah amended, smiling at her husband, "but maybe a misidentification of my jhorun."

Maelnar quizzically cocked his head. "How so, lass? You believe your jhorun is not teleportation?"

"I think teleportation is only one aspect of my jhorun. You wanted to know how I could move that chair?" Sarah asked, turning to her husband. "I view what I did as a form of teleportation. This time I asked my jhorun to keep the object in sight while it moved."

Once more the wizard's eyes opened wide. "A teleporter cannot simply make an object move about if they so desire!"

"How would you know, Shardwyn, until you try?"

"Because, milady," the wizard explained, "my father was a teleporter. A powerful teleporter. But even he could not teleport underground, and certainly not to a location he had never visited."

"What about moving something while keeping it visible?" Sarah wanted to know.

"My father was a teleporter, Lady Sarah. He could not move objects with his mind as you have so remarkably demonstrated."

"Maybe he could have if he'd tried," Steve suggested.

"After living a long, very full life, my father knew what his jhorun was capable of doing, young sir," Shardwyn quipped, perhaps harsher than he had intended. "Forgive me. I do not intend to be rude, I really do not. My father was a powerful teleporter. But that's all he was."

"So, then how can I look at a simple drawing and I'm able to visualize the scene in my head? So vividly that I can teleport to a place I've never been?"

Shardwyn shrugged helplessly and pointedly looked over at the dwarf. Maelnar was chewing thoughtfully on his pipe.

"What say you to this, master dwarf?"

"I would say that this is the strongest example of a teleportation jhorun that has ever been encountered."

"It's almost as if the lady has the aid of a jorii. Hmmm. Sir Steve, have you noticed anything unusual about your own jhorun?"

"Other than it working in our world? Or what about being able to recharge my jhorun using mimets that have been charged by someone else?"

Maelnar froze. He looked hard at Steve. "Say that again, lad."

"I said, why does our jhorun work in our world?"

"Nay, the other part."

"Right-o. Why can we recharge our jhoruns using mimets that have been charged by someone else?"

"Wizards be damned."

Shardwyn looked up.

"No offense, wizard."

"None taken, dwarf."

Maelnar nodded his head. "She did it. She said she would find a way and she did."

All of them leaned forward in their chairs.

"Excuse me?" Kri'Entu looked at Shardwyn, only the wizard was just as clueless as he was. "*Who* would find a way to do *what*?"

Lost in his own thoughts, Maelnar chuckled. "That explains much."

"It doesn't explain shit!"

Sarah turned to her husband and smacked him on the arm.

"Hon! Language!"

"Sorry. Pardon me." He turned to the dwarf. "Okay, you. Stop smiling and start talking. Explain yourself."

"My apologies, lad. I do not know why I did not think of her sooner."

"Who?" Sarah asked.

"A very powerful sorceress. Caladonia.

"Caladonia? I do not believe I have heard of her," Kri'Entu commented.

"Unsurprising, lad, as she died over five centuries ago."

"Caladonia," Shardwyn repeated, thinking hard. "I believe I have. If memory serves, she lived a life of seclusion by the sea. Her powers of premonition were unmatched then and are still so to this day."

"Premonition?" Suddenly understanding, Sarah nodded. "She's the one who made the prediction for the Bakkian, isn't she?"

Maelnar nodded, taking a goblet of ale from a serving girl who had just appeared. Swallowing loudly, the elderly dwarf sat back in his chair and studied the wizard.

"Didn't you ever wonder who made the premonition?" Noticing that Shardwyn had elected not to comment, the dwarf turned to Kri'Entu. "Haven't you ever asked yourself *whose* voice you were hearing when the premonition was read?"

"The Bakkian would only activate for those directly involved," Kri'Entu clarified. "We were therefore only able to hear the prophecy when Mikal touched the crystal. But aye, I have been curious."

The dwarf had taken a long swig of ale from his goblet when, once more, he hesitated.

"What did you say?"

"What part?" Kri'Entu wanted to know.

"Did you just say, 'the Bakkian would only activate'?"

"Aye. In order to hear the prophecy," Kri'Entu explained, "those directly involved had to be in physical contact with the Bakkian itself."

Maelnar stared a moment or two longer at the humans before chuckling to himself.

"I knew I was coming here to help clear up some confusion, but I had no idea the severity of said confusion."

"What do you mean?" Sarah asked, confused despite herself.

Maelnar ignored the question and, instead, turned to the king.

"Your Majesty, would you be so kind as to retrieve what

you believe to be the Bakkian, please?"

More confused than he cared to admit, Kri'Entu opened his private safe to pull out the familiar rusted chest. He gave it to the smiling dwarf.

"Are you telling us that this is not the Bakkian?" the king asked, bewildered.

"This," Maelnar said, plucking the crystal shield out of its holder, "is only the —"

Many years from now, it will come to pass …

"Not now, you blathering ninny." Maelnar pressed down on the crystal just so and it instantly fell silent.

Sarah jolted in her chair. "Wait. Wait a moment."

Steve turned to his wife. "What?"

"That thing is only supposed to reveal itself to those involved in the prophecy, right?"

Surprised, both Steve and the king turned to the dwarf.

"Why did it activate when you touched it?" Steve asked. "What role do you play in this?"

"I crafted it," the dwarf said, simply. "A minor role, but still a role nonetheless. It's just the vessel that holds Caladonia's premonition."

"Then what is the Bakkian?" Sarah asked.

"I believe it is finally time to use your key, Sir Steve."

Confused, Steve looked at the dwarf. "What does my key have to do with it?"

Maelnar hopped off his chair to retrieve the folded paper sitting on the table before them. Unfolding it, he read aloud the question Sarah had written down.

"Why does our green portal key take us to the middle of the forest from our home when it should take us back to the castle?"

The dwarf refolded the paper and placed it back on the table.

"That key takes you to that spot for a reason," Maelnar informed the two Nohrin. "Did you think I crafted a faulty key?"

"The thought had crossed my mind," Steve said under his

breath. He gave a lopsided grin when the dwarf looked his way. Maelnar chuckled.

"What's so special about that spot in the forest?" Sarah wanted to know. "There wasn't anything there."

"Ah, but there is," Maelnar contradicted, eliciting surprised looks from both of the Nohrin. "I am old. Were you to ask, I would be unable to answer how many years I can count. When you get that old, your memory starts to fade. That locale is too important to forget. So, I deliberately modified the key's destination to fall within range."

"Of what?" Kri'Entu, Steve, Sarah, Rhenyon, and Shardwyn all asked in unison.

"Caladonia's journal."

"What does it contain that's so important you'd go to those extremes to not forget its location?" Sarah wanted to know.

"All her research and notes pertaining to the Bakkian," the dwarf explained. "You wish to know more about the Bakkian and the nature of the Nohrin? Then you should start by asking the right question. For example, *what* is the Bakkian?"

"Enough questions." The king's statement silenced everyone. "We still have no answers. Maelnar, are you certain this journal will give us the information we seek?"

"Aye, Your Majesty."

"Very well. Sir Steve, may I have your green portal key? I will dispatch several squadrons to fetch it at once."

"Only the Nohrin can retrieve it," Maelnar cautioned, causing the king to frown.

"How do you know?" the king asked. All eyes turned back to the dwarf.

"Because only the Nohrin will be able to defeat the challenges she put in place."

"Challenges?" Rhenyon scoffed. "The Nohrin can easily defeat any challenges."

"While I appreciate the support," Steve began, clapping the commander on the back, "I'd appreciate all the help I can get."

"You have it," Rhenyon promised, glancing at the king

who nodded in agreement.

Always the pragmatic member of their group, Sarah caught the dwarf's attention. "What do you know of these challenges?"

"Only that it will take both of you to retrieve her journal."

"Wow, what's in this thing, anyway? The secrets of the universe?" Steve laughed at his own joke. No one else joined in. "Okaaaay. I'll shut up now."

Smiling fleetingly, Sarah turned back to Maelnar.

"What can we expect to find? I mean, can someone else find this journal and use its information for their own good?"

"Caladonia was a very meticulous sorceress," Maelnar informed them. "Anything she learned she noted in one of her many journals. She had shelves and shelves of them, lass. This particular journal details everything she learned about the young prince and the events leading up to his protectors' arrival."

Steve gave a visible start. "She specifically mentioned us? By name?"

"She mentioned your family," the dwarf clarified, drawing a gasp of shock from both of the Nohrin. "Remember lads, her jhorun was premonition. She could see how much danger the boy would be in so she did what was needed to facilitate your arrival. And that included describing how to link our world with yours."

"This journal explains all that? Can't you just tell us?"

"Do you not remember what I just said about age and memory?" Maelnar snorted, pulling out his pipe in the process. "Caladonia entrusted me with her journal, asking me to see to it that it falls into the proper hands. Together we fabricated obstacles that only the Nohrin would be able to overcome."

"Hah! So you do know what the challenges are," Steve accused. "Well, what are they?"

The dwarf smiled. "Over five hundred years, lad. Once you hit my age, see if you can remember what you were doing five centuries before."

"Okay, so what do you remember about my family?" Steve asked.

"Let me think." The dwarf finally coaxed a spark out of his chunk of flint. Blowing a smoke ring that refused to break, Maelnar turned to face Steve once more. "A hundred years ago, I remember a Lentarian soldier by the name of Luther —"

"Hey, Luther was the name of my great-grandfather!" Steve interrupted.

"Splendid. Now be quiet."

"Sorry."

"Luther recognized the importance of protecting this future boy, so when the request came for someone to willingly journey to another world, he volunteered, leaving all that he knew behind. In this new world, he constructed a portal, thereby linking that world with ours."

"Are you telling me," Steve began, staring hard at the dwarf, "that I'm part Lentarian? That this soldier and my great-grandfather are the same person?"

"Aye, unless you know of anyone else in your world who has a portal in their house?" Maelnar nonchalantly asked.

"So Luther created the portal. I had wondered about that," Sarah remarked. "How was he able to make that portal? I wouldn't think just anyone could do it."

"The knight was sent to the strange world equipped with all the necessary plans—and equipment—to make a return portal. However, it did not work."

"Sure it did," Steve countered. "We're here, aren't we?"

"Ah, but remember, young lad, what the prophecy said. Do you remember?"

"They had to be two foreigners," Sarah answered.

The dwarf's eyes lit up. "Excellent, Lady Sarah. By definition, two foreigners who were not born in Lentari. The soldier was no foreigner, so he was unable to use the new portal to return home."

"That's why my grandparents made it through. Both of them were foreigners."

"Precisely." Maelnar agreed.

Kri'Entu frowned. "It is just a portal. Could it not be simply activated and anyone could cross through?"

"All I can tell you, Your Majesty, is that Caladonia took

measures to ensure the Nohrin's arrival."

"The sorceress enchanted the portal?" Steve wondered aloud. "How was that possible? The portal was created after the sorceress passed away." He turned to his wife. "Right?"

Sarah shrugged. "Unless the plans Luther used to create the portal were drafted by the sorceress herself."

Heads were nodding.

"It is possible," the king conceded.

"So how did she manage to prevent the soldier from returning while allowing others to pass through?" Steve wondered aloud.

"If I were to venture a guess, I'd say that …"

"If she had the power to do that," Sarah speculated, interrupting the dwarf, "then she clearly had the means to see to it we retained our jhorun in our world. We could better protect Mikal if we had them, right?"

Steve turned to the wizard. "Is that even possible?"

"Caladonia was very powerful, very resourceful," Maelnar recalled. "I would say so."

"How is it that this has remained secret for so long?" the king demanded, growing angry. "How is it that no one has ever heard this story before today?"

"The writings of Caladonia were lost to obscurity until recently," Maelnar explained, sinking deeper into his cushion. "Nearly four centuries passed before her work was discovered by the king at the time, Kre'-, Kre', blast, I cannot remember the name. No matter. The king was an avid follower of all premonitions, no matter whether good or bad, so he viewed her tomes of predictions to be worth their weight in gold. You have to understand that most of Caladonia's premonitions held little or no value to the present day, but it so happened that the king learned of the existence of the tome detailing her research about the Bakkian."

Rhenyon whistled in amazement. "I personally would like to know how the Nohrin's world was selected and how they managed to send a soldier there."

"How it was done, or why their world was chosen, I am not certain, only that both sisters agreed a link must be forged with another world."

Steve shot up a hand. "Sisters? This Caladonia had a sister? Was she a sorceress, too?"

Maelnar nodded. "Aye. Both were very powerful sorceresses."

"They both were?" Rhenyon asked, impressed. "That strong of jhorun in siblings is exceedingly rare."

"And exceedingly powerful," Shardwyn said, also impressed. "I do not know much of the sister. What was her name, do you remember Maelnar?"

The dwarf stopped puffing on his pipe to stare at the wizard.

"That has got to be the first time in many years you have called me by my name, wizard. Shardwyn. There, you see? I can do it, too."

"How long have you two known each other?" Sarah suddenly asked.

"A great many years, milady," Shardwyn smiled at her.

"Back to the sister," Kri'Entu gently reminded everyone, hoping to steer the wizard and dwarf back on track.

"Right, the sister. Celestia."

"I am not familiar with any of her work," Shardwyn noted, briefly reminiscing the many hours he had spent in the Royal Archives scouring for information about the Bakkian over the years. "I knew Caladonia had a sister, but that's the extent of my knowledge on her."

"Unsurprising," Maelnar informed him. "Her tastes led to much darker spells and enchantments. I tried many times to convince Caladonia that deep within her sister's chest beat a heart of evil. Yet, as siblings often do, she turned a blind eye to what her sister was doing. Everything is chronicled in her journal, which her ancestors maintained up until a century ago."

"Why only a century?" Steve wanted to know. "Why not until the present day?"

"Once the bond had been forged with another world, it became a matter of *when* and not *if* the Nohrin would appear," Maelnar said.

"You wanted answers to your questions, Sir Steve," Shardwyn piped up. "It would appear this journal contains the answers."

"So, here is what we will do" Kri'Entu declared, catching and holding everyone's attention. "First, Shardwyn, you are to figure out what to do with this." He presented the small golden vial of his wife's jhorun to the stunned wizard. "I want to know how to return this to the queen, is that understood?"

The wizard nodded. "Completely, sire."

"Commander, you are to accompany the Nohrin tomorrow."

Rhenyon nodded. "Understood, Your Majesty."

"The castle remains on high alert. Thaden will want these items back. Alert your men."

"Consider it done, Your Majesty."

"Sir Steve, Lady Sarah."

"Let me guess," Steve interrupted, when the king took a breath. "Get the journal."

Kri'Entu smiled. "Aye, as fast as you can."

"You got it."

Chapter 14 — Journal

How do you propose we go about this?" Steve asked, surveying the familiar forest path. "What exactly are we supposed to be looking for?"

"Listen, do you hear that?" Rhenyon motioned for everyone to be quiet. "A waterfall is nearby."

"That's right," Sarah confirmed, twisting to point off in the distance. "It's that way. I think we should go check it out."

"Why?" Steve asked, also turning toward the distant sounds of falling water.

"Do you see anything around here that might be useful?"

"Well, no," her husband admitted, giving her a grin.

"Exactly. Let's go. It took us a half hour to reach it before."

"You'd think if we're supposed to check out that waterfall then we would have been dumped closer," Steve grumbled. He turned to his wife. "Just teleport us there. It'd be easier."

Sarah nodded. "I could, but we might miss something along the way."

Steve's grumbling started anew as he turned to follow his wife.

"Why are you headed that way?" Rhenyon called out, as husband and wife walked off. He pointed slightly southeast. "The waterfall sounds as though it is coming from this direction."

"Yeah, it does, but the path that leads to it is over here."

Frowning, Rhenyon looked at the ground and wandered off, pushing slowly past the knee-high ferns. "We can use this trail. It appears to be a more direct route."

Baffled, Steve approached his friend and stared down at the ground. Sure enough, a small trail appeared to originate from that very spot. Had that always been there?

"Figures. Never said I was a Boy Scout."

Curious, Rhenyon looked at Sarah, who smiled, and shook her head, putting a finger to her lips. The commander grinned.

"There wasn't much at that waterfall," Steve recalled, thinking back to what he could remember from their first visit to Lentari. "Pool of water. River flowing off to the east. Not much else, if memory serves. Any ideas on what we are looking for?"

"I have a feeling we'll know when we see it."

Taking the much shorter trail, they arrived at the falls in a scant ten minutes instead of thirty. Fortunately, no residents were utilizing the watering hole this time. Both husband and wife craned their necks to follow the flow of water up the rocky cliff.

"Hope we don't have to climb that sucker," Steve remarked.

"Why would we?" Sarah countered. "I can teleport us to the top in no time."

"And if what we seek lies behind the water half way up?" Rhenyon nonchalantly asked.

"Hmm." She hadn't thought of that.

"Let us explore the area," Rhenyon suggested. "If we have to look elsewhere, then we will, but only if necessary."

"Sounds good."

Their small group split up, figuring more ground could

be explored if they did so separately.

"I still don't know what we're looking for."

With a sigh, Sarah looked back at her husband. "I told you. Look for anything out of the ordinary."

"Anything out of the ordinary," Steve mimicked, shaking his head. "Thanks. That's a big help."

Sarah smiled and closed her eyes, sending out her jhorun to investigate the surroundings. Did anything feel different? Any tingles anywhere? Her jhorun flashed briefly in response: *no*.

Steve wandered over to the water's edge. He squatted down, peering closely at the lagoon. Maybe it was concealed under the surface? Would she have chosen such an unlikely place for hiding her journal? He snorted. Probably not. She wouldn't have wanted to risk her precious book getting wet.

"I believe I have found something!"

Steve's head snapped up. His wife had already joined Rhenyon and together they were pointing across at the falling water. They seemed to be peering at the base of the waterfall. He joined them moments later.

"Dude, that was quick. Whatcha got?"

Rhenyon pointed. "There, can you see it?"

Steve squinted at the base of the falling water. "What am I looking for?"

Sarah smiled. "Good eyes! I never would have seen that."

Steve turned to his wife. "What? What do you guys see?"

Sarah leaned close and pointed to the base of the falling water. "Look! Rhenyon has located a path behind the waterfall."

"He did?" Steve leaned to the left, then to the right. He couldn't make out anything. Besides, the noise of the cascading water was making it hard to concentrate. They all had to shout in order to be heard. "Where?"

Rhenyon gently tugged him a few feet his way while Sarah simultaneously guided his head so that his gaze would fall upon the area in question.

"That? That little ledge thing? You call that a path??"

Very delicately chiseled into the wall behind the waterfall was an outcropping of rock that was no more than six inches wide. Once again, unless you were standing in the right place, and looking just so, the tiny path would be invisible from the water's edge.

"That has the dwarves written all over it," Sarah speculated, turning to Rhenyon to confirm her suspicions.

"Aye, my thoughts exactly."

Steve was impressed.

"How did you find that so easily?"

"They deceived me once, down in the tunnels," Rhenyon gave a smug smile. "They will not do so again. It was just a matter of knowing what to look for."

"Great. So we're going to have to swim? That's just peachy."

Sarah let out an exasperated sigh. "Crybaby. I've got this, princess, so won't have to worry about getting your feet wet."

Steve's eyes widened. "Her aim striketh me to the core."

Sarah giggled. "Dork. Stay put."

She straightened, staring out across the water at the tiny ledge she was going to have to balance on. Standing stiff as a board, arms extended out to hug the non-existent wall, she vanished. Moments later she appeared fifty feet away, perched on the thin ledge. It had looked bigger, much bigger, from the water's edge.

"Be careful!" Steve called out as Sarah began inching along the ledge.

"Can you see anything, milady?" Rhenyon shouted to her.

Sarah shouted something back but it was lost in the roaring water. Continuing to inch along, she disappeared behind the falling sheets of water.

"Think there's anything back there?" Steve asked, turning to his friend.

Rhenyon nodded. "Aye, there must be. Why else would that ledge be there?"

Several minutes later, Sarah popped into existence a few feet away.

"Bingo. Let's go, boys."

"What's there?" Steve asked.

"What did you find, milady?" Rhenyon asked, at the same time.

"I'll show you."

Hooking an arm through each of theirs, she teleported the three of them to the cave she had discovered tucked away behind the falling water.

In such close proximity to the waterfall, talking became impossible. She couldn't hear her own voice even if she shouted at the top of her lungs. Giving Rhenyon a nudge to get his attention, the two of them followed Sarah as she disappeared into the darkness.

"How far does this go back?" Steve yelled out.

Sarah shrugged helplessly. She couldn't hear him. Steve lit his right hand and held it aloft. They were approaching the cave's back wall.

Rhenyon sidled closer. His mouth opened but almost immediately closed. He pointed at Steve's flaming hand, cupped both hands together, and slowly drew them apart. He ended his gesturing by pointing again at Steve's hand.

He nodded. More light? Not a problem. Both hands ignited and he pumped his jhorun into them, increasing the light.

Sarah squatted low to begin inspecting the wall. She looked back at her husband and made the same motion. She wanted more light, too.

Grunting, Steve held both arms straight out from his body, intensifying his jhorun as he did so. Both hands blazed brightly.

Rhenyon waved his arms to get his attention. With beads of sweat appearing on his brow, the commander held up both hands in a universal 'no more' gesture.

Steve slowly lowered his arms as he decreased the temp. Rhenyon nodded and began inspecting the cave.

"Don't come over here!" Sarah cried, not caring whether her husband could hear her or not, and backpedaled away as fast as she could. She mouthed the words *too hot* in the hopes he'd understand.

Steve nodded again. He backed away from his wife. Rising to her feet to inspect another section of the wall, Sarah scurried past their human torch, eager to explore a cooler section of the stone surface. Just then, something caught

Steve's eye. Her shadow, as she passed his flaming left hand, had just appeared skewed on a certain section of the cave wall, but only for a moment. He extinguished his left hand and then re-lit it.

Rhenyon glanced up. Steve pointed at him, forked two of his fingers in front of his own eyes, then pointed at the wall where the shadow had appeared misshapen.

The commander moved over to inspect. Whirling back around, he slapped Steve on the back. He was grinning. He flickered the flames as before, until she looked up. Rhenyon motioned for her to join them, pointing out the hidden dwarf tunnel. Sarah grinned as well, giving her husband an enthusiastic thumbs up.

Rhenyon ducked down to peer into the small tunnel, cautiously stepping inside moments later. Nodding his head with approval, he beckoned the others to follow. Proceeding deeper into the passageway, the sound of roaring water subsided enough where they could finally talk to one another.

"Nice job, honey!"

"Hey, even I can get lucky every once in a while."

The dwarf tunnel deposited them into a larger cave where they were able to straighten up.

"Wonder how big this one is," Steve remarked.

"Perhaps you should stand over there and remain stationary," Rhenyon suggested. "Lady Sarah and I can search for clues."

"All righty then." Steve walked to the center of the cave and stood still, stretching his arms out at a ninety-degree angle.

"Can you rotate a bit? Aye, that is perfect. Thanks."

Steve sighed. "Yeah, sure, no problem."

"Whoa! Go back a little to your right!"

Puzzled, Steve slowly rotated in place.

"There! Stop there!"

"What do you see?" Steve wanted to know, desperately curious.

"Rhenyon, take a look. What do you think?"

"I would say we have found what we are looking for, milady."

Steve cleared his throat. "What do you have? What'd you find?"

"Should have known they would have put this at their eye-level."

"Put *what* at eye level?" Steve asked, growing frustrated. "Hey, would you two stop ignoring me?"

Rhenyon straightened. "My apologies, Sir Steve. Behold. The mark of the griffin."

Letting one hand extinguish, Steve joined them at the wall and squatted down to examine a small metal disc that was embedded onto the surface. A familiar sight met his eyes: a stationary griffin with a single raised foreleg.

"Okay, so now what? That means there's something behind this wall, right? Another hidden door?"

Rhenyon and Sarah began methodically searching the wall's surface while Steve grudgingly resumed his duties as a human torch.

"This wall isn't that big," Sarah said, putting her hands on her hips. "It shouldn't be too difficult to find the door."

"The dwarf did mention that only the Nohrin would be able to retrieve the journal," Rhenyon helpfully supplied, glancing back at their torch, who nodded. "Think you can teleport us inside?"

Sarah nodded. She didn't see why not. She faced the wall, closing her eyes as she did so. Yes, a picture was forming.

"See anything?" Steve asked.

"Another cave. Bigger than this one. Fortunately, there's just enough light to make out the walls. Where the light's coming from, I'm not sure. Maybe more of that glowing moss from before? I'll go first, to check it out."

"Like hell you will."

"Methinks not, milady."

"The three of us," her husband declared. Rhenyon nodded in agreement. "Together."

Not in the mood to argue, Sarah took both of their arms and jumped them into the next cavern. Steve instantly reignited both hands and raised his right arm high into the air. Rhenyon wandered over to the closest wall and retrieved an unlit torch from a wall sconce. He held it out to Steve. Seconds later, he replaced the now lit torch back into its holder. By the light of the torch they could make out three other torches around the perimeter of the cavern. Steve flicked his gaze at each torch. Moments later, the four torches were blazing brightly. Together they stared at the center of the cavern.

Sarah laughed. "Gee, I wonder what we're looking for in here?"

Right smack in the middle of this cavern was a short stone dais, and sitting directly atop was a large wooden chest with a thin band of elegant metal scrollwork wrapping around the entire thing. Steve squinted at it. It didn't even appear to be locked. How easy!

"I trust this not," Rhenyon warned, glancing around the empty cave. "It cannot be this simple."

"Oh, come on. Why look a gift horse in the mouth!" Steve strode over to the chest. It was about the size of a metal footlocker Steve had seen for purchase at discount stores everywhere.

"Just be careful," Sarah cautioned. "You don't know what will happen if you touch it."

Her husband gave her a look that said *oh, please*, and nudged it with his foot. Nothing happened. Emboldened, he nudged it again, this time a little harder. The chest grated along the stone pedestal about a foot and a half.

"I don't think there's anything in it. It moved way too easily."

Steeling himself, he poked a finger at it. Again, nothing happened. With a shrug, he went to open the lid, only the chest refused to cooperate. Annoyed, he used one hand to brace the chest from sliding and used the other to pull back the top. The lid remained firmly mired in place.

"C'mon, sucker. Open up." Steve grunted with the effort. "What the hell? Is this thing super-glued shut or something?"

Rhenyon approached, running his fingers along the surface of the chest.

"No seam. This chest has no lid."

"Really?" Steve squinted at the chest. He had misidentified the small section of chest above the metal scrollwork as the lid when, in fact, Rhenyon was right. There was none. "So how are we supposed to open it?"

"By jhorun, clearly."

"Okay, I'll buy that." Steve turned to his wife. "Hon, can you teleport whatever it is that's in there out?"

"Without knowing what it is? Nuh-uh. Sorry. Until I know what's in there, I'm not bringing anything out."

"Can you see what lies inside, Lady Sarah?"

Sarah closed her eyes and asked her jhorun to inspect the chest's interior. The tingles appeared instantly, but flashed in annoyance: her jhorun had been blocked.

"I can't get a picture," Sarah reported, frowning. "Something's blocking me."

"See? I told you it would not be that simple."

"Yeah, yeah, okay, that's one for you. Zip it."

Rhenyon laughed as they all slowly walked around the chest, brainstorming ideas they could try in order to open it.

"Maybe we should just take the chest back to the castle and figure out how to open it there," Steve suggested. "You think Shardwyn could open it?"

"I don't think so," Sarah said, shaking her head. "Maelnar said that only we would be able to open it." She looked at her husband. "I think it's time you try to do something."

"Like what? How is fire going to open that thing? Do we really want to take a chance of burning that journal?"

"I could try my jhorun," Rhenyon suggested, drawing both Steve and Sarah's gaze to his own. "I have the ability to shape wood. I might be able to get it to collapse in on itself."

"Sure, give it a try, buddy."

Steve stepped back as a hand was laid on the top of the chest. Several moments passed as Rhenyon's brow furrowed with concentration.

"Doesn't appear to be working," Sarah observed, eliciting a grunt from the commander. "I can't open it, and neither can Rhenyon. If only the Nohrin can open it, then that means it has to be you."

Frowning down at the lidless chest, Steve approached. Igniting his right hand, he laid it on the container, fully expecting it to either pop right open or else catch fire. Disappointed, but not too terribly surprised, he grunted. He ignited his left and laid both hands on the chest. Naturally, nothing happened.

"See? It can't be me. It's not responding."

"That's all you're going to try?"

"What else do you want me to do?"

"Increase the temperature," Rhenyon suggested.

"Try touching only certain spots," Sarah added.

"Maybe you should be holding the chest." Rhenyon said.

"Maybe you should …"

"Okay! Enough!" Steve laughed, giving Sarah a smile. "Jeez! Fine, let me try something else."

Sarah and Rhenyon moved back to give him some room.

With both hands lit, he began poking fingers at various places. No luck. Taking Rhenyon's suggestion, he decided to pick the thing up and heat the entire chest at the same time. However, as he stooped to pick it up, the two handles were forcefully yanked out of his hands as he lifted. Figuring it must have just slipped out of his hands, he squatted again, each hand latching onto a handle. Slowly he lifted. The chest stayed put. Grunting with the effort, he tried to lift the chest from the stone dais. Whereas the chest easily slid along the ground, it utterly refused to be lifted.

Puzzled, Rhenyon approached and pushed the chest along the surface of the stone dais, but as it approached the edge of the pedestal, it stopped. As one, all three squatted down to stare at the bottom of the chest. As far as anyone could tell, there wasn't anything restricting the chest to the ground.

"Well, that answers the question about whether we could get this thing to Shardwyn," Steve commented. "Step back. I'm going to hit it with a stronger blast."

Rhenyon and Sarah moved to the mouth of the concealed tunnel and waited.

Cracking his knuckles as he flexed his fingers, Steve laid both hands back on the chest and sent a much stronger blast into its depths. Still nothing. He hit the chest with another blast, only this time he kept it going for about five seconds. The chest remained unchanged.

"Sir Steve!"

Steve glanced over at Rhenyon.

"Stop for a moment. We would like to see if the surface is warm to the touch."

"Umm, okay." Steve decreased his hands until they were back at standard torch level and stepped back.

Rhenyon approached and tentatively laid a hand on the chest. Surprised, he slapped his hand onto the surface.

"Cool to the touch."

"What does that tell us?" Steve asked.

"That whatever you're doing, it's not enough."

"Still think blasting it with fire is the way to go here?"

"For now, yes. Pretend it's that demon thing. Hit it as hard as you can go."

"Fine. You two should hide in the tunnel."

"We're way ahead of you. Rhenyon, come on. We need to clear out."

From the confines of the tunnel, Sarah and the commander eagerly watched as Steve conjured an impressive jet of fire, twirled it about overhead, and then slammed it into the chest. The wooden chest was blasted off the stone dais and smashed into the far wall. It fell to the ground while bits of gravel and broken rock rained down all around it.

"Hmmm. I think I hit it too hard."

Sarah and Rhenyon emerged from the tunnel.

"You think?"

"You said to hit it as hard as I could, so I did! Besides, I thought it was attached to the ground."

"As did we. It would appear the chest remains unharmed."

"Can't say that about the wall, though," Sarah added, glancing up the point of impact. Several chunks of stone had been gouged out of the wall's surface.

"Check the bottom. See if there was something holding it in place."

Nodding his head, Rhenyon tilted the chest up so they could all see the bottom. There wasn't anything to indicate that it had once been confined to the pedestal.

"Why'd it let go?" Steve wondered.

"It reacted to fire," Rhenyon pointed out. "That would clearly suggest that you are the one who needs to open the chest, Sir Steve."

"Hit it again," Sarah suggested, looking down at the chest. "But not as hard this time."

Once the area was clear, Steve summoned another jet of flames and hit it again, but not nearly as hard as he did the last time. As far as anyone could tell, nothing happened.

Hands still lit, Steve glanced back at his wife. He shrugged. "What now?"

"Can you hit it as hot as you can, but not as forcefully?" Rhenyon asked, stroking his goatee.

"Hot, but not hard." Steve snickered, shaking his head.

"Get your mind out of the gutter," Sarah said, shaking her head.

Still chuckling, Steve looked down at the chest. Ordering his jhorun to keep the size of the jet small, he blasted the stubborn chest and maintained the levels for about ten seconds. Still nothing.

"Well, we could try …" Steve trailed off as he suddenly squatted down low to inspect the chest up close. Something had caught his eye. A section of the decorative band encircling the chest was glowing! Was it just hot? Had it done that before?

"What's the matter?" Sarah called out. "What are you looking at?"

"Guys, come here a sec."

"What do you see, Sir Steve?"

"Look at that. See the section of that metal thingy there? It's glowing. Did it do that before?"

Rhenyon squatted down as well. He gingerly held out a hand, fully expecting the metal band to be radiating heat from Steve's jet of fire. However, it was cool to the touch.

"Is it warm?" Steve wanted to know, being immune to heat or fire.

"It is not."

"What'd you do?" Sarah asked, gently running her fingers across the glowing band.

"You saw what I did. I hit it with a blast of fire."

"Everywhere or just this one spot?" Rhenyon asked.

"Ummm, just this spot, I believe."

"Same temp?"

Steve thought for a moment. "No, I started at medium, then increased to hot."

"Repeat the test."

"Do it again."

Sarah and Rhenyon smiled at each other as each spoke at the same time.

"Do it again," Sarah repeated, "but at a different spot. See if you can get another section to glow."

Once the area was clear, Steve resumed his blast of fire at the chest, this time focusing on the other side. Deliberately aiming his jet at the decorative metal band, he ordered his jhorun to maintain the blast for an additional ten seconds. He extinguished his hand to inspect the scrollwork. Hah! Another section of the metal band was now glowing! However, as he leaned over to inspect the other side, he was dismayed to see that the first glowing section had faded.

"Did it work?" Sarah called out.

"Yeah, this side's glowing now, but the other side went out. Hold on, I'm going to hit both sides at the same time."

Creating two jets of fire, Steve hit both ends of the chest simultaneously. Blasting the metal scrollwork for another ten seconds, he let his hands resume torch levels and then inspected his work.

"Two spots are glowing now!" Steve called out, turning to face the mouth of the dwarf tunnel. "What do you want to bet I have to get the whole damn thing to glow before it'll open?"

Rhenyon tapped the decorative metal band. "I would agree. You will have to work fast. The band ceases to glow after only a few moments."

Giving the commander a sour look, Steve snorted. "Thanks, Einstein. I noticed."

Rhenyon quizzically turned to Sarah.

"Who —"

Sarah grinned. "He's being a smartass. He knows."

Grunting, Rhenyon turned back in time to see Steve re-ignite his jets and blast the chest again. However, trying to blast the entire metal band at the same time was proving to be more difficult that he had originally thought. From what he could tell, the decorative scrollwork needed at least ten seconds of direct contact with a blast of fire before it would start glowing.

Sarah and Rhenyon had both noticed, and were silent as they considered this latest puzzle.

"What do you want me to do here?" Steve asked.

Sarah held up a hand. "Just a second. We're thinking."

With a bemused expression on his face, he watched as his wife and the commander whispered between themselves. Sarah hooked her left thumb in his direction and made a circular motion with her right hand. Rhenyon nodded and said something else to her that he couldn't hear, and then motioned to the ground. Both nodded and then in unison looked up at him.

"What?"

"We think we have it."

"Hit me with your best shot."

"You need to create one of those ropes of fire that we've seen you do and then whip it around the chest. That way you could make contact with the entire metal band at the same time."

"Ropes of fire?" Steve repeated, puzzled.

"Do you remember the fire net?" Rhenyon asked. "Back when we were rescuing the queen, you ensnared the gang leader by weaving strands of fire together. We need you to create a single strand and wrap it around that."

"I have no clue how I made that net thing."

Sarah pointed at the chest. "Just now, when you hit that chest for the first time, you created an impressive blast. But before you hit it, you twirled strands of fire about overhead. Do you remember?"

Steve was silent as he thought about it. Okay, he did remember that. Could he produce a single strand of fire and whip it around the chest? What the hell, he thought. It's worth a shot.

Aiming his right arm away from the chest and away from the two of them, Steve blasted out a jet of fire, but this time he ordered his jhorun to not target anything. Sure enough, without an intended target, the jet whipped about like an unattended fireman's hose. He elevated his right hand. Now it looked like he was twirling a lasso over his head.

"I'm sure this makes me look like a dork."

Sarah laughed while Rhenyon suppressed a smirk.

"Yippee kai-ay, you ugly sucker." Steve lashed out his arm, briefly pretending he was Indiana Jones. However, as soon as he thought about latching it onto the chest, he inadvertently gave his jhorun a target. The jet whirled about overhead and the end of the fire rope cracked like a bullwhip, making contact with the chest. The chest was flung backward, smashing back into the stone wall.

"Whoops! Sorry, my bad! Rhenyon, can you reset that thing?"

Keeping a wary eye on the twirling jet of fire overhead, Rhenyon hastily retrieved the chest and set it back upright on the stone dais.

"Thanks. Okay, stand clear! I'm going to try again!"

It took four attempts before Steve managed to hit the chest at the right angle. The jet of fire neatly coiled around the metal band and held fast.

"Nice shot!" Sarah called from the safety of the tunnel. "Now *fry it*!"

With his left hand braced on top of his right, he sent a brutal blast down the strand. Fascinated, Steve watched the increased level of jhorun zip down his "bullwhip." Blazing brightly, the enhanced jet of fire finally made contact with the entire metal band at the same time.

They all heard the loud click.

Not sure how to extinguish this new fire rope thing, he let both hands snuff out, reigniting them at normal torch levels moments later. The decorative band that had been wrapped around the chest was now lying broken on the floor, the chest opened wide.

"Alright, honey! Nice going!"

"We'll call that one a group effort."

As one, all three leaned over to peer into the open chest. A tattered leather-bound book met their eyes.

Chapter 15 — Bakkian

Kri'Entu and Ny'Callé rose from their seated positions as people began filing into the room. The king indicated for everyone to take a seat in one of the chairs that had been brought in to join the four already set in a semicircle around the hearth.

"Are you sure I'm supposed to be here?" Annie hesitantly asked, turning to look at her sister.

"Lady Annie," Kri'Entu answered, drawing her attention, "as temporary protector of my son—" at this, the king frowned at Mikal, who sank deep into his own chair, "you are most certainly welcome here."

"Honestly, we do not know what would have become of Mikal if the two of you had not followed," the queen added, also turning to frown at her son, who somehow managed to sink even deeper into the plush chair. She looked over at her son's tall, quiet mentor. "You have our eternal thanks."

"No thanks are necessary, Your Majesty," Tristan insisted, bowing low.

"Son, perhaps this is not the best place for you right now."

Mikal turned to look at his father.

"All of you are talking about me. I want to be here!"

"Your father is right," Ny'Callé added, causing her son to pout. "Maybe you could …?"

"Why don't you take Peanut for a walk?" Steve suggested, coming to the queen's aid.

The boy's face lit up. "Aye! Where is she?"

"She was taking a nap on our bed earlier. All the serving girls have fallen in love with her."

"She is my dog," Mikal declared.

"Go on then," Kri'Entu instructed. "Be sure to stay close."

As Mikal ran from the room, Steve glanced again at the two empty chairs.

"So, where are the two lovebirds? Is Maelnar still working with Shardwyn or did he go back home?"

"Both have spent the last three days poring over Caladonia's journal," Kri'Entu answered, trying to suppress a smile.

Rhenyon leaned forward. "Together? I thought they did not care for one another."

Sarah nodded. "That's the impression I got, too."

"They may not care for one another, but both were surprised to learn that they do work well together."

"Maybe between the two of them they can figure out how to give your jhorun back to you." Steve sank down onto his chair, both knees popping loudly as he did so.

Sarah and Annie both turned to regard him with a pitiful look.

"Not one word out of either of you."

Ny'Callé smiled. "As it turns out, I do not believe I want it back."

"Your Majesty!"

"Excuse me?"

"You're kidding!"

Kri'Entu motioned for everyone to be silent. He smiled at his wife.

"Fear not. I believe an explanation is forthcoming."

All heads turned to the queen.

"It would seem my jhorun has been returned."

"So, Mikal was able to restore it?" Steve asked

"Or did you use the vial?" Sarah wanted to know.

The queen shook her head. "No one has touched the vial."

"Okay, then Mikal would have had to restore it. That's great! But I thought when Mikal restores someone's jhorun, he was actually taking it back from Thaden. Doesn't that make whatever's in that vial useless?"

"All will be revealed soon, Sir Steve."

Steve looked at the king and grinned. "The suspense is killing me, Your Majesty."

"You must be patient, Sir Steve." the queen added, smiling at her son's bodyguard.

"I know. It's just that there have been so many unknowns that it'll be nice to have some questions finally answered."

"Shardwyn has hinted you will not be disappointed," the king added. "He specifically mentioned that all those questions the two of you had asked earlier will be finally addressed."

Steve took Sarah's hand and held it tightly in his own.

"Really? Cool! This is gonna be awesome."

"Personally, I want to hear about Mikal's jhorun," Sarah added, receiving nods from both of the Kri'yans. "I want to know why Thaden wants him so badly."

"That makes two of us," Kri'Entu muttered under his breath.

At that moment, a door opened and then closed in the distance. A familiar voice sounded, arguing with yet another familiar voice.

"Are you daft? A kyte with a sprig of lavender in its beak does not indicate wyverian unrest. So you can —"

"And how would you know anything about kytes?" came the shrill reply. "Have many of them flying about in Borahgg?"

"Be that as it may," the dwarf grumbled, "I am only —"

Both wizard and dwarf trailed off as they noticed that every person in the room was staring at them as though they had just sprouted wings. Shardwyn shuffled by Maelnar to take an empty seat, the journal tucked under his right arm.

"Greetings everyone. We have made progress."

"What you have made are assumptions," the dwarf corrected. "*I* have made progress."

Hoping to stave off imminent hostilities, Kri'Entu gestured for the dwarf to be seated.

"Where shall I start, Your Majesty?" Shardwyn asked, addressing the king.

"Let us start with why *your* son wants *my* son," Kri'Entu suggested.

All heads turned to Shardwyn as he opened the journal to one of several bookmarked pages. He tapped the leather-bound diary and nodded sagely.

"Because of his jhorun," Shardwyn answered, running his fingers along the delicate script contained within the journal. "Lady Sarah's earlier assessment is quite correct. The prince's jhorun is not enhancement."

"Then what is it?" the king snapped, sighing moments later. "My apologies, Shardwyn, but my son's life is at risk. Please, can you tell us what Mikal's jhorun is?"

"Indeed I can, Your Majesty. His jhorun is the key to all this madness."

"Well?"

"Well what?"

"What is his jhorun?" Kri'Entu, Ny'Callé, and Sarah all shouted in unison.

"Caladonia searched relentlessly for the answer. She, too, knew the future prince's jhorun was significant."

"Shardwyn …" the king warned.

"Jhorun! His jhorun *is* jhorun!"

Steve blinked. He looked at his wife, who shrugged her shoulders helplessly.

"You need to clarify, lad," Maelnar added gently, seeing confusion on everyone's face.

"Young Mikal can create jhorun, Your Majesty," Shardwyn added.

The Antechamber fell silent. Sarah sat back in her chair as she thought about what that meant. As she considered, her eyes drifted to the table before them. Sitting on top was the all too familiar pewter goblet.

"Mikal can give jhorun to those who do not have it." Sarah suddenly sat up straight and stared at the dwarf. "*He* is the Bakkian, isn't he? You said before it wasn't that shield thing."

Maelnar and Shardwyn both bowed to Sarah.

"Well done, milady."

"Wait." Steve sat up straight. "Mikal is the Bakkian? And he can only give jhorun to someone who doesn't already have it? Then that certainly explains how we got ours."

"Actually, it does not," Shardwyn countered.

"Sure it does! Obviously, we didn't have jhorun when we first came here. Within a couple of days, we had some. It seems pretty straightforward to me."

Sarah turned to her husband. "You think Mikal gave us our jhorun? How? We didn't meet him until we made it to the castle. By that time, we already had our jhorun."

"Okay, I'll give you that one. Then how'd we get ours?"

Shardwyn held up the journal and gave it a little shake. "The answer is here."

"You found that, too?" Steve asked.

"That was Caladonia's last and most powerful gift," Maelnar answered.

"So, she's responsible for our jhorun?" Sarah asked.

"Not just any jhorun," Shardwyn explained, flipping the journal open to another of the bookmarked pages. "Caladonia knew the prince would be in danger once the nature of his jhorun was revealed, so she made certain his protectors would be capable of handling any threat that manifested, in this world or any other."

"The sorceress knew the Nohrin would take Mikal to their world?" Rhenyon whistled. "Impressive."

"Well, she had the premonition," Ny'Callé added, drawing a giggle from Sarah. "It should not be that surprising."

"You're saying she would have known we'd need our jhoruns in our world to help protect Mikal, is that right?" Steve asked.

"Indeed," Shardwyn nodded.

"How'd she do it?" Steve wanted to know.

"While she does not indicate how," Maelnar began, "what *is* known is she surrendered her own jhorun, and her very life, to cast the complex spell necessary to ensure the prince's survival."

Once more the entire room was stunned into silence.

Sarah was amazed. "She sacrificed herself? For Mikal? Wow. That's dedication for you."

"Aye," Kri'Entu agreed. "It is, indeed."

Steve turned to his wife. "I'm still unclear why she figured we'd need our jhoruns in our world. Who's here that could follow him there?"

"No one as far as I know," Sarah answered.

Rhenyon turned to the wizard. "Is there? Someone who could travel from this world to theirs? Lady Sarah can do it, but can anyone else?"

"There are several teleporters," Kri'Entu recalled, thinking back to the last countrywide census of notable jhorun, "but none who are strong enough to move that distance."

"That does make me feel a bit better," Maelnar murmured, more to himself than to anyone.

Curious, Sarah turned to the dwarf.

"Better about what?"

"Lass, do you have any idea how many sessions my council has held, trying to determine how you were able to breach the Barrier?"

"It's not my fault your safeguards to keep strangers out of your underground cities are weak."

Steve snorted with laughter. "Ooooo! Fight! Fight! Fight!"

Sarah smacked Steve on his left arm while Annie simultaneously hit him on his right. "Dork."

Maelnar choked on his ale. The coughs coming out of the diminutive dwarf were violent enough to warrant a few slaps on the back from the commander.

Grinning at the human female he was so fond of, the dwarf once more pulled his beard out of his belt and mopped up his spilled drink.

"They will be very relieved to learn that the Barrier remains secure. It was just our luck that the one human capable of defeating the enchantments happened to pay us a visit."

Rhenyon chose this time to clear his throat. The king looked his way.

"Yes, Commander?"

"Your Majesty, something puzzles me still."

Kri'Entu nodded, giving the commander permission to speak.

"If there are no teleporters capable of traveling to the Nohrin's world, then why ensure their jhorun can be used there?"

Everyone was silent as this was considered.

"With Mikal safe in the Kingdom of Idaho," Rhenyon continued, "why would it be necessary? The Nohrin should have no need of their jhorun there."

All eyes turned to the wizard, who was busy flipping through the journal.

"That would suggest," Rhenyon continued, "that even in their world, someone from ours would be able to reach him."

"Master Rhenyon makes a valid point," Maelnar observed, pulling out his pipe and pouch of tobacco.

Stymied by the commander's question, Shardwyn began skimming page after page of Caladonia's elaborate handwritten notes when he stopped and tapped the page.

"There's this flower again."

"What flower?" Maelnar asked, hopping down from his chair to lean over Shardwyn's shoulder.

"This one."

"That's larkspur, lad."

"Fine, then. It must be Caladonia's favorite. I have seen it on several different pages."

Maelnar stiffened.

"Dianthus were her favorite. Purple or red."

"At least she has good taste," Sarah added, smiling at the dwarf, who did not return the smile.

"What is the significance of larkspur, then?" Sarah asked, turning to their dwarf companion. "Do you know?"

"Aye, I do, lass. It was Celestia's favorite."

"The sister," Kri'Entu breathed.

"Aye, Your Majesty," Maelnar said, turning to regard the king.

"Is that important?" Annie asked, drawing everyone's attention to her. "So, her favorite flower is mentioned. How is that relevant?"

"Ordinarily it would mean nothing, Lady Annie," Shardwyn explained, not bothering to look up from the journal. "They were sisters after all. I had not paid attention to the flowers, attributing them to, uh, to simple random drawings."

"Doodles," Steve suggested.

"Aye. Doodles. But this doodle is of a flower that her sister favored. Coincidence?"

"Methinks she was suspicious of the sister," Kri'Entu suggested. "Perhaps, wherever you see the larkspur, it might pertain to something she suspected her sister knew."

Maelnar nodded. "Aye, my thoughts exactly. You should look for more of those flowers. I do not think I would be remiss in saying wherever you find the larkspur, you will find some mention of Celestia. See if there is anything you missed."

"If Caladonia's specialty was premonition, what was Celestia known for?"

Shardwyn stopped flipping through the journal to pointedly look at the dwarf.

"Her natural ability was being able to influence the passage of time."

"How would something like that work?" Steve wanted to know.

"Let's say you had domesticated a kyte," the wizard began. "The natural lifespan of such a creature is but a few years. Celestia could have extended the life of the kyte by many times."

"Domesticated kites?" Annie whispered to her sister.

"Birds."

"Ah, that's right. I forgot."

"Doesn't appear very impressive," Steve observed.

"It was not," the dwarf confirmed. "She could only affect items that she was in direct contact with for an extended period of time."

"But you said she was a sorceress, right?"

"Aye, Lady Sarah. They both were. Even though her power was minor, she could still manipulate time, classifying her as a sorceress. However, Celestia coveted her sister's jhorun. She believed her own was inferior, so she strove to replace it."

"How?" the king demanded.

"The only way she could. She shunned her natural jhorun to study enchantments and spells. She became quite gifted with illusions."

"Illusions? That can't be good."

The king turned to Shardwyn, who stopped skimming pages as he felt the king's gaze fall upon him.

"Does this sound like anyone else we are familiar with, Shardwyn?"

"It does, Your Majesty."

"What happened to the sister?" Rhenyon asked. "What was her fate?"

"No one knows," Maelnar admitted. "She vanished right before her sister sacrificed herself."

"Celestia disappeared?" the king asked, frowning at the wizard. "Before Caladonia sacrificed herself? Those two events must be related. You will make this your top priority. Ascertain Celestia's fate. Is that understood? I want to know when, where, how, and *if* she died."

"Understood, Your Majesty."

"If this sister has somehow survived by using her jhorun, and has the ability to threaten my son in the Nohrin's home world, then I want to know. Is that understood?"

"Completely, Your Majesty."

"Do you think she's still alive?" Sarah quietly asked.

"I do not believe in coincidences. The sister disappears, and not that long after that Caladonia sacrifices herself?"

"I believe she knew Celestia was a threat to the young prince," Maelnar added, puffing on his pipe. "The reason the jhorun they possess are so powerful is because it has been enhanced beyond wizarding levels. That much is clear."

"And just how do you enhance a jhorun beyond wizarding

levels?" Steve wanted to know.

"Well, could they have used a jorii? Did they exist back then?"

"They might have, Lady Sarah," Shardwyn said, shaking his head. "They did have several in their possession."

"Caladonia mentioned a fallout with her sister over the jorii," Maelnar explained. "We do not know what caused the fight, only that the sisters disagreed on what they would use the jorii for. That's when Celestia disappeared, taking her two jorii with her."

"Did Caladonia have two jorii as well?"

"Aye. She used both to power her spells. I believe —"

"*We* believe, dwarf."

"*We* believe," the dwarf amended, frowning at the wizard, "that she transferred this power to the ones who would someday protect the Bakkian, and that's how she forfeited her life."

"Our jhorun is stronger than a wizard's?" Steve asked, amazed.

"And that's why it works in our world and Tristan's doesn't?"

Wizard and dwarf nodded.

"Is that why I am able to teleport between this world and ours without a portal?" Sarah asked. "As well as teleport to a place that I've never seen?"

"Because your jhorun has been drastically enhanced, aye," Shardwyn agreed.

"What about the mimets?" Steve asked, raising a hand. "Why can we use power crystals charged by someone else?"

"Ah! I figured you would come around to that sooner or later." Shardwyn flipped open the journal and selected another bookmarked page. "The answer is here. Caladonia was obsessed with being prepared. Not only was she working on a method of storing extra jhorun, she also wanted the Nohrin to be able to use the mimets regardless of who charged them. She experimented on herself. It says here she was able to modify her own jhorun to coexist with someone else's. Her work is quite remarkable."

"So, the two of us can both draw power from a charged mimet because essentially our jhorun originally belonged to

Caladonia, is that right?"

"Correct, Lady Sarah."

"How do you modify someone's jhorun?" the queen wanted to know. "I did not realize two jhorun could coexist."

"The formulas are here, as well as her notes to recreate her experiments."

"That journal does not leave your possession," Kri'Entu decreed. "It must not fall into the wrong hands. As soon as you are finished with it, that journal will be placed in the vault under the strongest enchantments we can create."

The wizard nodded sagely.

"Why not just destroy it?" Steve suddenly asked. "Why risk it? It's only a book. Wouldn't take much to turn into a charcoal briquette."

"The thought had crossed my mind," Kri'Entu admitted, giving the fire thrower a smile. "And once we finish deciphering it, I very well may have you do just that."

"What will you do about Thaden?" Rhenyon asked the king, pointing at the goblet on the table. "He will want that cup back."

"He wouldn't dare try to make a play for that thing while it's here, would he?" Steve asked, glancing briefly at Shardwyn.

"While the goblet sits in this room, it is safely out of Thaden's grasp," Kri'Entu answered, before Shardwyn could take a breath.

"Wouldn't that suggest," Sarah began slowly, "that Shardwyn's son will just bide his time until he has a chance to steal it back or, more likely, create another one?"

Kri'Entu sighed. "It would, aye."

"Do you really think Thaden can find a way to steal it back?" Steve asked.

"I would be a fool to believe Thaden's reach does not extend to this castle." The king sat back in his chair, fingers pressed together as a multitude of potential disastrous scenarios ran through his head. "And I am no fool."

"Then, I say we go after him before he either comes after us or is able to make another of those damn goblets," Steve suggested. "Right now, *we* are the ones who have the advantage."

Rhenyon smiled, grateful that someone else shared his sentiment. He glanced at the fire thrower and gave a supportive nod of his head.

"And how do you propose we do that?" Sarah asked her husband, frowning. "I don't relish the idea of bringing him here."

"Nor do I," Kri'Entu agreed.

"Then don't."

Everyone turned to stare at Sarah's sister once more.

"What do you suggest, Lady Annie?"

"You have what he wants. Make him think he can get it."

"You mean lure him?" Sarah shook her head. "To where?"

"To wherever you want. Seriously, am I the only one who watches TV?"

The Lentarians stared blankly at her.

"Okay, bad example." Annie turned to Tristan. "Remember that show we watched before dinner, on the night before we came here? The one about the lady who was in trouble?"

Tristan nodded, puzzled.

"A lady had hired this guy to protect her," Annie explained to the others, "and when the good guy wanted to find out who was trying to harm the lady, he deliberately walked her around out in the open."

"So the aggressor would identify himself and ultimately put the lady in danger," Tristan finished for her. "If you remember, Lady Annie, I told you then the strategy was poor and not realistic."

"Do something like that here."

"I know what show you're talking about," Steve interjected, frowning. "I'm not sure I like where this is going, though."

"You have the leverage to get Thaden, or whatever his name is, to go where you want," Annie persisted. "If he wants Mikal and that cup as badly as you say he does, then why couldn't you pick and choose where to meet?"

"Thaden would not pass up the chance to reclaim his prize," Shardwyn confirmed, "nor would he pass up an opportunity to lay his hands on the boy. The question is, how do we lure him to a place of our choosing while keeping the prince safe?"

"I have a question."

Everyone turned to Sarah. The king nodded.

"I can teleport. Steve can control fire. Annie can heal. Is there anyone who can make someone look like someone else? For example, make someone look like Mikal?"

All heads turned to the king. Kri'Entu rose, activated his griffin safe, and retrieved an armful of scrolls. Breaking the seal on the first, he unrolled the parchment on his desk and started skimming the long list of names and their associated jhoruns.

Ny'Callé tapped her husband on his shoulder.

"Give me a scroll. Two can search faster than one."

Smiling appreciatively, Kri'Entu handed the second scroll to his wife. Rhenyon leaned forward and held out a hand. Without looking up from his census, the king handed the commander another of the scrolls.

With the search for a suitable illusionist in full swing, Sarah decided to walk around the Antechamber to stretch her legs. Her sister joined her moments later.

"By the way, that was a good idea," Sarah commented.

"What happens if they can't find anyone?" Annie wanted to know.

"I'm not sure," Sarah admitted. "There must be someone in this kingdom who can work with illusions."

"I can brew a potion that would do the job, miss," Shardwyn added, overhearing the question, but he frowned moments later. "However, there is not enough time to properly prepare the potion. I am sorry to say it would not be as effective as it should be."

The king looked up from his desk.

"How long would the effects last?"

"Since the potion would be unable to steep for the required amount of time, it would be severely weakened. A potion that complex, brewed in less than a day, would end up lasting no more than a half a day at the most. But--"

"That should be more than adequate for a doppelganger to convince Thaden that —"

"Your Majesty," the wizard interrupted.

The king sighed. "Yes, Shardwyn?"

"I do not believe a shifter potion will work for this particular circumstance."

"Why not?"

"It would only change the person's appearance," Shardwyn explained. "It will not change their mass."

There was a collective sigh from Sarah, Rhenyon, and the Kri'yans.

"Mikal is a little boy," Sarah said, nodding her head in comprehension. "There's no way a full-grown man, resembling Mikal in appearance, is going to convince anyone that they are the prince."

"You'd need someone the same size as Mikal," Steve deduced, frowning. He then looked at Rhenyon. "Do you have any guards who are that short?"

"I do not believe so," Rhenyon answered, frowning as he mentally reviewed the duty rosters. "But I will find out."

The commander composed a hasty message and instructed the closest guard to deliver it to one of his lieutenants.

"I am small. I will go."

"You will do no such thing," the king contradicted, turning to his wife. "You have been forcefully taken from us once before. There is no way I will give that man a second opportunity. I thank you for your bravery, my love, but the answer is no."

"What about me?"

All eyes turned to Sarah's sister.

"I'm only a little taller than Mikal. I'll bet I could pull it off."

"No way. There's no way you're doing that!" Sarah protested, frowning at her sister. "Do you have any idea how dangerous that'd be?"

"If I had kept a better eye on him in the first place, then we wouldn't be in this predicament, would we? I'm volunteering."

Rhenyon frowned. "I would never ask a lady to do a —"

Annie, Sarah, and the queen all turned to Rhenyon.

The commander cleared his throat and tried again. "That

is to say, I could never —"

"This is my choice, and I'll take it," Annie said, crossing her arms over her chest. "You need someone to pose as Mikal. I'll do it, so it's settled."

Tristan stepped forward. "Lady Annie—"

"Don't start with me, Tristan," Annie warned. "I'm responsible for this mess."

"Nice try," Steve interjected. "You didn't arrange to have his mom kidnapped, so you can't take the blame."

Annie rounded on her brother-in-law. "It was my job to—"

"Oh, would you let it drop?" Sarah said in exasperation. "Do you realize what you're asking? This other wizard will stop at nothing to get his hands on Mikal. Do you know what he'd do to you if he found out he had been tricked?"

"Sarah, I understand. That's why I'm counting on you and Steve to keep me safe. This is important to me. I'm going to do this."

Helplessly, Sarah turned to her husband. "You talk to her."

Instead, much to her shock, Steve turned to Rhenyon and motioned for all the men to form an impromptu meeting. Even Maelnar hopped down from his chair to join the others in their hushed conversation.

"I cannot ask Lady Annie to do this," the king said in a quiet tone.

Steve pointed in Annie's direction. "You heard her. She's pretty set on going. Besides, we can protect her. We took Thaden on once before, in his own lair. We can do it again."

"Do not underestimate my son, young sir," Shardwyn cautioned. "You caught him unaware before. This time, he will be prepared."

"How will we make certain Thaden learns only what we wish him to learn?" Kri'Entu asked, looking pointedly at each of them.

"Let us assume this castle has spies," Tristan began.

"No assumptions necessary," Rhenyon softly muttered.

"Precisely. Call for a meeting with your senior advisers. Announce your suspicions that your son is not safe within these walls, and that you feel the only way to protect him is to take him elsewhere. In this case, to Donlari. Let it be known we will conceal him somewhere in the village."

"Hide him in Thacken Lodge," Steve suggested, drawing a nod of approval from Rhenyon. "Sarah and I will be with him. Her. This is weird. Anyway, unless the two of us are there, it won't be believable. Besides, we know the area and the owner of the inn."

"I can have my guards everywhere," Rhenyon added. "Working at the inn, stationed outside, and even pretending to be drunks and farmers."

"So, you are insinuating that one of my advisers is a Ylanian spy?" Kri'Entu asked, frowning at Tristan. "I do hope you are wrong, Lieutenant."

"And if Thaden does not believe Mikal will leave the castle?"

"Let it also be known the Nohrin will be in possession of the goblet," Tristan suggested.

Shardwyn gasped.

"We cannot let that goblet fall back into my son's hands!"

"It won't," Steve promised. "Sarah will be there, so if things get dicey, she can zap that thing out of there."

Kri'Entu was silent as he considered.

"We can end this once and for all, Your Majesty," Steve insisted.

"Your son will remain safe, here in the castle," Rhenyon added.

The king still said nothing.

"The only risk is the goblet," Steve continued. "And if it looks like he'll make off with it, or if Sarah can't get it out of there, then I'll destroy it. You have my word."

The king finally nodded, straightening back up as he did so. The impromptu huddle ended; the men walked back to the women.

"Very well. Commander, see to the preparations in Donlari."

Rhenyon nodded and left the room.

"Lady Annie. You are to be commended for your bravery. Prepare yourself. Tristan, you are known to everyone as my son's mentor. In order to maintain this ruse, you must accompany Mikal, er, Lady Annie, to Donlari. In fact, I hereby appoint you as Lady Annie's personal guard."

Tristan bowed and forced himself not to smile.

"It will be my pleasure."

Annie turned to the tall soldier and raised an eyebrow. The gesture was not lost on her new guard.

"Sir Steve, Lady Sarah. You have done so much for us already, so I hesitate in asking this."

Steve held up a hand and ignited it.

"Then don't. Besides, you don't have to. Let's end this."

His eyes hardening, Kri'Entu nodded. He turned to regard the wizard.

"Shardwyn, prepare the potion. Make haste. The longer we wait, the higher the risk of your son making the first move."

"At once, Your Majesty." Shardwyn started heading toward the door when he paused and turned back. "Sir Maelnar, I, er, would, er, appreciate your assistance."

Surprised, bemused, and honored, the dwarf nodded, hopping off his chair to follow the retreating wizard. Once the unlikely duo had departed, Steve sat back and sighed. He turned to the queen.

"Your Majesty, I've been wondering something. If you don't mind me asking, how did you realize that the jhorun Mikal restored was not your original jhorun?"

"My natural jhorun was very difficult to suppress," the queen explained. "Therefore, I let it be active all the time. Now all I have to do is simply think about what it was like without my jhorun and within moments I can feel my jhorun diminishing. I could not do that before."

"What about the original vial of your jhorun?" Steve wanted to know.

"It remains sealed," Kri'Entu answered.

"Well, you could always use that cup thing to remove the new jhorun and put your original back in place, couldn't you?"

The queen nodded.

"Aye, I could, but I believe I prefer this one."

"Then what are you going to do with your original

jhorun?" Sarah asked.

"The vial with the queen's jhorun has been secured in a safe place," the king assured her. "It should never have to be used, but in case it's needed, we will have it."

Steve gestured at the cup. "Hey Annie, if you don't want your jhorun, now's the time to say something."

Annie smiled and shook her head.

"Actually, I think I'll keep it. Just remind me to thank Mikal for giving it to me."

"I'm curious. I wonder why Mikal gave you a healing jhorun?"

Tristan cleared his throat.

"I believe I can shed some light on this subject. I was, er, talking with young Mikal about, uh, Lady Annie after we had stopped to rest on the side of the road. It was right after it had been discovered I was injured."

Annie turned to Tristan. "You and Mikal were talking about me?"

Tristan's face reddened noticeably.

"About whether you might develop a jhorun seeing how Steve and Sarah developed theirs within a day or two of their arrival here."

"Are you saying you and Mikal were talking about what Annie's jhorun might be?" Sarah asked.

"How did healing come into the conversation?" Annie wanted to know.

It didn't seem possible, but Tristan's face reddened even further.

"We were discussing what type of jhorun you might get should you be fortunate enough to receive one. Mikal had speculated it may be a jhorun dealing with illusion, or possibly the ability to conjure food. I, er, might have suggested a jhorun of a more, er, nurturing nature."

"Nurturing nature?" Annie repeated, causing Tristan to blush even deeper. She was silent for a few moments. "Your words or his?"

"They were mine."

Annie stared at Mikal's tutor for a few moments more before the corners of her mouth turned upward into the beginnings of a smile.

"Nurturing, huh? Huh?" Steve playfully jabbed his elbow in Tristan's stomach.

"I was only theorizing."

"Just be careful," Steve advised, giving Tristan a playful slap on the back. "Annie has a wicked left hook."

"And on that note, I think I'm going to go for a walk." Sarah rose stiffly to her feet. "I've been sitting for too long. Would anyone care to join me?"

"I will." Steve also stood and took his wife's hand. "We can give the two love birds a little privacy."

This elicited another smack on the arm from his sister-in-law.

"I believe I will accompany you as well," the queen decided.

Annie jumped to her feet.

"What? Wait a minute. You're not going to leave me in here by myself. I think a walk sounds great!"

Tristan rose to his feet as well.

"Lady Annie, would you care for a personal tour of the castle? It would be my pleasure to show you around the grounds."

Annie shot a dark look at her sister and brother-in-law as they quickly bolted from the room.

"If you will excuse me," the king rose from his seat, trying very hard not to smile, "I have matters that I must attend to as well."

* * *

"I usually try to support the vendors once or twice a week," the queen was saying, several hours later.

"It shows that you care."

Ny'Callé turned to Sarah and smiled.

"I believe so, too."

The trio stopped at a cart with bright colorful bolts of fabric. Steve rolled his eyes as both women began looking through the various styles.

"This one is very pretty," Sarah was saying. "The gold

thread enhances the griffins' feathers."

The queen rubbed the knitted throw between two fingers.

"I do not know how they can get their yarn so soft, nor their weaving so fine. It is a skill I clearly lack. Sarah, are you a skilled weaver?"

"Ummm, no, I'm not. We get our clothes from a group of, um, weavers who call themselves JCPenney."

"They must be gifted women. I remember the clothes you were wearing when you first arrived. They do remarkable work."

"They really do," Steve agreed, suppressing a smile. "They send out advertisements all the damn time."

Sarah lightly smacked him on the arm.

They walked past several more rows of vendors as they left the castle's largest bailey and approached the northern gate.

"It's turning out to be a very nice day, isn't it?" Sarah observed.

"Aye, it is, Lady Sarah." Ny'Callé agreed, smiling at her as they approached the border of the orchard. "Perhaps we could find Mikal?"

Steve put his fingers to his lips and whistled. He waited a moment and then tried again. If Peanut were in the area, she should have started barking by now.

"They have to be around here somewhere."

Sarah put her arm on her husband's shoulder, bringing him to a gentle stop.

"Whistle again. I thought I heard something."

The queen covered her ears as Steve once again whistled long and loud for their furry companion. Now they all heard it: excited yipping. It was coming from somewhere ahead.

"Sounds like they're playing," Steve determined. "Usually she would have heard the whistle."

"I do believe you would be hard pressed to find someone who did not hear that whistle," Ny'Callé added, rubbing her ears.

"Must be one heck of a game. She's not responding."

Steve, Sarah, the queen, and an entire squadron of armed men headed toward the northern orchards where they encountered another armed squadron keeping an eye on the prince. There, running in zigzags through the many trees, was the young boy. He was laughing hysterically as his canine companion easily outdistanced him. Peanut deftly darted around Mikal's legs, and every so often would nudge a heel to send the giggling boy face first into the soft grass. Mikal would regain his feet, abruptly change directions and sprint to the next tree. Peanut always caught him just before he made it to safety. The young corgi tripped him up again, this time under a large jansa tree.

Even from their distance they could hear the muffled thump as the boy went tumbling to the fruit-strewn ground. Wiping remnants of smashed purple fruit off his trousers, the boy grinned at his canine companion.

"When my mother asks what happened to my clothes, you know who will get the blame, don't you?"

Peanut barked joyfully, enjoying this game of tag. As her human companion called for a rematch, the young dog hesitated and sniffed the air. A strange new scent had caught her attention. A quick backward glance at her playmate confirmed the scent did not originate from him. The winds picked up, bringing even more new scents to the excitable dog. She continued to remain motionless with one foreleg raised. She turned her head to sniff east and then west. When she finally turned to sniff the scents arriving on the southern winds, both of her ears jumped straight up as an enormous creature landed silently twenty feet away.

The massive emerald dragon slowly lowered its head to inspect the foreign creature. Inching forward until it was only a few feet away from the tiny being, the dragon hesitated. Very gently, dragon and corgi sniffed noses.

Deciding the huge dragon was now a part of her pack, Peanut invited her newest littermate to join in on the frolicking. With her head down low and her rear up high, she playfully yipped at the dragon.

Recognizing an attempt at play, the dragon folded its wings and dropped as low to the ground as its bulk would allow. The dragon feinted right. The young corgi bolted, barking maniacally as it ran around the dragon's enormous body.

Afraid the small creature would be squished flat if it moved, the dragon remained motionless, its tail swishing noisily through the grass. When the small creature finally completed her trek around the dragon's body, the corgi once again struck a playful pose. Once more the dragon purposely twitched, causing the small dog to take off in another frenzied sprint through the grass.

Unaccustomed to playing with a creature hundreds of times larger than she, Peanut flopped over after the third pass. Panting heavily, tongue sticking out of the side of her mouth, the young dog rested a few moments in the soft grass.

Nearly a hundred yards away, Steve and the others had held their breaths and watched with amazement as dragon and corgi had played with one another in the lush green meadow. When it was clear that no hostilities were forthcoming, he let out the breath he hadn't realized he'd been holding.

"There's a sight you don't see every day."

By the time the three of them approached the dragon, Peanut was regaining her feet.

"What manner of creature is it?" Pryllan inquired, looking down at the tiny fluff ball. "Is it injured?"

"She's fine," Steve called out as they approached the orchard. "In our world, it's called frap. It's supposed to stand for frenetic random activity period, but I personally like frantic random acts of play. Peanut is famous for it. Right about now she's probably thinking you're too big to run around."

Pryllan snorted once in amusement before raising her head back up. Her green reptilian eyes fixated on Steve's.

"I bring news from the north."

Chapter 16 — Showdown

Steve gazed up at the green dragon and started to ask a question, but before he could say anything, he was forcefully yanked backwards and thrown to the ground. The squad of men that had kept silent vigil behind them had abruptly decided to leap into action, forming an armored wall between them and the dragon.

Pryllan's growl was low and ominous, causing the human wall to beat a hasty retreat. Peanut leapt to the defense of her new playmate and added her own growl to that of the dragon's.

"Stand down."

The command, while it wasn't shouted, was easily heard by everyone. The authoritative tone brooked no arguments and received none. Several of the guards turned to look at the queen.

"The dragon is a friend. Stand down immediately."

"Aye, Your Majesty."

"If Pryllan wanted to do us harm, then she already would

have by now," Steve added, eliciting a grunt from the dragon. He turned to look at his enormous friend.

"So what's going on? What news do you have?"

The queen laid an arm on his.

"One moment, if you please. We must include my husband." The queen turned to one of the guards and motioned him over. "Go find the king. Tell him to come to the northern orchards."

The guard bowed and ran off toward the castle at a sprint.

"Good news or bad?" Steve wanted to know, turning back to the dragon.

Pryllan, who had leaned down for an additional inspection of the tiny dog, lifted her head back up.

"Informational."

"That can be taken either way!" Steve complained.

The queen turned to the guards still standing uncertainly about.

"The king will be here momentarily," she informed them, watching as all visibly straightened. "You might want to secure the perimeter before he arrives."

The soldiers managed to reform their ranks just as a second squadron of soldiers arrived, hot on the heels of the king.

Kri'Entu surveyed the enormous dragon and nodded his head.

"We have met a few times before. We are honored, Pryllan. To what do we owe the pleasure of this visit?"

"I give this information for you to do with as you please," Pryllan began, flicking her gaze between the king and the fire thrower. "An army of trolls has been spotted, advancing south. They will cross onto Lentarian soil by nightfall. At their current rate, they will be here by midday tomorrow."

The Kri'yans gasped with astonishment. Trolls were solitary creatures and not known for their social skills, so to hear of more than a few in close proximity was very surprising.

"How many comprise this army?" the king wanted to know.

"By my reckoning, nearly two-hundred."

"Two-hundred? Trolls?" Ny'Callé looked at her husband

in alarm. "What are we to do?"

"Wizards be damned," Kri'Entu muttered, cursing softly to himself. "So little time. We will have to—"

"I was not finished."

Kri'Entu paled and turned back to the dragon.

"My apologies. Do continue."

"The malwerns have also massed together and are traveling south."

"What's a malwern?" Steve asked, perplexed. A quick glance at his wife confirmed she didn't know what they were either.

"Malwerns are winged creatures that have a high-pitched shriek, causing a permanent loss of hearing with prolonged exposure," Kri'Entu answered, frowning as he did so. "Their bites and their claws are highly venomous. They are smaller than griffins, but are far more maneuverable in the air. Only the highest mountains are populated with malwerns, which means their principle habitat are the northern mountains of Ylani. Pryllan, do you have any idea on their numbers?"

"So many that they divided themselves into three groups," the dragon answered. "One appears to be headed toward a human settlement southwest from this location."

"Donlari," the king whispered.

"Another appears to be headed here."

Ny'Callé gasped and clutched her husband's hand tightly.

"What about the last one?" Sarah inquired, nervously eyeing her husband.

Pryllan snorted with disgust, as if recalling a bad memory. "We can only assume the third meant to attack the small human settlement nestled amongst the trees in the high north."

"Verdayn! They will decimate the village unless—"

"You have to do nothing."

Kri'Entu bristled with anger.

"I will do no such thing. I will not leave any village of this kingdom unprotected. I will—"

"You will do nothing," the dragon repeated.

"Why?" Steve asked, gazing up at his massive friend.

"Those filthy creatures chose to cross our valley. My

fellow dragons did not look kindly upon the intrusion."

"What happened? Did the dragons attack?"

"Ten of my brethren volunteered to address the threat."

"Were they able to drive them away?" Kri'Entu asked.

Pryllan snorted. "They refused to be swayed from their course."

"What did the dragons do?" Steve wanted to know.

"Eliminated the threat."

"Eliminated? Does that mean they took them out?"

"Only those that passed over our domain," the dragon clarified.

"So that's why I am to do nothing?" Kri'Entu asked, his eyes widening. "Because *nothing* is threatening Verdayn?"

The dragon nodded.

"It would appear Thaden knows we are planning on hiding Mikal in Donlari," Sarah observed.

Steve sighed. "Man, that was quick. Even for him. How'd he find out so fast?"

"I only informed my senior staff two hours ago." Kri'Entu exclaimed, deeply disturbed that one of his advisers was clearly a Ylanian spy. His brow furrowing, the king scowled, beckoning to one of the guards as he did so. "How could they have massed the trolls and malwerns in such a short amount of time? Regardless, get word to commander Rhenyon. Ylani has begun their move against us."

The soldier nodded and ran off.

"Lady Sarah. Where is your sister?"

"Taking a tour of the grounds with Tristan."

"She must prepare herself. I had hoped we would have more time, but clearly, we do not. It is time for her to assume the role of my son."

"She'll be ready. We'll be there every step of the way to make sure she's safe," Steve added, putting an arm around his wife.

"It's time to secure the queen and my son," the king stated, turning back toward the castle. Everyone hurried to catch up.

"Are you going to put them in the Antechamber?" Steve asked.

"In a manner of speaking, aye."

Returning to the heavily fortified chamber, the king dismissed the soldiers who were standing guard. He also sent for Shardwyn and Maelnar, figuring they had had an adequate amount of time to brew the complicated shape shifting potion. At least he fervently hoped they had. He strode over to the fake wall and activated his safe. Once the griffin had raised its paw, instead of hitting the concealed button, the king faced the statue and hesitated.

"Entu? What is the matter?"

The king turned to his wife. He gave her a smile, then turned to regard the rest of the people all staring curiously at him.

"I trust everyone here will keep this secret."

The king turned back to the griffin safe.

"*Entu anee wyverie.*"

"What'd he say?" Steve whispered to his wife. Sarah shrugged. She hadn't heard him either.

The safe's musical chiming suddenly changed frequencies, becoming higher pitched. The griffin statue lowered its right paw and then raised its left, revealing a second button. The king leaned forward to press it.

"What are you doing, Entu?" Ny'Callé asked, genuinely curious. She had never known there was a second button on the griffin safe, let alone the griffin could raise its other foreleg.

The floor rumbled slightly as the entire safe slid forward, out of the recessed area in the wall, revealing a steep tunnel leading down.

"Sir Steve," Kri'Entu turned to the fire thrower. "Can you please light the torches that you see there?"

Equally curious about the hidden chamber, Steve complied.

"Let me guess. No one knows about this room, right?"

"Only the commander and myself," the king confirmed. "The Antechamber is already enchanted against jhorun, so what better place to have a safe haven for the royal family?"

"It's a safe room," Steve decided, nodding his head. "Smart."

"Mikal and the queen will take refuge down there while

Lady Annie assumes the guise of my son. Accompanying the false prince will be the Nohrin, naturally, and Tristan, since it is well known that he is Mikal's tutor. This will maintain the illusion Mikal has left the castle for Donlari."

"Then, that means Annie must become Mikal here in this room," Sarah said. "Everyone saw all of us come in here, so they know Mikal is here. If Mikal goes down there, then everyone must see Mikal leave here as well."

The king nodded. "Agreed. That's why I dismissed the guards. Everyone must believe my son leaves this chamber."

Tristan and Annie arrived just then. Tristan bowed slightly before the king.

"You sent for us, sire?"

"Indeed, Tristan. Lady Annie, I had hoped we would have more time before it became necessary to transform you into my son, but we do not. Are you ready?"

Annie nodded. "I am."

As if on cue, Shardwyn and Maelnar arrived, in their customary fashion: they were arguing.

"You do realize you added rue when you should have added fragaria instead?"

"Dwarf, you need to have your eyes checked. I added —"

"Shardwyn, Maelnar, not now," Kri'Entu snapped. "Is the potion ready?"

Shardwyn gave a short bow, and held up a small container of a bubbling green mixture.

"It is, Your Majesty."

Annie stepped forward and took the potion from Shardwyn's outstretched hand.

"Will this hurt?"

Curious, Sarah turned to Shardwyn.

"Will it?"

"I have never had a need to alter my form, Lady Sarah. I do not know."

Before she could talk herself out of it, Annie broke the vial's wax seal and downed the bubbling concoction in a single swallow.

"I wonder how long we have to wait before something happens."

Steve turned to look at Shardwyn, who shrugged. By the time he turned back, the image of his sister-in-law had been replaced with an Annie-sized Mikal.

"Wow, that was quick!"

"What was quick?" the newest Mikal asked, using Annie's voice.

Sarah gently turned her sister until she faced a large mirror on one of the walls.

"Whoa! I didn't feel a thing!"

Annie raised her right arm and waved. The image of Mikal reciprocated the gesture in the mirror. Smiling, she turned to look at the real Mikal, who was staring at her with an open mouth.

"You look just like me!"

"That's the whole point," Steve explained, squatting down to Mikal's level. "You have to stay here, but we need other people to think that you're actually leaving with us."

"But —"

"You need to take care of your mom, okay? She's counting on you to look after her."

"Precisely," Kri'Entu agreed, putting his hand on his son's shoulder. "You must remain here, son. It is not safe outside this room."

The king strode to his desk to retrieve the box of portal keys. Steve, in the meantime, approached his sister-in-law.

"Annie, say something."

"Like what?"

"Hmm. Okay, new problem. Mikal here sounds just like Annie. Is there a way we can get her voice to match his?"

Kri'Entu hesitated as he retrieved his box of portal keys. "Shardwyn, you created a potion to change Lady Annie's appearance, but not her voice?"

The wizard turned to the king.

"My apologies, Your Majesty. I do not know what could have happened. Her voice should have matched the prince's, all the way down to the smallest vocal inflections."

"Still think you did not add any rue, wizard?"

With an exasperated sigh, Shardwyn turned to the dwarf, who sat smirking at him from his chair.

"If you saw I was reaching for the rue, then why did you not say so before?"

"I *did* say so before."

Kri'Entu plunked the chest of portal keys down on his desk a trifle more forcefully than necessary. Everyone fell silent.

"There's naught to do now but prepare Donlari. Sir Steve, take the key. You need to get to Donlari just as soon as you can. Mikal must be seen there."

Steve handed the brown crystal key back to the king.

"Thanks, but I don't need this."

Kri'Entu nodded, placing the key back inside the chest and sealing it shut. "I keep forgetting about Lady Sarah's remarkable jhorun. Very well. Just be sure you appear in the constable's office so it looks as though you used the portal."

"Got it. How long do you want us to parade our Mikal around?"

"If this ruse is to be believed, then not long at all. He must be taken straight from the constable's office and secured in the inn.

"So I can go then?" Mikal asked, turning his hopeful eyes onto his father.

"Absolutely not," the king reiterated.

"But you just said I need to be secured in the inn!"

"Son, I meant Lady Annie."

The young boy sighed. It had been worth a try.

While the king saw his wife and son tucked safely away within the hidden chamber, Steve and Sarah helped each other back into their leather armor.

"You'd think I'd know how to do this by now," Steve grumbled, holding up one of the many pieces of leather and trying to remember where it was supposed to be fastened.

"Your cuirass is upside-down, Sir Steve," Rhenyon helpfully pointed out.

"Hmm?"

Sarah tapped her husband's chest. "Your chest piece, honey."

"Oh. Thought that felt a bit weird."

"And that's a greave, Sir Steve," Tristan added. "It goes

on your shin, not your arm."

"That's okay," Sarah patted her husband's cheek reassuringly, "this is only the first time you've worn this, so it's understandable that—oh, whoops. My mistake."

"Smartass."

* * *

Tristan gently pushed the door open and peered outside. The sun had just set moments before, so while there was still enough light to navigate by, it wouldn't last.

"Let us be off. Thacken Lodge is just over there, down the end of that alley."

"Remember," Sarah told her sister, "as soon as you get out into the open, pull the hood up on your jacket, like you're trying to not be noticed."

"Got it."

"Expect danger," Tristan advised.

"Really?"

"No, but you need to appear as though you expect danger."

"Oh, okay."

The four of them hastily slipped out of the constable's office and headed off, walking carefully along the darkening street. Both Steve and Tristan hastily slung their rucksacks over their shoulders. Annie waited a few moments before pulling her hood tightly over her head.

"We need to avoid calling attention to ourselves, yet we do not want to appear conspicuous. We need to —"

"We got it, Tristan. Let's just keep moving."

The front door to Thacken Lodge was open wide. A steady stream of patrons were entering and exiting the inn, making entry into the lodge difficult.

"What's with all the people?" Steve whispered, looking over at Tristan. "What happened to keeping this discreet?"

"This *is* discreet, Sir Steve," Tristan whispered back. "I have spotted no fewer than two dozen men I am personally familiar with."

"Definitely good to know," Sarah softly murmured.

"Tristan, find out which room we have so we can get out of the open."

Mikal's tutor nodded and angled off toward the counter. The large proprietor, chatting amiably with a group of patrons, looked up as Tristan approached. Greetings were given, and Thacken, without giving the slightest indication of how much information he had been privy to, waved off the newcomer, instructing him to take any room on the top floor.

"He does know it's us, right?" Steve whispered, irked at their abrupt dismissal.

"Of course, he does," Tristan whispered back, steering all of them toward the staircase. "However, the civilians are under strict orders not to reveal anything to anyone. As far as he is concerned, we are simple travelers who need lodging for the night."

A skinny pimply-faced boy, still enmeshed in the throes of puberty, collided with Sarah and was knocked off his feet.

"Oh, I'm sorry. Are you okay?"

Steve leaned around his wife and held out a hand, waiting for the skinny youth to accept his offer to be helped back up.

"We didn't see you there. Are you okay, sport?"

"Of course, I am," the boy said in an unusually deep voice, one that everyone had heard before. "Wizards be damned. What did I do to that old fool to deserve this?"

Shocked, Steve stared into the kid's eyes.

"Rhenyon?"

"If this is his idea of a joke, I am not amused."

Sarah clapped a hand over her mouth to keep from laughing out loud. Steve had to look away before he started laughing, too. The boy scowled.

"Just keep moving. Secure yourselves in the room. Go on, make haste!"

Demonstrating remarkable restraint, Steve refrained from saying anything negative about the acne-infested visage his friend was now wearing. Rhenyon's disguise would definitely have to be the subject of some good-natured ribbing at a later date.

Several hours later, Steve was pacing in their small room.

"This is a waste of time. It's been, what, three hours and

nothing has happened! This isn't working."

Sarah took her husband's hand and gave him an encouraging pat.

"Be patient, Sir Steve," Tristan offered. "As far as Thaden is concerned, we have the two things he wants most in this world: Mikal and the goblet. He will come."

"I wish he'd just get this over with."

"Honey, when was the last time you ate something?"

"What's that supposed to mean?"

"Well, you do get a little cranky when you get hungry. Why don't you go downstairs and get something to eat? Then you can bring something back for the rest of us. Tristan, why don't you go with him?"

"Agreed."

"Come on," Steve said, crossly. "There's nothing else to do."

He pulled open the door and stormed out into the hallway. Tristan glanced back at Sarah.

"Make sure he gets plenty to eat," she advised.

Smiling, Tristan closed the door behind him.

* * *

From a discreet location several hundred yards away, the inn was watched. The bustling tavern was starting to settle down for the night. The flow of patrons coming and going had finally tapered to a trickle. The townsfolk who were lucky enough to depart the inn were ignored; they were irrelevant. The less people to deal with, the better.

"How long must we wait?" one man hissed in frustration.

"As long as it takes."

"Why are we not attacking? There are no guards, no soldiers. Easy pickings!"

A thin man was nervously wringing his hands together. He turned to regard the one who spoke. "Be silent. We were told to wait, so wait we will."

"I do not see why —"

"If you cannot keep your mouth shut," a sinister voice whispered out of the darkness, "then perhaps you would like me to do it for you?"

All traces of chattering instantly vanished. The thin man turned to the newest arrival.

"Do you think this wise, Master?"

"Stop your fretting, Warrick."

"But Master, I implore you to consider your actions. The Lentarians are fools, but I do not think even they are foolish enough to believe you will not try to reacquire your cup."

"You believe we are walking into a trap?"

Warrick emphatically nodded his head, hoping he was finally getting through to his arrogant master.

"Nonsense," Thaden huffed. "I do not fear peasants."

"But Master, I —"

"Enough of this. I have waited long enough for my vengeance. Tell me about the village. I trust you have secured the portal key?"

Warrick dropped his gaze to the ground, saying nothing. Thaden stared at him suspiciously.

"Imbecile, where is the key?"

"We were unable to acquire this village's key, Master."

Thaden glared at his fidgeting minion. The time had come to correct the mistake of taking this fool on as an assistant. However, thanks to his inept assistant, he now had more pressing problems to deal with.

"I will have words with you once this is over."

Warrick bowed his head, more in fear than shame.

"As you wish, Master."

Thaden turned to several of the hulking men he had brought with him.

"Ulrik, Wolfred."

Two muscular thugs looked up.

"I have a task for you. Fetch the portal key. It will be somewhere in the constable's office. Be back in less than ten minutes and you will get to choose your replacement jhorun."

A misshapen grin split the face of one of the brutes, displaying cracked and rotted teeth. They both slipped away into the darkness.

The blond wizard frowned. Communication with the castle had not yet been cut off. Phase two of his plan would have to wait until he was certain this backwater village would be unable to call for help.

While confident he could handle anything the foolish Lentarians could throw at him, Thaden decided there wasn't any harm in taking precautions. He prepared to cast several spells, designed to prevent anyone from teleporting. Once cast, even *he* wouldn't be able to break his own enchantment unless he moved away from the affected area. He reminded himself to also cast a ward of obscurity. No sense in attracting unwanted attention if it could be avoided.

With a sigh of exasperation, Thaden began to chant.

* * *

"But I have to go to the bathroom!"

"Can't you hold it?"

"I *have* been holding it. None of the rooms here have bathrooms in them. Trust me, I was stuck in one of them for a whole night, remember?"

"Just go with her," Steve instructed.

Sarah looked at her husband.

"The bathrooms are on the main floor. I don't want to go down there by myself."

Steve propped himself up on an elbow on the bed and eyed his wife.

"Want us to come along?"

"Yes, I do. Besides, we're supposed to be his bodyguards. Her bodyguards. Whatever."

"Makes you wonder, doesn't it?"

"What?" Sarah prompted.

"Just how accurate was Shardwyn's potion?"

That brought them both up short. Both sisters eyed each other and broke out in giggles. Sarah looked at the image of Mikal, who looked back at her and raised an eyebrow.

"Well, we're going to find out. Should I put my jacket back on?"

Sarah nodded. "Yes."

Reluctant to let his bag out of his sight, Steve slung the rucksack over his shoulder as they exited the room. Once they descended down the stairs to the main floor, they were grateful to see there were at least half a dozen undercover guards still seated at various tables.

The boy that Rhenyon had become was sitting at the table nearest the bar and closest to the front door. Glancing up, he stared at the four of them questioningly. Steve mouthed the word 'bathroom' and hooked a thumb over his shoulder toward his wife. Rhenyon nodded, turning his attention back to the door. Bolli, the innkeeper's wife, had just exited the kitchen and was wiping her hands on an apron. When she saw the two Nohrin and the king's soldier escorting a third person to the water closets behind the rear storeroom, she gave them a knowing smile and a slight nod of her head.

The front door opened and two small children, a boy and a girl, came inside. Both children were wearing the drab peasant clothes found on most peasant farmers. The girl smiled shyly at Rhenyon before she darted over to one of the tables and snatched a loaf of bread. In the meantime, the boy had grabbed a tankard of ale from the counter and bolted out the front door with his sister in hot pursuit.

Bolli was standing closest to the girl and almost managed to apprehend her as she ran by. With a shout, she followed the girl outside. Annoyed that a boy, and a young one at that, had managed to steal some ale from his tavern, Thacken bolted after his wife, intent on catching the two thieving miscreants. The half dozen undercover soldiers seated at various tables also took up the chase and disappeared out the front door leaving one very surprised youth staring at an empty room.

Tristan looked at the commander. The young boy met his eyes and nodded his head in the direction of the two children. Tristan nodded, sprinting through the open door to try and catch up to the two young thieves.

"What's going on?" Sarah asked, as she and Annie appeared from the back of the inn. "What'd we miss?"

"I'm not sure," Steve admitted, looking out the front door. "Two kids just darted in here and stole some bread and ale."

"Two kids? In the middle of the night? Anyone else think that's odd or is it just —"

Sarah's eyes rolled in her head and she toppled forward. Rhenyon made it to her first before she fell to the ground. However, his present form lacked the musculature necessary to hold her aloft, so the two slowly began to sink to the ground.

"Blasted wizards and their damn potions!"

Steve came to their aid before either could crack their head on the floor. He gently lowered both his wife and the boy to a sitting position.

"Are you okay? Sarah? Wake up! What's the matter?"

"Wizards be damned!" Rhenyon hissed, standing abruptly and drawing his sword. "She passed out before, when we were teleported from that cell, remember?"

"We were just teleported? Again? What, did he move the whole damn tavern? It still looks the same to me."

Rhenyon glanced around, scowling as he did so.

"The stairs are in the wrong location, the counter was curved before and it is not now, the tables —"

"Okay, I get it."

Sarah opened her eyes.

"I think we were —"

"Teleported, we know," Steve finished for her, looking around the new tavern in alarm.

So where were they now? Still in Donlari? Probably not. Steve paled. If they were in another village, then that meant the five squadrons lying in ambush all throughout the town had just been rendered useless. To make matters worse, the undercover guards who had been in the tavern had all given chase after those two kids, leaving them with no backup. No one to back them up outside, and now there were no soldiers to help them inside. That could only mean …

"Get behind something!" Steve snapped to Annie, igniting both hands. "Hurry! Hon, go with her!"

Both Sarah and her sister darted behind the long counter and ducked down low, scattering mugs and plates as they did so. In the next instant, a dozen men swarmed into the tavern, rapidly spreading out to cover all doors and windows.

He didn't wait. Before the newest arrivals could dive for cover, Steve fired twin blasts at Thaden's henchmen, watching with satisfaction as two of them were thrown through the front window. Rhenyon noticed another two men trying to make their way to the bar, so he leapt in front of them. Even in his weakened state, he was still a force to be reckoned with.

At that moment, ten more of Thaden's henchmen poured into the tavern. These men had bows already nocked with arrows. Three drew back and let loose.

Realizing he was about to be turned into a pincushion, Steve darted behind the closest table, tipping it over just in time to feel it shudder as the arrows struck. He silently pled with his jhorun to refrain from using one of his now famous detonations. His wife and sister-in-law were in the blast zone and would more than likely be hurt.

The sharp clang of steel on steel drew his attention. The two henchmen battling Rhenyon were savagely lunging and chopping at the young boy. If they thought they were truly fighting someone that young, they wouldn't be fighting as viciously, would they? Did they know who they were facing?

Steve ignited a chaser and threw it at one of Rhenyon's assailants. The goon saw the speeding fireball and ducked, causing the chaser to smash through the nearby window. It disappeared into the night. The hired mercenary sneered at him.

"Is that the best you can do?"

Steve held up a finger. "Wait for it."

"Wait for what?"

The errant chaser sped back through the broken front window and slammed into its intended target, engulfing the man in flames. Screaming, the thug dove through the broken window and disappeared.

Steve continued to fire jet after jet at Thaden's men, who kept popping their heads over the overturned tables, much like prairie dogs poking their heads out of their burrows. Comprehension dawned: *they were keeping him preoccupied.* He risked a glance behind him. Sure enough, one of Thaden's henchmen had managed to sneak past him. However, before Steve could shout a warning, one of the front doors ripped itself off of its hinges and floated in midair. Hesitating only briefly, it sped across the room to collide with the henchman who was just starting to climb over the bar. With a grunt of expelled air, the man collapsed.

Noticing that he could no longer hear the sounds of Rhenyon and his attacker, Steve risked a glance in the opposite direction. Neither were visible. Detecting movement in his peripheral vision, he snapped his gaze back to the front of the tavern. He could only hope Rhenyon was alright.

After seeing their companion flattened by the heavy wooden door, four men suddenly stood, figuring if they all stormed the bar at the same time then at least one of them should be able to make it to where the prince was hiding. Unfortunately for them, Steve was ready. Two were blasted through the open front doors before they could take a step.

"Anyone else care to try their luck? Come on guys, I double dog dare you."

The two men cursed with disgust and dropped behind their tables.

"Wait outside. I will deal with these impertinent fools."

Unsure of who spoke, the men cowering behind the tables looked toward the doorway. No one was there, therefore no one moved.

"I said leave. Now."

Now the voice was recognized. The remaining men scrambled out of the inn.

"No one kills him but me."

Steve snorted. He knew that voice. He had been wondering when Thaden was going to put in an appearance.

"Rather presumptuous, don't you think?" Steve looked around. "Are you actually hiding from me?"

The voice chuckled. "Insolent scum. I have this entire building surrounded. Surrender. Swear allegiance to me and you might live through the day."

Steve shook his head and laughed. "And I'm supposed to trust you to keep your word? Spare me."

Thaden appeared in the doorway, scowling. Without batting an eye, Steve threw a huge fireball at him. Thaden flicked his right hand, batting it aside. The fireball spiraled out the door and struck a henchman.

"Final chance, fire thrower. I will not make this offer again."

"Oh my goodness gracious me," Steve mocked, in a falsetto. "Whatever am I going to do? I am so scared! Perhaps I should just give up. In fact, come and get me."

Thaden snarled and thrust a hand into his robes. Moments later, he flung a handful of pebbles into the air. Each pebble became a dagger and streaked toward Steve, who grunted with surprise as an invisible force shoved him across the room. Sliding to a stop amidst a pile of tables and chairs, Steve grinned as several dozen knives all plunked harmlessly into a nearby wall.

"Thanks, hon!" Steve called out. He wasn't sure where his wife was hiding, but was very thankful she was keeping an eye on him. "Perfect timing!"

Thaden scowled. He threw a second handful of pebbles and watched with dismay as his opponent was shoved out of the way a second time.

"Okay, sport, I do believe it's my turn."

Thaden darted behind one of the inn's massive support posts as twin jets of fire sprang into existence and launched straight toward him. Noticing that the wizard was now hiding, Steve ignited a jet of fire and refrained from giving it a target, once more giving himself the appearance of holding a burning rope. Not wanting to give the wizard any time to think about retaliating, he whipped the rope around the top of the post, much like he did with the chest from the cave. Blasting extra jhorun through fire tendril, he watched as the wood post burned through, separating from the ceiling. Sarah was ready. As soon as the post was separated, she used her jhorun to push the post over.

Unfortunately, Thaden was ready for him. This time, he was holding a small open canister of grain, which he flung at Steve. Each piece of grain morphed into a full-sized arrow and sped toward the fire thrower.

Steve jerked up both hands, knowing full well what was coming. The problem was, for once, he didn't want the explosion, not with his wife and Annie in such close proximity. However, his jhorun didn't agree. The blast shattered the remaining windows that weren't already broken and incinerated the volley of arrows in midflight. The shock wave even slammed Thaden up against the nearest wall and scorched his blonde hair, turning it black.

While Thaden appeared to be stunned, Steve glanced over his shoulder to make sure Sarah and Annie were alright. Both were on their feet, looking for Rhenyon.

Sarah waved Annie over.

"Found him."

Annie joined her sister and knelt down to lay a hand on his chest.

"He's still breathing, but he's got a nasty cut across his chest."

"How fast can you heal him?"

"I have no idea. I haven't healed that many people."

"Drag him back behind the counter!" Steve instructed. "Hurry!"

Annie and Sarah each took an arm and dragged Rhenyon's unmoving form to safety.

"Do your thing," Sarah told her sister. "Try to heal him as fast as you can."

"I'll try," Annie said, laying her hands back on the boy's chest.

Hurricane force winds suddenly slammed into Steve, shoving him into the far wall and pinning him in place. Thaden smiled as he conjured a tiny ball of fire and added it to the blast of air that was holding Steve in place. The air jet turned to a roaring jet of fire and engulfed Steve, blocking him from sight.

"Burn, fire thrower!" Thaden hissed with delight. "There will be no—"

The wizard hesitated. The amount of jhorun he was using to maintain the fire jet had just drastically increased, to the point where he could feel his jhorun drain away. Something wasn't right. He let the jet lapse.

The flames shrank in size and vanished. Even the wooden tables and chairs that had caught fire were extinguished. Steve was grinning. He stretched his arms, and then his back.

"Thanks! I really needed that!"

Thaden's eyes narrowed as he realized the strength of Steve's jhorun had been restored. Had his jhorun been absorbed by his opponent? Closing his eyes, he chanted, seeking the closest source of water. Nearly a hundred feet below the tavern, Thaden detected a large body of water: an aquifer. Expelling more jhorun than he should have had to, he summoned a jet of water from the underground reservoir and punched it through the tavern's floor boards to coalesce above his head. He waited a few seconds for enough water to accumulate before he directed the water jet toward the fire thrower.

In a split second, Steve yanked the Nohrstaf free of its holder and thrust it out in front of him. The small club became a large shield. The force of the water slammed into him, pushing him backwards several feet. Jamming his right arm through the straps on the shield, he leaned into the blast, taking the full brunt of the jet onto his right shoulder. His left hand now was free to ignite a jet of fire, which he blasted at the wizard.

Thaden barely had enough time to adjust his water jet to intercept the flames. Fire met water and hissed in an angry protest. Huge clouds of steam collected near the ceiling as each combatant blasted the other with as much power as they could muster. However, neither was able to gain ground on the other.

"Surrender, fire thrower! You cannot defeat me!"

With the water jet now focused on blocking his own attack, the Nohrstaf reverted back to its default form. He jammed the small club into its holder on Mythrin's scabbard and ignited his right hand as he did so. Retrieving a mimet from one of its pouches, which wasn't easy to do with only one hand, he restored his jhorun a second time. Energized like never before, he re-doubled his efforts, forcing Thaden to retreat a few steps. Clouds of steam drifted along the ceiling, soaking everything it touched. The ceiling groaned in protest as it quickly became waterlogged.

With his jhorun tiring much more rapidly than he would ever admit, Thaden relinquished his grip on the aquifer, letting the jet of water collapse in on itself. He snarled in protest and darted behind another support post.

With his jhorun nearly at a full charge, Steve advanced

on the wizard. Making certain he kept an eye on Sarah and Annie's location, he withdrew two more mimets and held them in each hand. He leveled a blast at the post, causing the wizard to curse.

"How's that feel?" Steve called out. "Is that hot enough for you?"

Using both arms, he blasted two more jets at the post, watching with satisfaction as it charred and blackened.

Thaden broke from his cover and sprinted to the nearest overturned table. Steve hit it with a chaser, reducing it to splinters.

"Run, you coward!"

Shocked beyond words that he was now running for his life, his jhorun too weak to sustain any other elemental attacks, Thaden considered his options. To retreat now would lose considerable face in the eyes of his followers. However, as much as he didn't want to admit failure, he was rapidly running out of choices.

"You have not seen the last of me, fire thrower! I will have that boy!"

"Not today, nor any other day. That's my promise to whatever gods watch over this world! Do you hear me?"

Thaden cursed again and activated a teleportation spell to return to Ylani. However, nothing happened. Shocked, he repeated the spell and waited to be teleported. Again, nothing happened. His wards! He had forgotten about his own spells! He had been so preoccupied in keeping others from teleporting in, or for that matter, retreating, that he never figured he would be the one doing the fleeing. He was going to have to get away from the inn if he wanted to retreat.

Thaden darted out from behind the table and ran for the front door. A wall of flames erupted out of nowhere, barring anyone from using that as an escape route. A quick scan of the area revealed four windows, all broken, and all accessible. The wizard sprinted to the closest window, but slid to a stop as another wall of flames erupted in front of it. Three more walls of fire appeared before the other windows, sealing him inside the tavern.

Sarah and Annie cautiously poked their heads above

the counter to survey the damage. The great room was completely engulfed, and the flames were rapidly spreading. Steve glanced over at his wife

"You know what you need to do. Are you ready?"

Sarah nodded.

Thaden was dumbstruck. "Where's the boy? Who is that?"

Steve gave the wizard a smug smile. Annie's disguise had finally worn off and she now looked like herself again. "Mikal is safe and sound in the castle, where he's been all night."

Thaden began to curse in a foreign tongue. Steve turned to his wife again.

"Go."

Sarah nodded again, taking Annie's arm. She leaned down to grasp Rhenyon's hand.

"They will be going nowhere," Thaden sneered. "If I cannot teleport out, then neither will they."

Sarah vanished, taking Annie and Rhenyon with her. Thaden's jaw dropped open.

"Impossible!"

"Believe it, pal. And now, since it's just you and me, allow me to express how I really feel about you."

If Thaden thought the intensity of the jets of fire were extreme before, they were nothing compared to what was being fired at him now. He ran from hiding place to hiding place, seeking any location large enough to provide cover.

Angry, tired, hungry, and most importantly, frustrated by all the recent attempts on his life, on his wife's, and definitely on Mikal's, Steve eyed the burning room and encouraged the flames to burn hotter. *Burn everything.* If it meant that they could end this threat against Mikal once and for all, he'd burn the entire tavern down to the ground if he had to.

He watched as the wizard ran around the room, searching for an egress. The only way out now was in the kitchen, which was behind Steve, and he was pretty sure Thaden would be unwilling to chance a direct confrontation. He noticed the wizard was starting to sweat. Understandable. It must be roasting in here. No pun intended, Steve thought.

Thaden backed up against one of the last tables that

hadn't caught fire. There were remnants of several smashed plates and goblets decorating its surface. One goblet remained upright, filled with ale. His throat parched, Thaden gulped it down, hoping to quench his thirst.

Inexplicably, all the fires in the room extinguished with a soft whoosh. Thaden dropped the cup and faced the fire thrower, unsure of what was happening. He tried to think of something he could use for his next attack, hoping it didn't require a lot of jhorun.

The fire thrower walked toward him; his hands still ignited. Thaden backed away and watched as Steve walked over to the cup he had just dropped, and picked it up. He turned away and walked to the tavern's counter.

Thaden bristled with anger. The insolence! He dared to turn his back on him? On *him*?

Sarah and Annie reappeared. She looked at her husband. "Did he do it?"

Steve grinned and held up the goblet.

"Got it right here."

"What are you talking about?" Thaden demanded, growing fearful.

"You look a little worried there, pal," Steve told the wizard. "And you should be. Can I show you something?"

He turned the goblet over and pointed at the tiny purple gem adhered to the concave base. With his thumbnail, he pried the jewel off. The bronze goblet shimmered and became pewter. Twin lightning bolts appeared on the surface.

Thaden gazed in horror at the goblet. For several long seconds, he didn't say anything.

"Pretty cool, huh? Thanks for taking a drink, by the way. It's not a very good feeling, is it?"

Forgetting about the strain on his jhorun, Thaden summoned a blast of air. Nothing happened. He chanted the words to a levitation spell. Nothing.

"What have you done?"

"Oh, I'm just getting started."

Steve ignited both hands and held the goblet. The cup was glowing red in just a few seconds.

"No! You must not destroy it!!"

The wizard leapt for him, not really sure what he was going to be able to do to prevent the goblet's destruction, but knowing he had to do something.

Having a very low melting point, the pewter goblet melted. The liquid pewter ran through Steve's fingers and dropped to the ground, scorching the floor in the process.

"Noooooo!!!!"

Thaden fell to his knees as he stared at the scorched wood and the remains of his goblet. It was destroyed. His jhorun had been lost forever!

"The boy! The boy can restore my jhorun! Take me to him! Now!"

"Not a chance in hell."

"If you do not take me to him now, I will have every one of you killed! I swear I will do it!"

"By you and what army?" Steve asked, as he crossed his arms and leaned against the counter.

"You saw my men! They are all outside, waiting for my orders!"

"Really? Why don't we all go outside and talk about it."

Steve and Sarah calmly walked outside, followed closely by the fuming ex-wizard.

"Watch your step, my dear," Steve cautioned, steering his wife around a three foot hole in the ground.

He grinned as he glanced around the area, noting at least several dozen other holes in various places. There, filling the clearing, were two dragons. One was emerald green and the other a lustrous gold. Sounds of muted shouting were also heard, but were too faint to make anything out.

"W-where are my guards?" Thaden stammered.

Steve pointed at a hole. "Oh, they're still here. If you want to dig for 'em, that is."

"How did — what are dragons doing here? I would have detected them!"

"A ward of obscurity has been cast over this area," Pryllan answered, looking at the former wizard. "It masked our activities."

"How convenient!" Steve turned to Thaden, who appeared to be rooted in place. "Did you do that? That's so thoughtful."

Thaden glowered, but said nothing.

"We meet again, fire thrower," the gold dragon said.

Steve bowed. "Hey there, Kahvel. It's nice to see you. I take it you guys are responsible for the cleanup out here?"

Both dragons nodded. Annie finally walked outside.

"Omigod! Dragons! Real live dragons!"

Steve grinned. "Kahvel, Pryllan, I'd like to introduce Sarah's sister, Annie. Annie, this is Kahvel. He's the gold one. The green one is Pryllan, his mate."

"You know them? Personally?"

"Remember the gold dragon I told you about from our first visit here?"

Annie nodded.

Steve turned and held out an arm in Kahvel's direction.

"That's him."

"And the one who rescued you before, when you were lost? Is that the green one?"

"I wasn't lost, per se; I was just trying to —"

"He was lost," Kahvel confirmed, lowering his head to give Steve a condescending look, which earned him a giggle from Sarah. The huge dragon turned to regard Annie. "Sarah's sibling? A pleasure to make your acquaintance."

Having never been introduced to a dragon before, let alone two, Annie nervously smiled. "The, um, pleasure's all mine."

"One other item that needs addressing."

Everyone turned to Kahvel.

"Is this —"

Pryllan jerked her head up. She glanced at her mate.

"It just slipped away again."

Kahvel sighed and twisted his supple body so that he could face the other direction. He fumbled a moment in the grass and shrubs before he turned around, something held between two of his talons.

"Does this belong to you?"

Warrick dangled from the huge golden foreleg, howling miserably.

Steve snorted. "I know him. That's Thaden's right-hand man. Where'd you find him?"

"Fleeing north, raising quite a ruckus. Pryllan and I decided to investigate. We noticed that several wards had been cast over this area. Further investigation revealed a battle raging inside. We watched for a while and decided to intervene."

"You saw us fighting?"

Kahvel rose to his full height and nodded, turning again to inspect the dozens of holes he and his mate had made. He had been rather surprised to learn he had enjoyed pounding objects into the ground, even when those objects were fleeing humans.

"All I ask is that you speak on our behalf and explain our actions to the human king. Can you do that? I do not want to be responsible for dissolving the accord we have with the humans."

"You got it, pal. Trust me, I don't think you have anything to worry about. You and Pryllan did all of us a huge favor."

"Are you certain?"

"Quite certain, my friend," Kri'Entu answered, appearing from behind one of the nearby cottages.

Suddenly, armed Lentarian soldiers were everywhere.

"So, I take it we're still in Lentari?" Steve asked, looking at his wife.

"Yes. We're on the other side of Verdayn. Somehow, and don't ask me how, Thaden teleported everyone inside Thacken Lodge and brought them all here."

"Where's Tristan?"

"I would imagine he's still stuck in Donlari, chasing those kids."

"Oh, that's right. I wonder if he caught 'em."

Sarah giggled. "I'm sure he did."

"Is Rhenyon okay?"

"He's fine. Annie healed him completely. The king's personal healer is checking him now, just to be certain."

"Do not even speak to me."

Steve, Sarah, and the king all turned to look back at Thaden. Shardwyn was standing in front of him, sadly shaking his head.

"Never in my life have I been more ashamed of you, my son."

"I am not your son, nor are you my father."

"Is that the way you wish to be treated, then?"

"I would not have it any other way."

Giving another sad shake of his head, Shardwyn turned to the king.

"Your Majesty, I am —"

The king held up a hand. "Do not apologize for him. He speaks for himself, and is therefore responsible for his own actions."

"Think we could convince him to turn back the trolls and those flying things?" Steve asked.

"Unlikely, but not necessary," Kri'Entu said. "The griffins tell us the trolls have fled into the forest and the flocks of malwerns have scattered."

Steve nodded. "Makes sense. Thaden lost his jhorun, so he lost his hold over them."

The king turned to Steve. "It would appear so. I do not know how Thaden held sway over that many trolls, but I am extremely thankful that we will not have to face them."

"What are you going to do with my son, Your Majesty?"

Kri'Entu smiled at the wizard. "I have just the thing. Here's what I will need you to do."

Shardwyn listened to the king's instructions and started to smile.

Epilogue

Annie gently took her hand off the boy's forehead and replaced it with a damp cloth. The burning fever had finally broken. Whatever illness the boy had contracted had taken close to an hour to eradicate. She stayed by his side an additional three hours just to be certain all traces of the deadly disease was gone. Brushing her fingers against his cheek, the boy finally opened his eyes and smiled at her.

"Who are you?"

"I'm —"

"Where is my mother? I am hungry."

Aerlin struggled to sit upright. He stared at the many faces in his bedchamber. Some he recognized, some he did not.

Annie moved away as his grandfather knelt beside the bed.

"How are you feeling?"

"Good, grandfather. Can we get something to eat?"

Discreetly drying the corners of his eyes as he pretended

to blow his nose, King Ewam straightened, and then beckoned everyone to follow him out of the room.

"Entu, I am sorry. I was ready to wage war with you. I thought you were ignoring our pleas. If your wizard had not contacted my wizard, we would be marching into battle right now. I still cannot believe Wren did not detect another wizard in the castle."

Kri'Entu clasped Ewam's outstretched arm and inclined his head back at the room with King Ewam's grandson. "To be fair, Wren had more pressing matters to attend to. Let us put this whole misunderstanding in the past. I hereby make this promise to you: if you need our help, ask, and we shall answer. Had we but known your grandson was ill, I would have dispatched our finest healers. I think you would agree when I say that we need to find a more secure way to communicate. I do not want history to repeat itself."

"Nor do I."

"What's going to happen to Thaden?" Sarah wanted to know. "He won't be executed, will he?"

"He will wish he had been," King Ewam declared, his face hardening. He looked back at the small group of Lentarians and softened. "A renegade wizard hides in my kingdom and uses my own man to get me to do his bidding? He has caused enough mischief to last several lifetimes. The sentence of death, where appropriate in this case, will be commuted. He will atone for his crimes. Therefore, I have given Thaden a permanent position in my court."

Kri'Entu's eyebrows shot up. "You have? Is that wise?"

"Young Thaden has become Zaran's newest permanent stable boy."

"He's not a boy," Steve scoffed.

King Ewam leveled a gaze at the Nohrin.

"You object to him mucking out stalls on a daily basis?"

"Ah. Duly noted. Aren't you afraid he'll escape or else gather more followers?"

"He can still count one as a follower. Warrick has also earned himself a position."

Steve grinned. "Dare I ask?"

"Royal chamber pot cleaner."

Steve snorted with laughter while his wife suppressed a giggle.

"If he causes problems?" Kri'Entu asked, concerned.

The rotund king hefted the small leather pouch of jorii, a gift from the Lentarian King.

"I do hope he will try."

* * *

"But I want to come home!"

"Mikal, we must be patient. You heard your father. We do not know yet if it is safe here."

"Mikal." Kri'Entu squatted down next to his wife and son. "We know Thaden had followers here in the castle. We cannot allow you back until we are certain that no threat remains. Do you understand?"

Mikal nodded sullenly.

"Excellent. You will return to the Nohrin's world. As soon as it is safe here, we will send word. I promise, son."

Mikal sighed. Peanut appeared and snuggled up under his right arm.

"Are you ready to go back, girl?"

Peanut barked several times, her stump of a tail wagging happily.

"There will be no dragons there."

The young corgi didn't seem to mind as she pulled on her leash and escorted her human through the activated portal.

"We cannot thank the three of you enough."

Steve turned to the queen. He took his wife's hand and together they bowed to the Kri'yans. Annie, following their lead, also gave a short bow.

"I wish we could do more for you than simply give you medals," Kri'Entu said.

Steve, Sarah, and Annie stared down at the golden medals they were each wearing. The official ceremony had taken place last night, with all the pomp and circumstance the situation demanded. Sarah still hadn't cared for all the attention, nor had her sister for that matter. Steve, on the other hand, thrived on the attention, even though he'd deny it if asked. The Order of the Mythra Triad medal consisted of a golden ring with a gem-encrusted triangle attached in the center. A closer inspection of the center triangle revealed three separate cut gems: an emerald on the top, a ruby on the right, and a sapphire on the left. The center triangle was either a diamond or some type of clear crystal, with an etched image of a griffin with its foreleg raised.

"I think we're good," Steve assured the king. Sarah and Annie nodded in agreement. "We'll wait to hear from you before we do anything."

The Kri'yans nodded.

Tristan appeared and offered Annie an arm. Eyebrow raised, she took the proffered arm, giving him a warm smile in return. Together they walked back through the portal.

Steve hooked an arm through Sarah's. Amidst the clapping and cheering, they followed Tristan and Annie back through the portal.

Near the back of the portal chamber, a nondescript serving girl watched the proceedings as she ran her fingers along the delicate gold chain around her neck. The large group of people had started to disperse. She smiled at the two other girls also assigned to the kitchen staff. Together they walked back to the Great Hall, chatting amiably amongst themselves about how handsome several of the new recruits were and whether or not they were involved with anyone.

The girl hesitated just as the other two disappeared into the kitchen. She glanced back through the doorway into the smaller chamber. Her eyes narrowed. The boy had returned to the Nohrin's world. She still did not know how the castle portal was able to link to another world, but she would figure it out. After all, she had plenty of time on her hands and she was patient. She had to be. She'd been waiting for centuries.

~ ~ ~

To be concluded in:
The Amulet of Aria (Bakkian Chronicles #3)!

~ ~ ~

Author's Note

Thank you very much for reading this story. I never in a million years would have thought that I'd publish a book, let alone two. And to top it all off, I've started on the third and final installment of the Bakkian Chronicles.

For this second book, I decided Mikal needed a furry companion. Since my wife and I love corgis so much, the character of Peanut was added. And Peanut, just so you know, was originally suggested as a name for Keeley, but we decided against it. So, when it came to naming Mikal's feisty new pup, well, it didn't take long.

I originally wrote this when I was living in Lake Havasu City, AZ. I've since moved to Oregon, where the summers are much more pleasant. Trust me, the days of stepping outside when it was 120+ were getting old. Now, the summers are something I look forward to, since this area actually cools off at night. Again, nothing like Arizona.

One final request. The best way to show you enjoyed an author's work is to leave a review online. In this case, if you enjoyed the book, or didn't, please consider leaving a review wherever you purchased the book. It can be anything from several paragraphs or else nothing but a simple star rating. Amazon, Barnes & Noble, Goodreads, Smashwords, it doesn't matter. Any amount of publicity will always help a writer!

If you'd like to follow the progress on the latest book I'm working on, then I would encourage you to sign up for my newsletter, The Daily Scroll, so you'll never miss another book release, or contest, or any other bit of news that I pass along to the readers.

Again, thank you for reading! I truly hope you enjoyed the story as much as I enjoyed writing it!

ABOUT THE AUTHOR

Jeffrey M. Poole is a professional writer who writes in both the fantasy and mystery genres. His series are listed below. Jeffrey lives in picturesque Southern Oregon, with his wife, Giliane, and their Welsh Corgi, Kinsey. His interests include archery, astronomy, archaeology, scuba diving, collecting movies, collecting swords, and tinkering with any electronic gadget he can get his hands on.

In March, 2015, Jeffrey became a proud member of SFWA, the Science Fiction & Fantasy Writers of America! Jeffrey encourages readers to connect with him on Facebook (facebook.com/bakkianchronicles). Fans can also follow him online at: www.AuthorJMPoole.com. Scan the QR code to check it out!

BOOKS BY JEFFREY POOLE

Epic Fantasy
BAKKIAN CHRONICLES
The Prophecy
Insurrection
Amulet of Aria
Disneyland Debacle (short story)
Winter Wonderland (short story)

Epic Fantasy
TALES OF LENTARI
Lost City
Something Wyverian This Way Comes
A Portal for Your Thoughts
Thoughts for a Portal
Wizard in the Woods
Close Encounters of the Magical Kind
The Hunt for Red Oskorlisk (short story)
May the Fang be With You (Pirates trilogy #1)
The Hammer is Strong with This One (Pirates #2)
These are Not the Stones You're Looking For (Pirates #3)
Blast from the Past

Epic Fantasy
DRAGONS OF ANDELA
Harness the Fire
Strike the Spark
Clear the Water*

Mystery
CORGI CASE FILES
Case of the One-Eyed Tiger
Case of the Fleet-Footed Mummy
Case of the Holiday Hijinks
Case of the Pilfered Pooches
Case of the Muffin Murders
Case of the Chatty Roadrunner
Case of the Highland House Haunting
Case of the Ostentatious Otters
Case of the Dysfunctional Daredevils
Case of the Abandoned Bones
Case of the Great Cranberry Caper
Case of the Shady Shamrock
Case of the Ragin' Cajun
Case of the Missing Marine
Case of the Stuttering Parrot
Case of the Rusty Sword
Case of the Secret Staircase (short story)
*Case of the Unlucky Emperor**

* - *coming soon!*

www.ingramcontent.com/pod-product-compliance
Lightning Source LLC
Chambersburg PA
CBHW020559120726
47903CB00001B/311